"So, how do I compare to one of your heroes?"

Gideon had asked the question teasingly, but the way his hands roamed over her body left no doubt in Sarah's mind about what was to come next.

"You're stronger," Sarah murmured, kissing the tip of his nose. "Bigger." She kissed the hard line of his jaw. "Sexier." She kissed his mouth. "Much sexier...."

"Is that all?" Gideon was nuzzling her neck.

She leaned back against the couch, as if to postpone the inevitable moment of their union. "Well, the reality is much better than the fantasy version."

"And you're convinced I'm real?"

"I know the effect you have on me." She felt Gideon's hand tangle in her hair, forcing her to look straight into his eyes. Suddenly his mood had changed into one of stormy passion.

"I'm no hero," he warned, dragging Sarah on top of him.

"Yes, you are," she whispered passionately as waves of anticipation rolled through her. "You're the perfect hero...."

Author's Note

At the heart of every powerful romance story lies
a legend. There are many romantic legends and
countless modern variations on them, but they all
share one thing: they are tales of brave,
resourceful women who must gentle and tame the
powerful, passionate men who are their true
mates.

Those of us who love romance novels, readers and
writers alike, understand that it is because women
are willing to accept the difficult challenge of
bonding with men that civilization itself
continues. That, of course, explains the basic
appeal of our legends.

In the Ladies and Legends trilogy, I have written
three tales that are modern-day versions of three
classic romantic myths. I have created *The Pirate*,
The Adventurer and *The Cowboy*, all with heroes
of mythic proportion, tamed by women who
understand romance.

Jayne Ann Krentz

The Adventurer

JAYNE ANN KRENTZ

Harlequin Books

TORONTO • NEW YORK • LONDON
AMSTERDAM • PARIS • SYDNEY • HAMBURG
STOCKHOLM • ATHENS • TOKYO • MILAN

Published April 1990

ISBN 0-373-25393-1

Prologue

"DOES IT OCCUR to you that you might have become a little obsessed with this matter of the Flowers, Sarah?"

"Kate has a point, Sarah. During the past few months, you've talked about nothing else except the Fleetwood Flowers and that man Gideon Trace. Trace may be real enough, but I'm sure the Flowers are just an old legend. There are probably thousands of tales just like it and none of them has much basis in truth. Why get excited about this one?"

Standing at the window of her bright, cheerfully cluttered apartment, Sarah Fleetwood gazed at the street ten stories below and smiled to herself. "Because this legend is mine," she said enigmatically.

"You mean, because the woman who once owned the Flowers is a distant ancestress of yours?" Margaret Lark shook her sleek head. "That's no reason to think there's any more truth in this tale than there is in any other lost treasure story."

"If you ask me," Katherine Inskip Hawthorne said with a knowing wink, "it's not the tale of the Fleetwood Flowers that has you enthralled, Sarah, it's this man, Gideon Trace, the one you've been corresponding with lately, who really interests you."

Sarah felt the familiar little glow of excitement that always accompanied the sound of Gideon's name.

Gideon Trace. She had never met the man but already she knew a great deal about him. After four months of exchanging letters with him she was quite certain he was the real-life version of one of her own heroes, a man straight out of one of her novels of romantic suspense. Dark, enigmatic, mysterious and rather dangerous— the Beast waiting in a haunted garden for Beauty to rescue him from some curse.

Sarah knew she was no great beauty but she figured she could handle whatever curse had been put on Gideon Trace. In fact, she looked forward to the task with her usual boundless self-confidence and optimism. She glanced over her shoulder to where her two best friends sat on her shiny new, black leather Italian sofa.

"I can't explain it, Kate, but I know that the legend of the Flowers and Gideon Trace are linked. I'm going after both of them," Sarah said.

"You have no experience in treasure hunting."

"Gideon Trace will help me. I have a feeling about this particular treasure. It's mine. I'm going to find it with Trace's assistance."

Margaret raised her eyes to the ceiling. "Out of all those treasure hunters and salvage operators you contacted five months ago when you were researching *Glitter Quest*, why on earth did you fixate on Trace?"

"Something in his letters told me he was different from the others."

"Well, who am I to discourage you?" Kate said. "I wish you luck, my friend. I've had enough good fortune of my own recently. It's time you had a little, too."

Kate was dressed for travel in a flower-splashed turquoise cotton dress. She looked remarkably fit and healthy, Sarah noticed with great satisfaction. Her friend's eyes sparkled vivaciously and her tawny-brown hair gleamed. The tense, stressed-out look that had been hounding Kate had gone. There was nothing like a couple of months on a tropical island and marriage to a pirate to give a woman a shot of energy and the sheen of happiness.

"I suppose Kate has a point," Margaret said slowly. "We probably shouldn't try to talk you out of this. If a treasure hunt is what you want, go for it. Your intuition has always been extraordinary. Maybe it will lead you to the Flowers."

"Or at least to Gideon Trace," Sarah said, thinking, not for the first time, that her friend Margaret had that wonderfully elusive, subtle quality known as panache. Margaret managed to appear casually elegant just sitting there with one leg tucked under the other. She was dressed with her usual restrained flair, the collar of her pale yellow silk blouse turned up to frame her attractive face. Her black slacks had been beautifully tailored by an expensive designer and her fashionable black pumps had been made in Italy.

"And meeting Trace is the more important goal?" Margaret asked, her gaze shadowed with faint disapproval.

"Oh, yes, definitely. There's something in his letters, something I must . . ." Sarah paused to glance out the window again, her eye caught by a flash of yellow on the street. As she watched, a cab pulled over to the curb and a lean, dark-haired man dressed in jeans and a casual cotton shirt got out. He was followed by a miniature version of himself. "Jared and his son are here, Kate."

"So much for their whirlwind tour of the Space Needle and the waterfront. Guess it must be time to head for the airport." Kate got up to walk over to the window. Her eyes were warm and soft as she watched Jared Hawthorne lean down to say something through the window to the driver. Then he vanished with his son into the lobby ten floors below.

"How does it feel to have found your pirate?" Sarah asked softly.

"What can I say? I'm a new woman."

Margaret laughed from the couch. "That's certainly true. I take it Sarah and I are forgiven for having shanghaied you into that trip to Amethyst Island three months ago?"

"Given the way it all turned out, I'm more than willing to let bygones be bygones. What's a little matter of kidnapping and impressment among friends?" Kate's wedding ring gleamed in the reflected glow of a late afternoon sun. "I just wish you two could be as fortunate." She looked at Sarah. "Do you really think this Trace person is going to be someone special?"

"Yes." Sarah knew her sense of serene assurance was evident in her voice. "Very special."

"Don't be mislead by a few cryptic letters," Margaret advised. "The man publishes a low-budget, treasure-hunting magazine, for goodness sake. It caters to a bunch of gung-ho males of questionable intelligence who actually believe they're going to find a lost gold mine or Amelia Earhart's plane. Frankly, that puts Gideon Trace just one notch above a con artist."

"That's not true," Sarah said quietly. "He sells dreams. Just like I do."

"Never discount the value of a good dream," Kate added with a note of satisfaction as the doorbell rang. "I'll get that."

Sarah watched her friend walk across the room to open the door for her husband. No doubt about it,

Jared Hawthorne was just right for Kate. Those gray eyes and that wicked grin made Hawthorne a real-life, walking, talking pirate who could have stepped straight from the pages of one of Kate's historical romance novels. What was more, he had the forceful personality a man needed to run a tropical resort or deal with a woman like Kate. Jared did both very well.

"Hi, honey," Jared bent his head to give his wife a brief, enthusiastic kiss. "All set? I told the cab to wait. We've got a plane to catch."

"I'm ready." Kate smiled at her stepson. "How was the Space Needle?"

"It was great. You could see the whole city and the mountains and everything," David Hawthorne enthused. "I told Dad we should build one on Amethyst but he said all we had to do was climb to the top of Hawthorne castle and look out."

"He's got a point."

"Yeah, but I like it here. I hope we come back to Seattle, soon."

"So do I," Sarah said from the other side of the room.

"You and Margaret will have to come on out to Amethyst one of these days," Jared said easily. "Don't worry, we've got plenty of room."

"A whole resort," David clarified. "I'll show you how to snorkel, just like I showed Kate."

"Sounds terrific," Sarah said.

"Promise me you'll both make plans to visit us soon," Kate said. "I miss you both."

Jared's brows climbed as he glanced at his wife. "I don't see why. You spend enough time on the phone talking to them."

"Got to keep in touch with the business," Kate informed him loftily.

Jared grinned at Sarah and Margaret. "As I said, come on out for a visit. The airfare's bound to be less than the phone bills the three of you are running up."

Kate wrinkled her nose. "That's not true."

"Wanna bet?" Jared moved toward the pile of luggage in the corner. "Come on, Dave, give me a hand with this stuff. You know Kate never travels light."

"Okay, Dad." David threw a quick grin at Kate as he hurried toward the luggage.

Sarah hugged Kate at the door. "Don't worry, we'll get to Amethyst, one way or the other," she promised as she blinked back a few tears.

"Thanks," Kate whispered. "And thanks again for sending me on that first trip to the island. I owe all my happiness to you and Margaret."

"Oh, Kate, I'm so happy for you." Sarah smiled mistily and stepped back as Jared and David started through the door with the luggage.

"It's been great to see you these past two weeks, Kate," Margaret added, getting to her feet to give her friend a farewell embrace. "It's good to know we'll be able to visit with you at least once a year when Jared brings his son to the States to see his grandparents."

"Don't worry, you'll see her more often than that," Jared said from the doorway. "But right now I'm taking her home to Amethyst. I've got a resort to run. Place has probably started crumbling into the sea during the two weeks I've been gone."

"It wouldn't dare." Kate slung her purse over her shoulder and followed Jared and David through the doorway. "Goodbye, you two. It's been a wonderful visit. Can't wait to see you on Amethyst. Sarah, good luck with your treasure hunting. Margaret, take care. And thanks again."

Sarah went out into the hall to wave the small family into the elevator and then she returned to her apartment. She shut the door behind her with great care and walked over to where Margaret stood at the window.

"Well, you were right when you said Amethyst Island was the place to send Kate," Margaret remarked. "She looks radiant."

"She's happy and relaxed." Sarah watched Kate, Jared and David pile into the waiting cab.

"Good for her. Now, about your plans for the immediate future..."

"What about them?"

Margaret frowned, turning away from the window. "You're really going to look him up?"

"Gideon Trace? Absolutely. I'm driving over to the coast at the end of the week to try to find him."

"You've got an address?"

"Just the post office box number on the envelopes he's sent me. The towns on the coast are all small. The one he's in is barely a dot on the map, the kind of place where everyone knows everyone else. Someone will be able to tell me where the publisher of *Cache* magazine lives."

"You haven't told Trace you're coming, have you?"

"No, I plan to surprise him."

Margaret looked at her ruefully. "You're always so blissfully sure of that intuition of yours, aren't you?"

"It's only failed me once. And that was my own fault. I wasn't paying attention to the warnings it was giving me." Sarah walked toward the kitchen. "How about a glass of wine before dinner?"

"Sounds good. Well, at least Trace hasn't tried to talk you into investing a few thousand dollars in some crazy expedition to find a lost World War II plane that supposedly crashed on a Pacific island with a load of gold on board."

Sarah giggled. "You mean the way that guy Slaughter did?" Jim Slaughter, owner of a business called Slaughter Enterprises, had been one of the professional treasure hunters she had contacted five months earlier. She had found his ad along with several others in the back of a sleazy adventure magazine for men.

He had written her several letters on impressive letterhead and tried phoning a few times in an attempt to interest her in his scheme to find the plane full of gold. Sarah had politely declined several times.

"He was a slick one, wasn't he?"

"I'll say. But that's my whole point, Sarah. People involved in the business of treasure hunting are probably all borderline hustlers or outright crazies. They just want you to pour thousands into their projects to find lost gold mines or something. Then they take your money and disappear."

"Not Gideon Trace. He's different." Sarah managed to find two clean wineglasses in the cupboard. She made a mental note to run the dishwasher soon. She was almost out of clean dishes. "Trace certainly hasn't tried to convince me to invest a dime in any crazy treasure-hunting scheme. In fact, he's tried to discourage me from wasting my time going after the Flowers."

"I don't know, Sarah. I just don't like the whole idea. But it's your decision." Margaret sauntered after her, pausing to glance at the evening paper that was lying on the counter amid a motley collection of yellow pads, romance novels and pens.

Sarah felt a twinge of uneasiness. Hand on the refrigerator door, she turned her head just as Margaret flipped through the newspaper to find the business section. "Margaret, wait, I don't think you ought to read that section."

But it was too late. Margaret was already staring down at the photo of a hard-faced man in a western-style business suit. "Don't worry about it, Sarah," she said quietly. "He makes headlines in the business world. He always has. You can't expect me to stop reading the paper just because I'm occasionally going to run across an article about him." She refolded the paper and raised her head, smiling grimly. "Besides, that's all in the past."

"Yes." Sarah busied herself with a bottle of Chardonnay and sought a way to change the subject. "Want to go out for a bite to eat in the Market?" she asked as she tossed the cork in the vague direction of the trash basket. It missed. Sarah promised herself she would pick it up later.

"All right. Then I think I'd better go back to my own apartment and get some writing done. I haven't accomplished much in the two weeks Kate's been visiting us and I've got a deadline coming up next month."

"You'll make it. You always do." Sarah poured two glasses of the clean, polished Washington Chardonnay and handed one to Margaret. "Here's to Kate and her new family."

"And here's to your treasure-hunting expedition," Margaret added as the glasses clinked. She took a sip and her gaze turned serious. "Promise me you'll be careful, Sarah."

"Hey, my middle name is Careful."

"No, it's not. Your middle name is Impulsive and I'm afraid that one of these days that intuition of yours, which you trust entirely too much, is going to land you in a heap of trouble."

"I'm thirty-two years old, Margaret. Trouble is starting to look promising. Now, no more lectures. Let's get down to serious business. What do we want for dinner and where do we want to go to eat it? I vote for pasta."

"You always vote for pasta."

TWO HOURS LATER, pleasantly stuffed with hazelnut tortellini, Sarah turned the key in the lock of her front door. She wandered through the cheerful, vividly decorated one-bedroom apartment, turning on lights as she went.

When she reached the desk where her computer sat like some ancient monolith rising from a sea of notes, magazines, empty tea mugs and research materials, she stopped.

It only took her a minute to find the stack of Gideon Trace's letters. Margaret was right, Sarah thought with a small smile as she reread one of them. Gideon's notes did tend to be a bit cryptic. An uncharitable observer might even call them somewhat dry. There was certainly very little hint of the fascinating man she just knew he had to be.

Dear Ms. Fleetwood:
In regard to your most recent inquiry concerning the legend of the Fleetwood Flowers, I'm afraid I have very little to tell you that you don't already know. The tale dates from the late eighteen hundreds and is not unlike many other stories of lost treasure. Such stories tend to become greatly exaggerated over the years.

The Flowers were supposedly five pairs of earrings fashioned from gemstones. According to the legend, Emelina Fleetwood, a spinster school-teacher, spent a summer searching for gold in the Washington mountains near her cabin. It was not unknown for women to try their luck at gold mining on the frontier and some gold was found in Washington, as you probably know.

At any rate, she is said to have discovered a small vein, worked it all summer and then went back to teaching the following year. She never told anyone where her strike was or if she'd gotten anything out of it. But the legend claims she had the earrings, which she always referred to as her Flowers, made up by a San Francisco jeweller and that she paid him with gold nuggets.

Before she died, Emelina Fleetwood is said to have buried her earrings somewhere on her property and drawn a map showing the location. If there ever was a map, it has long since disappeared.

I'm surprised you are familiar with the legend. It is an extremely obscure one. My professional opinion is that there is not much merit to the tale. Any search for the Flowers would probably be a waste of time.

If I can be of any further help, please feel free to contact me. Thank you for your check. I have renewed your subscription to *Cache* for another year.

Yours,
G. Trace

P.S. Thank you for the recipe for pesto sauce.

"Well, Mr. G. Trace," Sarah said as she put the letter back down on the desk, "I appreciate your professional opinion but I'm not going to abide by it. I'm going to find the Flowers and what's more, you're going to help me."

1

IT WAS THE BIGGEST, ugliest cat Sarah had ever seen. A true monster of a cat, twenty or twenty-five pounds at least and none of it fat.

Its fur was a mottled, blotchy color somewhere between orange and brown with here-and-there patches of black and tan for added color interest. It had one torn ear and a few old scars, but otherwise looked to be in excellent physical condition. Sarah decided this particular cat probably won most of the fights it chose to start. She doubted it had ever purred in its life.

"Excuse me," Sarah said to the cat, which was sprawled across the top step, effectively blocking the entrance to the porch. "Would you mind if I knocked?"

The cat did not bother to lift its head but its tail thumped once in warning. It opened its eyes to mere slits and regarded her without enthusiasm. Sarah found herself pinned by a stone-cold, green-gold gaze.

"I can see you're not the eager, welcoming type. Somebody should have traded you for a Beagle years ago. What are you? Some kind of guard cat?"

The cat said nothing but continued to watch her with its remote, gemlike gaze. Sarah glanced around, hoping for signs of human habitation, but there weren't many.

The big, weather-beaten Victorian-style house she had finally managed to locate after much diligent searching was perched on a bluff overlooking the sea.

The view of the Pacific was hidden this morning behind a veil of fog that hung over the water like a sorcerer's dark spell.

The house with all its aging architectural embellishments was as faded, forbidding and aloof as old royalty.

The nearest neighbor was some distance away, concealed by a heavy stand of trees. The distant roar of the sea and the whisper of restless pines were the only sounds. For all intents and purposes, Gideon Trace's home was isolated in a universe of its own, with only the cat to indicate that anyone actually lived here.

Sarah took another look at the large cat. "I'm very sorry," she said firmly, "but I am going to knock on the door, whether you like it or not."

The cat stared at her.

Sarah cautiously moved to the farthest edge of the steps so that she would not have to actually step over the creature. She went briskly up to the wide porch, ignoring the irritated thumps of the cat's tail. But the animal made no move to stop her as she went over to the door.

She had her hand poised to knock when a faint tingle of awareness went through her. The door was suddenly opened from the other side. Sarah looked up and found herself pinned for a second time that morning by a pair of icy, green-gold eyes. This time, at least, the eyes were human. Sort of.

"Who the hell are you and what do you want?"

For an instant Sarah felt as if time had been temporarily suspended. She stood there on the porch, staring up at the man in front of her, mesmerized by his jungle eyes and the gritty, rough-textured sound of his voice. For the first time since she had set out on her quest it occurred to her that she might have bitten off a little more than she could chew.

Gideon Trace looked large, cold-eyed and dangerous.

"Yes, of course," she said finally. "It makes sense that you would look a little like the cat."

The man's gaze narrowed in a way that reminded Sarah of the beast on the porch step. He did not move— just stood there in the doorway, big and unwelcoming. He was clad in jeans and a faded blue work shirt. "Are you selling something, lady?"

Sarah rallied quickly and summoned up her most engaging smile. She held out her hand. "In a way. I'm Sarah Fleetwood. I've been looking forward to meeting you. You are Gideon Trace, aren't you?"

His gaze dropped to her outstretched hand as if he didn't know whether to shake it or bite it. When he glanced up again Sarah thought she saw a barely concealed flare of surprise in his eyes. "Yeah, I'm Trace." His big hand closed briefly around hers, nearly crushing her fingers. He let go of her instantly, frowning. "You're the Fleetwood woman who's been writing to me for the past few months? The one who wrote me about the legend of the Flowers?"

"That's me." Sarah clutched the strap of her oversized black, white and yellow shoulder bag. "I wanted to talk to you in more detail about the legend because I've decided to look for the Flowers. To be perfectly honest, I'm hoping to convince you to go with me as a sort of consultant. That's what I meant when I said I was here to sell you something. In a way, I am. I'm hoping to sell you on this great idea I've got. You see, I..."

"Hold it." Trace held up a hand to silence her.

Sarah ignored the upraised palm, much too excited to stop now that she had located her quarry. "I haven't had any experience with treasure hunting and I thought you could advise me. I'll pay you, naturally. What do treasure-hunting consultants go for these days? Is there a price break if I buy you for a week at a time, or is it the same as the day-to-day rate? I'm sure we'll be able to work something out. I've given this a lot of thought and I . . ."

"*I said, hold it.*" Gideon Trace's expression was as austere and forbidding as that of his cat. "Are you always this, uh, enthusiastic?"

Sarah blushed. "Sorry, I was kind of rushing into things, wasn't I? My friends say I'm sometimes a little too impulsive. But what do they know? At any rate, I'm so glad to have found you, Mr. Trace, because I just know our association is going to be an extremely advantageous one for both parties." She gave him another of her most winning smiles.

The smile appeared to make Gideon Trace more wary than ever. His strong face was set in distinctly unenthusiastic lines. His green-gold eyes glittered as he looked down at her. "How did you find me?"

"I asked at the gas station."

"Maybe I should go ask someone at the gas station what I'm supposed to do with you now that you're here."

"I think what you should do next is invite me in for a cup of tea."

"Is that right?"

Sarah swallowed. "I think it would be an excellent idea."

"I don't drink tea. I haven't got a tea bag in the house."

"No problem. I always travel with my own." Sarah plunged a hand into her oversized shoulder bag and whipped out a tea bag with the words English Breakfast on the tag. "All I need is some hot water. You do have that, don't you?"

Gideon was clearly searching for an appropriate response to the question when a soft, inquiring meow sounded from the vicinity of his feet. Sarah knew that gentle tone could not have emanated from the great beast on the front steps. She glanced down to see a small, delicately built silver-gray cat watching her with warm, golden eyes.

"Oh, isn't she lovely?" Sarah crouched and offered her fingers in greeting.

The silver-gray cat stropped her tail once or twice against one of Gideon's well-worn boots and then glided forward. Politely she investigated Sarah's fingers and then rubbed her sleek head against the proferred hand.

Sarah looked up a very long way to where Gideon was scowling down at the scene taking place around his legs. "What's her name?"

"Ellora."

Sarah was delighted. "After the mysterious cave temples in India?"

"Yeah." There was another flicker of surprise in his eyes.

Sarah scratched Ellora's ears and the cat began to purr. "I hardly dare ask the name of that monster on the front steps."

"Machu Picchu."

"Oh, yes, the lost city of the Incas." Sarah turned to look at the big cat who hadn't moved from his position in the middle of the step. "The name sort of fits, doesn't it? Massive and immovable."

Gideon ignored that. "I take it you drove over from Seattle this morning?" He made it sound as if she had done something exceedingly stupid.

"Yes, it was a lovely drive. Hardly any traffic."

"Well, as long as you've made the trip, you might as well come in for the tea."

"Thanks." Sarah gave Ellora one last pat and rose to her feet. "Your two cats certainly have different personalities, don't they? How do they get along?"

"Ellora keeps Machu Picchu wrapped around her little paw." Gideon sounded resigned to the situation.

"Hard to believe," Sarah muttered.

"What do you expect? He's just a simple-minded male. Ellora has no trouble with him at all. This way." Gideon Trace turned to lead her into the house.

Sarah followed quickly, glancing around with deep interest. The inside of the old Victorian seemed dark and forbidding. It was also chilly.

"Must cost a fortune to heat one of these old houses."

"Yeah, but I don't need a lot of heat."

Sarah eyed the faded drapes, unpolished wooden floors and aging furniture. It was obvious publishing *Cache* did not provide a high profit margin. Either that or Gideon Trace simply didn't believe in investing in his personal surroundings. The place did not appear neglected, she finally decided, just dark and gloomy.

It was also incredibly tidy.

Magazines were filed in a terrifyingly orderly fashion in a rack. There was a huge assortment of books but they were all arranged with great precision in the floor-to-ceiling bookcases. The surface of the coffee table was completely clear, unmarred by so much as one empty coffee mug.

Even the chess game that had been set up on a table in one corner looked neat and orderly. Sarah glanced at the carved wooden pieces and wondered who Gideon played chess with. From all appearances he was a very solitary man.

She hurried after her reluctant host as he went through the living room into the kitchen. Here the windows all faced the sea, providing a ringside view of the dark fog that hovered over the water. The room itself was spacious in the manner of old kitchens and somewhat lighter and more inviting than the living room. But the impression of grim orderliness still prevailed.

Sarah realized she had not anticipated that her hero would be quite so organized. But she refused to be daunted by petty details.

"Have a seat."

Sarah needed no second urging. She dropped her huge bag onto a ladder-back chair with a thud and took a seat at the old claw-footed table. "This is certainly an interesting place you have here."

"I like it." Gideon filled an old steel kettle at the sink.

"Have you lived here long?"

"Almost five years."

"Is that how long you've been publishing your treasure-hunting magazine?"

"About."

The man obviously was not good at small talk. That didn't surprise Sarah. Gideon Trace was not a small talk kind of person. "I certainly have appreciated your help during the past few months, Mr. Trace. The inside information you provided on the subject of treasure hunting was invaluable to my story. You'll be happy to know I sent the manuscript of *Glitter Quest* off to New York on Tuesday."

"Delighted," he agreed caustically. "You said in one of your letters that it was some sort of romance novel?"

"That's right. I write romantic suspense."

"Sounds like a contradiction in terms."

"Not at all. I think romance and suspense go together beautifully. Danger and adventure heighten the sensual tension in the story and vice versa."

Gideon looked distinctly skeptical as he set out two cups and spooned instant coffee into one.

"I take it you don't read in the genre?" Sarah ventured, a little disappointed after all these months of corresponding with her he had apparently not bothered to buy one of her books and read it.

"No, can't say that I do." Gideon put the kettle on the stove.

Sarah studied him as he turned to face her. He leaned back against the edge of the counter and folded his arms across his broad chest. Either a forbidding scowl was habitual for him or else she had interrupted something important. Perhaps he had been in the middle of one of his articles for *Cache*. She knew how it felt to be interrupted in the middle of writing.

"Look, if I've caught you at an awkward moment, I could come back later," she offered.

"Good idea. How much later?"

"In a couple of hours, say?"

The edge of his mouth lifted faintly. The hint of amusement vanished almost instantly. "Forget it. Might as well get this over and done. I get the feeling you're the persistent type. Tell me why you've suddenly decided to go treasure hunting, Ms. Fleetwood."

"It's time," Sarah said simply.

"What do you mean, it's time?"

"I just have a feeling about it."

"How long have you known about the legend of the Flowers?"

"Almost a year. The story has been handed down through the women of my family for years but no one ever paid much attention to it. When my aunt died a year ago, however, she left the map to me."

Gideon didn't move but there was a new intensity in his eyes. "What map?"

"The map Emelina Fleetwood made. You mentioned it in your letter, remember? You said you doubted its existence, but it's quite real. My aunt had it most of her life until she willed it to me." Sarah reached for her purse and started scrabbling about inside. "I made a dozen copies and put the original in a safe-deposit box. I brought one of the copies with me." She hauled out a clear plastic envelope that protected a sheet of paper with a crude sketch and some words written on it.

Gideon reached for the envelope with the first show of genuine curiosity he had yet exhibited. He frowned over the cryptic drawing. "Treasure maps are a dime a dozen. Someone's always claiming to have one or trying to sell one. Ninety-nine point nine percent of them are fake. What makes you think this one is genuine?"

"My aunt once had the map analyzed by a lab to make sure the paper at least dated from the right period. It did."

"That doesn't mean the map is genuine or even that it was ever meant to lead anyone to the Flowers. It could have been drawn for any number of reasons."

"It's the real thing."

Gideon's head came up, his eyes brilliant. "You sound very sure of that."

"I am. I have a feeling about it." *And I've also got a feeling about you, Gideon Trace, but we'll get to that eventually.*

"Even if it's genuine, what makes you think you'll be the Fleetwood to find it?"

"I've got a—"

"A feeling. Right. Do you get these feelings often, Ms. Fleetwood?"

"Often enough to know I should pay attention when one hits." There was a soft meow from the floor. Sarah looked down as Ellora jumped lightly into her lap and proceeded to curl up.

"I think I should point out that I don't do the kind of consulting work you're looking for," Gideon stated, his gaze on Sarah's hand as she stroked his cat.

"I know you're in the business of publishing *Cache*, but I thought you might be interested in this project. Right up your alley. It's such a fascinating legend. Think what a great article it would make for your magazine."

"I've heard plenty of other tales just as fascinating, if not more so. Few of them ever lead to a real find. The most anyone ever actually uncovers is an old bit of rusted metal or a button or a stray rifle ball. Treasure hunting is just a hobby for most people. No one gets rich. Believe me, there's more money in publishing *Cache* than there is in actually hunting for the goodies."

"Well, I'm going to give this a whirl and I really think you should consider coming along with me, Gideon."

He blinked. "Me? Why?" Then he quickly held up a palm to forestall her answer. "Wait, don't tell me. You've got a feeling, right?"

"Right," she said, delighted he understood. "Now, how soon can we leave? I've got enough stuff packed in my car to last for a couple of weeks. I figure if you're not particularly busy on an issue of the magazine, we could take off tomorrow morning."

He stared at her. "Just like that? Are you out of your mind? You don't even know me. I could be a mass murderer, as far as you're concerned."

"Don't be ridiculous. I feel like I've known you for months. Ever since I got your first letter, in fact."

Gideon looked slightly stunned. "You're either incredibly naive or amazingly foolish. You shouldn't be allowed out except on a leash."

"I promise you, I'm neither particularly naive nor foolish. I know what I'm doing. I usually do."

"You're serious about this, aren't you? You materialize out of thin air on my doorstep, wave an old map in my face and expect me to immediately sign on for the duration of your idiotic expedition?"

"I like to think of it as a quest. All quests need a knight-errant. You're elected."

"Who are you? The beautiful princess or something?" He slapped the envelope with the map down on the table.

Sarah grinned. "What you see is what you get. I left my tiara at home. How about it, Mr. Trace? Are you available for hire?"

"No, I'm not available," he muttered as the kettle began to whistle. "I write about lost treasure. I don't waste my time looking for it."

"But you won't be wasting your time. I'll pay you."

"Look, lady, treasure hunting costs money. A lot of money. People have poured millions into projects aimed at locating sunken ships and lost gold mines." He picked up her tea bag and dropped it into a cup. Then he poured boiling water over it. When he was finished he poured water over the instant coffee in his own cup. Every movement was economical and controlled. It was the kind of motion that indicated underlying strength and power.

"I'm not suggesting we attempt a major expedition to find a sunken treasure ship. I'm only after Emelina Fleetwood's Flowers. And I've got a map. What could be simpler?"

Gideon shook his head in disgust as he carried the cups over to the table and sat down across from her. "Listen carefully, Ms. Fleetwood, while I spell out a few facts of life. Treasure hunting is almost never successful. At least not today. A hundred, two hundred years ago it was still possible for an amateur to stumble across something like the temple caves of Ellora or a forgotten pharaoh's tomb. Today, the only people who get that kind of thrill are professional archaeologists and even for them, the thrills are few and far between."

"I'm only trying to find a few pairs of earrings, not a lost civilization."

"Then that puts you in the ranks of the hobbyists. You'd be better off buying yourself a metal detector and heading for the beach to hunt for lost change."

"You're really determined to be difficult about this, aren't you?"

"I'm attempting to give you a realistic picture of what you're contemplating."

"Where's your spirit of adventure? You must have a genuine interest in treasure hunting or you would never have started a publication like *Cache*. Don't you feel the lure of the lost treasure? The excitement of the search? The lust for a dazzling fortune in lost gems?"

Gideon's eyes glittered briefly behind harrowed lids. "I try to focus my lust on more accessible objects."

Sarah blinked and then smiled. "Are you trying to frighten me, by any chance?"

He sighed. "I get the feeling that would be difficult."

"Impossible," she said crisply.

He watched apprehensively as she yanked the tea bag out of her cup, squeezed it quickly between thumb and forefinger and glanced around for a place to toss it. When she showed signs of hurling it across the room into the sink, Gideon moved.

"Here, I'll take that." Gideon plucked the tea bag from her fingers and got to his feet. He went over to the sink, opened a cupboard door underneath and carefully dropped the dripping tea bag into a trash bin. Then he came back to the table and sat down again.

"Everybody's afraid of something, Ms. Fleetwood."

"True. And I'm no exception to the rule. But I'm not afraid of you."

"Because you've got a feeling about me?"

"Right."

"You know something, Ms. Fleetwood?"

"Call me Sarah. What?"

"You're one very bizarre female."

"Yes, I know," Sarah admitted humbly. "My friends have often told me that."

"Wise friends. Have they attempted to diagnose your condition?"

"They say my problem is that I tend to think sideways. As I said, what do they know? Now, about our project."

"Already it's *our* project?"

"I've been thinking of it as our project right from the moment the idea occurred to me."

"When was that fateful moment?"

"I believe I was in the shower at the time. I get many of my best ideas in the shower, you know."

"No, I didn't know." Gideon looked unwillingly fascinated.

"At any rate, I suddenly knew that it was time to look for the Fleetwood earrings and that I was the one to search for them. I got out of the shower, put on a robe and walked out into the living room. Your latest letter with the research data on salvage operations that I needed for *Glitter Quest* was on my desk. I glanced at it and immediately knew I wanted you to help me in my search."

"This is amazing."

"Isn't it, though? I expect it will be a lot of fun, too. And very educational?"

"Educational?"

"Sure. The material you sent me on treasure hunting for *Glitter Quest* was extremely interesting, but rather academic, if you know what I mean. This way I'll have a chance to learn about the process of a real-life treasure hunt from the ground up, so to speak."

Gideon sipped his instant coffee. "What if I tell you I'm not free at the moment to take off for two weeks?"

"Well, I could come back at a later date, I suppose."

"How much later?"

"Tomorrow?"

"Or the next day, maybe? Never mind. It's obvious you're not going to go away for good."

"I really could postpone this for a while if it was absolutely necessary. After all, those earrings have been lost for a long time. But I sort of thought this was the right moment to start the search. And something tells me you have to be involved in the hunt. I really can't explain it, but I sense it's inevitable. I trust my intuition."

"You do realize that financing this little expedition is going to be a major project in itself? Two weeks in the mountains including meals, lodging and gas are not going to come cheap. Can you afford it?"

"I've budgeted for it. I'm a reasonably successful writer, Gideon, and I assure you I can handle the tab for this venture. I'll consider it my annual vacation."

"You want to spend your annual vacation digging around in the dirt for something that probably doesn't even exist?"

"You have to learn to think positive, Gideon," she said earnestly. "The earrings exist and we'll find them."

"Tell me, Sarah, do you usually have to strong-arm some man into accompanying you on your annual vacations?"

"Now, don't be sarcastic. To tell you the truth, I've never met one who was worth the effort before. And it does appear to be an effort, doesn't it? I didn't realize it would be quite this difficult."

Gideon fixed her with a strangely baffled look. "I'm worth the effort because I can show you how to read that map or something?"

"Sarah pursed her lips and scratched behind Ellora's ears. "Not exactly. Maybe. You've certainly had more experience with treasure maps than I've had. But I'm not sure if that's why I need you along. It's hard to explain. I just know I want you with me. Somehow the Flowers and the map and you are all linked together."

He frowned suspiciously. "You're not under the impression you're psychic or something, are you?"

"Of course not."

"Are you sure?"

"You're teasing me, aren't you? Don't worry, I'm not weird or anything. Just sort of intuitive. The minute we started corresponding, for example, I knew I was going to like you very much. I certainly hope you feel the same way about me."

"I'll be blunt, Sarah Fleetwood. I can't even begin to figure out how I feel about you."

"Well, you don't need to make up your mind this instant."

"I don't? What a relief."

She smiled sunnily and dove into her oversized bag for a piece of paper and a pen. "Here's the name of the place where I'm staying tonight. It's a tiny little motel a couple miles down the road." She jotted down the name. "Know it?"

He scowled at the slip of paper. "Sure, I know it. We don't have that many motels around here. What about it?"

"I suggest you pick me up for dinner around six o'clock. The motel clerk said there was a nice little restaurant nearby. You'll probably be more relaxed if we settle the details of our association over dinner."

"*Dinner.*"

"You do eat dinner, don't you?" Sarah gently lifted Ellora from her lap and set her on the floor. The cat purred more loudly than ever.

"Yeah, I eat dinner. That's not the point. The point is . . ."

"Don't worry, I'm buying." Sarah picked up her bag. "Please, Gideon? This is very important to me and I feel certain that once you've had a chance to think about it all, you're going to want to accompany me on my search for the Flowers. Have you got anything else you have to do tonight?"

"What if I said I had a date?"

Sarah was thunderstruck. "Good grief, I never even considered that. Have you got a date?"

Gideon groaned. "No."

"Wonderful. Then it's all settled. See you at six." Sarah whipped around and headed toward the front door, digging the car keys out of her pocket. "Just give me a chance, Gideon," she called back over her shoulder. "I know I can talk you into this. And you won't lose by it, I promise. I'm prepared to pay you a very decent wage. You can apply it toward the heating bill for this house."

She waved from the doorway at Gideon, who was still sitting at the kitchen table, and then she turned to lope down the porch steps. Machu Picchu had not moved from his throne. He slitted his eyes as Sarah stepped carefully around him.

"It's okay, beast. I know what I'm doing. I'll take good care of him." Sarah grinned at the cat and went down the walk to get into her car.

Inside the house Gideon sat unmoving until the cheerful hum of the compact's small engine had faded into the distance. Then he looked down at Ellora.

"You know something? She reminds me of you. She moved right in on us the same way you moved in on me and old Machu a year ago. What the hell am I supposed to do now?"

He got up slowly and carried the cups over to the sink. He had long ago discovered that if he didn't pick up the dishes, they never got picked up. He was willing to bet that Sarah Fleetwood's apartment would be littered with old tea mugs that needed washing.

"The Flowers. Why in hell did it have to be the Flowers? And why her?" Gideon stalked into the living room and paused for a moment beside the unfinished chess game. He had carved the pieces himself. They weren't great art, but they were functional. He picked up the queen and turned it over and over in his hand, examining it from all angles.

He was interrupted in his contemplation of the queen by a grumbling roar from the front door. Gideon went to open it. Machu Picchu ambled inside, pausing briefly to slap his tail heavily against Gideon's boot before he heaved himself up onto his favorite indoor position on the back of the sofa.

"Dinner. I'm supposed to drop everything and pick her up for dinner. Where does she get off giving orders like that? Who the hell does she think she is?"

The cats blinked lazily and watched as Gideon strode along the hall to his study. There, carefully weighted down by a big chunk of rose quartz, he found the stack of letters he had received from one Sarah Fleetwood. For some reason he couldn't explain why he'd kept them all.

The earliest dated from four months ago when she had first contacted him for information on modern treasure hunting. The latest dated from last week. He picked it up and scanned it again. It was in the same style as all the rest, breezy, enthusiastic, cheerful and inexplicably captivating.

Dear Mr. Trace:
It's midnight but I had to let you know I am nearly finished with *Glitter Quest*. I want to tell you how much I appreciate your research assistance. It really made a difference. The plot is much more intricate and involved because of some of the details you provided. It's been fascinating working

with you. This has been such a fun book to write.

I must tell you I have truly enjoyed our corre-spondence these past few months. In fact, I have been inspired, but I'll explain just how at another time.

By the way, if you're still suffering from that cold you mentioned in your last note, I suggest you try hot tea with a shot of lemon and honey. Works wonders.

Yours,
Sarah

P.S. Am enclosing a cartoon I cut out of the paper this afternoon. I thought you would enjoy it.

The cartoon featured a pair of cats. It was only a co-incidence that the cats, one beefy and one quite small, vaguely resembled Machu Picchu and Ellora, Gideon told himself. After all, he'd never mentioned either fe-line in his letters to Sarah.

He glanced at the old clock in the corner. It was still early in the day. Plenty of time to find an excuse for not taking Sarah Fleetwood to dinner.

But the woman knew too damned much about the Fleetwood Flowers, Gideon reminded himself. And now she had managed to locate him. That made her a distinct threat to the quiet, well-ordered existence he had carved out for himself.

Gideon had learned long ago that it was good policy to neutralize potential threats before they got to be real problems.

He'd better take the lady to dinner.

2

IT WASN'T as if he had anything better to do, Gideon told himself as he climbed out of his car in the motel parking lot. It was either this or another evening alone with Ellora, Machu Picchu and a good book. Not that the evenings alone were all that bad. For the most part he found them comfortable.

But a part of him still hankered after an occasional shot of excitement and, for better or worse, Sarah Fleetwood had managed to whet his appetite. He had to admit it was the first time in a long while that a woman had been this interesting. What few relationships he'd gotten involved in since his divorce had tended to be quiet and extremely low-key.

There was nothing quiet or low-key about Sarah Fleetwood.

The door of one of the motel rooms was flung wide as he started toward the office to inquire about Sarah's room number.

"Hi, Gideon," Sarah called out across the parking lot. "I'm ready."

He turned at the sound of Sarah's voice and saw her furiously locking the door behind herself. She must have been watching for him from the window. Gideon couldn't remember the last time a woman had waited impatiently for him at a window. Leanna had always been much too poised or preoccupied with her work for that sort of thing, at least when it came to waiting for him.

Of course, he should bear in mind that Sarah Fleetwood was not just waiting for a dinner date. She was after five pairs of jeweled earrings known as the Fleetwood Flowers. That was bound to make any woman eager.

"You're late," Sarah informed him as she hurried across the parking lot. Her high heels clicked on the pavement in a way Gideon found surprisingly sexy. The sound made him think of soft feminine sighs and sudden passion in the middle of the night.

Annoyed with himself, he took his mind off sex and glanced at his watch. "Five minutes. You going to fire me for a lousy five minutes?"

She gave a gurgle of delighted laughter as she hopped into the car without waiting for him to get the door. "Does that mean you've decided to let me hire you in the first place?"

He slid behind the wheel and turned the key in the ignition. "I'm thinking about it."

"Then it's all set." Sarah sat back, clearly bubbling over with satisfaction.

"Not quite." He spun the wheel and drove out of the small lot. "I said I'm thinking about it. I'll let you know my answer when I'm ready."

"Okay, okay. Be that way. In the meantime, I'm hungry. Does this place called the Wild Water Inn have pasta?"

"I've never noticed. Whenever I go there, I order fish. That's the house specialty."

"Maybe they have some pasta and fish dishes. Linguine with clams or something."

He slanted her an appraising glance. "I wouldn't be surprised. Even if it's not on the menu, I'll bet the chef will bend over backward to make a special."

Sarah's eyes widened in surprise. "Do you really think so? He must be a very accommodating chef. What's his name?"

"Mort."

"Mort. I'll remember that. What a nice man."

"You've never even met him and you don't know for sure yet if he'll go to the trouble of preparing something special for you." But Mort probably would do it, Gideon conceded. There was something about Sarah Fleetwood that made a man want to please her just to see the delight reflected in her face.

Any man or just him? he wondered with a sudden sense of foreboding.

Gideon studied her out of the corner of his eye as she watched the rugged coastline sweep past. He knew he was checking to see if his first impression had been wrong. But his earlier reactions this afternoon did not undergo any drastic revision now.

He guessed her age at around thirty, give or take a couple of years, although she might have been younger. Those clear, deep hazel eyes were just as unsettling now as they had been when he'd first opened his door to her, her small, elfin features just as piquant.

The red silk sheath she wore played lightly over a slender, surprisingly sensuous body. There were veins of gold running through her light brown hair. She had brushed the heavy mass straight back from her forehead and tied it in a cascading ponytail that somehow managed to look chic instead of youthful. There was a sleek delicacy about her that would make anything she wore look stylish.

All in all, she still reminded him of Ellora. Gideon briefly regretted that he hadn't put on a tie. He suddenly felt vaguely underdressed in his jeans and white shirt.

"This scenery is magnificent, isn't it?" Sarah said, turning away from the window reluctantly. "I'm going to have to set a book here. It's the perfect backdrop for a romance with intrigue and suspense. Lots of drama and impending danger. Where did you live before you moved to Washington, Gideon?"

"Here and there."

"Ah-ha. A world-weary wanderer who's finally decided to settle down. I knew it. What did you do before you started publishing *Cache*?"

"This and that."

"Real-life treasure hunting, I'll bet."

He gave her an irritated glance. "What makes you say that?"

"Well, we already know you're not a mass murderer and I don't see you as a sales rep. So what else would give you a background in this and that?"

"The inability to hold a good job for any length of time?"

"Nah. You could do just about anything you wanted to do. If you wanted to hold down an ordinary job, you'd have done it. But I don't see you as an ordinary sort of man, Gideon. You're like one of the heroes out of my books and I never write about ordinary men."

"Look, Ms. Fleetwood, we'll probably get along a whole lot better if you don't try to romanticize me."

"How can I help it? You're a very romantic figure."

"You call being forty years old and living alone in an old house with two cats romantic?" He glanced at her in sheer disbelief.

"Very."

"You've got the wrong man. You want someone like Jake Savage."

She was immediately fascinated. "Who?"

"Jake Savage." Gideon wasn't surprised by her reaction. Women always reacted that way to Savage. Just the sound of his name was enough to do it for this particular female, apparently.

"What a terrific name. Do you think he'd mind if I used it some day in a book?"

"I doubt it, he's dead."

"Too bad. What was he like?"

"He was the kind of guy you're trying to make me into. Savage was a real-life adventurer. Liked to live life on the edge. Ran a business called Savage & Company."

"What did Savage & Company do?"

"Just about anything in and around South America and the Caribbean that paid enough. Flew supplies into the jungles for various governments, including our own. Transported equipment up rivers for tourists, photographers and scientists. Handled shipments of medicine and clothing for charitable organizations. Acted as guides and outfitters for archaeologists and the occasional team of journalists. And once in a while Savage and Company did some actual treasure hunting. Oh, you'd have loved Jake Savage, all right."

"What happened to him?" Sarah demanded.

"The story is he went off on a particularly dangerous job one day and never came back out of the jungle."

"And thus passed into legend. Great story."

"Thought you'd like it."

"Did Jake Savage go alone on his last expedition?"

Gideon hesitated. "Savage had a partner who usually accompanied him."

"Did the partner die in the jungle, too?"

"Apparently. He didn't return, at any rate, but hardly anyone noticed. Savage was the big name."

"So his obit got all the attention."

"Right. Without him the company folded."

"All very interesting, but we don't need Jake Savage along on our expedition. We've got you."

"You must drive people nuts with all this boundless optimism and enthusiasm."

She bit her lip. "Am I driving you nuts?"

"Yeah. But don't worry about it. I haven't got anything better to do tonight."

She grinned. "I didn't think so."

Ten minutes later when he walked into the restaurant with Sarah Fleetwood beside him, it seemed to Gideon that every head in the place turned in his direction.

That wasn't strictly true, of course. The customers from out of town had no interest whatsoever in the very ordinary sight of a man walking into a restaurant with a woman. But all the locals, from the hostess to the busboy, were instantly intrigued. Gideon swore silently. He was not accustomed to being the center of attention and he didn't like it. It was all Sarah's fault.

"Nice to see you again, Gideon. It's been a while. Follow me, please." Maryann Appley, the young hostess, smiled very brightly as she led the way to a seat by the window. "I hope you enjoy your dinner, ma'am," she added to Sarah as she pulled out the chair.

"Thanks, I will," Sarah said cheerfully, reaching for the menu. "Look, they do have linguine and clams. What luck." As soon as the hostess disappeared she leaned forward. "Why is everyone staring?" she asked in a stage whisper.

"It's been a while since I brought a lady here." Gideon picked up his menu.

"Oh." She looked thoughtful. "Does that mean you don't date much?"

"It's a small community. Not many single women around. They all head for Portland or Los Angeles because there aren't many single men around here, either."

"There's you."

Gideon looked up. "What are you trying to do? Figure out why I'm not married?"

Sarah blushed a charming shade of peach and looked down at her silverware. "I suppose so. Frankly, I couldn't believe my good luck when I realized from your first letter that you weren't married."

"I don't recall mentioning the fact."

"No, but I could tell. In my age group the men always seem to be married. Or if they're single it's because they've just recently been divorced and are all messed up in the head. Or they're gay." She looked briefly anxious.

"I'm not gay and I'm not recently divorced."

She relaxed back into her infectious smile. "Perfect."

"You think so?"

"Definitely. Have you ever been married, Gideon?"

"You get real personal, real quick, don't you?"

"Not normally but I feel like we've known each other for four whole months."

"Funny. I feel like I just met you today."

"I'm going too fast for you, aren't I?"

"That's one way of looking at it. What is all this personal stuff leading up to? You planning to propose marriage to me?"

Sarah cleared her throat delicately and studied her menu. "Don't be ridiculous. It's much too soon for that."

Gideon stared at her, his head reeling. "Maybe we'd better take this one step at a time."

"My thoughts exactly. We don't want to terrorize you."

"I'm beyond terror. I'm in the Twilight Zone. I feel the way Machu Picchu did the day Ellora arrived on the doorstep."

Sarah laughed and closed her menu with a snap. Her eyes sparkled as she studied him across the table. "What did Ellora do first?"

"Moved right in on Machu's feed bowl. Normally, Machu would have bitten off the head of any intruder who got within twenty yards of his food."

"But not Ellora."

"No. That's when I knew we were done for. I think she baffled him at first. By the time he figured out what was going on, it was too late. She was a permanent resident. You ever been married?"

That caught her off guard. Gideon experienced a definite twinge of satisfaction at having finally achieved the near impossible. He had a feeling Sarah was almost never caught flat-footed. She was too quick, too animated, always one step ahead. A sideways thinker. He watched as she played with a fork for a minute.

"I was almost married once," she said finally. "About four years ago."

"What happened?"

"Got stood up at the altar."

He was astounded. "Literally?"

"Literally. Very embarrassing, to be honest. Church full of people. Spectacular dress. Reception waiting.

And no groom. It was all very dramatic, I assure you. Enough to put a woman off marriage for life. But nothing is ever wasted for a writer. One of these days, I'm going to do a romance that starts out with the heroine being left at the altar. Snappy beginning, don't you think?"

"How's it going to end?"

"At the altar, of course. With the right man this time."

"But you're not ready to write that story yet?" he asked on a hunch.

"No. The whole experience left me feeling a little raw, if you want to know the truth. Even if it was all my own fault."

Gideon scowled. "What do you mean, your own fault?"

"You're suddenly full of questions. Does this mean you're not bored?"

"You might be a pain in the neck at times, Sarah, but I seriously doubt you could ever manage to be boring."

"I'll take that as a compliment."

"You didn't answer my question."

She sighed and appeared to be marshaling her thoughts. Gideon got the feeling she was just about to open her mouth when Bernice Sawyer, the waitress, arrived to take their order. He swore silently.

"I'll have the linguine and clams," Sarah announced. "And please tell Mort I was thrilled to see it on the menu. I love linguine and clams."

Bernice blinked. "Uh, sure, I'll tell him. How about you, Gideon?"

"The salmon," he told her dourly, wishing she would go away so he could get the answer to his question.

"Right. Salmon. As usual." Bernice smiled, undaunted by his obvious irritation. "Glass of wine?"

"Yes, please," said Sarah instantly.

"Why not?" Gideon thrust the menu at Bernice, hoping she'd take the hint and leave quickly.

"Be right back," she promised and sauntered off in the direction of the kitchen.

"Really, Gideon, there's no need to be rude," Sarah murmured in a low, chiding tone.

"Was I?"

"Yes, you were."

Bernice materialized again with the wine. Gideon possessed himself in patience until Sarah had taken a sip. When her gaze went toward the view of rocks and crashing surf, he tried again. "So why was it all your fault?"

"I beg your pardon?" She looked politely blank, as if she hadn't followed his train of thought.

Gideon knew instantly she was faking it. "Getting left at the altar. Why was it your fault?"

"Umm. Well, I should have seen it coming." She took another sip of wine.

"You've already told me you're not exactly psychic. How could you have seen it coming?"

"For a man who thought I was coming on a little too strong a while ago, you're awfully interested in my private life all of a sudden."

"Think of this as an interview. I'm still trying to make up my mind about whether or not to accept your offer of a job."

Sarah smiled. "How is my answering your question going to tell you what sort of employer I'll be?"

"I won't know until I hear the answer."

She drummed her fingers on the table, contemplating that. "It's hard to explain. I just knew later that I should have understood Richard didn't really want to marry me. He was on the rebound and he only thought he wanted to marry me."

"How did you feel toward him?"

"Well, you have to understand that I was at a point in my life when I was trying to be terribly realistic about relationships. I had convinced myself that the man of my dreams was pure fiction and I would only get hurt looking for him. Richard was sexy and charming and very nice, really. We had a lot in common and he gave me a whirlwind courtship. Very romantic."

"What happened?"

"The night before our wedding his ex-wife decided she had made a mistake and called him up. He went to meet her. I thought he was going off to his bachelor party. Some bachelor party. At any rate, he didn't show up the next day in church. All for the best, of course. Imagine getting married and then having him change his mind."

"Richard sounds like a real son of a—"

"That is, naturally, one point of view. I'm inclined toward it, myself." Sarah's eyes gleamed with mischief. "The reason the whole thing shook me up so much was that I'd never really made that kind of mistake before. I had plenty of warning and enough hints that he was still emotionally tangled up with his ex-wife, but I didn't pay any attention to them. I felt like an idiot later."

Gideon eyed her thoughtfully. "It threw a scare into you, that's what really happened. You'd always relied heavily on your intuition and it failed you."

"No. I keep telling you, my intuition was fine. I just wasn't paying attention."

"You got a scare. It should have taught you a good lesson about trusting your so-called intuition, but I'll bet you didn't learn a damn thing from the experience."

For the first time since she had landed like a whirlwind in his life, she looked genuinely annoyed with him. "Look, Gideon . . ."

"Forget it," Gideon said. "This brings us to the little matter of your hiring me as a treasure-hunting consultant."

"It does?"

He was finally beginning to feel like he was catching up with her. At this rate, he might even gain the upper hand for a few breathless minutes. "It does," he confirmed. "It's obvious that you can't really be any more sure of me than you were of this jerk, Richard."

"Not the same thing at all."

"How do you know?"

"I know."

"Got a feeling, right?" he mocked.

"Yes, I do, damn it. Don't make fun of me, Gideon."

"I wouldn't think of it."

She glowered at him. "And don't, whatever you do, turn out to be one of those people who *lectures*."

"God forbid." He sat back and swirled the wine in his glass. So much for trying to make her think twice about the whole project. He wasn't sure why he had bothered. Maybe just to see how deep her certainty ran.

"That was the only thing that worried me a tad, you know," she said finally.

"I've lost you again. What was the only thing that worried you?"

"That you might have a tendency to lecture. I picked that up here and there in some of your letters. But it's a relatively minor flaw and one I'm sure we can work around."

"You think so?" Gideon met her mischievous gaze and the vague tension that had been gnawing at him for several hours suddenly coalesced into a powerful urge to take her into his arms and wipe some of that feminine assurance out of her eyes. He knew just how he would kiss her. Hard and deep and very thoroughly.

"I think so. Say, I've been meaning to ask, did you ever try that recipe for buckwheat noodles I sent you last month?"

"No. The local stores don't run to fancy stuff like buckwheat noodles."

"You should have told me. I'd have sent you some."

"I was thinking about it," he admitted. "But you showed up on my doorstep before I got around to writing the letter." No point telling her that all the recipes she'd sent him during the past four months were neatly filed in a kitchen drawer. He took them out and read through them regularly but he had never actually tried one.

"I see."

Gideon watched her closely. "You're determined to go after the Flowers, aren't you?"

"Absolutely."

"What will you do if I don't agree to come along?"

"Gideon, I'm counting on you to help me."

"Forget the big-eyed approach. I don't respond to it." Like hell. His whole body was responding. "Any idea how much the earrings are worth?" he asked casually.

"Not really, but I'm sure it's a great deal. Each pair was made out of a different gemstone. One pair was made out of sapphires, one out of rubies, one out of diamonds, one out of opals and one out of pearls. The story is that Emelina Fleetwood knew she would never marry and she was determined to give herself the kind of jewels a rich husband would have given her. She wanted to prove she didn't need a man to shower her in luxury. She could do it all by herself."

"And you want to follow in her footsteps?"

Sarah frowned. "Not exactly. I don't think you understand. The Fleetwood Flowers are a piece of history, my personal history."

"You're really fixated on those earrings, aren't you?"

"They're family heirlooms. Naturally I'm interested in them."

"Sure. Family heirlooms. They hold no monetary interest for you at all, do they? Just pure historic value. I suppose you're going to tell me you're not going to sell them if you find them?"

Sarah put down her glass of wine with great care. The laughter had completely vanished from her eyes. "What is this?" she asked quietly. "You think I'm some sort of opportunist? A gold digger? A scheming little hussy trying to get rich quick?"

"I didn't say that."

"You don't have to say it." Her gaze narrowed. "Look at it this way, Gideon. Unlike most treasure hunters, I'm at least going after a fortune that belongs to me."

"You think that because those earrings belonged to someone in your family who lived way back in the late eighteen hundreds that you now have a claim on them?"

"More of a claim than anyone else."

"I've got news for you. Treasure that old belongs to whoever is clever enough to dig it up."

"I plan to be the one who's clever enough to dig it up."

"Take it from me. Amateurs never find real treasure. You'll be wasting your time, Sarah."

"I was right. You do have a tendency to harangue."

Gideon glanced up and saw Bernice heading toward the table. "Let's change the subject. Here comes our fish."

Sarah lifted her eyes ceilingward in an expression of utter disgust and snapped back in her chair. "Wouldn't want to spoil your appetite."

"You won't."

Five minutes of oppressive silence followed. Gideon decided he wasn't going to be the one to break it. The salmon was good, as usual. Mort really could cook.

"Gideon?"

"Yeah?"

"You don't really think me a cheap, scheming opportunist just because I want to find the Flowers, do you? Do you genuinely believe I'm just trying to use you?"

He put down his fork. "I'm not sure what to think. It's possible you've spent the past four months establishing a sort of relationship with me so that when you finally asked for help, I'd be more likely to say yes and work cheap."

"Damn. It never occurred to me you'd see things in that light. I was so sure . . ."

He picked up his fork again. "You're an unusual woman, Sarah. And that's putting it politely. I don't know what to make of you, yet."

"I really have got you terrorized," she said, her voice unnaturally flat.

"I wouldn't say that."

"Does this mean you truly aren't interested in helping me find the Flowers?"

"I didn't say that."

"Well, what are you trying to say, for heaven's sake?"

"Don't get mad."

"I'm not mad. I just want to know where I stand. Are you going to help me or not?"

"I'm still thinking about it."

"Was your ex-wife a gold digger?" Sarah demanded suddenly. "Is that why I'm making you nervous? Do I look like her or something?"

"No, you definitely do not look like her. Leanna liked success in whatever form it took and she liked flash. But I wouldn't call her a gold digger. She had too much class for that."

"Flash? What do you mean by flash?"

"Never mind. Eat your linguine."

"Gideon, are you going to help me with my treasure hunt or not? Tell me now. I don't take suspense well."

"You should, since you write it."

"That's different. What's your answer?"

"I don't know yet. I'll let you know later."

"Oh, yeah?" She glowered at him. "I'm not so sure I need or want your answer now or later."

"Okay."

"Don't be so bloody difficult, Gideon. Let's just forget the whole thing."

"Fine."

Her fingers clenched around her fork. "I can't believe I was so wrong about you. Can't we at least talk about this some more?"

"Not right now. I said I'd give you my answer later and I will. Let's talk about something else."

"Like what?"

He shrugged. "Pick a topic."

She paused. "All right. What kind of academic background do you have?"

"Does it matter?"

"I was just curious. You said to pick a topic. I picked a topic. If you don't like it, you're free to choose another."

"School of hard knocks. I graduated with honors." When she said nothing in response, Gideon began to feel guilty. He had only himself to blame for sabotaging her buoyant spirits. "What about you?"

"Does it matter?"

He winced. "No. Just trying to make conversation."

"I've got a better idea. Let's not try. I think it would be best if we both shut up for a while."

This time the silence that hung over the table stretched until Bernice arrived with the check.

Well, Trace, you've managed to dazzle her with your usual devastating charm, haven't you? You're hell on wheels with the female of the species, all right. You had to work real hard this time, didn't you? She didn't get discouraged easily. You had to really push. But now you've done it. You've managed to turn her off completely. Nice going. Even Machu had the sense not to screw up this badly when Ellora turned up on the doorstop.

Gideon was startled at the unexpected sense of loss he felt.

THE MAN MUST HAVE BEEN MAULED rather thoroughly at some point in the past, Sarah decided some time later. She sat quietly in the passenger seat of Gideon's car as he drove back to her motel. She no longer knew what to say. She couldn't believe she had been so wrong about him, but there was no doubt he didn't seem to want to have much to do with her.

Had she misjudged him completely?

It was possible. She had managed to fool herself once before.

Another curtain of fog was closing in from the sea as Gideon parked his car in front of Sarah's room. A yellow lamp illuminated the number on her door. She started to dig out her keys without much enthusiasm.

"Good night," Sarah made herself say without any emotion. "Sorry I took up so much of your time. Good luck with your magazine. Maybe I'll contact you again some day if I ever decide to do another treasure hunt story."

Gideon didn't move from behind the wheel. He just sat there, large and forbidding in the deep shadows. "Is the offer still open?"

Sarah's hand froze on the door handle. "Yes."

"I'll take the job."

"Gideon." All the doubts of a moment before dissolved in a second. Without a moment's hesitation she threw herself across the seat and into his arms.

3

IT CAME AS A DISTINCT SHOCK to Sarah when Gideon's arms abruptly tightened around her in a crushing grip. His mouth came down over hers with devastating swiftness as he pinned her against the back of the seat.

Belatedly she tried to pull away from the overwhelming embrace as she realized what she had initiated. She had been intending only a quick, impulsive, friendly hug. She should have known better than to let herself get this close to him. She was too vulnerable.

It had finally dawned on her over dinner that Gideon had not fallen for her during the past four months the way she had fallen for him. Her letters had meant nothing to him. He had not been thinking about her as anything more important than just another *Cache* subscriber asking for assistance. He was nowhere near ready for a relationship.

But now she found herself trapped in an embrace that was more shatteringly intimate than any she had ever known. It was only a kiss, her mind cried out. But she had never been kissed like this. It was, after all, her first kiss from Gideon. Gideon with whom she had slowly, surely fallen in love during the past few months.

Gideon, her own personal dream hero come to life.

Except that he didn't see himself in quite the same light. What's more, he saw her as a nuisance.

"Gideon?" She could barely speak his name. She gripped his shoulders with feverish intensity as four months of gathering desire welled up inside and threatened to swamp her.

"You're so delicate and fragile," Gideon muttered against her mouth. His hands moved over her with incredible sensitivity, learning the shape and feel of her. "I could crush you."

"You won't." She could not think clearly now that he had finally touched her. She clung to him even more tightly, her arms curving around his neck, her head tipped back against the seat. He was so wonderfully solid and substantial—so real. She'd known all along she couldn't have been wrong about him. Perhaps he was finally beginning to realize it, too.

His mouth moved against hers again. The kiss was far more satisfying than she had dared to dream it would be. There was an exciting, intoxicating hunger in him that she responded to instantly. She felt the edge of his teeth nibbling on her lower lip and she trembled.

He held her in a grip of iron, as if he was afraid she would evaporate. One of his hands slid down to her hip, squeezing gently. She splayed her fingers over his broad shoulders, savoring the strong, smoothly muscled contours. The masculine power in him drew her like a magnet. She moved beneath his crushing weight.

"Sarah?" His voice was ragged.

She murmured softly, a small, choked cry of delight and need.

"It's okay, Sarah," Gideon said harshly. "You don't have to fake it."

Sarah froze as if someone had just poured ice water over her. Frantically she tried to pull her scattered senses back into a coherent pattern of thought.

"Fake it?" she gasped. "What do you mean, fake it?"

"I've already said I'll help you look for the earrings. You don't have to pay me off with sex."

She struggled frantically to wriggle out of his arms. When he didn't release her, she managed to get one hand free. She swung wildly, aiming for the side of his face.

The blow never landed. Gideon caught her wrist when her palm was less than two inches from the target. "There are limits, lady. I'll be damned if I'll let you slap me."

"Let me go." She was frightened now, thoroughly aware for the first time of just how vulnerable she was.

"You started this, remember?"

"Get away from me, Gideon. Go back to your big, cold house and your cats. I don't need you to help me find those earrings. I'll do just fine on my own."

He looked down at her as she lay trapped and helpless in his arms. His eyes glittered with dangerous, unreadable emotions. Sarah held her breath.

Then, very slowly, he released her.

Sarah didn't hesitate. She scooted rapidly across the seat and yanked at the door handle.

"Wait." Gideon leaned across the seat and snagged her wrist, effectively chaining her when she tried to get out of the car.

"Let go of me."

His hard face tightened. "You're a temperamental little thing, aren't you? Simmer down. I've said I'll help you and I will. What did you expect me to think was going on a few minutes ago when you threw yourself into my arms?"

"You weren't supposed to think anything sordid or cheap or tacky about me, that's for sure." Sarah stared stonily ahead at the yellow light over her motel door.

"I tend to be impulsive when it comes to things like affectionate little hugs."

"That was no affectionate little hug we had going there."

"You're the one who tried to turn it into something more. And then you had the nerve to throw it in my face when I . . . when I . . . Never mind."

He swore softly. "Would it help if I said I'm sorry?"

She slid a sidelong glance at him. "Are you?"

"Yeah."

"For kissing me or for what you said afterward?"

He was silent for a heartbeat. "Not for kissing you."

"How about for calling me an opportunist and a gold digger earlier?"

His mouth kicked up wryly at the corner. "I didn't call you those things."

"You implied them. Are you sorry for that, too?"

"I guess."

She wrinkled her nose. "You sound like a five-year-old. *I guess I'm sorry for that, too.* But you aren't. Not really. Because deep down you still wonder if I am just a cheap, hustling bimbo looking for a fast buck. You have sadly disappointed me, Gideon."

"I can see that," he said dryly. "Obviously I'm not turning out to be heroic material. Let's forget about the personal side of this for a minute. Do we still have a deal?"

She tried to tug her wrist out of his grasp and got nowhere. "I don't know. Now I'm the one who will have to think about it. Your attitude is changing everything. I'll give you my answer in the morning."

"You do that. And one other thing. If I go with you on this treasure hunt, it won't be as your employee. I don't work for anyone. We'll be partners. I won't be taking salary from you."

"What do you want?"

"I'll want a share of whatever treasure we find."

She scowled at him. "But you've already said we probably won't find anything."

"I'll take my chances. Are you willing to split the profits?"

"Well, I don't know. I hadn't actually planned to sell the earrings. I was going to keep them."

"Fine. You keep four pairs. I'll take the fifth. My choice of the lot."

"I'm not sure that's fair. What if one pair turns out to be far more valuable than the others in today's market? The diamond pair, for instance?"

"That's the risk you take."

"I don't have to take any risk at all, Gideon. I'm the one with the map, remember?"

"Expert advice doesn't come cheap."

"You've already told me you're not a professional treasure hunter. You just write about treasure hunting."

"I'm a lot more professional than you are."

Her resentment flared. "Too bad I can't get hold of the famous Jake Savage, isn't it? Then I wouldn't need you."

His mouth thinned. "You said you thought I'd do just fine, remember?"

She wrenched her wrist free of his grasp at last and shoved open the car door. "I'll make my decision in the morning."

He didn't try to stop her as she stalked toward her room, flexing her hand to see if her wrist still functioned. It did. He hadn't really hurt her. He was a powerful man but one who was very much in control of his own strength.

Just like one of her heroes.

She refused to give Gideon the satisfaction of glancing back over her shoulder as she opened the door of her room. He didn't start the car until she was safely inside. Hurrying over to the window, she peeked through a small opening in the curtains to watch as he drove off into the night.

When the parking lot was silent again she switched on a light and sank down on the edge of the bed to think.

No doubt about it. Her impulsiveness and blind faith in her own intuition had gotten her in trouble again. She had moved too fast without taking the time to analyze just what she was dealing with.

Just because she had started to fall in love with Gideon Trace from the moment she had opened his first letter did not mean that she understood him. The man was turning out to be much more of an enigma than she had anticipated. The fact that he could even begin to suspect her motives was proof of that. She did not see how he could possibly doubt her.

Sarah twisted her hands in her lap, aware of a chilled feeling in the room that was not entirely a result of the gathering fog outside. She did not want to face the obvious, but she had to force herself to do so.

She had to wonder if she was making the same kind of mistake she'd made with Richard. She had to wonder if she was turning a blind eye to the obvious warnings.

Margaret was right. Impulsiveness was a dangerous quality.

With a wretched sigh, Sarah got to her feet and went about the business of getting ready for bed. There was nothing she could do tonight. She would wait and see if dawn brought a clearer notion of how to handle the situation.

GO BACK TO YOUR BIG, cold house and your cats.

Hours later it occurred to Gideon that he had been sitting for a long time in the darkened living room. There was a half-empty glass of brandy on the table in front of him. Ellora was curled up against his thigh, purring contentedly. Machu Picchu was stretched full length across the back of the sofa.

Gideon hadn't bothered to turn on any lights. It was almost midnight. And the house was cold. He wondered if it was worth building a fire.

"The place was just fine until she arrived. It didn't seem cold at all until after she'd been in it and left," he told the cats.

Machu flicked his ears, not bothering to open his eyes. Ellora slithered around a bit until she was more comfortable.

"No offense, but you two aren't the world's greatest conversationalists."

Gideon got up off the sofa. He picked up the brandy glass and walked over to the table where the chess pieces had been set out. Idly he fingered the wooden figures for a moment and then he set them out in a slightly different pattern.

Machu rumbled inquiringly.

"Think she'd have made the deal with Jake Savage if the bastard was still around, Machu? Savage always had a way with women. He sure wouldn't have screwed up the way I did tonight. He'd have charmed her straight into bed."

Machu didn't answer but his gem-hard eyes watched Gideon intently.

"You and me, we're not exactly loaded with charm, are we, pal?" Gideon studied the new positions of the wooden figures. The balance of power had now shifted to his side of the board. "But Savage isn't here. I am. And she wants the Flowers. I can lead her to them. The question is, do I really want to get mixed up with her? We've been doing pretty well here on our own."

Ellora lifted her head and meowed silently.

"So why does the house seem cold, damn it? It's almost summer."

GIDEON TRACE was at Sarah's door before she had even finished dressing for the day in a pair of white jeans and a lemon-yellow shirt. Deliberately she made him wait while she anchored her hair in an off-center twist over one ear. Then she went to open the door.

"Hi." She offered nothing further. He looked larger than ever standing there in the cold, gray light of a new day.

"Good morning." Gideon braced himself with one hand against the doorjamb. "Make up your mind, yet?"

"I had no idea you were waiting on pins and needles."

He gave her his faint, twisted smile. "I know I'm early. I was afraid if I left it too long, you'd sneak off to go after the Flowers without me."

"I was only going to sneak as far as the coffee shop." She turned to pick up her windbreaker, aware that he was scanning her room from the doorway. She was suddenly very conscious of her nightgown lying in a heap on the bed, the open suitcase with a sock trailing out of it and the collection of toilet articles littering the dresser. She closed the door very quickly.

"I'll join you for breakfast," Gideon said. "I didn't get a chance to eat before I left the house this morning."

"Your own fault." She locked the door behind her and started across the street to the small coffee shop. The lights were just coming on inside. To the right, the narrow, two-lane road vanished around a bend into the fog-shrouded trees.

"You hold a mean grudge, don't you?" Gideon paced beside her. His hands were thrust into the pockets of a sheepskin jacket.

Sarah said nothing more until they were seated in a booth in the corner of the coffee shop. She studied Gideon for a long moment, remembering all the fleeting thoughts, hopes and dreams that had come to her in the night. She fought back the sense of longing that threatened to overwhelm her and tried to make herself speak coolly and logically. There would be no more impulsiveness on her part, she vowed silently.

"Let me get this straight," she said. "You think I'm an opportunist who uses sex to get what she wants, but you're willing to help me search for the earrings if you get to keep one pair for yourself, right?"

His big hands folded around the mug in front of him and his eyes met hers in a level gaze. "I'll help you search for the earrings. Let's leave it at that."

"All right. I guess that makes us both opportunists, doesn't it? At last we have something in common."

He stared at her unblinkingly, the way Machu Picchu would stare at a mouse. "We're in this together? We've got a deal?"

"Sure. Why not? I came to you in the first place because I don't know anything about treasure hunting.

You do. That makes you very useful to me and I'm willing to bargain with you for your talents. Since you claim it's unlikely we'll ever find the earrings, I'm getting a heck of a deal, aren't I? If there aren't any profits in this, I won't have to split anything with you."

"I see you've decided on the role of tough little cookie this morning. Just for the record, it doesn't suit you." Gideon took a swallow of his coffee.

"You like me better as a scheming little seductress?"

He grinned reluctantly. "I really ruffled your feathers, didn't I?"

She glared at him. "I made a serious mistake in dealing with you the way I did yesterday. I can see that now. I should have been restrained and businesslike right from the start. Unfortunately that's not my normal nature."

"I gathered that much."

"That does not mean, however, that I can't behave in a restrained and businesslike manner when I put my mind to it."

He looked frankly disbelieving. "Think so?"

"Of course. And a restrained, adult, businesslike manner is precisely what I will project from now on. No nonsense. I shall just think of you as a business partner and deal with you as I would with one." She put her hand across the table. "Very well, Mr. Trace, we have a deal."

He stared down at her extended palm and then slowly reached out to solemnly shake her hand. She allowed him to crush her fingers for about two seconds and then she quickly withdrew her hand to safety. "What about your cats?"

He shrugged. "They'll be fine for a week or so. I've left them on their own before. My neighbor will check their food and water."

"How long will you need to pack?"

"I packed last night."

"You're suddenly very eager for the hunt."

"When do you want to leave?"

She took a breath. "I'll be ready as soon as I settle the motel bill."

"Fine. We'll take my car. You can leave yours at my place."

Sarah looked at him and wondered if she was really intuitive or just plain crazy.

Half an hour later she signed the credit card slip in the motel office while Gideon waited out in the parking lot, leaning against the fender of his car.

"You a close friend of Trace's?" The inquisitive-eyed little clerk glanced out the window and back at Sarah. He was a thin, balding man in his sixties, dressed in brown polyester pants and an aging polo shirt. He had been pleasant enough, but it was clear he had a keen interest in local gossip.

"We're business associates," Sarah said crisply. She finished her scrawling signature with her usual flourish.

"Business associates, huh? Didn't know Gideon had any business associates. Thought he worked on that treasure-hunting magazine of his all by himself."

Sarah smiled loftily. "He's acting as a consultant for me. I'm doing some research on treasure hunting for a book."

"That right? Interestin'. Never met a real-life writer before. Except for Gideon, of course. And he don't exactly write books, just articles for that magazine of his. The two of you goin' somewhere together?"

"A business trip."

"Right. A business trip." The clerk chuckled knowingly. "Wished we'd had business trips like that in my day. Well, at least this time Trace won't be goin' off alone on one of his business trips."

That stopped Sarah just as she started to turn away toward the door. "He's gone off on trips before?"

"Well, sure. 'Bout once a year he just ups and disappears for a while. Sometimes as long as a month." The clerk winked. "I asked him once where he went and he said on vacation. You the one he's been vacationin' with all these years?"

"I don't really think that's any of your business." Sarah closed the door behind her on the sound of the desk clerk's cackling laughter.

Gideon straightened away from the fender and unfolded his arms. He scowled. "Old Jess give you a hard time?"

"Not really."

"Why's he falling all over himself laughing in there?"

"He thinks he's a stand-up comedian."

They drove both cars back to the big old house on the bluff. Machu Picchu sat placidly on the top step watching as Gideon transferred Sarah's luggage from her car to his. Ellora flitted about with an air of delicate concern. The silver-gray cat hung around Sarah, tangling herself up between Sarah's feet and asking to be picked up and held.

When Sarah obligingly lifted Ellora into her arms, the cat purred.

"I think she wants to come along," Sarah announced.

"That's all we'd need. A couple of cats to keep track of while we're traipsing around the Cascades. Forget it. The cats are just fine staying here by themselves."

Sarah held the cat up so she could look Ellora straight in the eye. "Hear that? You have to stay behind. But we'll miss you."

There was a low, grumbling cat roar from the top step. Sarah glanced over and saw Machu looking more cold-eyed than ever. "You, too, Machu. You take good care of Ellora while we're gone."

Machu Picchu looked away, his ears low on his broad head, tail moving in a slow, restless arc.

"He hasn't got the most charismatic personality in the world," Gideon said, "but you can count on old Machu. He'll do a good job of taking care of Ellora and watching over the place, won't you, pal?" Gideon scratched the oversized cat briefly behind the ears. Machu tolerated the caress in stony silence.

"When you're that big, you don't have to be charming, I suppose," Sarah said with a small smile.

"Does that logic apply to human males or just to cats?" Gideon asked.

"Just to cats." Sarah made a production out of checking the back seat of her car. "I guess that's everything," she said a little uneasily as she realized she was about to be cooped up with Gideon for several hours.

"Don't lose your nerve now." Gideon calmly locked his front door.

"I wasn't losing my nerve."

"Having second thoughts?"

"A few."

"Don't worry. Something tells me you're going to like the treasure-hunting business. It's tailor-made for bright-eyed, gullible types like you."

Sarah paid him no attention as she patted Ellora one last time. "Goodbye, Ellora. Don't let that beast push you around too much."

Ellora purred more loudly, looking not the least bit concerned about being bullied by Machu Picchu. When Sarah put her down she trotted over to the steps and bounded up to station herself beside the big cat. Machu unbent so far as to touch noses with her in greeting. Then his big tail curved around her neat hindquarters. Ellora looked shamelessly smug.

"Are you sure they'll be all right?"

"They'll be fine. Stop looking for an excuse to delay things. We've got a long drive ahead of us."

Sarah slid into the front seat and adjusted her seat belt. "I have to tell you, Gideon, that your sudden enthusiasm for this venture is making me nervous. What changed your mind? Did you decide the map and the legend are real, after all?"

"I figure it's worth a shot." He swung the car out onto the narrow highway. He was silent for a minute or two before he said, "Couple of things you ought to know about treasure hunting, Sarah."

"And you're going to tell me what I should know, right?"

"Right."

"I've told you, I don't like being lectured."

"You came to me for advice. I intend to earn my share of the loot."

"*If* we find it."

"I thought you were already sure we would." He gave her a fleeting, mildly derisive glance.

She ignored that. The truth was, she was almost certain they would find the Flowers. The problem now was what might happen when they did. "All right, expert.

Tell me the couple of things I ought to know about the treasure-hunting business."

"The most important thing is that we don't make a public production out of it. The less attention we attract, the better, especially if we do get lucky."

"Why?"

"Use your head, Sarah. If we do find the Flowers, we're talking about a tidy little fortune in gemstones. People have killed for less, believe me."

That shocked her. "Good grief, I never thought of that."

"Somehow that doesn't surprise me."

"I can't believe we'd attract the attention of a killer."

"That's the worst possible case. It's far more likely we'd attract the interest of other treasure hunters, curious tourists and little kids who would want to follow us around and watch while we dig. There might also be legal complications. Do you know who owns the old Fleetwood property now?"

She smiled, vastly pleased with herself. "Yeah. Me."

"You do?" That obviously startled him.

"I bought it two months ago. It was incredibly cheap because it has no real value. It's lousy farmland by today's standards and it's not a good building site for a modern home. I'll sell it right after we find the Flowers."

Gideon whistled softly. "I'm impressed."

"About time."

"All right, you've taken care of the major complication, the legal ownership of the land. But I still recommend we keep our plans quiet. Nothing pulls attention like a hunt for real treasure and attention usually means trouble for small operations like ours. If this were a major salvage operation to find a sunken ship, that would be one thing. We'd want investment money and plenty of media hype. But the two of us operating alone are highly vulnerable. We go in and we get out without making waves."

Sarah debated briefly the wisdom of confiding that she'd mentioned the Flowers to one Jim Slaughter of Slaughter Enterprises and then decided not to say anything to Gideon. After all, she'd definitely told Slaughter she wasn't interested in either hiring him to help her find the earrings or in financing his downed-airplane-full-of-gold project. He was definitely out of the picture and if she mentioned him to her new consultant, Gideon might get nervous. Things were tricky enough at best right now.

"Okay," Sarah said easily. "Very low profile. I understand. I figure we'll just check into a couple of rooms at a motel in the little mountain town that's near the property. We'll make the motel our home base. Who's going to notice our coming and going?"

"Probably everyone in town," Gideon said.

Sarah thought about that. "You really think so?"

"Yes."

"Well, what do you suggest we do?" she asked, irritated. "Camp out? I warn you, I'm not big on roughing it."

"We don't need to go as far as setting up a tent."

"Thank heavens." Sarah shuddered.

"My suggestion is that we act like a couple of city folks on vacation in the mountains. You know, tourists who've come to take photographs of the spring wildflowers."

"I didn't bring my camera."

"I brought one."

"That was very clever of you," she said with genuine admiration.

His brows rose. "Thanks. Wait until you hear the rest of the cover story."

"Cover story." Sarah tasted the words, her excitement reawakening rapidly. "I've always wanted to have a cover story. What's ours?"

"As I said, a couple of people on vacation." He shot her a cool, assessing glance. "But it's going to look strange if we don't act like a real couple. A man and a woman traveling together are either lovers or business associates. Since we don't want anyone to know we're business associates, we have to look like lovers."

Sarah turned her head to stare at him in amazement. "What on earth are you trying to say, Gideon?"

His expression hardened. "We can't risk taking separate motel rooms the way you planned. Someone might notice and start asking why we always take off together during the day but don't sleep together at night."

"Oh." She tried to absorb that slowly.

"The legend of the Flowers is not unknown in the region where we're going. Someone with enough curiosity might put two and two together and decide to follow us. If they did, they'd see us head for the old Fleetwood property to dig every day and then we'd have problems."

"You're suggesting we pass ourselves off as a couple of lovers? You think I'm going to share a room with you? After the way you've been treating me? Forget it, Gideon."

"Don't get upset. This is business, remember? I'm not saying you have to sleep with me."

"How very accommodating of you." Sarah crossed her arms under her breasts. "I don't like this cover story. Come up with another one."

"It's the best one I can come up with at the moment." He glanced at her again. "Oh, hell, Sarah, don't act like I've just threatened your virtue. All I'm saying is that the best cover we can have is to look like two people involved in a relationship who are on vacation in the mountains. Nobody will pay any attention to us."

"You do this a lot?"

"Hell, no. What makes you say that?"

"Old Jess, the motel clerk, said you have a habit of disappearing on vacation at least once a year."

"A man's got a right to get away for a while."

Sarah eyed him thoughtfully. Gideon looked annoyed but otherwise innocent of any lecherous intentions. "You're sure that traveling as a couple is the only good way to handle this?"

"I think it's the best way under the circumstances." Gideon concentrated on watching a car in the side mirror. "Also the simplest. Simple explanations always work best."

"You sound very knowledgeable on the subject."

He shrugged. "Just using a little logic. Don't forget this is my field of expertise."

She chewed on that for a moment. "You guarantee separate beds?"

"For a woman who was convinced yesterday that I was the romantic hero of the century, you've sure changed your tune."

"Gideon, I'm warning you—"

"Sure. Separate beds. I've already taken care of it."

She sucked in her breath. "You have?"

"A friend of mine has a cabin up here that's not too far from your property. I called him last night. He said we could use it for a week.

Sarah felt dazed. She had the distinct feeling that she was somehow losing control of the situation. She tried to imagine what it would be like sleeping under the same roof with Gideon Trace and her mind reeled. If he'd been falling in love with her during the past four months the way she had with him, that would be one thing. But this business of a one-sided attraction was very dangerous.

On the other hand, the situation was fraught with tantalizing possibilities if she could just keep her head. She would have a chance to work on Gideon, a chance to let him get to know her.

"All right. I'll go along with your idea for the sake of our cover story," Sarah said with sudden decision.

He glanced at her and then shook his head in silent wonder. "You really are something, aren't you?"

"Why do you say that? Because I trust you enough to share a cabin with you?"

"Uh-huh."

"This is now a business relationship, right?"

"Right."

"Well, I've known you long enough to be quite certain you'll be an honest, dependable, reliable business partner."

"Amazing. As I said, you shouldn't be allowed out without a leash."

"Stop complaining. This is all your idea and you are the expert, aren't you?"

"I keep telling myself that."

4

GIDEON RISKED A FEW GLANCES at Sarah's face as he set the luggage on the bare floor of the rustic cabin. He closed the door carefully, unable to tell what she was thinking. He wondered if she was wrinkling her nose in that interesting fashion because she didn't like the looks of the old, run-down place or because she was starting to have a few additional reservations about sharing it with him.

Personally, he was still stunned by his own daring and astounded by the success of his small coup. He couldn't quite believe he'd pulled it off. *She was here with him under the same roof.* In fact, she'd hardly put up any argument at all.

He still didn't know whether to be insulted or delighted or irritated by her ready trust, though. It was possible she'd gone along with the idea of posing as a couple on vacation simply because she had written him off completely as a potential lover.

Or had she abandoned the notion of seduction as a tactic now that he'd agreed to go on the quest for a share of the profits? Either way, he had no reason to feel so euphoric. But he did.

The fact of the matter was that, after blundering in where an intelligent angel would fear to tread, Sarah had tried to pull back to safe territory and he had rather neatly prevented her from doing so. Gideon was quite pleased with himself. He had managed to salvage the situation after nearly wrecking it.

"Not much, is it?" He followed her glance around the cabin they had rented for a week. There was one bed in a small room off to the left and a sagging couch near the old brick hearth. The kitchen was tiny but it had a refrigerator and a stove and all the necessities. They wouldn't be forced to locate a restaurant every day.

"Actually it's quite picturesque." Sarah set down the bag of groceries she had bought en route to the cabin. She wandered over to the hearth, her hands thrust into the back pockets of her jeans. "Very atmospheric, in fact. A lonely cabin in the woods. Who knows what might have happened in a place like this in the past? Maybe one of these days I'll—"

"Use it in a book?"

She smiled briefly. "Yes."

"Think you'll ever use me in a book?"

"I already have. Several of them."

He wasn't sure how to take that, but it sounded positive. "The guy who rented this place to me said the couch pulled out into a bed. I'll take that."

"It doesn't look very comfortable."

"Is that an invitation to share the other bed with you?"

"Of course not," she snapped. "Don't tease, Gideon. This is a business relationship now, remember? That's the only kind of relationship you seem to want."

Sure. That's why I spent an hour on the phone last night trying to locate the owner of this place. That's why I agreed to pay him in-season rates even though it's not summer yet, Gideon thought. "Sorry about the cabin," he muttered gruffly. "I guess the motel rooms would have been more comfortable."

Sarah turned her head, her fey eyes registering surprise just before she stepped into the bedroom. "There's nothing wrong with the cabin. It's a perfect location for an adventure. This may be a business deal to you, Gideon, but for me finding the Flowers is still an exciting idea."

She closed the door before he could think of an adequate response.

Some time later, after a meal of ravioli with pesto sauce that Sarah had somehow magically produced in the kitchen amid incredible chaos, Gideon wandered around the cabin, checking the locks on the windows. They were about what he'd expected—not much better than paper clips.

Things seemed to have gotten off to a promising start. Of course there had been that one brief moment of panic on Sarah's part when she'd realized the kitchen didn't have a dishwasher but she'd calmed down when Gideon had made her an offer she couldn't refuse.

"You take care of the cooking and I'll handle the cleanup," he'd suggested.

"It's a deal. I told you that you had all the makings of a real hero," she'd retorted cheerfully.

He studied the decrepit sofa, wondering if it would fall apart completely when he pulled it out into a bed. He gave it a tentative yank.

It survived the jolt but the lumps did not look promising.

He stood looking down at it while he listened to Sarah rustling around in the bathroom. It had been a long time since he'd shared quarters with a woman. The realization of just how long it had been made him feel old.

On the other hand, the fact that he was getting aroused just listening to Sarah undress behind the closed door had definite youthful implications. *You're only as old as you feel, Trace.* Right now he felt he could hold his own with any young stud of twenty. Too bad the lady was no longer throwing herself at him.

He had what he'd decided he wanted last night as he'd sat brooding in the shadows of his aging house. He'd set up this scene in his own heavy-handed way but now he wasn't certain how to play it. Sarah no longer showed any signs of wanting to be swept off her feet by him.

As usual, his timing was excellent with everything except women.

Gideon wondered if he'd lost his only shot at playing hero.

The door of the bathroom opened.

Sarah stood there enveloped in a green velour robe that she'd belted around her small waist. Her hair was loose around her shoulders and her face was freshly scrubbed. She looked touchingly vulnerable and at the same time incredibly sexy.

"It's all yours," she said as she headed toward the bedroom.

He figured she meant the bathroom, not the body in the velour robe. "Thanks." He knew he was staring. The bedroom door closed firmly.

Gideon sighed, picked up his shaving kit and headed for the bath. The small room was still warm and moist. He felt big and awkward standing in the middle of the tiny place, as if he had accidentally invaded a medieval maiden's private bower. A bright yellow toothbrush stood at attention in a glass on the sink and a hairbrush lay on the counter next to the toothpaste tube.

The top had been left off the toothpaste. Automatically Gideon replaced it.

Ten minutes later he went back out into the main room. No crack of light showed under the bedroom door. He stood for a moment, trying to think of something clever to do next. The only action that came readily to mind was to open the bedroom door and that was out of the question.

Business partners.

"Damn." So much for sweeping her off her feet. He wondered if she'd brought along any of her books that featured his doppelgänger as a hero. Maybe he could figure out how to proceed if he saw himself in action.

His mouth quirked ruefully as he undressed and slid into the cold, uncomfortable bed. It was disconcerting to think of himself as a hero in a novel of romantic suspense. *Be interesting to read the sex scenes.*

Half an hour later he was still awake, his hands folded behind his head, his mind playing with the image of Sarah wearing nothing but a pair of antique earrings, when the bedroom door opened softly. He went very still.

"Gideon?" Sarah's voice was low and hesitant.

"Yeah?"

"Are you asleep?"

"Not any more."

"Good. Because I've been thinking."

She came farther into the room. Gideon turned his head and looked at her in the shadows. He could just barely make out the fact that her feet were bare on the hardwood floor. Her hands were thrust into the sleeves of her robe.

"Something wrong?" he asked, wondering if she'd already seen through his flimsy excuse for sharing a cabin and had decided to complain.

"Yes." Her chin came up determinedly. "Yes, there is something wrong. Very wrong."

So much for his cleverness. "What is it, Sarah?"

"I have to know something." She started pacing the length of the room, looking more medieval than ever in the darkness as the robe floated around her small, bare ankles. "I realize that I should probably just let it go, but I can't. I have to find out what went wrong. I can't believe I was this mistaken a second time."

"Sarah . . ."

She stopped him with a raised hand. "Just tell me the truth and I promise I won't ask anything personal again." She went as far as she could in the small space available, swung around and started back in the other direction. "Why don't you trust me?"

That caught him off guard. "It's not a matter of trusting you," Gideon said cautiously.

"Yes, it is. You don't. Why?" She was still pacing. "I mean, is your inability to trust me based on some significant event in your past? Do you distrust all women? Did your marriage sour you on the female of the species? Or is it something about me, personally. Did I just come on too strong? Was that it? I know I'm not always subtle."

Gideon groaned. "Look, I'm not real good at conversations like this."

"Talk, Gideon. I've been your friend for four months. The least you can do is tell me why you still don't trust me."

"Damn it, why do you have to take it personally?"

"Because it is personal."

He began to get annoyed. "You're a demanding little thing, aren't you? Demanding and arrogant."

"*Arrogant.*"

"Yeah, arrogant. Who do you think you are, Sarah Fleetwood? You just explode in my life like a firecracker. You tell me you think we're meant for each other on the basis of a handful of letters as if you're my mail-order bride or something and, oh, by the way, would I help you recover a fortune in lost jewels. And you wonder why I've got a few questions about your motives?"

She paused at the far end of the room again. He could see she was nibbling on her lower lip. "Put like that, it does sound a little strange, doesn't it?"

"Strange is right."

"I still think there's more to it than that." She resumed her pacing. "Are you sure there isn't something in your past that's making you extra cautious about trusting me?"

"Sarah, I'm forty years old. I'm not exactly a naive, trusting innocent. And if you had any sense, you wouldn't be, either. The world does not reward naïveté. I would have thought getting left at the altar would have taught you that much."

"I am not naive, damn it. And leave Richard out of this. You're evading the point."

"What do you want? A complete history of my life to date so you can psychoanalyze my reasons for being cautious about you? Don't hold your breath."

"What was your wife like?"

"Good Lord, you don't let go of something once you've glommed onto it, do you?"

"No. Was she pretty?"

"Yeah."

"Was she kind?"

That made Gideon flounder for a split second. He had never thought of Leanna as kind. She had been too wrapped up in her career and her own emotional problems to be kind to others. She had needed kindness, but she hadn't dispensed much of it. On the other hand she certainly hadn't been vicious, he reminded himself. Just a little mixed up about what she wanted.

"You think kindness is important in a beautiful, sexy woman?" he asked derisively.

"Of course, it is. It's important in anyone."

"What cloud have you been living on? Look, everyone liked Leanna and, as I recall, she was fond of small animals so she certainly couldn't have been unkind, right? She was also very intelligent, very attractive and very sophisticated."

"Oh."

Gideon smiled grimly in the darkness. Sarah sounded woefully disappointed. Obviously she'd been hoping to hear that Leanna was a bitch. But Leanna had not been a bitch, just an unhappy, confused young woman who'd turned to Gideon at a low point in her life and then realized her mistake.

"She was also published," he added, not knowing why he felt compelled to twist the knife. It was as though he had to find a way to rip through the iridescent veil of Sarah's bright-eyed optimism and discover what lay underneath.

"She wrote?" Sarah sounded more wretched than ever. "Like me?"

"No, not like you. She was an assistant professor at a small college in Oregon when I met her. She wrote articles on archaeology for academic journals."

"I see. Important, scholarly stuff." Sarah was obviously getting more depressed by the minute.

Gideon suddenly felt as if he'd been pulling wings off a fly. "The only problem Leanna and I had was that she wasn't in love with me. She just thought she was for a while. She tried, I'll give her credit for that."

"What happened, Gideon?"

"We split when she realized she loved someone else."

"Someone with flash, you said?"

"Did I?" Gideon frowned, remembering the brief conversation on previous marriages he'd had with Sarah yesterday. "I did say that, didn't I? Yeah. She found someone with flash and she went for it the way a trout goes for a bright, shiny lure."

"Did you try to stop her?"

"I tried to tell her she was making a mistake. The guy she fell for didn't have it in him to be faithful to any woman for long. I warned her she wasn't going to be happy with him. But she thought she could change him."

"She married him?"

"No. They got engaged as soon as our divorce was final, but he was killed before the marriage could take place."

"How sad. For all of you. But maybe that way Leanna never had a chance to find out what a louse he really was."

Gideon shrugged. "Maybe. I never saw her again after the divorce. I heard she remarried a couple of years ago. A college professor. With any luck she picked the right man this time."

"That's very generous of you," Sarah said with obvious admiration. Her voice glowed with approval.

"It is, isn't it?" He grinned briefly and was surprised by his own amusement. It was certainly the first time he'd ever found anything at all humorous about his divorce. Something about Sarah seeing him as benevolent, kind and generous was very entertaining, however.

"Does this mean you're not carrying a torch for her?" The hope in Sarah's voice was unmistakable.

"Carrying torches is a waste of time."

"Well, that's certainly true. Unless, of course, you're thinking of someday trying to fan the flames?"

"I'm not. I learned a long time ago never to look back."

There was silence from the far end of the room. Gideon could feel Sarah mulling over the information he had given her. Her head was bent in concentration.

"This man your ex-wife married," Sarah said at last, "the one with flash, was he a friend of yours, by any chance?"

Gideon didn't move. His momentary flare of amusement evaporated. "I knew him."

"Ah. So he was a friend of yours. A close friend?"

He didn't like the sound of that. "It's not what you think, Sarah."

"Sure it is." She obviously felt she had hold of something important now. She started pacing the floor again. "Your wife betrayed you with your best friend. Very simple. Tragic, but simple. It explains everything, especially your inability to trust me."

"What the hell are you talking about? Do you always leap to conclusions like this?"

"Sometimes. Gideon, having your wife betray you with your best friend is not a minor event. Wars have been fought over less."

"I'm not planning on starting any wars. Besides, I told you, the guy's dead and Leanna's remarried. There's nothing left to fight over even if I was so inclined."

"Which you're not. A very hopeful sign. Okay, now I think I've finally got a handle on our relationship. This is the curse from your past that needs lifting, isn't it? Just like in the story of 'Beauty and the Beast.'"

"What the hell are you talking about?"

"Relax, Gideon. I was just using a familiar metaphor from the old fairy tale. Put in modern terms, the fact is, I was missing some of this information from the beginning. That's why I botched up our initial meeting. It was all my fault. I rushed things."

Gideon was beginning to get that uneasy sense of being left behind in her dust again. "Sarah, don't go flying off on some new tangent, okay?"

She ignored him as she paced faster and faster. A fresh sense of anticipation was radiating from her in waves of energy Gideon could almost feel.

"I realize now you need plenty of time to get to know me so that you'll be able to see how totally different I am from both your best friend and your ex-wife," Sarah said.

"You've never even met either of them."

"That doesn't mean I can't figure out what their problems were."

"What is this? Instant psychoanalysis?"

"Common sense and a touch of intuition. I know a lot about you now, so I can make some good guesses about the other two people who were involved in this mess." Sarah spun around at the far end of the room and buzzed past Gideon, robe flying. "Let's take Leanna first: neurotic with problems of her own that she was trying to use a husband to resolve."

Gideon blinked owlishly, taken back by the accuracy of that comment. "Of all the idiotic conclusions," he growled. "You don't know what you're talking about. You don't know any of the people involved, except me."

"Knowing you is enough. Any woman who couldn't see what a terrific husband you'd make is immature, neurotic and probably trapped in her own emotional problems. I'm sorry to have to tell you that, Gideon, but I'm afraid it's the truth. How old was Leanna when you married her?"

He propped himself up on one elbow, scowling at her as she went whizzing past the bed again. "Twenty-five, I think, why?"

Sarah was nodding to herself. "Twenty-five going on seventeen. Some people, male and female, are still awfully immature at twenty-five. They often don't know what they really want. Some people go through their whole lives never knowing what they really want. Add to that immaturity a certain lack of brainpower or a lot of personal problems and you've got a powder keg of a marriage."

"I've already told you my ex was not exactly a dummy."

"I'm talking about common sense, not academic ability. There's a world of difference. It's common sense that makes people act intelligently, not education. All education does is give you a wider frame of reference to utilize when you're using your common sense to go over your options. A lot of people with Ph.D.'s make stupid decisions because they lack common sense. Now, then. Give me a minute to think this through."

"Take your time." Gideon was exasperated. He wondered how he'd ever gotten involved in this crazy discussion.

"Don't be sarcastic. This is important. Critical to our whole future together, in fact."

He shook his head, watching her in disbelief as she went to stand at the window. He was suddenly out of patience. If she came waltzing by the sofa one more time he was going to grab her and pull her down beside him. "Sarah, I don't know what's going through that weird brain of yours, but I think it would be best if you went back to bed."

She turned to face him. "Yes, you're probably right. I can finish thinking about this in my own room. No need to keep you awake while I go over all this information in detail. Good night, Gideon."

Anger surged through him. How dared she presume to analyze and dissect him like this? He made a grab for her as she glided past him on her way back to the bedroom.

He heard her soft gasp of surprise as his fingers locked around her wrist. "You think you know it all, don't you?" he muttered. He drew her inexorably toward him, playing seriously with the idea of dragging her down onto the bed. It would be so easy. She was so small and delicate.

"Gideon?" Her eyes were very wide now.

"Somebody ought to give you the lesson you need."

"You may be right," she agreed tremulously. "But, please, not tonight. I'm not sure I could handle it." She leaned down and gave him a quick, fleeting kiss on his cheek.

Gideon jerked back as if he'd been burned. Unthinkingly he released her. Sarah instantly sailed on past him into the safety of her bedroom. Gideon rubbed his cheek and scowled into the darkness as her door closed softly behind her.

Intent on inducing a little healthy fear in her, he had been expecting a struggle, not the small, gentle caress he had received. Her reaction had startled him and he'd let her go before he'd realized quite what he was doing, he told himself, thoroughly irritated.

He lay there for a moment, aware that he was breathing a little heavily and feeling baffled. Then he rolled onto his back and stared at the shadows on the ceiling. This must have been how poor old Machu Picchu had felt in the first days after Ellora's arrival.

SARAH ROSE AT DAWN the next morning, feeling very much her normal cheerful, optimistic self again. After several intense hours of close thought during the night, her mind was clear and serene once more. She was back on track at last and she knew what had to be done. Hurrying over to the wooden chair in the corner, she grabbed her robe, slipped into it and opened the bedroom door.

Gideon was still asleep, sprawled on the sofa bed, the sheets and blankets bunched at his waist. He was lying on his stomach and the sleek expanse of his well-muscled back was a riveting sight in the early light. Sarah longed to stroke him, the way she would have stroked one of his cats.

But she knew that would be a mistake. He would only assume she was still trying to seduce him for her own nefarious purposes. Which she was, of course, she thought with a grin. She was determined to make him fall in love with her. But the seduction was going to take a slightly different form than originally planned. This was not the time to be obvious.

She hurried through her morning routine in the bathroom, trying not to use up all the hot water. Gideon would not appreciate a cold shower. On the way back to her own room, she saw that he had not moved. She took one last, wistful look at his powerfully built shoulders and went to finish dressing.

A few minutes later, wearing jeans and a shirt, her hair tied up out of the way at the back of her head, she made her way into the kitchen. It didn't take long to locate the pans she needed. She opened the refrigerator.

Within minutes she had filled the cabin with the inviting aroma of fresh-brewed coffee. The counters were cluttered with utensils, plates and a frying pan she had set out.

She was humming to herself as she whisked pancake batter in a large bowl when she realized she was no longer alone in the kitchen. She glanced over her shoulder and saw Gideon standing in the doorway. He had put on his jeans and nothing else. He scanned the kitchen, rubbing absently at the dark shadow of his beard.

"Do you always make this much of a racket in the morning?" he asked.

"Uh-huh. Are you always this grouchy?" She put a pan of syrup on the stove to heat.

"One of the things about cats is that they don't complain about my mood in the mornings. What are you making? Pancakes?"

"Yep. With real maple syrup. None of that caramel-colored sugar water for us. Run along and take your shower. Everything will be ready as soon as you get out of the bathroom."

"Why?"

"Why what?"

"Why the fancy breakfast?"

She debated briefly how much to tell him and then decided he might as well know what he was facing. "Because it's the first step in the courtship, if you must know the truth."

"*Courtship.*" He looked dumbfounded. "What the devil are you talking about now?"

She stopped whisking the pancake batter and turned around to face him. "I figure your problem is that I went too fast."

"My problem, huh?"

"Right. Thanks to our conversation last night and all the thinking I did afterward, I have a much better idea of how to handle you now."

His eyes flashed with something that might have been amusement. "That's certainly a relief to hear."

"Laugh if you must, but it's true." She pointed the dripping whisk straight at him. "I can see that when I arrived on your doorstep, I was already light-years ahead of you in terms of my position within our relationship."

"Hell. Are you still on that kick?"

"Of course. What we need to do is let you catch up with me. Your progress has been severely retarded by the fact that you've got a few unpleasant events in your past that have made you gun-shy when it comes to relationships. In short, you're afraid I might be as foolish and as uncertain of what I really want as your ex-wife was. You don't trust my judgment."

"I didn't say Leanna was foolish or uncertain."

"No, but it's obvious she was if she actually thought she wanted someone else instead of you."

"I don't know what makes you think I'm such a hell of a catch, but—"

"On top of having your wife desert you, you also had the traumatic experience of being betrayed by a close male friend. In short, you've got a legitimate fear of being betrayed by people you trust. You're carrying some serious scars. You've obviously learned to keep yourself aloof from people who try to get too close to you. You've gotten in the habit of questioning everyone's motives. It's entirely understandable."

Gideon stared at her. "No kidding?"

"Don't act so insulted. We're all shaped emotionally by our pasts even when our rational mind tells us we don't have to repeat our mistakes. If we're reasonably intelligent, we're afraid we might repeat those mistakes. If we're not too intelligent or self-aware we go on repeating them. Either way, it's hard to break the cycle."

Gideon propped one shoulder against the doorjamb. He looked fascinated. "What hang-ups have you got from your traumatic experience of being left at the altar?"

"Well, for one thing, you'd never find me waiting in a wedding dress in front of a church full of people again, that's for sure."

"You don't plan to marry?" he asked slowly.

"I didn't say that. I just wouldn't risk a big wedding with all the trimmings. Believe me, if I ever decide to try it again, it'll be a quick trip to Vegas or Reno." She grinned. "See? We all have our scars. Rationally I tell myself that I wouldn't screw up and make such a major error in judgment again. I'll be sure of what I'm doing the next time and it will be perfectly safe to plan a big wedding if that's what I wanted."

"But you won't plan one?"

She shook her head swiftly. "No, I won't. Emotionally I couldn't face it. I couldn't bear to risk that sort of humiliation again, no matter how sure I was of the man I was marrying. Just the prospect of addressing invitations to all the people who witnessed the first fiasco is enough to make me cringe." She shook off the old pain and smiled reassuringly. "You see? That's how our mistakes affect us. We try to learn from them, to protect ourselves and in doing so we sometimes err on the side of caution."

He watched her intently. "If I'd have been there, I'd have nailed the bastard's hide to the wall."

Sarah was instantly warmed by the unexpected words. She smiled mistily. "Gideon, that's about the nicest thing anyone's ever said to me. Thank you."

"Forget it." He came toward her.

Sarah felt the immediate tingle of sensual awareness ripple through her. She wasn't sure what the determination in Gideon's eyes meant, however. Instinctively she stepped back and found herself up against the kitchen counter. "Gideon?"

He didn't halt, just kept coming toward her until he was looming over her, crowding her against the counter. He was overwhelming when he was this close. Sarah was mesmerized by the pattern of crisp, curling hair on his broad chest. She gripped the whisk handle as if it were a lifeline to sanity.

Deliberately he reached out and removed the bowl of pancake batter and the whisk from her frozen fingers.

"Gideon, I don't think . . ."

"Sarah," he muttered, his voice lower and grittier than usual as his hands slid up her arms to her shoulders, "let's get something understood here. You don't

have to go through a lot of crazy rationalization or try
to see me through rose-colored glasses if all you really
want is for me to take you to bed. I'll be glad to lay you
down on that sofa over there right now."

Sarah panicked. "Don't you dare do this to me, Gideon Trace. This is a relationship we're building here. I'm
not about to let you reduce it to nothing more than a
roll in the hay."

"I wasn't going to do that."

"Yes, you were. That's exactly what you were going
to do and I won't have it, do you hear me?"

He winced as her voice rose hysterically. "Believe me,
I hear you."

"I mean it. Every word. This is very important to me.
I gave it hours of thought last night and I know how I'm
going to handle everything. Things are back on track
now and I won't let you mess it all up with sex."

He smiled faintly, his mouth very close to hers. "I
kind of like the thought of messing it up with sex. I'm
not the knight in shining armor you seem to think I am,
but I'll certainly do my best to give you what you want
in bed."

"*No.*"

He kissed her before she could find a way to deflect
him. Sarah struggled furiously for a moment and then
capitulated with a small, trembling sigh as his mouth
moved on hers. He was so real, this man who had filled
her thoughts and her heart for the past four months.
How could she resist his kiss?

It was no wonder she was vulnerable on this front,
she thought fleetingly. Everything felt so *right* when he
kissed her. She flexed her nails experimentally on his
shoulders and he responded with a heavy groan.

She could feel his strong thighs pushing against her and there was no mistaking the solid evidence of his early morning desire. His beard scraped along her cheek in a way that was unbelievably sexy.

"Gideon." His name was torn from her in a breathless gasp. She could feel his teeth on her earlobe now. The sensation was driving her wild. Frantically she fought to hold on to her common sense. "Gideon, no. Not like this. Not until you're ready."

"I'm ready. Believe me, I'm ready."

"No, damn it, not yet. Please."

He broke the kiss at last, but he didn't release her. His eyes were as green as emeralds as he looked down into her upturned face. She knew she was trembling and she also knew the heat she felt was probably evident on her flushed cheeks.

"You really want me, don't you?" Beneath the blatant, masculine desire in his gaze was an odd, bemused look. "You really do want me. I've never had a woman look at me quite the way you're looking at me now."

"Of course, I want you." She glowered at him, trying to hide her flustered emotions. "I've never made any secret of that. But that's got nothing to do with it. You need time to realize you want me, too."

"I do want you."

"I mean, really want me."

"I really want you." Sexy amusement lit his eyes again.

Sarah grabbed the dripping whisk and threatened him with it. "Stop teasing me and go take a shower, you beast. And when you come back into this kitchen, you are going to behave yourself, is that clear?"

He grinned slowly, his eyes alight with a sensual promise that made her ache to throw herself back into his arms. "Real clear. Be interesting to see how you enforce your own rules." He turned and sauntered out of the kitchen.

5

Two days later, Sarah again succumbed to serious self-doubts. Conducting the courtship of a man might be a feasible notion if the object of the effort was shy and retiring by nature but Gideon was definitely not shy or retiring.

What he was, was difficult and maddeningly unpredictable. He was also proving dangerous on a sensual level.

Having discovered just how vulnerable she was to his kisses, he tormented her with them. He seemed to delight in catching her off guard and pulling her into his arms for a quick, stolen caress that inevitably left her feeling giddy and breathless.

But whenever she tried to introduce a serious, personal topic or questioned him about his past, he became as silent and uncommunicative as a mountain.

She could not tell if she was making any progress at all.

And the courtship wasn't the only area that wasn't progressing with satisfying rapidity. They had not broken the code on the map and Sarah was getting frustrated. She had expected the actual treasure hunt to go smoothly.

"You're too impatient," Gideon remarked as they tromped back and forth across the heavily wooded acreage that had once been owned by Emelina Fleetwood.

There was very little left of Emelina Fleetwood's home, just a tumbledown cabin that was completely bare inside. Some distance away from where the house stood was the collapsed wall of what might have been the barn. A few feet from the back door of the cabin itself were several boards left from what might have been an outhouse. Rusty nails and a couple of pieces of metal from some old farm equipment were scattered around the ruins.

Almost everything had long since been reclaimed by the forest. The multitude of owners who had tried to farm the place since Emelina's time had not made any noticeable improvements.

"Two whole days, Gideon, and we've gotten nowhere."

"People spent most of the century looking for the *Titanic*. They're still looking for Kidd's and Laffite's gold. And they still haven't found Amelia Earhart's plane. Treasure hunting requires time and effort and plenty of patience."

"But we've got a map."

"You keep saying that. Your precious map isn't a magic talisman, you know. It's just a crude sketch that could have been made by almost anyone at any time and mean almost anything."

"I'm sure the map is genuine. It's a family heirloom."

"You got any idea of how many family heirlooms are nothing but junk?"

"This isn't junk. There shouldn't be any problem. Darn it, this is your area of expertise. Why can't you figure out what this code means?" She scanned the odd notes in front of her. "Sixty, ninety and a straight line connecting two dots with the number twenty-five beside it. Then the phrase, 'White rock at intersection of

B and C. Ten paces due north.' I tell you, Gideon, we're overlooking something obvious here."

"Yeah. A white boulder."

"That, too. Where do you suppose it is?" She looked around as she had countless times during the past two days and saw nothing of a white rock.

"It probably got washed away or covered up with mud and debris years ago. People who bury treasure expect to dig it up again within a few months or years at the most. They often use transient points of reference like an outhouse or a tree or something else that could easily be gone by the time the next generation comes looking for grandpa's gold."

Sarah wrinkled her nose. "An outhouse?"

"Sure. That was a favorite place to bank the retirement funds in the old days. Who would go looking for gold in an outhouse?"

"You, obviously." She laughed up at him. "Ever find any that way?"

"I refuse to respond to that on the grounds that it may make me look like an idiot."

Sarah giggled. "You did, didn't you?"

"It was a long time ago." Gideon came to a halt. "Isn't it time for lunch, yet?"

"You know, Gideon, there are times when I get the feeling you're only in this for the food. You've been showing an uncommon interest in mealtimes since I cooked that first dinner for you."

"Hey, how was I to know you could cook? And what are you complaining about, anyway? The way to a man's heart is through his stomach."

Sarah slid him a sidelong glance. "Is that true? Am I getting closer?"

He threw a heavy arm around her shoulders and pulled her against his side for a moment. His lips moved sensually in her sun-warmed hair. "You're welcome to get as close as you want, Sarah."

"Unfortunately your idea of close is not the same as mine. Not yet, at any rate."

"Are you sure of that?" He boldly let his hand glide over the curve of her breast.

"Positive." She pushed free of the tempting embrace and stalked across the small clearing in back of the old cabin to where she had left the picnic basket.

Gideon followed more slowly, his eyes thoughtful. "What happens if we find the earrings, Sarah?"

"*When*, not *if*, we find them." She knelt on the ground and spread out the red and white checked cloth she had brought along in the basket. "And what happens is that you get one pair and I get the other four. Just like we agreed."

"And then you go back to Seattle and I go home to my place on the coast?" He settled down on the ground, one leg drawn up.

She thought about that as she unwrapped tuna fish sandwiches. "No, of course not. This is a long-term plan I'm working on here. But I haven't made all the decisions. I'm not exactly sure how to handle our relationship after we find the earrings. I can't just move in with you, yet. You're not ready for that."

"I'm not?" He took a big bite out of his sandwich.

"No. So it looks like it'll be a long-distance commute for a while. Which won't be easy because I'm scheduled to start a new book next month. Once I start working on it I won't have a lot of free time."

"And I've got a magazine to get out by the first of every month."

"Things will get complicated, won't they? But we'll manage somehow."

"More likely once we find the earrings you'll go back to your real world and that'll be the end of my courtship," Gideon said flatly. He took another large bite of his sandwich.

"No, that's not the way it will be."

"I think it will be exactly that way, Sarah."

"Damn it, you really do think I just brought you along so you could help me find my treasure, don't you? You think that once we've found it, I'll give up courting you."

"I think I'd assign a high probability to that scenario."

"Is it so hard for you to develop a little faith in me?"

"I'm supposed to have faith in you after knowing you for all of three days?"

"Stop saying that. We've known each other for four whole months."

"We were pen pals for four months, not lovers."

Without any warning, Sarah found herself very close to losing her temper. "Pen pals. Yes, that's what we were and you liked it that way, didn't you? In fact, I'll bet you preferred it that way because you didn't have to take any risks or make any commitments. Letter writing is a very safe way to conduct an affair, isn't it?"

"It has a few advantages," he agreed, obviously satisfied at having provoked her. "But it also has a few distinct disadvantages." He leered cheerfully at her. "Now that I've met you in the flesh, I can see what I was missing when all I was getting were recipes."

With a supreme act of willpower, Sarah pulled herself back from the brink. She had been on the verge of flying into a genuine rage, she realized, shaken. Gideon had done this deliberately.

"Stop teasing me, Gideon."

"I'm not teasing you. I mean every word. What do you say we make a deal? You've had your four months of letters. Let me have four months of you in bed, regardless of whether or not we find your earrings. Then we'll decide what sort of relationship we've got."

Sarah refolded the sandwich wrapper with shaking fingers. "Don't talk like that, Gideon."

"You don't like the terms?" he asked, voice hardening. "That doesn't surprise me. You don't get much out of it under those conditions, do you? All right, I'll make the deal contingent on finding the earrings. If we do turn them up, I get my four months."

"I said stop it damn you." She threw the unfinished portion of her sandwich back into the basket and leaped to her feet. The sunlight still poured into the clearing but the warmth had gone out of the day. She was suddenly feeling very cold.

There was a long silence during which Sarah stood with her back to Gideon, her hands thrust into the pockets of her jeans. A lazy breeze ruffled the delicate wildflowers scattered around her feet. She could not bring herself to turn around for fear Gideon would see the hint of tears in her eyes.

The sound of another sandwich being unwrapped behind her finally broke the spell.

"Sorry," Gideon growled. "I was pushing it, wasn't I?"

"Yes, you were." Sarah turned back to watch as he wolfed down another of her sandwiches. "Why?"

"Why?" He looked momentarily blank. "Because I want to take you to bed. Why else?"

"You're going about it the wrong way."

"Yeah, I got that feeling. Sit down and eat the rest of your lunch, Sarah. I'll work on keeping my mouth shut."

Moodily she dropped back down onto the ground, folding her legs tailor-fashion. Her appetite was gone. "I was so sure this was going to work, but I'm not getting anywhere."

"You've only been looking for the earrings for two days. There's a lot of territory left to cover around here."

"I didn't mean the treasure hunt."

"I see. You meant our famous relationship. Well, don't get impatient about that, either. You haven't given it any more time than you've given the treasure hunt."

"I've given it four whole months."

"More like three whole days."

She dropped her forehead down onto her updrawn knees and took ten deep breaths. When she raised her head again, her emotions were calmer once more. "Let's talk about the treasure, since we don't seem to be able to discuss our relationship."

"That'a girl. Stick to the real stuff. The stuff you can count on. Nothing like knowing you're sitting somewhere near a cache of jewels to take your mind off a courtship, is there?"

Sarah lost it then. All the self-control she had been practicing for the past few minutes disintegrated in a flash. "You sarcastic, hateful, son of a.... Don't you dare talk to me like that. Do you hear me? Not ever. I won't tolerate it. I'm trying to give you a proper courtship—trying to give you time to catch up with me in this relationship. The least you could do is be polite."

Gideon narrowed his eyes, his expression suddenly fierce. He reached for her, caught her arm and dragged her across his lap to cradle her in a grip of steel.

"I'm sorry," he muttered over and over again as his big hands stroked her. "I'm sorry. You're right. I'm not used to trusting people and I'm not any good at dealing with women. If you want gallantry and charm and trust, you're going to have to look somewhere else."

She huddled against him, aware of the tension that was tightening his whole body. Her fury evaporated. "You really are a beast, aren't you? Your first instinct is to bite that hand that's trying to feed you."

"I said I'm sorry," he said again. His fingers moved in her hair.

"I don't know if I can believe that."

"It's the truth. I shouldn't have pushed you like that." He drew his head back to look down into her glistening eyes. "But I can't guarantee you it won't happen again."

"You have a long way to go to catch up with me, don't you? A lot further than I thought at first."

"So? Are you going to give up on me?"

She shook her head slowly. "No."

"Sarah . . ."

She put her fingers over his lips. "And don't, I warn you, make any cracks about me not giving up on you until you've helped me find the Flowers. If you say anything even close to that, I swear I won't be responsible for my actions."

He shut his mouth and squeezed her so tightly she thought her ribs would crack.

THE NEXT MORNING Sarah awoke with more doubts. The gentling of Gideon Trace was proving to be a formidable task.

The man was like a wild animal that had once been wounded. The bleeding had stopped long ago and he had recovered physically, but the scars would forever make him cautious about trusting anyone.

The coffee was brewing and the biscuits were in the oven. In a few minutes she and Gideon would sit down to breakfast just like two people who were involved in a real relationship.

She was deliberately trying to give Gideon a taste of what living with her would be like but she couldn't tell yet if she was having any impact.

Perhaps the treasure hunt had been a bad idea. She considered that thought very seriously as she slipped outside to taste the morning air while she waited for Gideon to finish shaving.

It was beginning to dawn on her that she might have made a drastic mistake in using the treasure hunt as an opening for contacting Gideon Trace.

Perhaps the truth was, she had only herself to blame for some of his wariness.

How would she have felt if some stranger with whom she had conducted only a casual correspondence suddenly showed up on her doorstop and said he wanted to have a relationship while they searched for a fortune in jewels?

Sarah grimaced and dug her toe into the ground. Perhaps she should call a halt to the treasure hunt for now and go back to square one. She had been convinced somehow that the Fleetwood Flowers and Gideon were linked and it had seemed natural to pursue the two of them together. But she might have been wrong about that part of things.

Certainly her relationship with Gideon was the most important part of the equation. Perhaps she should give it her full attention for now.

Equation.

Sarah blinked in the morning light, inhaling the sweet scent of the evergreens. *Equation.*

She stood staring a moment longer at the stand of trees that edged the clearing. Then, moving slowly, she turned and went back into the cabin.

Gideon was just emerging from the bathroom, tucking his shirt into his jeans in an intimate, somehow very sexy gesture. But, then, Sarah reminded herself, everything about Gideon was sexy to her. He took one look at her face and his brows rose questioningly.

"What's wrong?"

"Nothing. I just thought of something."

"What?"

"Emelina Fleetwood was a schoolteacher."

"So?"

"So in those days a good schoolteacher emphasized the basics, reading, writing and arithmetic."

"And?" He went into the kitchen to help himself to a cup of coffee.

"Gideon, it just hit me that one very logical way for a retired schoolteacher to make the directions to her treasure was with a classic mathematical equation. One she was never likely to forget. The most likely sort of equation to choose for that kind of thing would be one from geometry. You know, triangles."

"Triangles?"

"You can make all sorts of measurements if you know just a little bit of information about a particular triangle. Heck, the Egyptians built whole pyramids based on stuff they knew about triangles."

Gideon regarded her for a moment as he sipped his coffee. His eyes were very green. "It wouldn't be the first time someone used that technique. It requires that whoever hid the treasure be familiar with geometry, but you're right, a schoolteacher would have been."

"We're sitting here with a map that's just loaded with info that could be elements of an equation." Excitement flowed through Sarah as she moved over to the kitchen table to look down at the map in the plastic envelope. "Look at these numbers. Sixty and Ninety and twenty-five. A ninety-degree triangle is a right triangle. Right?"

"Right."

Sarah frowned. "So maybe what we've got here is a right triangle. Maybe the sixty refers to the size of one of the other angles. Right triangles with sixty-degree angles in them are common in geometry."

"What about the number twenty-five? My geometry is rusty but I seem to recall that the angles of a triangle have to add up to 180 degrees. Sixty, ninety and twenty-five don't add up to that."

"Maybe twenty-five is the length of one of the sides of the triangle. The distance between the two small squares on the map, perhaps." Sarah was getting more excited by the minute as she examined the markings on the copy of the Fleetwood map. "Given a couple of angles and the length of one side, you could solve for the remaining two sides, right?"

"Sounds like we're talking your basic Pythagorean theorem here."

"Yes, of course. The square of the length of the hypotenuse of a right triangle is equal to the sum of the squares of the lengths of the other two sides."

"Congratulations to your memory."

"Don't congratulate me, congratulate Mrs. Simpson. Math was not my strong point in high school," Sarah said as she continued to study the map. "But Mrs. Simpson drilled some of the basics into me. Little did she know I was going to become a writer and never need the stuff. Until now, that is. I guess you never know. Now, if we assume twenty-five is the length of one side…Gideon, we're going to need a calculator. I'm not *that* good at the basics. Got one?"

"Not on me, but we can pick up a cheap one in town this afternoon. We're almost out of milk, anyway."

"Let's go now."

"Sarah, it's only seven o'clock. The stores won't be open until nine or ten."

She sat back, disgusted with the delay. "This is it, Gideon. I know it. I have a feeling."

"Uh-huh. I have a feeling there's something getting very close to being done in the oven."

Sarah's eyes widened. She leaped to her feet. "My biscuits."

"First things first," Gideon said. "The Flowers can wait. I'll get the honey."

LATER THAT MORNING, with the help of a five-dollar calculator, they ran the numbers. Sarah was beside herself with excitement. She practically danced around the table as they drew triangles and labeled the sides.

"We've got the length of all three sides and we know there's supposed to be a white rock at the point where B and C intersect," she said, delighted with the results.

"None of this does any good unless we can figure out what points Emelina used to measure her triangle," Gideon noted.

"Well, she gave us the length of one side of the triangle, twenty-five feet. She must have been using familiar points of reference. You said yourself, people tended to do that. Gideon, this is so thrilling. I've never done anything like this before." She looked up when there was no response from his side of the table. "But you have, haven't you?"

"Once or twice." He sat watching her with an unreadable expression in his eyes.

"Like once or twice a year when you go off on one or your mysterious vacations?" Sarah asked shrewdly.

He exhaled heavily. "Magazines are expensive to run. *Cache* needs an infusion of cash periodically."

"So you go out and dig some up. Wonderful."

"It's not quite that easy, Sarah. More often than not, you don't get lucky."

"Still, you know more about second-guessing someone like Emelina Fleetwood than I do. What do you think she used as points of her triangle?"

He hesitated for a long time. Then, as if he had reached a decision, he pulled the map closer. "We're assuming that all these figures apply to a right triangle. We could be totally off base with all this. The numbers might mean something else entirely."

Sarah shook her head. "No, I don't think so."

His mouth curved faintly at her air of certainty. "Yeah, I know. You've got a feeling. All right, we'll assume your intuition is valid and go from there." Gideon leaned over the map. "My first hunch is that she was using the distance between the outhouse door and the back door of her cabin. Twenty-five feet sounds about right for that. But she might also have used a clothesline or a tree as a marker."

"No, no, I think you're right. Brilliant idea. Lucky you've had experience with outhouses, isn't it?"

He gave her a warning glance. "One more outhouse joke and I'm through as a consultant."

She grinned, undaunted. "Let's go see if we can find enough left of that old outhouse to tell us where the door was."

"It probably faced the main house." Gideon glanced wistfully toward the kitchen counter. "What about lunch?"

Sarah started to protest any further delay and then thought better of it. There was something in Gideon's expression that made her think another picnic lunch was important today. "I'll make us some sandwiches."

Forty minutes later they paced off the distance between the toppled outhouse and the sagging back door of the cabin. Sarah held a tape measure in one hand and Gideon took the other end.

"Twenty-five feet," he called from the back door of the cabin.

"All right," Sarah sang out. "I'm sure this is it, Gideon. Now, if we assume that the right angle was at her back door, then the one at the outhouse door was the sixty-degree angle."

"She could have drawn the triangle to either the right or the left of her base line," Gideon remarked.

"We may have to measure it twice and see which point is near a white rock." Sarah glanced to the side. "Let's try it off to the right, first. The woods on that side of the house look promising. Got the measuring tape?"

"I've got it."

Five minutes later they came to a halt in a grove of pine and fir.

"I only hope we're walking a reasonably straight line," Sarah said as they started to pace off the remaining side of the imaginary triangle.

"I think we can gauge it fairly accurately this way. You getting hungry yet?" Gideon was carrying the picnic basket and seemed more interested in its contents than he did in locating the white rock.

"No. I'm too excited. Aren't you feeling any thrill at all? We're so close."

"Ninety-nine times out of a hundred you end up with nothing but a pile of dirt at the end of this kind of hunt."

"Don't be so pessimistic."

"Sarah, we walked all over this section of ground yesterday and found nothing."

"We'll get lucky today. Today we know what we're doing."

"I'm glad one of us does."

But when they finished, there was no white rock at the point where the B and C of the triangle supposedly intersected. Sarah looked around, utterly baffled.

"I don't understand it. I was so sure we'd find it using the triangle formula. Maybe we should try the other side of the clearing."

"Maybe." Gideon glanced up at the sky. "Lunchtime."

"Is it?"

"Yes, it is. I vote we take a break and eat right here." Gideon settled down on the ground right at the point where the intersecting lines of the triangle should have revealed a large white boulder. He spread the checkered cloth on the thick carpet of dried pine needles and started unwrapping sandwiches.

Reluctantly Sarah plopped down beside him. "Do you think maybe this really is a wild-goose chase, Gideon?"

"How should I know? You're the one with the map and the sense of intuition. Here. Have some carrot sticks."

She took a carrot and munched absently. "I wonder if I've blown this whole thing out of all proportion. This morning I was wondering if I'd been mistaken in thinking that you and the earrings are linked."

He slanted her a glance. "Which is more important? Me or finding the earrings?"

"You, naturally." She wrapped her arms around her knees and gazed straight ahead into the forest. "But I can't quite figure out why meeting you seemed so bound up with my finding the earrings. It's kind of weird when you think about it."

"It was *Cache* that put the idea into your head. The coincidence of the fact that I publish a treasure-hunting magazine is probably what made you connect me to the idea of hunting down the earrings. It's logical."

"Yes, but I don't usually operate on logic."

"I've noticed. Have some lemonade." He poured her a cupful from the Thermos.

"Things are getting confusing, Gideon."

"I can see your problem. It always gets confusing when you mix a fortune in gems with the great romance of the century."

She took that seriously. "Yes, it does. I'm worried that if we do find the jewels, you'll think I used you. How am I going to convince you that you're more important?"

Gideon leaned over her and brushed his mouth against hers. "You are one wacky female."

"*Interesting.* I'm an interesting female. Not wacky."

"If you say so." He kissed her again. "You taste like lemonade."

"So do you."

He rolled onto his back. "What do you say we take a nap?"

She shook her head automatically. "I never take naps."

"I do. When I'm lying out in the middle of the woods on a warm afternoon, that is."

She smiled. "Do you do that a lot?"

"No." Gideon folded his arms behind his head and closed his eyes. In a moment he was sound asleep.

Sarah watched him for a while, the sweet longing deep inside making her feel unaccountably sad. She wished he belonged to her so that she could touch him; make love to him.

A few minutes later she pillowed her head on his strong shoulder and fell asleep.

When she awoke a long while later, Gideon's fingers were on the buttons of her shirt and he was leaning over her with a compelling passion blazing in his gemlike eyes.

"You want to prove to me that I'm more important than finding the earrings?" he challenged softly. "Let me make love to you. Here. Now."

Dazed with sleep, sunlight and a sudden, searing sense of longing, Sarah reached up to put her arms around his neck.

6

AN ALMOST UNBEARABLE SENSE of excitement washed through Gideon as he watched Sarah awaken with a smile of sensual welcome in her eyes. It suddenly occurred to him that he had been waiting all of his life to see just that look in a woman's gaze. The feel of her arms stealing around him was more satisfying than finding hidden treasure. His hand trembled from anticipation and desire as he touched her.

"Gideon? What is it?"

"I want you. So bad I can taste it."

He winced inwardly at the sound of his own voice. It was harsh and raspy in his throat. He wanted to murmur in her ear; he wanted to charm her; coax her into making love with him; persuade her into sensual surrender. He longed to reassure her—to tell her he would be careful with her, infinitely careful. He would do everything he could to make it good for her.

But the only words he could get out were the ones that told her he was starving for her. He wondered if he'd frightened her.

"I'm glad you want me," Sarah said. "So glad."

She wasn't trying to pull away from him, he realized. She still wanted him as much as she had seemed to want him whenever he had kissed her during the past few days.

Gideon relaxed slightly. He touched her throat, inhaling the scent of her, and felt her fingers move in his hair. The gentle caress sent passionate chills down his spine.

When he finally got her shirt open he thought he would lose what remained of his self-control. He lifted his head to stare down at the curves of her small, full breasts. His whole body was tight, hot and heavy now.

"So sweet." He bent his head to kiss the soft, inviting fullness of her. "Soft. Hot." He caught her nipple gently between his teeth. It grew taut and firm almost instantly and his whole body clenched in response.

"Oh, Gideon."

Her leg shifted, sliding alongside his, and Gideon was suddenly impatient with the clothing. He splayed his fingers over her warm belly and slid his hand down to the fastening of her jeans. He hesitated, waiting to see if she would resist this next step.

She didn't. She simply lifted her hips so that he could push the jeans off entirely. When he saw the scrap of red lace she wore as panties, he thought he would go out of his mind.

"I've never seen anything sexier in my life," he whispered as he slipped one finger beneath the elastic edge of the delightfully shameless undergarment.

She laughed softly and buried her flushed face in his shoulder. "Good. I wore them just for you."

"Does that mean you intended to let me make love to you today?"

"I've got six other pairs just like these with me. I bought them in Seattle before I came to meet you. I've worn one of the pairs every day since I found you. I never knew when this was going to happen, you see. I wanted to be prepared."

He was torn between laughter and a frustrated groan. "What about your famous intuition? Didn't that warn you when this would happen?"

"My intuition is always at war with my common sense when I'm around you," she complained softly. "You make it hard for me to think straight. Things aren't always clear for some reason."

"I'm glad. And I can't wait to see the other six pairs." He covered her mouth with his own, his tongue surging intimately between her lips. He knew he was seeking advance knowledge of what it would be like when he claimed her completely. The sample he got was enough to make his head whirl.

His fingers found the hot, flowing warmth of her and he almost came unraveled.

"I love the feel of you," Sarah said, her eyes narrowing with desire. "Your hands. Yes, please, touch me, Gideon. Such wonderful hands." She sucked in her breath. "That feels incredible."

Gideon watched her hair spill over his arm, the soft, thick strands turning to honeyed gold in the splintered light. He was enthralled with her response, mesmerized by it. He'd never had a woman come alive like this under his touch. She was literally melting for him. He could see the heat in her cheeks and feel her racing pulse.

A glittering host of emotions rocked him as she twisted and lifted herself against his probing hand. He was at once filled with a sense of raw, masculine power and great tenderness. He wanted to bury himself in her and find his own release before the gathering pressure drove him out of his mind. But at the same time he longed to bring her such pleasure that she would never even want to look at another man.

"My jeans," he muttered abruptly. "Give me a second, honey." He released her to fumble with his own clothing. All his actions seemed unbelievably awkward suddenly. She was so sleek and sinuous and delicate. He felt like a great, rutting male animal next to her.

But Sarah didn't seem to mind. In fact, she seemed to find him endlessly fascinating. Her eyes were glowing with a shimmering heat as she helped him tug off his pants. When she saw him reach into one pocket for a little plastic packet she grinned teasingly.

"Obviously I'm not the only one who's been running around prepared for this," she said.

He felt himself redden as he busied himself for a few seconds but he merely shook his head. "No, you're not. But I wasn't relying on intuition, just hope." He took a deep breath and tugged off the red panties. For a long moment he could only stare at the tangled triangle of hair that was revealed. He was held in thrall by the promise of what awaited him.

Sarah seemed equally enchanted. She touched him, wonderingly at first and then more boldly, stroking him as if he were a big cat. Under her fingers Gideon began to feel like one. A sense of his own fluid grace and power filled him, washing out the awkwardness.

She did this to him, he thought. She made him feel this way, made him glory in his own manhood.

"I don't know if I can wait very long for you," he warned her. "I'm going up in flames. You have a hell of an effect on me."

"That's only fair. Because you have the same effect on me."

She kissed his throat and shoulder. He felt first her tongue and then her small teeth on his skin and he shuddered.

She seemed to sense when he was at the end of his tether. When he grasped the ripe curve of her thigh and pushed tentatively, she went easily onto her back, reaching up to draw him down to her.

Gideon fought for control as he watched her part her legs for him. Her silent invitation was the most compelling action he'd ever witnessed. It said without words that she was giving herself to him—that she was his.

He could no more have resisted the siren call of her in that moment than he could have flown into the sun.

With a short, muttered exclamation of need he slid between her thighs, astounded at the silky feel of them. He hesitated an instant, afraid once more that he was going too fast, that he might hurt her.

But she was beckoning him into her with that ancient summons in her hazel eyes.

He pushed slowly against her hot, damp opening, seeking an easy, gentle entry. But she was small and tight, in spite of her obvious willingness.

"Sarah?"

"It's all right." She stroked him gently when she felt his hesitation. "You're just right for me."

She lifted her hips, urging him to complete the union. Gideon groaned as the last of his control left him. He surged into her, pushing through the brief resistance of small, tight muscles and on into the clinging warmth that awaited him.

He went still for a few seconds, savoring the sensation of being inside Sarah. It was like nothing else he'd ever experienced.

"Buried treasure." He kissed her breast.

"What?" She was breathing quickly through her parted lips, her eyes glittering as she adjusted to him.

"Nothing. Never mind."

He began to move in her, slowly, powerfully. He got his hand down between their bodies and found the tiny nub hidden in her soft thatch of hair. She went wild when he touched her then.

"*Gideon.*"

Suddenly she was clutching at him, her eyes widening briefly with distinct surprise before they squeezed shut. Gideon held her as she shivered in his arms. The emotions that flooded through him in that moment were chaotic and indescribable.

Before he could even begin to sort out his feelings, the full force of his own release roared through him. The power of it drove out all other sensation.

He heard himself call Sarah's name and then there was only a sweet, blissful exhaustion.

SARAH DRIFTED SLOWLY up out of the dreamy web of satisfaction that had held her for several minutes. She was aware of the great weight of Gideon Trace on top of her. The deliciously crushed sensation made her smile. Her hands moved slowly on his smoothly muscled back, exploring the powerful, lean contours. He felt so right.

There had never been any real doubt. Gideon was her knight in shining armor, her moody, taciturn, difficult hero whose grim facade hid a passionate, loyal heart.

She had been wrong to worry about letting the lovemaking happen too soon. There had been no reason to hold off until she was sure of him. She was already sure of him. She had been since the beginning. Her intuition had not failed her.

And even if it had, it was too late to worry about it. She was head over heels in love with the man. She had been in love with him for months.

Sarah looked up into the trees, aware that it was now midafternoon. Branches rustled overhead. The sun that filtered through the leaves was still warm. The rock digging into her back was getting very hard.

Gideon exhaled heavily and raised his head to gaze down into her eyes. Satisfaction and an amusing, rather arrogant, vaguely leonine contentment gleamed in his eyes.

"You look a little like Machu Picchu," Sarah said.

Gideon smiled slowly. "Fair enough. You look like Ellora." He kissed her lightly on the mouth. "Any regrets?"

"None."

"That's good because I don't think I could go back to playing your courtship game."

"It wasn't a game. I just wanted to be sure you knew what you were doing."

He kissed her shoulder. "How'd I do?"

"Beast. You knew what you were doing, all right."

He raised his head again, laughing down at her with his eyes. "Thanks. I'll assume that's a compliment."

"The resemblance to Machu Picchu is getting stronger by the minute."

"How's that?"

"Well, you're getting quite heavy, for one thing." She wriggled her shoulders, trying to find a more comfortable spot on the ground.

"And you're such a delicate little thing, aren't you? Wouldn't want to squash you." Gideon moved, rolling over onto his back and dragging her with him so that she sprawled on top of him. "Now about this treasure hunt we're on...."

She shook her head, framing his hard face between her palms. Frowning with serious intent, she looked deep into his eyes. "Forget the treasure hunt. As of this afternoon, the earrings are no longer important. I'm still not sure why searching for them was so linked to finding you, but everything is much clearer now than it has been for the past few days."

His brows rose in silent laughter. "Sex has made it clearer?"

She smiled. "I suppose so. The point is, you're my important discovery, Gideon. I don't need the earrings now. They can wait." She brushed her mouth against his.

His arms closed around her, hard and tight and strong. Sarah was sure that his kiss was saying everything he did not yet seem able to say with words. He wanted her, needed her, loved her. It was enough, more than enough for the present.

When he freed her mouth, she was breathless again. She saw the look in his eyes and laughingly shook her head. "Oh, no. Not a second time on the ground. Not unless you're on the bottom."

"Not that comfortable, huh?"

"Like being trapped between a rock and a hard place."

He grinned wolfishly. "So how did I compare to one of your heroes?"

"Bigger." She kissed the tip of his nose. "Harder." She kissed his cheek. "Stronger." She kissed the strong line of his jaw. "Sexier." She kissed his mouth. "Much sexier. To sum it up, the reality was much better than the fantasy version, but I like to think that creating you over and over again in my books prepared me for the real thing when you walked into my life."

"I didn't exactly walk into your life. You walked into mine."

"Details, details. Same result. A happy ending."

The wicked satisfaction in his eyes was echoed in his laughter. "Are all romance writers experts at happy endings?"

"It's our stock and trade. You only get two fundamental choices in the world when it comes to philosophies: optimism or pessimism. Romance writers are basically optimists at heart, just like treasure hunters."

He gave her an odd look. "I've never thought of myself as an optimist. God knows, I'm no Pollyanna."

"Nonsense. Under that gruff, grouchy, bristly exterior beats the heart of a man who secretly believes in the same things I do. You're just too macho to admit it."

"You think you know me so well, don't you?"

She smiled serenely. "Naturally. I've been studying you since I was old enough to figure out the basic differences between men and women. That's how long you've been in my head."

He touched her hand. "You were studying a fantasy creation, not a real man."

"I know the difference between fantasy and reality," she assured him as she sat up and reached for her shirt and jeans.

"And you're convinced I'm real?"

She paused in the act of buttoning her shirt, aware already of the faint soreness in her thighs. She flashed him a rueful grin. "Very real. I can still feel the effects."

His gaze grew serious. "Did I hurt you?"

"No, of course not. I was just teasing." She patted his cheek and began struggling into her jeans.

"Sarah?"

"Umm?"

"Never mind." Gideon got slowly to his feet, pulling on his own clothing with quick, efficient movements.

She watched him out of the corner of her eye as she began to pack up the picnic basket. Something important was going through that inscrutable mind of his but she couldn't begin to guess what it was. Perhaps he was searching for a way to tell her he loved her, she thought happily.

Gideon leaned over to catch hold of one corner of the red-checked cloth. He pulled it back slowly, as if not sure how to refold it.

"Here, I'll do that," Sarah offered, taking the corner of the cloth out of his hand. She shook out the old tablecloth as Gideon walked around, kicking at pine needles. "What are you doing?" she asked finally.

"Just making sure we don't leave any sandwich wrappers behind." He used the toe of his boot to sweep back another layer of needles.

Sarah glanced down and saw the tip of moss covered rock thrusting up out of the earth. "That's what was digging into my back when you were making love to me. No wonder I felt as if I were trapped between a rock and a—" She broke off. "Oh, my God. A rock. Gideon, it's a *white* rock. Look at it."

He glanced down. "It looks like a green rock to me."

"Rocks aren't green. It's just got a lot of moss growing on it." Sarah dropped the red cloth and knelt on the ground for a closer look. Experimentally she scraped off some of the moss with her fingernail. "It is white."

Gideon crouched beside her. "Think so?"

"I'm sure of it." She looked up at him with growing delight. "Gideon, this is so exciting. Maybe we've found the jewels after all. Help me dig away some of the dirt."

Obediently he reached out and pulled away a few clods of dirt. More of the white boulder was revealed. "If this is your famous rock, it's no wonder we didn't see it when we went looking for it. It got covered up long ago in a mud slide."

"Yes, that's exactly what must have happened." Sarah sat back on her heels, frowning. "We'll never be able to uncover it with our bare hands. We'll need tools."

"An excellent observation." The distant sound of an engine shattered the stillness of the forest. Gideon was on his feet instantly, tugging Sarah up beside him.

"What's wrong?" she asked, taking the picnic basket as he thrust it into her hands.

"Nothing. But it sounds like we may have company coming. The cardinal rule of treasure-hunting expeditions is you don't reveal the location of the treasure to strangers."

Sarah hugged the basket to her and hurried to follow him out of the woods, past the old Fleetwood homestead and on to the cabin they were renting. The sound of the engine in the distance grew louder. "Do you really think we might have found the white rock that marks one of the points on Emelina Fleetwood's triangle?"

He threw her an amused glance over his shoulder. "What does your famous intuition tell you?"

She frowned, trying to sort out the jumbled impressions in her head. "I'm not sure," she said slowly. "I think that white rock is the one we've been looking for, but . . ."

"But what?" The engine roar was closer now.

"But I just don't feel much urgency about the whole thing." She grinned. "Not that finding a fortune in gems is totally uninteresting, of course. I'm not that laid back about it all."

"I'd wonder at your sanity if you were."

"Well, it certainly would be great fun to turn them up. But like I said, they're not as important as they once were." Sarah abandoned the effort to explain. "Never mind. Here comes our visitor and you're right about one thing—I don't want some stranger to get his hands on them. Those earrings are Fleetwood earrings."

A black Jeep roared around the bend in the road. Instead of going on past the isolated cabin, it turned into the long, winding drive as if whoever was behind the wheel knew exactly where he was going.

"You tell anyone else you were coming up here?" Gideon asked, his gaze on the Jeep as it drew closer to the cabin.

"Sure, a couple of people, including my friend Margaret Lark. But she doesn't own a Jeep and neither does anyone else I know. Maybe it's our landlord."

"No, I don't think so." Gideon reached the front step of the cabin and drew her to a halt beside him as the Jeep entered the yard. His gaze never left the vehicle.

The Jeep came to a halt in a cloud of dust. Sunlight glinted on the windshield, obscuring the view of the driver. Sarah experienced a sudden shaft of deep uneasiness.

"Gideon?"

He didn't respond. His whole attention was on the Jeep. She sensed the tension in him.

The door of the Jeep cracked open with a flourish. A black boot, so brilliantly polished that it caught the sun, hit the ground. Something silver glinted at the heel.

"Hell," Gideon said.

The man who got slowly out of the Jeep was as spectacular as his boots. He moved with laconic grace, well aware he was making an entrance and obviously enjoying it. His hair was as black and gleaming as his footwear. His eyes were blue, a bright, devilish sapphire blue.

There was no doubt the stranger had been ruggedly good-looking at one time. He still was, to be perfectly honest. The chin and nose and cheekbones were all well chiseled. But Sarah could see that there had always been an underlying weakness and the years were starting to reveal it.

He wore khaki pants tucked into the tops of the high, dashing boots and a shirt that had a large number of pockets, epaulets and flaps on it. The clothes fit him so precisely they might have been hand-tailored.

"He looks like something out of a men's fashion magazine," Sarah whispered.

"Plenty of flash, all right. But, then, he always had that."

She frowned up at Gideon but he was still watching the newcomer. The stranger smiled, an easy, knowing, charming grin that revealed sparkling white teeth. Sarah's sense of unease grew a hundredfold. She knew she was not going to like this man, whoever he was.

"Hello, Gideon. I hear the last name is Trace now, is that right? Nice touch. That's all you left behind when you changed your identity, wasn't it? Just a trace. It's taken me a while to find you but it looks like I finally did it with the help of Ms. Fleetwood here. Long time, no see, Gid. How's it going, buddy?"

"Sarah," Gideon said, "meet Jake Savage."

"My pleasure, Ms. Fleetwood. But I believe we already know each other."

She stared at him. "We do?" But her intuition was already giving her the answer. Something about this man was awfully familiar even though she knew she had never met him. That voice . . .

"Jim Slaughter, owner and operator of Slaughter Enterprises, at your service. We had the pleasure of exchanging a few letters and a couple of calls regarding an expedition to find a downed plane full of gold, remember? You declined to invest. I'm still hoping to change your mind on that subject, by the way. I think we could do a lot for each other, Ms. Fleetwood."

"You're Slaughter?" She was horrified. It was beginning to dawn on her that she was the one who had led him to this place. She'd mentioned the Fleetwood Flowers to him. "Why did you change your name? I don't understand any of this."

"I had to change my name about the same time as Gideon here changed his, ma'am. But that's all in the past now."

"I thought you were dead, Mr. Savage," she said.

Savage chuckled. "So did a lot of people, including my old partner, here, right, Gid?"

Partner. Sarah looked at Gideon. "You were his partner? The partner you said disappeared in the jungle along with Mr. Savage?"

Gideon didn't bother to reply. His eyes were still on the swashbuckling figure of his former associate. "What brings you back to life after all this time, Jake?"

"Got some big plans, Gid, old pal. Thought you might be interested in going back into partnership. Like I said, I've been looking for you for a while. I had a hunch you weren't any more dead than I was. You're a hard man to kill. Who'd have guessed I'd have found you through the charming Ms. Fleetwood? Piece of luck, huh?"

Gideon's brows rose sardonically. He slid a speculative glance toward Sarah. "How *did* you find me through the charming Ms. Fleetwood?"

"Simple enough," Jake said easily. He grinned his engaging grin at Sarah. "The little lady contacted me five months ago wanting to know if I'd be interested in helping her do some research. I did a little research myself and decided Sarah and I could be very useful to each other. So I offered her a chance to participate in a real-life search for lost gold."

"At a price," Sarah muttered.

"Well, naturally," Jake said, still smiling. "A fine investment opportunity. And just picture the publicity we could get: romance writer and one of her heroes go hunting for a fortune in the South Pacific. We could have drawn money and media like crazy. We'd have had people lined up for blocks wanting in on the deal."

"I take it you declined the offer, Sarah?" Gideon glanced at her.

"Yes." She clutched the picnic basket more tightly to her chest.

"I was pretty sure I could talk her into it, given a little time," Jake said with irrepressible self-confidence. "I mean, it's easy money, right? Hey, we take the investment cash but we don't actually have to *find* anything. How many treasure-hunting expeditions get lucky? Almost none. None of the investors squawk too loudly because they all know the odds going in."

"Easy money," Gideon agreed dryly.

"But in the meantime, she's led me to you, Gid. And that changes everything. I've got a deal for both of you."

"Forget it. I changed my name for a reason, Jake. I'm out of the business."

"I don't believe it for a minute. If you're out of the business, what are you doing here looking for the Fleetwood Flowers?"

"This is personal," Gideon said softly.

Sarah risked a quick glance at Gideon. He was grim-faced, his eyes very cold.

"Hey," said Jake, "so it's personal." He winked at Sarah. "I can understand that. But that doesn't mean the three of us can't do a little business. I've been thinking this through and I've got it all planned out."

"I'll bet," Gideon said.

"Now just listen, pal. Here's how it shapes up. Slaughter Enterprises gets a nice splash of publicity by turning up the Fleetwood Flowers for a pretty little romance writer, see? Lots of press on that. Then, when we're riding the wave of that announcement, we let it be known that Sarah is going to join us on an expedition to the South Pacific to find a plane full of gold. Like I said, money and media will pour in. It's dynamite, Gid. Dynamite. Better than the old days, huh? No risking our necks in some godforsaken South American jungle this time. First class, all the way. And get this—with you along, we'll probably find the damned gold."

"No thanks," Gideon said.

"Think it through," Jake urged. "Give it a chance to sink in, that's all I ask. We made a hell of a team in the old days. You know it and I know it."

"What makes you think we're going to find the Fleetwood Flowers?" Gideon asked.

Jake Savage looked at him in astonishment and then to Sarah's surprise, he burst out laughing. "Hey, Gid, this is me, your old buddy, Jake, remember? I know you, pal. You never go after anything but a sure thing. If you've agreed to help Ms. Fleetwood here, it's because you've cut yourself in for a slice of the action and you're damned sure there's going to be some action. Neither of us ever worked for free, even when it was *personal*."

7

"I DESERVE A FEW ANSWERS, Gideon." Sarah took the tops off several stalks of fresh broccoli with a few ferocious strokes of her knife. She dropped the broccoli into a colander and picked up a carrot and a peeler.

There had been a taut silence in the small cabin after Jake Savage had driven off to find a motel in the nearby town. He'd seemed unoffended by Gideon's failure to offer him a bed for the night. Sarah had the feeling that it took a lot to offend Jake. He was so accustomed to wowing people that it would never occur to him that he was being insulted.

"What do you want to know first?" Gideon was sitting at the kitchen table, a cold beer in front of him. He looked remote and austere, the way he had the day she'd arrived on his doorstep.

"Well, we could start with your real name, I suppose," Sarah said tartly as she whacked strips off the carrot.

"My real name is Gideon."

"Gideon what?"

"Does it matter?"

"It matters, damn it. What's your legal name?"

"My legal name is Trace. I've got a bunch of credit cards, a social security number and a driver's license under that name. How much more legal does it get?"

"What was it before it was Trace?" she asked through set teeth. "Back when you were the partner of the famous Jake Savage?"

He ran a hand through his hair. "Carson."

"Carson." She tasted that for a minute. "Not bad. But I like Trace better. Maybe it's because I met you under that name." *Maybe because you made love to me under that name.* "All right, let's go on to the next question. What really happened back in that jungle where the two of you were supposed to have disappeared? What jungle was it, anyway?"

Gideon was quiet for a moment. "It doesn't really matter now. I told you Savage & Company occasionally did odd jobs all over South America."

"And?"

"And this was one of the odder ones. The kind where you don't ask a lot of unnecessary questions and you take your pay in cash. On delivery. Savage and Company never got involved in anything illegal on general principle, but there were times when it walked a fine line."

"You would never do anything illegal," Sarah declared.

Gideon's mouth twisted faintly. "The problem is that the definition of legal varies a lot once you get south of Tijuana."

"I can imagine. Okay, go on."

"As I said, it was a job. For which Savage and Company was supposed to be paid a great deal of money. We were to take a shipment of supplies to a group of archaeologists excavating an old Indian ruin deep in the jungle. But it turned out the folks waiting for the supplies weren't legitimate researchers. They were in the business of smuggling antiquities. We saw more than we should have seen and they didn't want any witnesses."

"Dear heaven," Sarah breathed. "What happened?"

"We were ambushed on the way back out of the jungle."

"By the so-called archaeologists?"

Gideon nodded. "It had to be them, although I didn't stick around to take a close look."

Sarah stared at him in shock. "How did you escape?"

"With a little luck and the usual advance research on the terrain that I had done before we went in. That was my speciality, Sarah. My contribution to Savage and Company. I did all the research on a job, made all the preparations, checked out all the people involved. I went over every detail ahead of time, envisioned all the worst case scenarios and planned for them. Getting stiffed by the client is one of the worst case possibilities. I always allowed for it."

"What did Jake Savage contribute to the company?" Sarah asked dryly.

Gideon gave her a derisive look. "Flash. What else? You've seen him. He brought image and style to the team. A natural salesman. He was everything people wanted to see when they hired a professional adventurer of any kind. He made people think we could handle anything. And we did. We had a hell of a reputation down south. We always got the job done."

"And you always took a cut of the action," Sarah concluded quietly.

Gideon shrugged. "It was business. At least for me. Jake liked the money, too, of course. He needed a lot of it because he tended to go through it like water. But the truth was, he got most of his kicks from being a living legend. He was addicted to his own image. He could walk into any bar from Mexico City to Buenos Aires and the women would fall all over him. And the men all wanted to be able to say they'd met him and bought him a beer."

"But you were the one who really made Savage and Company work, weren't you?" Sarah said, knowing she was right. "You were the strategist, the planner, the one who knew the terrain."

"Jake had his uses as an image. He drew business and investors like flies. But the truth is, he couldn't find candy on Halloween night without help."

Sarah started to giggle before she could stop herself. When she realized Gideon was watching her curiously, she took a swallow of wine to give herself time to regain her firm demeanor. She was not going to stop grilling Gideon until she got all the answers.

"So Savage and Company wouldn't have lasted a week without you behind the scenes."

"It was a partnership. And for the most part it worked well for both of us. We made a lot of money. Did a lot of fast living. You can get addicted to adrenaline just like you can to anything else."

Sarah eyed him sharply. "Do you still crave the excitement?"

Gideon smiled slightly. "Nothing more than what I can get once a year when I go on vacation and do a little treasure hunting."

"All right," Sarah continued forcefully, determined not to be sidetracked, "what happened at the scene of the ambush? Why did you and Jake get separated and each think the other might be dead? What went wrong?"

Gideon took a mouthful of beer and thought about the question. "I don't know."

"What do you mean, you don't know? You were there."

"I was there, all right. But that doesn't mean I know what went wrong. All I know is that one minute we were alone in a Jeep on the trail. We were carrying the cash the so-called archaeologists had paid for their supplies. The next minute I just sort of knew we weren't alone."

"You *knew* it?" Sarah's attention was caught by the odd phrasing. "What does that mean?"

Gideon moved his hand impatiently. "Just what it sounds like. There was no one in sight ahead or behind us, but I had a feeling we were in deep trouble. I told Jake I thought we'd better get out of the Jeep and get into some cover. I knew a place we could disappear to until the coast was clear. Usually he trusted my instincts. In fact he always did. This time he insisted I was crazy. But I was driving. I stopped, picked up the suitcase full of cash and headed into the jungle. Jake didn't have any choice but to follow."

"But he didn't want to go with you?"

"No." Gideon was quiet for a moment, reflecting on some private vision. "About two minutes after we had left the Jeep we heard gunfire back on the trail. Then a lot of noise in the undergrowth. Whoever had attacked the Jeep had realized it was empty and was looking for the principal stockholders of Savage and company. I took off in the direction of a cave I had found on one of the maps. Jake kept stalling. I couldn't figure out why he was having such a hard time keeping up with me, why he kept arguing."

"He was probably disoriented and scared."

"Hell, I was scared, too, but at least I wasn't disoriented. I never get disoriented."

"Instinct again?"

"Whatever. At any rate, I got Jake and the money into the cave and we found the cavern tunnel that an old guide had told me about. It led through the heart of a small mountain and out the other side. The perfect escape route. I'd earmarked it for just that kind of emergency."

Sarah momentarily forgot about her need to stay firm. She was enthralled with Gideon's story. "That was brilliant of you."

His mouth quirked. "Well, it was the best I could come up with under the circumstances. Unfortunately there was a narrow ledge over a gorge on the other side of the cave. Only room for one man at a time to cross it. I went first with the money and Jake started to follow. Then he seemed to lose his nerve. He told me he'd take his chances hiding in the cave. I yelled back that he was a fool and I tried to throw him a vine to use to steady himself. But he panicked and raced back into the cave."

"And you never saw him again," Sarah concluded.

"Not until today. When I walked out of the jungle a few days later, I discovered we were both supposed to be dead. The local gossip, though, was that there was a price on our heads if we did happen to show up. The smugglers wanted us to stay dead. I obliged. I got off the island on a fishing boat and that was the end of it."

"Why did you change your name and create a whole new identity for yourself?"

Gideon turned the beer can in his hands. "It's hard to explain. The truth is, I saw it as an opportunity to start over. I wanted out of the kind of business Savage and Company did. Twelve years is long enough in that line. Thirteen years in it could get a man killed. But it's not always easy to walk away. I wasn't famous like Jake, but a lot of people knew me, knew the kind of work I'd done in the past. Some held a few grudges, like those smugglers who had tried to get rid of us after the last trip. All in all, it was simpler to just start fresh."

Just like one of my heroes, Sarah thought with a surge of empathy. Gideon had turned his back on the past in search of another life. "What about Jake?"

"I wasn't sure Jake was dead. In fact, I figured there was a good chance he wasn't. It took several months and a lot of research but I eventually found out he was very much alive and doing business under the name of Slaughter."

"You've known who he was and where he was all this time?"

"I told you, I like to cover all possible contingencies," Gideon explained quietly.

Sarah picked up her wine and sat down across from him, thinking quickly. "You didn't want him to find you again, did you?"

"No."

"Because you were afraid he'd pressure you into going back into business with him and you wanted out of that kind of work?"

Gideon hesitated. "That was part of it, I guess, but not all of it. I could have resisted the pressure easily enough. But the truth is, I just didn't want to deal with him ever again. Or any of the people from that old life." He searched her face. "Does that make sense?"

"Of course. You had a right to try a new path. What better way to do it than under a new name? But why did Jake change his name when he came out of the jungle?

Oh!" Sarah clapped her hand over her mouth as the realization hit.

"What is it, Sarah?"

"Yes, I see now. He had to change his name, didn't he? He thought you were either dead or determined to stay missing and he knew that with you gone Savage and Company was effectively out of business. He knew he couldn't run it without you. Better to go out a legend than to go on as a has-been who can't hack it on his own. He had his image to think of and from what you've said, his image was everything to him. He couldn't bear to destroy it by proving how incompetent he was to run Savage and Company without you."

Gideon studied her. "You really think that was the reason he changed his name?"

"It makes perfect sense when you think about it."

"I always figured he used a new name because he was afraid of running into those smugglers again," Gideon said slowly. "Or someone like them. Who knows what other deals he had cooking behind my back?"

"That may have had something to do with his decision to change his name, but I doubt that's the reason he made it permanent." Sarah leaned forward. "Tell me something. You say you've been keeping tabs on him. What's he been doing in the past five years?"

"Small-time stuff for the most part. Nickle and dime guide jobs for tourists who want to picnic in the jungle near an old ruin. That kind of thing," Gideon said vaguely. "I haven't paid close attention. All I cared about was having him stay out of my way."

Sarah bit her lip. "But now he's very much in your way, isn't he? And it's all my fault. I led him straight to you."

Gideon gave her a wry look. "Just how many so-called treasure hunters, salvage operators, amateur adventurers and assorted riffraff did you contact when you first started doing research on *Glitter Quest*?"

"A couple of dozen, at least," she admitted. "I wasn't sure what I was looking for at first, you see."

"A couple of dozen. Hell."

"Don't worry," Sarah assured him hastily, "I only mentioned the Flowers to you and Slaughter, or Savage, or whatever his name is."

"That's something to be grateful for, I guess." Gideon gave her a direct look. "Two dozen. What made you pick me out of the pack?"

"Two reasons. First of all, I knew as soon as your letter arrived that I wanted you and no one else to help me in my research."

"The famous Fleetwood intuition strikes again."

"Don't laugh. It was true. But there was a second reason I picked you. You didn't ask for money. In fact, after I mentioned the Fleetwood Flowers, you actually tried to talk me out of wasting my time, remember?"

"I remember. For all the good it did me."

"All of the others turned out to be screwballs or outright frauds who wanted me to invest in their various schemes. I was invited to pour money into every lost gold mine from here to Australia. Jim Slaughter, I mean, Jake, turned out to be more persistent than the rest, though. He liked the idea of teaming up with a writer. I got the feeling that, in addition to wanting me to finance him, he had visions of me doing a book on him or something."

"Or something," Gideon agreed coldly.

She ignored that, frowning intently. "What did your family think about you changing your name?"

"That wasn't a problem."

"No family?"

Gideon shook his head. "No."

"And no wife," Sarah said as she put the rest of it together for herself. "Because Leanna had already divorced you by that time, hadn't she?"

"Yeah."

"And she was waiting for Jake Savage, wasn't she?"

Gideon was silent for a long moment. "That's about the size of it."

"Savage and Leanna. Those were the two people who betrayed you."

"Don't make it sound so melodramatic. Leanna fell in love with Jake and I was in the way. That was all there was to it."

"Hah." Sarah was incensed all over again. "It was an outright betrayal. The worst kind. How dare they do that to you? Your wife and your best friend. Impossible to forgive or forget."

"I wouldn't put it that way."

Sarah glared at him. "Have you forgotten?"

"No, but that doesn't mean I'm still holding a grudge."

"You've got every right to hold one. No wonder you never wanted to see Jake Savage again."

"If you say so. Look, could we change the subject?"

"To what?" Sarah asked.

"How about we discuss the little matter of Emelina Fleetwood's earrings? We've got some decisions to make now that we've located that white rock."

Sarah scowled and got up to go back to peeling carrots. "Good point. What are we going to do about Jake? I don't want him hanging around the Flowers."

"I agree. He's got his eye on those earrings, all right. And on you."

"You mean because he thinks he can use me for publicity purposes? You may be right. In any event, he's definitely the type who will step in at the last minute to claim all the credit. I can see him having a photographer and a couple of reporters waiting in the bushes to cover his big discovery of the Fleetwood Flowers."

"Yeah, that's Savage, all right. He always liked to have a photographer or a reporter around."

"So what should we do?"

"Leave."

"Leave? After finding the white rock? We can't just walk away and let Jake Savage dig up my earrings. It's not fair."

"I've told you, he won't find them on his own. They're as safe now as they've been for the past few years."

"You really think so?" Sarah asked doubtfully.

Gideon watched her, his legs stretched out in front of him. "Trust me on this. I know Jake Savage."

"I'm not so sure he's as incompetent as you say he is."

"Those earrings are getting more important again, aren't they?" Gideon asked softly. "This afternoon you said you weren't very concerned about them at all, but now you're getting downright agitated on the subject."

"It's the principle of the thing. This afternoon I didn't know Jake Savage was going to pop up. He has no right to get his hands on those earrings."

"He won't."

"You sound awfully confident," Sarah said resentfully. "But I have a funny feeling about him. I know he's going to try to claim the Flowers, Gideon." She shivered as her intuition conjured up an image of Jake Savage reaching for the earrings. "I just know it. He has no right."

"I was his partner for a long time," Gideon said. "I know his limitations."

"One of his limitations is that he has no scruples. A man with scruples does not steal his best friend's wife."

"He didn't steal her. She fell in love with him. It wasn't anyone's fault."

"The heck it wasn't. Neither one of them had any scruples if you ask me. How did you get mixed up with a couple of bozos like those two, Gideon?"

"The same way you got mixed up with Richard Whatshisface and managed to get yourself left at the altar. These things happen."

She sighed. "I guess."

There was silence for a moment as the vegetables cooked on the stove. Sarah drummed her fingers on the countertop and stared at the cloud of steam that drifted up from the pot.

"Sarah?"

"Yes, Gideon?"

"About what happened this afternoon...."

She glanced over her shoulder and met Gideon's intent eyes. "What about it?"

"I know I sort of pushed you into it."

"You didn't push me into it."

"Yes, I did. You'd been trying to resist for the past few days."

She smiled. "Not very successfully."

"Are you sure you don't have any regrets?"

"I'm sure. What about you?"

He looked surprised at the question. "Hell, no. Why would I have any regrets?"

"Why, indeed?" she muttered as she dished up the vegetables.

Three hours later Gideon won another hand of gin rummy. He had been winning steadily since they'd begun the game shortly after dinner. "You're not concentrating," he accused.

"I know." Sarah propped her elbows on the table and rested her chin on her folded hands.

"Thinking about the earrings again?"

"No."

"Savage?"

"No."

Gideon leaned back in his chair. "Then what were you thinking about?"

"Us."

His eyes narrowed. "What about us?"

"I'm wondering what to do next, if you must know. Nothing has gone quite the way I thought it would since I met you."

"I knew it," Gideon said swiftly, "you are having regrets."

"I am not having regrets," she snapped. "I'm just feeling confused about a few things."

"Such as?" he challenged roughly.

"Such as what to do with this courtship."

"The courtship's over," Gideon announced, getting to his feet.

Sarah looked up in astonishment. "It is?"

"That's right. We're no longer involved in a courtship. It ended this afternoon when I seduced you on that white rock. We are now involved in an affair."

He came around the table, bent down and scooped her up out of her chair.

"What do you think you're doing?" But her pulse was already racing with anticipation.

"What does it look like I'm doing?" He stalked out of the kitchen, carrying her weight easily. "I'm taking you to bed."

"Oh."

"Is that all you can say—*oh*?" He carried her through the bedroom door and dropped her lightly down onto the bed.

She smiled in the shadows. "The truth is, it's so terribly romantic, I'm left speechless."

He grinned as he began stripping off his clothing. "You're bound and determined to think of me as a romantic hero, aren't you?"

"It's not a fantasy, you know. You are a fascinating, romantic man and I—" She broke off abruptly as he came down beside her on the quilt. It was not yet time to tell him how passionately in love she was. He was not yet ready to let himself believe in love even though she was certain he was in love with her.

"You what?" Gideon gathered her close, nuzzling the delicate curve of her shoulder.

"I think you're also the sexiest man I've ever met." She leaned over him, tasting him with her tongue, tangling her legs with his.

"I don't know about that," Gideon said as he began unfastening her jeans, "but I do know for a fact that you're the most exciting thing that's ever walked into my life." He stopped working on her jeans and framed her face between his big hands. "Sarah?"

"Yes?"

"Promise me you won't walk out again for a long time."

"Never, Gideon. I swear it."

"Don't make impossible promises," he advised. "Just swear you'll give me a little time."

"All the time in the world." She brushed his hard mouth with her own.

He took the silent offer of reassurance, his arms closing fiercely around her and then there was no more talk.

SARAH WAS MIXING THE BATTER for blue corn griddle-cakes the next morning, listening to the sound of the shower so she could gauge when to start cooking when she heard the roar of the black Jeep in the drive.

"Damn him, anyway," she said beneath her breath as she went to the window and watched Jake Savage step out of the vehicle. The man looked as rakishly handsome as ever. She wondered if he traveled with a valet. No normal man could keep such a perfect crease in his khakis or such a polish on his boots.

As he walked to the steps, Sarah saw that Savage had something in his hand. It was a bunch of flowers. She groaned as she went to open the door.

"Good morning. Ms. Fleetwood." Savage held up the flowers with a flourish. "I thought these might brighten up the place a bit. This cabin Gid rented isn't exactly the Ritz, is it?"

Automatically Sarah took the flowers. "The cabin suited us perfectly." Behind her the shower was still going strong. She wished Gideon would hurry and get dressed. She did not like being alone with Jake Savage. "What can I do for you; Mr. Savage?"

"Invite me in for breakfast? I can't remember when I last had a real home-cooked meal. Is that coffee I smell?"

Sarah wondered if there was any civilized way to refuse him a cup. But it was difficult to think of an excuse while she was holding the flowers he had brought. "I'll get you some. Gideon should be out of the shower in a minute."

"Thanks." Jake's smile had just the right touch of boyish masculine charm and gratitude as he followed her into the kitchen. "I guess I make you a little nervous, don't I?"

"Yes, you do."

"Relax. I'm not after the earrings, if that's what's worrying you," Jake said as he took Gideon's seat at the table. "But I can arrange some great publicity for you as well as myself when you find them. A little PR never hurt a writer, did it?"

Sarah felt chilled. Very carefully she put the flowers into a pan of water. "How did you find me up here in the mountains?"

"One of your neighbors told me you'd gone over to the coast to meet the publisher of a magazine called *Cache*. After that, one thing led to another. I talked to a few of Gid's neighbors, including the one who was letting you use this cabin. It finally hit me just who Gideon Trace really was. When I showed an old picture of him to the guy who runs the motel where you stayed, I knew for certain. Hell of a coincidence, huh? Turning up Gid along with you?"

"Amazing."

Jake looked briefly contrite. "Hey, I didn't mean to scare you."

"You didn't scare me." She poured a cup of coffee and put it on the table in front of Jake. "Where have you been living since you got out of that jungle?"

"Gid told you the story, huh? Did he tell you about me getting trapped in that cave while he escaped?"

"He told me you didn't make it out with him," Sarah said cautiously.

Jake shrugged. "No hard feelings. I don't blame Gid for leaving me behind. That's the way it goes. Sometimes you've got to look out for number one and let your partner take his chances. Who knows? If I'd been in his place, maybe I'd have done the same." But his wry smile and clear blue eyes said he'd never abandon a partner in a million years. A man could count on a guy like Jake Savage.

Sarah watched him with increasing fascination. She poured herself some tea and sat down. "That's very broad-minded of you, Mr. Savage."

"Call me Jake. Or Jim. Doesn't matter. Hey, this coffee's terrific. Trust old Gid to find himself a woman who could cook this time around. He never makes the same mistake twice. You and Gid been together long?"

"We've known each other for over four months," Sarah said.

Jake nodded. "When did you tell him about the Fleetwood Flowers?"

"Why?"

"Just curious. Wondered if Gid was still doing business in the usual way. Did he ask for up-front money and a cut of the action? That was the usual policy."

Sarah stirred her tea, thinking of Gideon's demand for one pair of earrings—his choice. "I haven't paid him a dime."

Jake grinned, showing an expanse of sparkling white teeth. "Fair warning, little lady, Gid never works for free. If he didn't take any up-front money from you, then that means he really does believe in the treasure and it means he's got his eye on a chunk of it. You sure you don't have a contract guaranteeing him a slice of the pie?"

"We have a verbal understanding," Sarah said stiffly.

"Hell. That's too bad." Jake gave her a pitying look. "Then my advice is to be very careful, Sarah. Very, very careful. Gid and I had a verbal understanding before we went into that jungle five years ago. I not only didn't get my cut, I nearly died in that damned cave."

Sarah heard the shower stop but her entire attention was on Jake Savage. "You're trying to frighten me, aren't you? Trying to make me distrust Gideon."

"All I'm saying is, watch your back. And your treasure. If you don't know how to do either, hire me. I'll do it for you. I've had experience in both departments."

"*Hire* you?"

"Why not? Call me a consultant. I'll handle the media and Gideon for you. Gideon's useful but you've got to keep your eye on him."

"And in return all you'll take is a nominal fee and full credit for finding the Flowers?"

"I think you'll realize that I'm worth every penny, Sarah. Just ask any of my old clients." Jake reached across the table and covered her hand with his own. His blue eyes were serious and full of understanding. "All you want is the Flowers. All I want is the publicity so I can attract some really big investors. This downed-airplane-full-of-gold thing is going to be a major score. You and me, we can work together, even without Gideon. Like I said, we don't actually have to find the treasure."

"What about Gideon?" Sarah removed her hand from under Jake's.

"Yeah," said Gideon from the doorway. "What about me?"

Sarah jumped and turned her head to see him buttoning his shirt as he walked into the room. She saw the cold expression in his eyes and knew he'd seen her hand under Jake's. She wanted to go to him and reassure him that everything was all right, but he was already helping himself to the coffee.

"If you join us you'll get your cut, as usual," Jake said easily. "I'm just trying to convince Sarah here to let me handle the press for her."

"We don't need any attention from the media," Sarah said, her eyes on Gideon.

"Right," said Gideon. "The last thing we need is an orchestrated media blitz. It's time for you to leave, Jake."

"We can do each other a lot of favors, Gid. We were big once. We can be again."

"No."

"Think about it, Gid. And don't tell me you don't miss the old days. Or the money."

"Get lost, Jake."

"Come on, Gid, this is me, your old buddy talking."

"Get out of here," Gideon said very softly. "Now."

Sarah froze at the steel in Gideon's voice. She looked at Jake and saw frustrated rage flash for an instant in his blue eyes.

But the anger was gone almost immediately as the self-assured gleam came back into Jake's gaze. He got to his feet. "Okay, okay. Take it easy. Hey, I'm gone already, right? So much for old times. You've changed, Gid." He turned to Sarah. "Listen, if you change your mind, Sarah, let me know. You can leave a message at this number any time of the day or night."

Jake scrawled a phone number on the back of a business card and reached across the table to press it into Sarah's hand. He folded her fingers around it with an intimate gesture and then he got to his feet and sauntered out of the room. A moment later the Jeep roared off down the drive.

Sarah looked down at the card in her hand. *Slaughter & Co. James Slaughter, President.* There was no address, just a box number in Anaheim, California. That made a certain sense. Anaheim was the home of Disneyland. She looked up and saw Gideon watching her over the rim of his cup.

"The two of you got involved in a nice, cozy little chat while I was in the shower, didn't you?"

"Don't get defensive. It's not my fault he showed up this morning."

"Is that right?"

"It certainly is. Now stop trying to bully me."

"Let's eat breakfast and get packed, Sarah."

"Packed?" Sarah frowned. "Gideon, I did a lot of thinking last night and I still feel we shouldn't leave the Flowers behind. Not now that Jake Savage is hanging around. Something tells me he's going to try to find the Flowers, that he'll come close, maybe even get his grubby hands on them. I've got this feeling . . ."

"I've told you he won't find them. Damn it, Sarah, don't argue with me. We don't have the time. The Flowers are safe enough for now. We're getting out of here."

"Not without the Flowers, Gideon."

"Forget the Flowers. We'll come back for them. Eventually."

"But, Gideon . . ."

"I want to be out of here by eight o'clock."

Sarah shot to her feet, exasperated. She planted both palms on the table and glared at him. "I'm in charge of this little expedition, remember? I say we stay and dig up the earrings so Jake Savage won't get his hands on them."

"No." Gideon sipped his coffee. "You're not in charge. We're partners."

"Oh, yes, that's right. You're in this for a cut of the action, aren't you? I almost forgot."

"I'm sure Savage reminded you."

"He did say something about the fact that you never work for free," Sarah retorted. "But I was beginning to think our partnership was a little more than a mere business arrangement."

"Did you think I'd give up my claim to one of the Flowers just because we're having an affair? Is that why you're sleeping with me? You figure you can persuade me not to take my cut when this is all over?"

He might just as well have slapped her across the face. Sarah gasped with shock. She took a step back from the table, her eyes widening in hurt and anger.

"You're right," she whispered, aware that she was trembling from head to foot. "The sooner we get away from here, the better. I'll go and pack."

8

SARAH STARED at the mountain scenery through the car window. "You can drop me off in Seattle." They were the first words she had spoken since they had left the cabin.

"I'm taking you back to the coast with me." Gideon's refusal was quiet but resolute.

Sarah shot him a seething, sidelong glance. "What are you going to do? Kidnap me until you can figure out a way to get your hands on all of the Fleetwood Flowers?"

"I'm not kidnapping you. I'm giving you a lift back to where you left your car. It's still at my place, remember?"

"I remember." She sank down low in her seat, her arms folded tightly beneath her breasts. He had a point. "You're right. I'll need my car." She looked at her watch. "We'll be at your place shortly after noon. I'll drive back to Seattle this afternoon. I'll be home in plenty of time."

"Plenty of time for what?"

"For whatever I want to do."

"Planning on going after the Flowers by yourself?"

"It's none of your business what I do about the Flowers. Our partnership is hereby dissolved. Finished. Terminated. Liquidated."

"I'm not ready yet to be fired."

"Oh, yes, you are. You and Jake Savage had both better stay out of my life from now on. If I catch either one of you anywhere near my property, I'll have you both arrested for trespassing."

"Sarah, you're not being rational about this. How are you going to catch Savage or anyone else hanging around your property when you're in Seattle?"

"I'm heading back up here just as soon as I can," Sarah vowed. "This time I'll bring my own shovel and a shotgun."

"Have you got a shotgun?" Gideon asked.

"No, but I expect I can get one. Guns are readily available these days."

"You don't need a shotgun or anything else to protect your damned Flowers," Gideon said wearily. "I've told you a hundred times, Savage won't find them."

"Is that right? Well, what about you?"

"If you want to make certain I don't dig them up on my own, all you have to do is stick around and keep an eye on me."

"I'm a busy woman, Trace. I've got more important things to do than try to keep tabs on you. No, the fastest solution to this problem is for me to dig up my earrings before either you or your old buddy gets to them."

"I don't think that would be a good idea."

"I don't care what you think any more," Sarah said. "I've told you, you're fired as a treasure-hunting consultant and as my partner."

There was a long silence from the driver's side of the car. Gideon concentrated on the narrow, twisting road that was taking them down out of the rugged terrain to where the main freeway sliced through the mountain pass.

"Does it occur to you that you might be overreacting a bit?" Gideon said eventually.

Sarah gritted her teeth. "Overreacting to what, pray tell? Do you think it's possible I've gone a bit overboard in my response to your insults? Perhaps I should have just laughed off the accusation that I slept with you in order to get you to help me find my treasure. Maybe I overreacted to being accused of trying to use sex to stiff you out of your cut of the action."

"Sarah . . ."

"Or perhaps I'm being just a tad irrational now that I've come to my senses and realized I've been deluding myself about you right from the start. The famous Fleetwood intuition screws up again. I can't say I wasn't warned. Hell, you warned me, yourself."

"Sarah . . ."

"Then again, maybe I'm being a bit petty and overly defensive now that I've discovered I've got to protect the Fleetwood Flowers from not one, but two professional opportunists. Yes, I can see where I might be overreacting. I'll have to watch that, won't I?"

"Do you get worked up like this a lot?"

"What do you care? I won't be around you long enough for it to be of any great concern to you." Sarah continued to scowl out the window for a minute. "I wonder if I should just turn around and drive straight back up here this afternoon instead of going back to Seattle for the night. I know you don't think Savage can find the jewels on his own, but my intuition tells me he can and will. And now there's you to worry about, too, of course. Yes, I think I'd better get right back up here today."

"Forget it, Sarah. You're not coming back into these mountains to dig up the Flowers on your own."

"Who's going to stop me?"

"Me."

"I knew it, you *are* kidnapping me. Well, you won't get away with it. If you think you can just lock me away in your cellar or something and have no one notice I'm missing, you're crazy. My best friends in the whole world know I went to find you and if I turn up missing, Margaret and Kate won't rest until they've found out what you did to me. And Kate's husband will probably help them look."

"I'm beginning to see why you're successful at writing novels of romantic suspense. You have a very unique imagination, don't you?"

"And that's another thing. Better not forget what I do for a living. I've got an outstanding contract to complete. If I don't finish the last book on it, my publisher and my agent will come looking for you, too."

His mouth flickered suspiciously, but all Gideon said was, "I'll keep that in mind before I do anything rash."

Satisfied she'd made all the threats she could for the moment, Sarah lapsed back into a brooding silence. She needed her anger. At the moment it was all that was keeping her from tears.

"Sarah, I know you're in no mood to listen to explanations."

"You're right."

"But I'd like to point out that it's not entirely fair to blame me for wondering about your motives. You landed on my doorstep like a small tornado and I feel as though I've been swept up and carried along in a high wind ever since. From the first day you acted as though we were long-lost lovers—as if we'd known each other for ages. You practically begged me to make love to you every time I kissed you. You told me you were going to court me, which is another way of saying seduce me. You went wild when I did finally make love to you, as if I was some irresistible, private fantasy of yours that had come to life. It was crazy, Sarah."

"So I made a teensy little mistake."

"That was one explanation," Gideon said dryly. "But the other, more likely one is that you had a few private motives for wanting to ensure you had me tied up in knots. I don't blame you. You figured you needed some expert help finding the Flowers."

"Shut up, Gideon."

"I'm not saying you were faking your response in bed. I don't think any woman could give that convincing a performance, although that may just reflect my own lack of experience. I haven't been involved with that many women and none of them ever had sufficient reason to want to—"

"I said shut up and meant it," Sarah hissed. "If you dig that hole any deeper, you may never be able to crawl out of it."

"I'm just trying to point out my side of this."

"You've made your point. Damn. When I think of all the excuses I made for you based on the trauma you'd been through with your ex-wife and Jake Savage, I could just spit. You don't need any excuses for the way you've been acting, do you? You come by it naturally. Let's change the subject."

"To what?"

Sarah chewed thoughtfully on her lower lip. "Why didn't you want us to dig up the Flowers before we left this morning? Jake was gone. If we'd hurried, we could have gotten them without him ever knowing. Are you planning to come back on your own and take all of them for yourself?"

He didn't rise to the bait. "I didn't want to start digging for them knowing Savage was still in the neighborhood."

She caught her breath. "You mean you think he might wait until we've dug them up and then try to steal them from us? I never thought of that."

"I know."

"But he was your *partner*."

"I'm aware of that."

"Of course, he did steal your wife. I can see where you might wonder a bit about his trustworthiness in other matters."

"It's not because of what happened with Leanna that I'm worried."

"It's because of what happened on that last trip you two made into the jungle, isn't it?"

Gideon concentrated on the slow-moving truck ahead of them. "I can't help but wonder how he survived."

"You survived."

"I'm better at it than Savage." There was no arrogance or ego in his voice. It was just a simple statement of fact.

"So you're wondering how he got out of that jungle?"

"I'm wondering how he managed to get out of that cave alive, let alone find his way out of the jungle."

"How do you think he managed?" Sarah asked slowly.

"I think it's possible he had help."

"But the only help around from what you've said would have been the smugglers and they were the ones who staged the ambush."

"You've got it."

Sarah was shaken by the implications. "You think it was a conspiracy? That Jake was part of it?"

"I think it's a possibility."

"That would mean he deliberately set you up that day. That he intended to get you killed. But the plan failed because you sensed trouble."

"Savage was never very good at the planning side of things. Believe me, it would be totally in character for him to have screwed up the timing on the ambush."

"I don't get it. Why would he want to kill the goose that lays the golden eggs?"

"A goose, hmm? I never thought of myself that way, but I guess that's one point of view. To answer your question, all I can say is, there was a lot of cash involved."

"How much of it did you get out of the country?"

"All of it except what I spent bribing the captain of the fishing boat. I used the remainder to set myself up in business with *Cache*."

"Good heavens. You did lead an adventurous life, didn't you? I see what you mean about adrenaline. So what this all boils down to is you're afraid we'll be standing there plucking the Fleetwood Flowers from the ground and your old buddy Jake might show up to take them away from us at gunpoint."

"I'd just as soon not take any risks."

"I can understand that. You've got a lot to lose. Just one pair of those earrings will be worth a lot of money. I've got an even bigger problem, though, don't I? I have to figure out a way to protect the Flowers from you and Savage."

"Sarah, if you continued to make not-so-veiled accusations about my trustworthiness, I'm eventually going to lose my temper."

"The way I lost mine when you started making nasty cracks about my reasons for sleeping with you?"

Gideon shook his head ruefully. "Something like that. For the record, and not that you've bothered to ask, I give you my word I'll abide by our original bargain."

"We don't have a bargain. I fired you, remember?"

"I warned you that I don't fire that easily."

"Which, translated, means you're not going to give up your claim to the jewels."

"I don't suppose it's occurred to you that I'm more worried about you than I am the Flowers?"

"No."

"Sarah, be reasonable. As long as Savage is hanging around, it's dangerous for you to even think about digging up the earrings. Leave them where they are until he gets bored and leaves the vicinity."

"What makes you think he'll get bored?"

"I know him. If he believes I've really given up on the Flowers, myself, he'll give up on them, too. He got used to trusting my instincts. And he never hangs around too long if there's no percentage in it. One of these days he'll disappear and leave us in peace. When he does, we'll go back and get the Flowers."

"It might interest you to know," Sarah said slowly, "that Jake doesn't trust you any farther than you trust him."

"What the hell does that mean?"

"We had quite an interesting conversation this morning while you were in the shower. Jake tells a slightly different version of what happened that day in the jungle. According to him, you more or less abandoned him to his fate."

Gideon's head snapped around, his eyes blazing. "He said I cut out on him?"

"Yup."

"And you believed him?"

Sarah was feeling resentful enough not to respond immediately to that.

"*Sarah*. Of all the ... You didn't believe him, did you?"

"What is this? I'm supposed to have complete, unswerving faith in you even though you can have serious doubts about my integrity?"

"For God's sake, just tell me if you actually believed him."

Sarah blinked, startled at the intensity of Gideon's reaction. "Calm down. I didn't believe him. Although I have to say I think it's entirely possible that in the stress of the moment each of you could have misinterpreted the other's actions."

"Thanks for that much, at any rate."

"You're welcome. How long do I have to wait for my apology this time?"

"Until hell freezes over."

"Never mind. I can see your heart's not in it. Getting back to how we deal with Jake Savage. I'm supposed to just twiddle my thumbs until the coast is clear?"

"Patience is a virtue."

"I was patient for four long months until I decided it was time to look you up. It turned out to be a futile exercise in virtue from every viewpoint."

"Give me some credit. I found your white rock for you, didn't I?"

"After seducing me on top of it."

He smiled briefly. "It was kind of symbolic, wasn't it?"

"Of what?" She felt goaded now.

He shrugged. "Making love to you was a lot like finding buried treasure."

She shot him a suspicious glance, trying to see if he was making fun of her. But he looked perfectly serious. Sarah couldn't help it. She tried to ignore what he'd said, but she wound up hugging his incredibly romantic words to herself even though she tried not to read too much into them.

MACHU PICCHU and Ellora were waiting on the front porch when Gideon pulled into the drive. Machu stayed posed regally on the top step, waiting for Gideon to get out of the car and come over to be recognized. But Ellora glided happily down the steps and trotted over to greet Sarah.

"Hello, sweetheart," Sarah murmured as she bent to pick up the cat. "Did you miss us? Did that big, old Machu bully you while we were gone the way Gideon bullied me?"

Ellora purred and butted her head against Sarah's chin. Then she wriggled free, leaped onto the roof of the car and padded over to welcome Gideon. He gave her an affectionate pat on the head and went back to unloading the luggage.

"Hold it," Sarah called out as she saw him start toward the front steps with her bags. "You can put those right into my car."

Gideon was already on the top step. He put down one suitcase and bent to scratch Machu behind the ears. "I think it would be better if you stayed here with me for a few more days, Sarah."

"No."

"We already went over this in the car. I don't trust Savage and I don't want you having to deal with him on your own. You told me, yourself, you've got two weeks to play with. You'll stay here where I know you're safe and when the time is right, we'll go dig up the Flowers together."

"I didn't agree to anything in the car. I'm leaving. I'll be perfectly safe in Seattle."

"Savage knows where you live," Gideon said patiently. "He's liable to come calling on the old divide-and-conquer theory. If he decides you can lead him to the earrings on your own, he won't hesitate to try to talk you into doing just that."

"Don't worry, he can't talk me into doing anything I don't want to do. Furthermore, I'm not about to cut you out of the deal and then turn around and let him in, instead."

"Savage can be very convincing. Especially with women," Gideon said. "I've seen him in action."

Especially with women. Sarah opened her mouth to protest the idiotic assumption that she could be swayed by someone like Jake Savage, but something stopped her. She was getting a familiar, faint tingling sense of awareness. Her intuition was kicking in again. She stood there, hands on her hips and contemplated Gideon and his big cat.

All this emphasis on Jake Savage's untrustworthiness was beginning to sound like overkill. Obviously Gideon was not physically afraid of the man. She couldn't imagine Gideon being afraid of anyone. Furthermore, she wasn't at all sure there was anything to Gideon's vague, farfetched theories about Jake having somehow set his partner up with the smugglers.

But the one thing about Jake Savage that Gideon had genuine reason to worry about was the man's effect on women.

It was true Gideon had said some terrible, hurtful things back there in the mountains, but for the first time Sarah was calm enough to realize he might have been lashing out from the depths of his own uncertainty. She remembered the look on his face when he'd walked into the kitchen that morning and seen Jake's flowers sitting in the pan of water.

And Jake's hand covering her own on the table.

And Jake looking intently into her eyes, telling her they'd make a great team.

Maybe what Gideon had really seen in his mind's eye was his ex-wife, Leanna, falling so easily for Jake's good looks and easy charm. Gideon should know by now that she, Sarah, was not at all the same sort of woman Leanna had been. But men could be awfully thick-headed about things, especially men like him who had been savaged in the past by people they had trusted.

"You have nothing to worry about," she told him finally.

"Nevertheless, I will worry. You're staying here, Sarah."

"Stop telling me what to do, damn you." Sarah whirled around and raced toward her car, fumbling in her bag for the keys.

She wasn't even halfway there when Gideon's arm caught her around the waist and jerked her to an abrupt stop. The breath was driven out of her lungs.

"I said, you're staying."

Sarah gasped for air as he turned and hauled her back toward the porch. "Gideon, you can't do this."

"Watch me." He took the keys from her hand and dropped them into his pocket. "We can do this hard or we can do it easy, Sarah, but one way or another, you're staying."

He meant it. Sarah slanted him a speculative glance out of the corner of her eye and read the implacable determination in Gideon's face. In that moment he looked more than ever like one of her dangerous heroes.

"If I do decide to stay," she said in her most imperious tones, just as if she had a choice, "it will be for only a few more days and it has to be understood that we're not going back to our old relationship. Is that very clear?"

Gideon's brows rose as he cautiously released her. "Old relationship? It seems like a fairly new relationship to me. We've barely gotten started."

"You know damn well what I mean." Sarah started toward the steps. "No sex."

"You said that once before but you changed your mind."

"That was different. This time I won't be changing my mind." Her chin was high as she swept past him into the gloomy old house. "I'll pick out my bedroom right now. You can leave my luggage in it."

Gideon muttered something under his breath. Then he looked down at Machu Picchu. "How the mighty are fallen, huh, pal? Yesterday I was a legendary lover. This afternoon I've been demoted to bellhop."

"I heard that," Sarah yelled from inside the house. "And you're absolutely right. Furthermore, if I were you, I wouldn't expect much of a tip. Where's the thermostat in this place? It's freezing in here."

Gideon hoisted the luggage again and followed her into the living room. He glanced around at the familiar

bleak, faded, excessively neat interior. It didn't seem all
that chilly to him. But he knew that was because Sarah
was already running around inside, opening the old
drapes to let in the light, putting hot water on the stove
for tea and generally warming things up with her ef-
fortless, effervescent vitality.

SEVERAL HOURS LATER Gideon sat alone on the sofa,
Machu draped in his usual position along the back. Ellora was nowhere in sight and Gideon suspected she
had accompanied Sarah to bed.

"Just us guys left out here," Gideon muttered to the
big cat. "But at least she stayed without too much of a
fight."

He was damned lucky she had given in as easily as
she had and he knew it. He'd thought for a while there
that he'd ruined all his chances when he'd asked her if
she'd played sensual games with him in an effort to get
him to give up any claim on the Flowers.

Nearly done in again by his own mouth.

One of these days Gideon hoped he would learn not
to fire from the hip. He was getting too good at shoot-
ing himself in the foot.

But the sight of Savage's flowers sitting in that pan
in the cabin's kitchen had rendered him cold with rage.
He'd been furious, not only with Jake who was, after
all, only acting in character, but with Sarah who'd accepted the flowers. Furthermore, she'd let the bastard
put his hand over hers. He'd *touched* her.

Gideon knew now she hadn't meant anything by ac-
cepting the flowers or letting Jake get close. She seemed
to be able to see right through the facade in a way no
other woman ever had. Sarah's problem was that she
just didn't understand how dangerous Savage could be

when it came to women. She was too naive, too trusting.

Just look how quick she'd been to trust one Gideon Trace, he reminded himself morosely as he took a large swallow of brandy. The little fool had come skipping cheerfully into his life just as if he really were one of the heroes out of her books.

No common sense, Gideon told himself. That was Sarah's whole problem. She was good-hearted and sweet and fascinating in many ways, but she obviously needed a strong-willed man to take care of her. She needed someone to keep her from getting into trouble. Someone to protect her from the likes of Jake Savage.

Jake Savage. Why the hell did he have to show up after all this time? Why couldn't he have done one decent thing in his life and stayed dead?

But it was typical of Jake to come back now, Gideon thought.

Just when things had been starting to fall into place between himself and Sarah. Just when he'd figured he was getting a handle on her. Just when he'd started an affair with her and he'd begun to realize how important she was to him.

Gideon got to his feet, brandy glass in one hand, and went up the stairs and down the dark hall to the room Sarah had chosen. She'd picked the bedroom at the far end, the one that would catch the first rays of morning sunshine.

He tried the antique glass doorknob. It twisted easily in his hand. He wanted to take that as an invitation but he knew it was more likely Sarah simply hadn't found the key in the bottom bureau drawer.

Gideon cracked the door a few inches and peered into the shadows. Ellora stirred, meowing silently as she watched him from the depths of the big, old four-poster. The cat was curled up against Sarah's leg. Sarah, herself, was a small, curved shape under the quilt. Her hair spilled out in a dark fan across the pillow. She was sound asleep, one hand curled near her chin.

Gideon wondered what she would do if he got into bed beside her. He stood there for a long while, sipping his brandy while he studied her in the dim light that filtered through the partially opened door.

Every time he had taken her into his arms, she'd melted for him, even when she'd claimed she didn't think he was ready for a sexual relationship. She'd always responded when he touched her.

In fact, she couldn't really resist him, Gideon told himself.

He opened the door a little farther and stepped into the room. She didn't move. He put the brandy glass down on the bureau and began to undress slowly.

A few minutes later, naked, he started toward the bed.

"Take one more step and I'll scream the house down," Sarah said from the shadows.

Gideon halted, feeling like an idiot. The sensation made him angry and fueled his sense of outraged frustration. "Why? You like it when I make love to you in my arms. Don't try to deny it."

"If you think I'm going to let you sleep with me after some of the things you said this morning, you're out of your mind. Go to bed, Gideon. Your own bed."

Gideon didn't move. "What do you want from me? Damn it, Sarah, I don't understand you."

"That's obvious. The answer to your question is that I don't want anything from you tonight. Go to bed."

"Sarah." He hesitated, some deep, primitive part of him urging him to ignore her protests. He was certain that if he just climbed into bed with her and took her into his arms, she would cling to him the way she always did. "Give it a chance. You want to communicate? This is one way we communicate just fine."

"Not tonight, Gideon. I mean it."

"Damn it, you want me to say I'm sorry? To apologize for what I said at the cabin? Is that it? All right, I'm sorry."

"That's not enough. Not this time."

"What more can you ask?"

"I want you to admit why you did it."

"Why I did it?" he asked blankly.

"Yes. Why you did all of it. Why you said those things about the reasons I was sleeping with you, why you whisked us away from the cabin and why you're so determined to keep me here instead of letting me go back to Seattle."

He stared at her, wishing he could see her face. "But I told you why I did all those things."

"You gave me a fine song and dance about having legitimate reasons to question my motives and how you were going to protect me from Jake Savage in spite of myself, but that's not the real reason."

"It's not?"

"No, it's not. I've been doing a lot of thinking and I've finally figured out what's going on inside that thick skull of yours. It's time you admitted to me and to yourself the real reason you've been acting the way you have today."

"All right, I give up. What is the real reason?"

Sarah sat up against the pillows, her eyes glinting in the shadows. "Actually, there are two reasons. First, you're afraid to admit how much you've come to care for me, and second, you're jealous of Jake Savage."

"*Jealous?*"

"You're afraid he's going to steal me, not the Flowers, aren't you? Isn't that the truth? Isn't it? Come on, Gideon, say it. You've finally started to realize you're in love with me and you're afraid I'm going to get swept off my feet by Jake Savage. That's the real motivation behind your actions, isn't it?"

Gideon felt as if he'd been sandbagged. "Is that why you didn't put up much of a fight about staying here with me?"

"Of course it is. If I didn't think there was hope for you, I'd have gone straight back to Seattle. But I finally realized the real reason you were acting like a lion with a thorn in its paw and I decided to give you a little time to understand your own actions. But I'm not about to sleep with you again until you finally acknowledge how you really feel about me. Then we'll discuss your little problem with jealousy. Don't worry. It's nothing we can't work out."

For once Gideon managed to keep his mouth shut, although how he managed it, he never knew. Jealous? Jealous of Savage? The blood was pounding in his veins, but not from desire. He hadn't been this furious in a long time. He turned on his heel, picked up his discarded clothes and stormed out of the room. He slammed the door so hard the wall trembled.

He was damned if he would admit he was jealous of Savage. He would not give Sarah that much power. Never in a million years. He would never again give any woman that kind of power over him.

Besides, she was a hundred miles wide of the mark. He wasn't jealous, he was just cautious. He was keeping her out of Savage's reach only because he was trying to protect her from her own naïveté. If she couldn't see that, she was a fool and a manipulative one at that.

If she wanted to think she was in love with him, that was fine, Gideon told himself. But it would be a cold day in Hades before he set himself up to be betrayed again by his woman and his ex-partner. This time around he was going to stay in charge of the situation.

He'd learned a long time ago that the only safe way to exist was to keep his emotions under rigid control. Sarah Fleetwood was not going to force him to break the rules under which he had been living successfully for the past five years.

SARAH TRIED HER BEST to ignore Gideon's foul mood for the next two days. She pursued a variety of activities as if she were on vacation, experimenting with new recipes in the kitchen, taking long walks on the beach, reading books from Gideon's extensive library.

She was unfailingly good-natured and upbeat, even though she had to grit her teeth on more than one occasion when Gideon turned on her like a cornered cat. In truth, there were some very discouraging moments.

But Sarah was determined that one way or another Gideon was going to learn that this relationship worked on trust, not good sex.

"How long do you think you can keep this up?" Gideon demanded as he washed dishes on the second night.

"Keep what up?" Sarah reclined at the kitchen table, her feet propped on a chair as she recovered from her labors. Dinner had been a particularly spectacular affair, one of her best efforts yet. The Thai-style noodles, hot-and-sour soup and raspberries in filo had been a culinary triumph as far as she was concerned. Gideon had made no comment as he'd worked his way steadily through the meal. He'd risen to do the dishes without a word.

"You know what I'm talking about." Gideon rinsed the dishes under a spray of hot water. "How long are you going to flit around here acting like you're my roommate or a boarder I've taken in for the summer?"

"Oh, that. As long as it takes, I guess."

A pan clattered loudly in the sink. "As long as it takes to do what, damn it?"

"As long as it takes for you to realize that we're supposed to be building a relationship."

He swung her a brief, angry glance. "If your crazy intuition is telling you this is the way to create a good relationship, you've got bigger problems than I thought."

"What do you want me to do, Gideon?" Sarah asked as Ellora plopped into her lap. "Sleep with you on demand even though you don't trust me and won't admit you love me? What's in it for me?"

"What the hell do you want from me?"

"You know what I want."

He snagged a dishtowel and began drying plates with swift, violent motions. "You started throwing yourself at me the minute I met you. I thought for a while you wanted me."

"I do."

"You don't seem to be having much of a problem pretending I'm just the landlord lately."

"That's not true," Sarah said. "This is as hard on me as it is on you. I'm suffering, too, you know."

"Not as far as I can see." He slung the dishes into the cupboard. "How does this new tactic work? If I go down on my knees and swear I love you and will trust blindly in you forever, do I get to go to bed with you?"

Sarah held her breath. "That would certainly be a promising start."

He shot her a scowling look as he put the rest of the dishes away. "Don't press your luck, Sarah."

She sighed. "It's all Savage's fault. If he hadn't shown up out of the blue when he did, you'd have made much more progress by now. I just know you would have. I wish he'd stayed gone."

"You and me both." Gideon closed the cupboard door and stalked over to stand in front of her. "Come here." He reached down to grab her hand.

She looked up warily. "Where are we going?"

"If you're going to act like a roommate or a summer boarder, you might as well give me a few of the benefits I'd expect from one."

"Gideon, I told you . . ."

Ellora squawked in annoyance as she was dumped unceremoniously from Sarah's lap. It wasn't Sarah's fault. Gideon had yanked her to her feet and was pulling her through the doorway into the living room.

"Sit." Gideon used a hand on her shoulder to propel her into a chair in front of the chess table. He took the seat across from her and studied her as she sat scowling at him.

"You ever play chess?" Gideon asked.

"Nope."

"Somehow I thought that might be the case. Well, if you're going to hang around here, you'd better learn. I need a regular partner. My neighbor obliges once in a while but he's not always around when I feel like a game."

Sarah felt a sudden glow of pleasure at his words. Her expression softened instantly. "You want me to play chess with you? Gideon, I'm touched. It's wonderful that you're starting to see me as something more than a convenient sex object."

"You were never that."

"Never a sex object?"

"Never very convenient. In fact, you've been nothing but inconvenient since the day you arrived." Gideon began setting out the chess pieces. "Pay attention. The first thing you're going to have to learn about chess is that you can't rely solely on your famous intuition."

"Why not?" She surveyed the pieces with deep interest.

"Because you'll lose if you do. Chess demands foresight, planning and strategy."

"That's the sort of thing you're supposed to be so good at."

Gideon smiled grimly. "Right. You're going to have to work hard if you want to beat me."

"I don't mind learning to play, but I should tell you I don't have the killer instinct when it comes to games. Somehow it's just never seemed all that important to win." Sarah was increasingly fascinated by the carved wooden chess figures. She picked up a knight. It felt good in her palm. "Did you make these?"

"Yes." He eyed her as she fingered the knight. "One winter when I had a lot of spare time. Why?"

Sarah shrugged and put the knight back down on the board. "Oh, I don't know. They're just interesting. Unusual. Maybe you have heretofore undiscovered talents as a sculptor."

"I doubt it. All right, we're all set. You ready?"

"That depends. Are you going to yell at me a lot if I don't learn fast enough to suit you?"

"Probably. I'm not feeling real patient at the moment."

Sarah glared at him. "If you start yelling, I'm outta here. Understand?"

"Don't bother issuing threats, Sarah. You've already got me tied up in knots. There's not a whole lot more you can do to me."

She reached across the table and impulsively put her hand on his. "Gideon, I'm sorry. Please believe me, I'm only trying to do what's best for both of us."

He eyed her laconically. "Sorry's not good enough, remember? You told me that, yourself."

She flushed and took her hand off his. She stared unseeingly down at the chess pieces. "I get the feeling this is going to be a perfectly miserable experience."

"Must be your intuition at work again."

But it really wasn't all that bad, Sarah decided two hours later. Gideon proved to be a surprisingly patient instructor, in spite of his veiled threats. At one point Machu Picchu lumbered over to take up a position in a nearby armchair and Ellora curled up beside him. The two cats supervised Sarah's progress with placid expressions.

"Not bad for a sex object," Gideon said finally. "I think you've got possibilities as a chess partner."

Sarah's head came up swiftly, unsure if he was teasing her. Gideon's eyes held a rare spark of humor, however, so she gave him a saucy smile. "Does that mean I have some practical uses, after all?"

"I could think of ways in which you'd be infinitely more useful."

Sarah got to her feet and went around the table to kiss him lightly on the cheek. "Good night, Gideon."

"Sarah?"

"Yes?" She halted at the foot of the stairs, her attention caught by something in his tone. She looked back and saw that he was toying with one of the chess figures.

"Never mind." Gideon put down the chess piece and reached for the brandy decanter. "Go to bed."

She went on up the stairs, Ellora trotting at her heels. Machu Picchu stayed behind, apparently feeling obliged to offer silent masculine support to the other male in the household.

Sarah lay awake a long time waiting for the sound of Gideon's footsteps in the hall. She did not go to sleep until after she heard him climb the stairs and go past her room to his own.

THE FOLLOWING DAY Sarah awoke to a world of infinite gray. The morning fog blanketed everything just as a strange feeling of uneasiness shrouded her normally exuberant emotions.

She looked out the window and realized she could not even see the beach. She was not usually depressed by fog. In fact, as a writer, she generally found it curiously exciting and even inspiring. But this morning was different.

She felt moody and restless. It was as if she sensed something ominous hovering out there in the fog.

But it made no sense to feel this way, she told herself as she showered and dressed in jeans and a sweater. Last night had gone rather well, all things considered. Gideon had seemed content to teach her chess and she had taken his interest in doing so as a good sign. He was trying to find other avenues of communication.

So why was she feeling so strange this morning?

Out in the hall she saw that the door to Gideon's room was half-open but all was quiet inside. Machu Picchu appeared in the opening and Ellora skipped forward to greet him. He touched noses with her and then stalked past Sarah as if she didn't exist. Sarah had the unsettling feeling that the big cat had somehow adopted Gideon's attitude toward her. When Ellora offered a silent apology for her companion's behavior, Sarah smiled.

"Don't worry about it," she told the small cat. "I understand. Men are very stubborn at times, aren't they?"

She followed the cats downstairs and went into the kitchen. The old Victorian lacked any semblance of cheerfulness today, even after she got the drapes open. Everything was dark, cold and depressed-looking. None of her plans for sprucing things up appealed this morning. Sarah tried to come up with some interesting ideas for breakfast but failed.

The fog hung heavily outside the window, drawing her in some strange way. Part of her longed to lose herself in the physical manifestation of the moodiness that seemed to have engulfed her during the night.

Intuition was sometimes a curse, especially when one didn't know how to interpret the vague warnings it was giving out. Sarah realized she wanted to go for a walk.

Without questioning the impulse, she found her windbreaker and let herself out into the chilled morning air. A few minutes later she was on the long, craggy beach below Gideon's house. She started walking, her hands thrust deeply into her pockets. The fog ebbed and swirled around her. She felt alone in the world and at the same time, threatened by something she did not yet understand.

One by one the doubts began to creep in and take root.

Maybe she was handling everything all wrong, she thought. What did she really know about dealing with a man like Gideon? It was true that in some mysterious way he was the personification of the heroes in her books, but she was also discovering that there was a lot she did not know or fully comprehend about those heroes. They were a part of her and yet they were strangers—alien lovers about whom she understood certain aspects but not others.

She had the ability to fashion exciting stories around such male characters but the raw truth was that she could not make real life turn out as neatly as a novel of romantic suspense. She had landed on Gideon's doorstep fully prepared to live out the fantasy of "Beauty and the Beast."

But in real life a man like Gideon Trace was not so easy to rescue from the curse of his past, not so easy to gentle and tame. He was more complex, more unpredictable and far more powerful than any fictional hero.

Sarah came to an abrupt halt near a small tide pool as a familiar sense of tingling awareness went through her. She definitely was not alone on the beach. She stood very still, waiting.

A moment later Jake Savage materialized out of the fog, not more than ten feet in front of her. He was dressed with his usual flair, polished boots and khakis and a leather jacket that, although it appeared to be brand new, was designed to look well worn and extremely macho. His black hair was damp from the fog and his bright blue eyes were alive with an almost feverish anticipation. Sarah suddenly wished that Gideon was not sound asleep in the house.

"Hello, Sarah. I'm surprised Gid let you out of his sight. Or did you slip the leash?"

"I just felt like taking a morning walk. What are you doing here, Jake?"

"What do you think I'm doing here? I came to find you. I've been keeping an eye on the house since yesterday, waiting for a chance to talk to you alone for a few minutes. I caught a glimpse of someone coming down the path through the fog a while ago and decided to see if it might be you."

"You've been spying on us?"

"Like I said, just waiting to talk to you. I knew Gid wouldn't let me anywhere near you if he had anything to say about it."

"Why did you want to talk to me?"

Jake smiled wryly. "I know it's none of my business, but I thought you ought to be told a few facts. Call me sentimental, but I didn't want to see you go through what Gid's wife went through."

"Oh, yes, Leanna. She cheated on him with you, didn't she?"

"Is that what Gid told you?"

"Isn't that what happened?"

Jake ran a hand through his hair, tousling it rakishly. "She was a very unhappy woman, Sarah. She turned to me for comfort. I guess I felt sorry for her."

"But not sorry enough to marry her after she left Gideon for you, right?"

Jake frowned. "Leanna wanted rescuing and I'm not much into the role of knight in shining armor."

"You prefer the role of seducer and betrayer."

Jake's eyes narrowed. "Gid really told you a story, didn't he?"

"No. I've managed to piece a lot of it together for myself, thought. It's pretty obvious what happened. Leanna was an immature, unhappy woman who was probably initially attracted to Gideon's strength but later dazzled by your flash. I suppose one could say she got what she deserved, which was nothing, but that doesn't make you any less guilty of betraying your partner. Why did you do it? Surely one woman more or less wasn't that important. A man like you can probably have his pick of women."

"Is that supposed to be a compliment?"

"No. An observation. Why, Jake?"

"That's none of your damned business. I took what was being offered on a silver platter, that's all. Hell, Leanna was a beautiful woman. If Gid couldn't keep her satisfied, that wasn't my problem."

Sarah shook her head thoughtfully. "No, I think there was more to it than that. You were jealous of Gideon, weren't you? Sleeping with Leanna was a way of getting even with him."

"Are you nuts, lady? Why in hell would I be jealous of Gid?"

"Because you were nothing except a hustler without him and deep down inside, you knew it. He was the one who made the partnership work. He was the one who had the skill and the talent to find whatever you two went looking for."

"The hell he was."

"You knew that you were totally dependent on him and eventually you must have come to hate him. All you brought to the partnership was image and flash. Did you really scheme with those smugglers to betray him? What did you think was going to happen if you did get him killed? Savage and Company couldn't have survived very long without him. But maybe your jealousy was too strong at that point for you to see reason. Or maybe there was enough money involved to make it worth the risk of dumping your partner."

"You little bitch, I'll tell you what happened that day. Gid left me behind while he escaped with a suitcase full of cash, that's what happened. You think Carson, or Trace, or whatever he calls himself now is the nice, honest, up-front type? You think he's some kind of good guy, a hero out of one of your books who's going to help you find those earrings? Wise up, little girl. He's using you. When he does find your treasure for you, he'll also find a way to keep it for himself. That's his real specialty, you see, looking out for himself. And he's real good at it."

"You're lying."

"You think so? Just remember what I told you. When Gid goes out on a job, he never comes back empty-handed. And people who get in the way can get killed."

"You look very much alive to me."

"I was damned lucky. You better hope you're equally lucky, hadn't you?"

Jake swung around and vanished into the swirling fog.

Sarah waited a couple of minutes, but the tingling feeling of awareness did not ease. Frowning, she turned around to head back toward the bluff path.

And walked full-tilt into a large, solid object that had been shrouded in fog.

"Gideon."

His gemlike eyes were the only sparks of color in the swirling world of gray. "Do you believe him?"

Sarah took a step back. The depressed, moody feeling she had awakened with closed in upon her more heavily than the fog. "Does it matter?"

"Yes, damn it, it matters."

"Why?"

"Don't play games with me, Sarah."

"I'm not playing games. I have, however, finally come to the conclusion that I don't owe you anything more than what you're willing to give me in exchange.

And I haven't gotten much trust from you, have I, Gideon?"

He caught hold of her arm as she made to step around him. "Where are you going?"

"Home."

"Seattle, you mean?"

"Yes."

"He got to you, didn't he? Just like he got to Leanna."

Sarah's eyes stung with tears. She dashed the back of her hand across them. "No, he didn't get to me the way he got to Leanna. You can't even give me credit for having more sense than your ex-wife had, can you? I've told you once and I'll tell you again. Leanna was a brainless little floozy without an ounce of common sense. Any woman should be able to tell at a glance that Jake Savage is a mirage of a man. All image and no substance. Amusing, perhaps, on occasion and definitely a sharp dresser. The kind who might look good escorting a woman to a fancy party. But that's about the end of it." She pulled her arm free of Gideon's grasp.

"Damn it, Sarah, you can't just walk away like this."

"Don't worry, I'm not running off with Jake Savage."

"You're not running off with anyone."

"Right. I'm going all by myself."

"Savage will try to use you," Gideon warned roughly. "Especially if he thinks we've split up. Remember what I said about him using the divide-and-conquer technique."

"I'm not going to lead him to that white rock."

"He'll find a way to make you." Gideon's voice was raw. "Tell me, Sarah, is it easy to walk away from me?"

She paused and looked back at him. His face was harsh in the gray mist. He stood there on the beach, a stark, bleak figure—a man who'd learned the trick of withdrawing completely into himself while he told the rest of the world to keep its distance.

"I was a fool to think you needed rescuing."

"Rescuing? What the devil do you mean by that?"

"Never mind. You like being alone, don't you? You like not having to take the risk of trusting anyone. No, Gideon, it's not easy to walk away from you. But I don't have much choice. Maybe you and my friends were right all along. I really shouldn't rely so heavily on my intuition." She smiled faintly. "At least this time I didn't get left at the altar, though, did I? Maybe things are looking up after all. Or else I'm getting smarter."

He made no move to stop her as she turned and started up the path toward the house.

GIDEON HUNCHED his shoulders against the chilled fog, his hands thrust into his jacket pockets, and listened to the sound of Sarah's car pulling out of his driveway.

She had done it. She had left him. A part of him could not accept it and he wondered if he would ever be able to fully accept it.

He could not believe how much he had grown accustomed to her foolish conviction that they belonged together. She had been so positive that they were made for each other, so convinced he was the hero of her dreams.

But he hadn't known how to deal with her at first. She had knocked him off balance right from the moment she had descended out of the blue onto his doorstep. And she had moved much too quickly for him. He was, by nature, not the type who could take the risks of real intimacy easily and he knew it. So he tried to resist Sarah at every step along the way, always looking for hidden motives, always searching for the cold reality that he knew had to lie beneath her warm, affectionate surface.

When they had become lovers that day in the mountains he had relaxed somewhat because he'd finally found a way in which he could trust her, a way in which he could feel sure of her. From the beginning he'd never really doubted the genuineness of her physical response.

Now, thanks to Savage, he was right back where he'd started. Alone.

But this time it hurt. He felt as if something inside him was cracking open, exposing him to the kind of pain he had protected himself from for years.

The worst of it was that even as he began to climb slowly along the path toward the house, Gideon knew he couldn't blame Jake for this latest disaster. He had no one to blame but himself.

Machu Picchu was sitting at the top of the bluff, tail coiled around his paws. He watched with idle interest as Gideon climbed the last few steps.

"She's gone, isn't she, Machu? I didn't even get breakfast."

The big cat followed him into the kitchen where Ellora sat in Sarah's chair. The silver-gray cat glared at Gideon with accusing eyes.

"Hey, don't blame me. She's the type who appears out of thin air and vanishes the same way. Here today, gone tomorrow. Flighty. Know what I mean?" Gideon put the kettle on the stove for instant coffee. *No, not gone tomorrow—gone today. Now. This minute.*

The cats continued to regard him in profound silence. Gideon poured hot water over the coffee and stirred absently. "I shouldn't have let her drive off in this fog," he announced after a minute. "The roads could be real bad."

The cats licked their paws.

Gideon climbed the stairs with his mug of coffee in one hand and went to see if Sarah had packed absolutely everything or if she'd left in such an all-fired hurry she'd forgotten a few items.

In her room he found no trace she'd ever been there. In a totally uncharacteristic gesture, she'd even made the bed up neatly.

Gideon went back downstairs wondering why the house felt so damned cold again.

The cats were sitting at the bottom of the staircase, watching him with their otherworldly gaze.

"I know, I know," Gideon said. "I shouldn't have let her leave alone. Not in this fog. Too dangerous. If she's got any sense she'll stop at a café and have a cup of tea or something until the fog lifts. I'll bet she's at one of the coffee shops in town. On the other hand, common sense is not her strong point. I probably ought to check on her. Make sure she waits awhile before heading for Seattle."

Ellora started to purr.

Gideon picked up his car keys and walked to the door. Behind him Machu rumbled plaintively. "You've got enough food and water to last for a couple of days," he told the big cat. "Don't worry. I'll only be gone for an hour or less."

But there was no sign of Sarah's car at either the coffee shops or the local gas station. The fog was not nearly as bad now as it had been a while ago. Sarah had probably not encountered any great trouble at all in getting to the main highway.

Gideon stopped at the edge of town and thought about going back to the big, cold, empty house.

He could not bear the thought. He started driving.

A few hours later he found himself in Seattle.

There was no great difficulty in locating Sarah's apartment building downtown. After four months of corresponding with her, he'd long since memorized the address.

HER WARM, CHEERFUL, sunny apartment wasn't nearly as inviting as it ought to have been. Sarah halted just inside the front door, her hastily packed suitcases in her hands. She glanced around uneasily. Something didn't feel right. She stood there a moment longer and then put down the luggage.

With a gathering sense of disquiet, she wandered around the living room. Everything seemed pretty much as she'd left it.

Until she got to her desk. It took her a minute or two to realize that the normal, exuberant clutter didn't look quite right. The desk was still a mess, of course, but it looked different somehow.

Someone had been through her things.

The maps.

On a hunch, Sarah gasped and yanked open the filing cabinet drawer where she had carefully stored the ten photocopies of her precious map. They were gone. All of them.

"Oh, you're back, are you, Sarah? Have a nice trip, dear?" Mrs. Reynolds from across the hall paused for a moment in the open doorway. "There was the nicest man inquiring about you after you left. A real charmer. Did he find you?"

"Yes, Mrs. Reynolds. He found me." Sarah slowly closed the cabinet door. Jake Savage had stolen the maps.

"Excuse me. I'm looking for Sarah Fleetwood's apartment." Gideon's gritty tones came down the hall from behind Mrs. Reynolds.

"Well, bless my soul, it's another one. Never rains but it pours, eh, Sarah, dear?" The elderly woman winked conspiratorially at Sarah. "Right this way, sir. Never knew our Sarah had such an active social life. Call me if you need help entertaining all these interesting young men, Sarah, dear." Still chuckling, Mrs. Reynolds disappeared into her own apartment and closed the door.

Sarah stared at Gideon as he came to a halt in the doorway. "What are you doing here?" she whispered.

"What the hell does it look like I'm doing? I followed you. I should have caught up with you long before you got to Seattle. The fact that I didn't means you drive too damned fast, Sarah."

She ignored that, feeling strangely weak. The stolen maps were forgotten. All the anger and hurt and frustration she'd been feeling since she'd left the coast were forgotten. All that mattered was that Gideon was here, glowering at her in his familiar, lovable, beastly manner.

"You *followed* me? All this way? You actually came after me?"

"Well, I didn't drive this far just to see the Space Needle."

"You came after me," she breathed, giddy with relief and euphoria. "You tracked me down to the ends of the earth so that you could drag me back to the coast, didn't you?"

Something warm and tender that was tinged with amusement flickered in Gideon's eyes, softening the grimness that had been there a moment ago. "I never really thought of Seattle as the ends of the earth, but I guess it's all relative, isn't it?"

"Gideon." She flew across the room and into his arms. When he caught her close, holding her in a grip of iron, she breathed a deep sigh of relief. "I was so afraid. I thought you just couldn't care enough, after all, that I didn't mean enough to you even though in the beginning I was so sure . . ."

"Sarah, honey, it's all right."

She clutched at him. "I don't mind telling you I was scared to death that it really was hopeless. You never seemed to be able to bring yourself to trust me. I couldn't believe I'd been so wrong about us, but you never know for sure. I've been wrong before and all the way back from your place I've been terrified that I'd made another mistake."

"Sarah, hush."

"Gideon, I love you so much and I've been so miserable. All those lonely hours on the road. It was the longest drive of my life, I swear. I just wanted to get home so that I could cry in the privacy of my own apartment."

"Sarah—"

"I've been telling myself I was a fool. I almost had myself believing it, too. But now here you are. You've come after me just like one of the heroes in my books and everything's going to be all right. I wasn't wrong about you, after all."

"Sarah, I'm here. Let's leave it at that for a while, all right?"

She raised her glowing face to his but before she could say anything else, he was kissing her. She parted her lips for him, pressing herself close into the comfort and strength of his big frame.

Gideon groaned, kicked the door shut with the heel of his boot, and picked Sarah up in his arms. Without breaking the kiss, he carried her over to the black leather Italian sofa.

10

SHE WAS CLINGING TO HIM, holding onto him as if she'd never let him go. Gideon staggered a couple of steps and then fell onto the sofa, dragging Sarah down on top of him. He still couldn't believe the depths of the welcome he'd seen in her eyes when he'd stepped through the apartment doorway. He didn't think he'd ever forget it as long as he lived. He'd been right to follow her. *She'd wanted him to come after her.*

The thing inside him that had cracked open and caused so much pain was healing with miraculous speed.

"I'm no hero," he warned one last time, wondering why he felt compelled to try to set the record straight. It was getting hard to think. Her mouth was so warm and sweet and spicy as she persisted in raining kisses over him.

"Yes, you are," Sarah whispered passionately. "You're a perfect hero. I always knew it. It just took you a while to figure it out, too, that's all."

"Hell, who am I to argue? You're the expert." He tugged at her sweater, pulling it off and tossing it down onto the carpet. Her fine, gently rounded breasts tumbled into his waiting hands and he inhaled sharply as his whole body tightened.

When she wriggled against him, sliding her hips across his, Gideon gave a husky, choked laugh and tugged at the fastening of her jeans. Her small, gentle hands were already fumbling with the buttons of his shirt. As soon as the garment fell open he felt her fingers trailing through the hair on his chest. Waves of anticipation rolled through him.

He looked down at the scrap of turquoise she wore beneath her jeans. He knew he was looking at one of the seven pairs of brightly colored, sexy panties she had bought especially to wear for him.

"You knew I'd come after you, didn't you?"

"No. I just hoped you would."

"Come here," Gideon whispered, urging her down so that her breasts brushed against his bare skin. He could feel her taut little nipples against him. "That feels so good, sweetheart."

"I love you, Gideon." She kissed his shoulder and then his own flat nipple. "I've been feeling so awful for the past few hours. I could hardly stand it."

"You should never have left."

"Maybe not. But I couldn't bear to stay, either. Not with you refusing to admit that we have something special together. Not when you couldn't let yourself trust me. But now you're here and everything's the way it should be."

He slid his hands down the length of her back to the sensual curve of her buttocks. He began coaxing the jeans over her lushly rounded derriere, allowing his fingers to stray into all the secret places. She moved delightfully against him once more and he lifted his lips against hers, seeking the sweetness of her. There was still far too much denim in the way.

"Easy, honey, easy," he breathed, holding her gently away from him so that he could slide off the sofa and stand up long enough to get out of his own clothes.

When he finished with the boots and the jeans and all the rest of it he sat down and reached for Sarah.

She came to him willingly enough as he finished undressing her but when she started to lie down and pull him to her he shook his head.

"This way," he mouthed in her ear, as he half-sat, half-sprawled against the leather cushions. Hands on her thighs, he parted her legs and eased her down so that she sat astride him. He felt her tremble.

"Gideon." She braced herself, kneeling on the cushions. Her fingers entwined in his hair. Her eyes glowed with excitement.

"Yeah. Like that." He took one nipple gently into his mouth and simultaneously touched her intimately. He found her warm and damp and ready for him. When he eased one finger into her she clenched almost violently. Gideon caught his breath.

"So sexy, baby. That feels so good," he muttered. He drew the tip of his finger across the small pearl hidden in the delicate nest and had the satisfaction of feeling her shiver again in his arms.

"Gideon, my wonderful, fabulous, Gideon." She nibbled on his ear, moving against his head. "I love it when you touch me."

He guided himself slowly into her, feeling her open to him and then close tightly around him. She gasped and began to slide up and down as he indicated with his hands on her waist. Then she began to set the rhythm, growing more confident and more forceful until Gideon could think of nothing except the powerful hunger that was sweeping through him.

When he could stand the ravening forces no longer, he surged into her one last time seeking the full satisfaction that he knew was waiting. Gideon felt Sarah shudder and cry out and then he was lost in the thrill of her release as it mingled with his own.

SARAH SMILED TO HERSELF as she languorously stroked Gideon's shoulders. "I like this position," she murmured.

"So do I. But, then, I like any position with you." His eyes were closed. He continued to sprawl against the cushions, his well-muscled legs relaxed, his hands moving absently on her thighs. "Sarah, promise me you won't run off like that again."

Her leaving had shaken him, she realized. He really did care for her. But, then, she had been certain of that the moment she saw him standing in her doorway.

"What made you come after me?" she asked softly. "You must have left shortly after I did." She was consumed with curiosity now, needing to hear every detail of what he had been thinking when he made the decision to pursue her. "When did you finally realize you couldn't let me go?"

"Sarah?"

"Yes, Gideon?"

"Just promise me you won't do that again. Please."

She sighed, resigned to the fact that Gideon was never going to find it easy to talk about his emotions. "All right. I promise."

"I could sure use a cup of coffee."

She collapsed against him in a fit of giggles. "What a romantic."

"I try." His smile was slightly lopsided, his eyes bemused as he played with her hair. "But I'd better warn you, there are probably going to be times when I'll mess up."

"You think so?"

"I keep telling you, I'm no hero. But you won't run off again if I do occasionally fail to live up to your expectations, will you? Sarah, I don't want to have to be afraid that every time I screw up, you'll leave."

Sarah's amusement slipped away in an instant as she saw the seriousness in his steady gaze. She shook her head vigorously. "No, never. I won't run off."

"You did this morning."

"That was different."

"How?"

"This morning I was feeling depressed. I knew somehow that I'd gone as far as I could. It was up to you to make an effort or give me some sign. If you were never going to be able to let yourself love me or trust me I had to find out now. I knew I had to leave." Sarah smiled. "And you came after me."

Gideon moved his head slightly on the cushions, his eyes warm. "I think you're a little crazy, but that's all right." His gaze shifted to the room around them. "So this is your place? It looks like you. I knew there'd be unwashed cups on the coffee table."

"Thanks a lot." She rose reluctantly from his thighs and reached for her clothing. "Look at the bright side. Now that I've got you, I'll be able to let my weekly cleaning service go, won't I? I'll make you some coffee while you get dressed. The bathroom's down the hall. Give me a minute and then you can have it." She clutched her shirt and looked down at him. "Gideon, I'm so happy."

He smiled slightly, his eyes very intent. "The cats will be pleased. They didn't approve of your running off the way you did this morning."

"You'll all just have to understand that I had my reasons."

Gideon's eyes hardened. "It was more than depression, wasn't it? We could have talked about that. And more than wanting me to give you some sign that I cared. It was Savage finding you on the beach that made you give up on me."

"I didn't give up on you."

"He upset everything. You were all right until he showed up again. You were adjusting to being with me. Getting used to it. But then he cornered you on the beach and it was all over. He always had a knack for being able to throw a spanner into the works."

"That's not the way it was at all. My feelings had nothing to do with Savage. I left because I wasn't sure I was getting through to you. It was time to give you a strong nudge."

"You'd have gotten through to me a lot faster if you'd let me make love to you instead of trying to build a relationship without sex," Gideon muttered. "It wasn't natural, Sarah. I felt you were trying to manipulate me by withholding yourself and then when Savage popped up again, I—"

"*Savage.*" Sarah's eyes widened in belated anger as reality came back with a thud. "Good grief, I almost forgot. How could I? The man's a thief."

"I'm in agreement with you on that point. But you didn't really believe all those things he was saying about me, did you?"

"Of course, I didn't believe him. But that's not why I'm furious with him now. I'm mad because he broke in here and stole all my extra copies of the map, Gideon."

Gideon's eyes hardened. He reached slowly for his shirt. "The bastard."

"He's going to dig up the earrings," Sarah said with a sigh. "I know he is."

"He won't find them."

"Gideon, I keep telling you, I can almost feel him finding them. My intuition tells me he's very close to getting his hands on them. Maybe he couldn't get close without the map, but now that he's got all ten copies of the thing he's bound to figure it out."

"Sarah, be reasonable. Ten photocopies won't do him any more good than one. They're all the same. I guarantee you he won't get the earrings."

She gave him a speculative glance. "You're very certain of Jake Savage's incompetence."

Gideon grinned briefly. "As I've always said, he's got his talents, but finding treasure isn't one of them." His grin vanished as quickly as it had come. "But he's gone too far with this business of breaking into your place."

"That's certainly the truth. I won't have it. What are we going to do, Gideon? Call the cops? How will we be able to prove it was Jake who broke in?"

"We probably won't be able to prove it." Gideon shrugged into his shirt. "But I think it's time I had a private chat with my ex-partner. I've had it with him."

"What are you going to do?" Sarah asked anxiously.

"I'm not sure yet, but one thing's for certain, I liked him a lot better when he was supposed to be dead."

"Gideon, you wouldn't, would you? You can't be serious. I mean, you can't actually, uh, that is. . . ."

"See that he goes back to being dead? Permanently this time? It's an interesting possibility. As a solution, it definitely has its merits."

"Gideon."

"Weren't you going to fix me some coffee?"

Sarah wasn't certain what to make of the blandly innocent expression in his cool green eyes. It occurred to
her that on some level she had always understood that
Gideon Trace was dangerous. She just hadn't ever
expected to see that side of him. She still wasn't sure she
was seeing it. There were definitely parts of this man she
did not completely know or understand yet. The
knowledge was disconcerting.

"I'll be right out," Sarah mumbled. Clutching the remainder of her clothing, she hurried off to the bathroom.

Gideon watched her until she disappeared down the
short hall. He felt a lot better now than he had when
he'd first arrived, he realized. Everything was going to
be okay again. He could relax. Sarah had just succumbed to a brief storm of feminine emotion, that was
all. She hadn't done anything drastic like change her
mind about him.

She still thought he was some sort of romantic hero
and apparently he had only reconfirmed her belief by
chasing after her.

As if he'd had any alternative, he thought as he got
to his feet and pulled on his jeans. He would never tell
her, of course, but the truth was, it hadn't been any
grand, romantic impulse that had brought him to Seattle. He'd been operating on instinct and his instincts
had told him that he could not let her disappear from
his life.

Gideon fastened his jeans and began wandering
around Sarah's colorful, modern living room. The
place fascinated him. It was so completely different
from his own home. Everything was bright, breezy and
exuberantly chaotic. Magazines that ran the gamut
from *Cache* to *Vogue* were piled willy-nilly on the sec-

ond level of a two-tier glass coffee table. A collection of bizarre paperweights occupied the top of the table. An unwashed mug or two stood proudly amid the clutter.

The furniture all looked as if it had been designed in an art studio, with more emphasis on abstract lines than functionality.

The walls were filled with posters of the Pike Place Market, photos of Sarah with two other women and framed book covers. He paused in front of one, studying it more closely.

The cover of *Dangerous Talent* showed a rugged-looking, dark-haired man braced at the edge of a jungle cliff. The man had apparently forgotten to button his rakish, khaki shirt that morning, Gideon noted. It hung open, revealing a lot of chest.

In addition to his unbuttoned shirt the guy in the picture was wearing boots and a wide leather belt. There was a knife strapped to his leg. In one hand he held a large revolver aimed at some unseen menace and with the other he embraced a beautiful woman.

Gideon wondered idly why the heroine had worn a sleek, sophisticated designer gown and high heels into the jungle. The glittering dress was already badly ripped and was probably going to get even more severely torn in the near future. Both characters looked far more concerned with how they were going to make love on the edge of a cliff than they were with whatever threatened them.

Gideon shook his head in mild amazement and then spotted an open box with a publisher's return address on it. Inside the box were several copies of *Dangerous Talent*. Unable to resist, Gideon lifted one paperback out of the box, opened it and turned to the first page.

Hilary sat frozen behind the wheel of the broken-down Jeep and watched helplessly as the man with the gun sauntered toward her. Around her the jungle was alive with brooding menace. But nothing it offered seemed even as remotely threatening at that moment as the cold, deadly expression in the eyes of the human predator in front of her.

Green, Hilary thought fleetingly as she stared, mesmerized through the windshield. She could see that his eyes were emerald-green like those of a jungle cat and just as chilling.

Her friends had told her Jed McIntyre was dangerous—a man who made his own rules out here in the wilds of Rio Pasqual. But Hilary, as usual, had refused to listen to good advice.

She had insisted on setting out to find McIntyre and now she was very much afraid that she had done exactly that. The man coming toward her with such casual, graceful menace certainly fit the description Kathy had given her.

Dangerous.

Jed McIntyre was perhaps ten paces away from the Jeep when Hilary came to her senses and remembered the pistol she had stuck in the glove box. Jerking herself out of her momentary trance, she lunged across the seat for it.

She never made it.

Gideon closed the book and put it back in the stack as he heard Sarah's light footsteps behind him.

"See what I mean?" Sarah asked as she went on into the kitchen. "All my heroes are like you."

"Other than the color of Jed McIntyre's eyes, I didn't see much resemblance."

"Then you didn't read far enough." Sarah switched on the coffee maker and put a kettle of water on the stove.

Gideon shrugged. If she wanted to see him as dark, dangerous and sexy, who was he to complain? "Just tell me one thing. Do I have to start carrying a gun and wear a knife strapped to my leg?"

"Good heavens, no. You don't need one. In that sense, you're a lot more interesting than Jed. Jed, I'm afraid, tended to rely a bit too much on brawn instead of brain. But brawn works nicely in a romance novel."

Gideon smiled at that. "Well, that's a relief. I've never liked guns or knives. Or khaki, for that matter. Stuff wrinkles like crazy." He went down the hall to the bathroom, which smelled of lemon-scented soap. Automatically he plucked the used towel that was hanging askew off the rack and tossed it into the hamper. He located a fresh one in a small closet.

A few minutes later when he got back to the kitchen he found Sarah pouring freshly brewed coffee. The stuff really was a lot better than instant, he decided. He was getting used to it. He sat down in a high-backed stool at the counter and picked up the red mug.

In front of him on the counter lay an assortment of odds and ends including a couple of large yellow notepads, a glass jar holding a dozen pens and a stack of romance novels.

"All right," Sarah said as she plunked herself down on the seat beside Gideon. "What are we going to do about your pal, Jake?"

"As I said, I'll have a talk with him." Gideon sipped his coffee thoughtfully.

"But how will you convince him to stop pestering us about the earrings? This little matter of going through my files is more than I can tolerate, Gideon."

"I agree and I'll deal with it."

She looked skeptical. "If you say so."

"Don't tell me you're losing faith now?"

"No, it's not that." She broke off, her thoughts clearly taking her in other directions. "But I can't help worrying about those earrings. I don't like leaving them buried up there in the mountains. I don't have as much confidence in Jake Savage's lack of competence as you do, I guess."

"Okay," Gideon said, coming to a decision. This had gone on long enough. Time to end it. "We'll go get them."

Sarah swung around on her stool and stared at him in surprise. "We will?"

"I want you to be able to relax and stop worrying about them. Obviously the only way to do that is to dig them up and put them in a safe place. We'll go see if we can find them in the morning."

"What about Jake Savage?"

"With any luck, he's still over at the coast, looking for an angle or contacting a talk-show producer. If he saw me leave, he probably assumed I followed you to Seattle."

"Gideon, this is wonderful. Do you know what this means? Do you realize what you're saying?"

He eyed her warily. "I'm saying we're going to dig up the earrings. If we can find them."

"No, no, no." She shook her head with obvious impatience. "That's not what you're saying at all."

"It's not?"

She smiled, her bright eyes triumphant. "What you're really saying is that you finally realize it's all right to help me dig up the earrings because you no longer think I'm just using you to get them."

Gideon absorbed the statement slowly, struggling with the convoluted feminine logic. "You really do have a talent for leaping to conclusions, don't you?"

"Go ahead. Tell me I'm wrong. Tell me you haven't decided to trust me at last," she challenged happily.

Gideon studied her for a long moment, enthralled by the warmth and delight in her vivid gaze.

"You win. I trust you."

He became aware, even as he said it, that it was the truth. He wondered if he'd known it all along on some instinctive level or if it was some grand realization that had just hit him. He decided not to worry about it. How and when he had come to trust her was no longer important.

What he couldn't explain to her was that this business of going back into the mountains to dig up the Fleetwood Flowers proved nothing at all about his trust in her.

GIDEON'S SHOVEL hit metal and clanged loudly in the morning stillness.

"Oh, my God, that's it," Sarah exclaimed. "You've found them. You've found the earrings. Gideon, this is so exciting. I can hardly believe it."

She leaned closer to examine the small pit they had dug precisely ten paces due north of the white rock. She had dragged Gideon out of bed very early so that they could get to Emelina Fleetwood's old cabin by mid-morning. Gideon had hardly complained at all.

"Stand back and let me get a little more of the dirt out of the way. It might not be the earrings, Sarah. It could be nothing more than an old tin can that was covered by mud years ago. Or a hubcap. Or a hunter's trap. Anything."

"It's the earrings. I know it is." Sarah used her own shovel to pry out more dirt. Slowly but surely an old metal box came into view. "Look at that, Gideon. It's a locked chest."

Gideon studied the rusted metal lid of the box. "An old strongbox. And you can bet Emelina didn't bury the key along with it."

"Maybe it's not locked."

"If it's not, then I doubt there's anything valuable inside," Gideon said reasonably.

Sarah knelt in the freshly turned earth to reach down into the pit and drag out the heavy box. She studied it intently. "Darn it, you're right. It is locked." She brightened. "But, as you said, I guess that means the earrings are still inside."

"We'll get it open."

"But how?" Sarah shook the box but it was impossible to tell if there was anything inside. She could hardly stand the suspense. "This is killing me. I can't wait to get it open. This is such an incredible experience. I've never done anything like this before in my life. Imagine. We've actually dug up buried treasure. We decoded the map and found the cache. Just like in a book."

Gideon leaned on his shovel and watched her with a curiously enigmatic smile. "Don't tell me, let me guess. You're going to use the experience in a romance novel, right?"

"Probably, but first I'm going to savor every minute of it for myself. I have to get a picture of this." She dug her small camera out of her bag. "Good thing I thought to bring this along, isn't it? Here, you stand next to the box."

Gideon shook his head and put down the shovel. "No, you're the one who should be in the picture. This is your treasure hunt. I just came along to consult, remember?" He took the camera from her and went to stand a few paces away.

Sarah hesitated for an instant, wanting him in the shot with her. But that was impossible. She scooped up the old strongbox and held it in front of her. Laughing with delight at her trophy, she stood posing for the shot. Gideon raised the camera to his eye, smiled again and pressed the shutter release.

"Now all we have to do is figure out how to open this strongbox," Sarah said, examining the rusty container.

"It will take a little time but we'll find a way," Gideon said, putting down the camera and picking up the shovel. "I've had some experience with that kind of thing."

"Somehow that doesn't surprise me." Sarah glanced up from the locked box. "What are you doing?" she asked as she saw him lift a spadeful of dirt and toss it back into the hole he had just finished digging.

"Filling in the hole."

"Why?"

He gave her an odd glance. "I don't see any point in advertising the fact that we've been here and dug up something valuable."

Sarah smiled with sudden appreciation. "Good idea. Why leave tracks for someone who might want to steal our treasure from us? I told you that you were smarter than Jed McIntyre."

"As long as I'm a little smarter than Jake Savage, we'll be okay," Gideon muttered.

"What did you say?" Sarah asked, uncertain she'd heard him correctly.

"I said, it's going to be a long drive back to the coast this afternoon."

"We could stay here or in Seattle tonight," she suggested.

"No," said Gideon. "We'll go back to my place. I didn't have a chance to ask my neighbor to take care of the cats."

"We'd better get back there, then. Poor things. They'll be starving."

"Not likely. Machu can still hunt when he has to, although he doesn't much care for the effort involved. He'll see that Ellora eats if it's necessary but he'd much prefer someone opened a can for both of them."

Sarah grinned. "He's a lot like you, isn't he?"

Gideon cocked a brow. "Because he doesn't mind eating canned food?"

"No, because he can still hunt if it becomes necessary."

SHORTLY AFTER MIDNIGHT Machu Picchu landed on Gideon's bare back with a heavy, near-silent thud. Gideon stifled a soft groan. The cat stepped off his back and sat on the edge of the bed, tail moving restlessly as he waited for a response.

Gideon rolled over slowly so that he wouldn't waken Sarah who was curled up beside him. He eyed Machu's implacable face for a few seconds and then he slid carefully out of bed.

Machu leaped soundlessly down onto the floor and started toward the bedroom door. Gideon paused long enough to collect the revolver he always kept in a shoebox under the bed and quickly put on his jeans. Barefoot, he went down the stairs as silently as Machu had.

At the bottom of the staircase, Gideon turned right and went down the hall to his study. He stopped outside the open door and peered into the shadows. He was not unduly surprised to see the figure of a man hunched over the locked file cabinet where the strongbox had been stored earlier. Keeping the revolver hidden behind the half-open door, Gideon reached just inside the room and flicked on the light switch.

The intruder jumped and whirled around to face him, his mouth open in shock and alarm.

"Forget it, Jake," Gideon said calmly. "Even if you managed to get the file open, you'd only find an empty, rusted out strongbox with nothing in it. The Fleetwood Flowers are long gone. Somebody got to them years ago."

Jake's hands fell away from the file cabinet. "Damn it, Gid, you always did have a way of sneaking up on people."

"Sarah kept saying she was afraid you'd get close to the earrings. I guess this was what she anticipated, wasn't it? That you'd break in and find the old strongbox. Looks like I've got to start paying more attention to that woman's intuition."

Jake hesitated, relaxing slightly when Gideon didn't move or say anything else. Then his brashness returned in a rush. With a cocky grin he stalked across the room and threw himself down in Gideon's desk chair. Legs stuck out in front of him, hands behind his head,

Jake continued to smile the rakish smile that had never failed to charm.

"Tell me the truth, Gid. This is your old partner here so you can be honest with me. I know you went back into the mountains this morning. I followed you. And I know you did some digging. I saw where you'd filled in the hole. You really didn't find the earrings?"

"Just an old strongbox. The earrings might have been stored in it at one time, but the box is empty now."

"Why keep it in a locked cabinet?"

"Sarah doesn't know yet that the strongbox is empty," Gideon explained patiently. "She's looking forward to opening it in the morning. I didn't want to spoil the surprise."

"But you couldn't resist taking a quick look for yourself, is that it?"

"That's it. You know me. I get curious about locked boxes."

"And you're telling me there was nothing inside, huh?"

"Right."

"I don't believe you." Jake Savage shook his head slowly. "You never came back empty-handed from a job."

"This wasn't my treasure hunt. It was Sarah's. I just went along as a paid consultant."

"Bull." Savage suddenly sat up straight in the chair, his eyes glittering with frustrated anger. "I think you found the earrings. I think you found them the same way you always find what you go looking for, you bastard."

"No. There's nothing inside. Take a look." Gideon opened the file cabinet and removed the strong box. Then he twisted a strip of metal in the old lock until something clicked. Then he raised the lid to expose the empty interior. He waited a few seconds while Jake stared into the box and then Gideon closed and re-locked it.

Jake eyed him uneasily. "Come on, Gid. We can do a deal. Just like old times. All I want is the publicity and a chance to draw in some big bucks. I need a big score.

"Be content with staying a dead legend."

Savage slapped his hand on the desk. "Why the hell should I do that? I'm not dead and I've discovered during the past five years that I don't like being a nobody. They don't know who I am any more, Gid. I walk into a bar and no one even knows me."

Gideon exhaled thoughtfully. "That's not surprising, I guess. You did a good job of disappearing five years ago."

"As good a job as you did."

"Tell me something, Jake. What really did happen that day we both supposedly got killed in that damned jungle? Did you set up an ambush with those smugglers? Were you working with them all along and finally decide I'd become a handicap? I was the one who saw too much that day we made the delivery, wasn't I? You already knew what was going on. You were in on it."

Jake's eyes flickered. He sat very still behind the desk. "You figured it all out, didn't you?"

"I've had a lot of time to think about it."

Jake's hand tightened into a fist. "You want to know why I did it? I'll tell you. There was big money involved. Enough to set me up for a long, long time. Enough to ensure that I wouldn't need to rely on you any longer, you bastard."

"I thought we were supposed to be partners, Jake," Gideon mocked softly.

"Yeah, but we both knew you were the one with the magic, the one who made Savage and Company a legend. And I was sick of knowing I had to depend on you. Sick of trusting you. Sick of relying on you."

"So you saw your big chance and decided to end the partnership. Except it didn't quite work out the way you'd planned, did it?"

"No, you son of a bitch, it didn't. But it will." Jake's hand shot under the desk and Gideon knew he was reaching for the small pistol he'd always carried strapped to his leg beneath his pants.

"Forget it." Gideon moved his own hand from behind the door and aimed the revolver almost absently at Jake. Savage froze, one hand still under the desk. "You were never that fast or that lucky and we both know it. The truth is, Jake, you were always better as a legend than you were as a reality."

11

GIDEON WATCHED, fighting to hide his amusement, as Sarah paced up and down the living room. The cats had long since grown bored with her diatribe against Jake Savage. Machu Picchu was sprawled in his usual position across the back of the couch, his ears flat against his head and Ellora was curled up, sound asleep, alongside Gideon.

"We should have turned him over to the police. He was guilty of everything from breaking and entering to being a damned nuisance. And the man lied through his teeth. How could you just let him go like that, Gideon?" Sarah turned and stalked back across the living room, robe flapping around her ankles. Her hair was anchored in a topknot that was coming adrift from it's moorings.

"He won't bother us again, Sarah."

"We don't know that for certain. We should have had him arrested. Why didn't you?"

"Jake would never have survived prison," Gideon said, thinking about it. "Assuming we could have actually gotten him convicted and sent up, which is highly doubtful. We'd have been lucky to make the charges stick. He didn't actually steal anything and he doesn't have a record. The most he would have gotten would have been a few months."

Sarah reached the far end of the room, spun around and headed back the other way. "I don't think that's all of it. I think you went easy on him for old time's sake."

"Old times sake?" Gideon cocked one brow.

"Sure. After all, he was your partner for several years. You'd been through a lot together. And you're the loyal type."

"I am?"

"Certainly. Don't laugh at me. It's your nature. I suppose it's one of the things I admire about you. But that still leaves us with a problem. What if he comes after the Flowers again?"

"He won't."

"I don't see what's to stop him this time."

"I told him that if anything happened to that strongbox, I'd destroy the legend I helped him build. That's all he's got left, Sarah. His own legend. It's the most important thing in the world to him."

Sarah paused and nibbled on her lip. "And you could do it? Through your magazine?"

"I could do it by sending letters to certain collectors and dealers telling them to take a second look at some of the South American artifacts they've acquired lately through Slaughter Enterprises."

Sarah's eyes widened. "You said you'd kept tabs on him. That's what he's been doing for the past five years? Selling antiquities?"

"Uh-huh."

"And some of them were fraudulent?"

"Right. Smuggling the real stuff is a better bet. Dedicated collectors and dealers won't ask too many questions about sources so long as the pieces are real, but they'll be mad as hell if they think they've been taken in by a fake."

"So Jake has been reduced to selling fake South American antiquities. What a comedown for him." Sarah shook her head. "That must have grated. No wonder he was looking for a way back to fame and fortune."

Gideon stroked Ellora. "Some people would say that publishing a small treasure-hunting magazine like *Cache* is even more of a comedown."

Sarah glared at him. "It certainly is not. You're in publishing, the same as I am. You're an author. Just like me. You write for people who can still dream, the same way I do. We perform a very valuable function for a very important group of people, Gideon Trace, and don't you forget it. As this world of ours gets more high-tech and more endangered, it needs its dreamers more desperately than ever."

"I never thought of it quite that way," Gideon murmured, amazed as usual by her highly biased view of him. It was very heartwarming.

Sarah turned away again. "I suppose somehow Jake is a dreamer, too, isn't he? Unfortunately he's just kind of screwed up in general."

"Unfortunately." Gideon yawned. "You were right, by the way, about why he set up that ambush five years ago. He was trying to prove something to himself. Trying to get free of his dependence on me."

Sarah nodded. "Trying to prove he didn't need you to be a success. You're sure he'll stay out of our lives from now on?"

"Reasonably sure."

"What about the Fleetwood Flowers? He wanted those very badly."

Gideon felt Ellora stretch languidly beneath his hand. "I told him the Flowers didn't exist."

Sarah stared at him, clearly startled. "But he kne we had the strongbox."

"I told him there was nothing in it."

Sarah smiled slowly, with obvious satisfaction "That was very clever of you, Gideon. Did he believ you?"

"Not entirely, but I think that after a while he'll con vince himself I was telling the truth. He'd rather be lieve there were no Flowers than that he failed to ge hold of them."

"Yes, exactly. He'll convince himself there was n treasure. And since we have no reason to advertise th fact that we found the earrings, Jake will never know the difference."

Gideon leaned his head back against the cushion and watched her through narrowed lids. "It's possibl that when we get the strongbox open tomorrow it really will be empty. You probably shouldn't get too excited about finding anything inside, Sarah."

"They'll be in there." She hugged herself happily. " can't wait to go to work on that old lock tomorrow. It's going to be such a perfect ending to this whole adven ture."

"What about us, Sarah? Does finding the Flowers mean the end of that, too?" Gideon asked quietly.

She smiled serenely. "Don't be an idiot, Gideon. You and I are just starting our adventure."

"You really mean that, don't you?"

She paused and gazed out into the night. "I've told you before, Gideon. In some way I've never been able to explain, the Flowers are linked to you, but they have nothing to do with our relationship. Do you see the difference?"

"I think I'm finally beginning to understand." Gideon glanced toward the stairs. "It's nearly two in the morning, Sarah. Let's get some sleep. Knowing you, you'll be up at the crack of dawn trying to jam a hairpin into that old lock."

She chuckled, reaching for his hand. "I don't have a hairpin with me. But that's all right. We'll rely on your professional skills."

Gideon rose from the sofa and put his arm around her shoulder. With his other hand he lifted her chin. When his mouth closed over hers, she parted her lips for him and wrapped her arms around his neck.

Gideon picked her up and started toward the stairs.

"I love it when you do this kind of thing," Sarah said, her eyes cloudy with desire as Gideon carried her into his bedroom. "You're so good at it."

"You think so?" He put her down on the bed and came down beside her. Slowly he untied her robe and opened it. She was so lovely, he thought as he bent his head to kiss her breast. And she wanted him. *Him*, not Jake Savage or anyone else. Just him.

"Yes. Perfect." She caught his head and held him to her, lifting herself invitingly against him. "Absolutely perfect."

"Perfect," Gideon agreed softly. His hand slid down to her thighs. Gently he parted her legs and made a place for himself near her warmth.

This was what he wanted out of life, Gideon realized; it was all he asked for of the Fates. He had been cold for far too long. Now he knew he would be content if he could spend the rest of his days warming himself at Sarah's hearth.

SARAH AWOKE SHORTLY after four o'clock when Ellora shifted slightly against her leg. Automatically she turned to find Gideon on the other side of the bed.

He was gone.

Sarah listened to the silence of the big old house for a moment or two and then she pushed back the covers and got to her feet. Her robe was on the back of a chair. She put it on, tied the sash and went very quietly out the door. Ellora followed at her heels.

Sarah crept down the stairs, avoiding the ones that creaked. At the foot of the staircase she hesitated and then turned down the hall toward Gideon's study. There was a thin wedge of light showing through the opening in the doorway.

Sarah tiptoed to the door and peered through the crack. Gideon was sitting at his desk dressed in only his jeans. Emelina Fleetwood's strongbox was open in front of him. Nearby sat five of the carved wooden chess pieces.

As Sarah watched, fascinated, Gideon picked up one of the chess pieces, removed the base and pulled out a small object wrapped in black velvet. He put the object into the strongbox and reached for the next chess piece.

Machu rumbled from somewhere inside the study and Ellora brushed past Sarah's bare feet. The little cat pushed through the crack of the doorway and trotted into the room. Gideon glanced up. He saw Ellora first and then he saw Sarah standing in the shadows of the hall.

A curious stillness gripped him. He sat as if made of stone, his green eyes glittering with an unreadable expression.

"Well, well, well," Sarah murmured. She pushed the door open wider, crossed her arms and leaned against the doorframe. She wanted to shout her happiness to the world.

"Couldn't sleep?" Gideon asked.

"Something woke me up."

"Probably your world-famous intuition."

"Probably." Sarah couldn't stop the smile that she knew was starting to light up her whole face.

Gideon sighed wearily and leaned back in his chair. "I guess you want an explanation."

She shook her head violently. "Not necessary."

"It's not?"

"No. Gideon, this is the most romantic thing that has ever happened to me in my entire life."

He glanced at the open strongbox. "It is?"

"Definitely. It proves you love me. Proves it beyond a shadow of a doubt."

"It does?"

"Oh, yes." She walked into the room and came to a halt on the other side of the desk. She planted both hands on its polished wooden surface.

"Sarah . . ."

"Admit it," Sarah said, wanting to laugh out loud at his wary expression. "Go on, admit it. Tell me you love me. Tell me that you're doing this—" she waved a hand to include the array of chess pieces and the open strongbox "—because you're wildly, madly, passionately, head-over-heels in love with me."

"Well . . ."

"Gideon, this is the sweetest, most romantic gift I've ever had. You knew how much I was enjoying my treasure hunt. You know how excited I was about opening that strongbox. And you couldn't bear for me to find it empty, could you? You wanted to give me a gift and letting me find the Fleetwood Flowers at the end of my big adventure was your present to me. Gideon, I am so thrilled, so incredibly touched. *You love me.*"

Gideon gazed down at the knight still in his hand. "You're amazing, you know that? Some women would look at a scene like this and assume right off the bat that they had been or were about to be robbed, cheated or otherwise swindled out of a fortune. You look at it and assume it's evidence that I'm in love with you."

Sarah grinned. "It is and you are. Aren't you?"

Gideon's answering smile was slow. His eyes lost their wariness. A deep, aching tenderness took its place. His hard face seemed to gentle in the lamplight. "I must be to have gotten myself into a situation like this."

Sarah laughed, her delight bubbling up inside like champagne. She darted around the edge of the desk and threw herself into Gideon's lap. "Tell me," she demanded. "Say the words."

He touched the side of her face wonderingly. "I love you, Sarah."

"Since when?" she pressed.

"I don't know. Does it matter?"

"No." She put her fingertips on his lips. "It doesn't really matter. The only thing that matters is that you're sure now."

"I'm sure."

She put her head down on his shoulder, nestling close. "I figured you must or you wouldn't be putting the Fleetwood Flowers back into that strongbox for me to find in the morning. When did you dig them up?"

"About four years ago. I needed the money to expand *Cache* and since I was now supposed to be an expert in treasure hunting I decided to do some. I went

rough a file I had put together on old treasure stories
at sounded promising—the real stuff, you under-
tand, the kind of tales I never print in *Cache*."

"The kind you pursue yourself when you go on va-
ation?"

Gideon nodded. "The Flowers was a story that had
ossibilities and it was fairly close to my home here on
he coast. So I did a little research, scraped together
nough for a down payment on the land and bought the
ld Fleetwood property for a few months. As soon as I
ound the Flowers, I sold the land again."

"Just the way I had planned to do it. I guess this
roves that great minds really do run in the same track,
doesn't it? Why didn't you sell the earrings if you needed
he money?"

"Believe me, I was going to sell them. It was the rea-
on I'd dug them up in the first place. They'd definitely
ring a nice chunk of change. Take a look."

Gideon unwrapped one of the black velvet pack-
ges. A pair of glittering sapphire earrings set in an old-
ashioned design tumbled out onto the desk. They lay
here like brilliant blue flowers. He opened another
velvet bundle and a set of beautifully matched pearl
earrings cascaded onto the desk. Then he unwrapped
he next three sets of Flowers. Rubies, opals and diamonds winked in the light.

"Emelina Fleetwood's buried treasure," Sarah
breathed. "They're beautiful."

Gideon gazed down as the small fortune lying in
front of him. "I intended to sell them off quietly, a stone
at a time, but I kept making excuses not to do it. Then
one day I realized I wasn't going to be able to ever sell
them at all. For some insane reason, I felt I had to hang
on to them."

"Of course you did. You were waiting for me to com
and claim them. It all fits together now. I always knew
the Flowers were linked to you. I just didn't understan
quite how. But now it's perfectly clear. You were hold
ing them, waiting for me to show up in your life, weren'
you? You just didn't know it. You've got intuition, too
Gideon."

"You think so?" Gideon wrapped his arm around he
waist, holding her tightly to him.

"Definitely. Why do you think you were the one who
made Savage and Company a legend? Why did you
sense that ambush five years ago? Why do you think
you found the Fleetwood Flowers without even a map?"

He gave her a wry look. "Why did I marry the wrong
woman the first time around? Why did I trust Jake
Savage to be my partner and friend?"

Sarah waved that aside. "I guess your intuition works
better with treasure and danger and that sort of thing
Mine seems to work mostly with people. We'll make a
great team."

"I think we will." He kissed her throat.

"You let me go through the whole treasure hunt from
start to finish so I'd have the thrill of actually finding
the Flowers on my own, didn't you?"

"I don't know if that was my initial plan," Gideon
said. "I wasn't thinking that clearly in the beginning. I
just knew I had to keep you around for a while and hiring on as your consultant and partner was a way to do
that."

"And naturally you stipulated that you'd get to keep
at least one pair of the earrings. After all, you'd already
found the whole bunch. You had some rights in the
matter."

"That's very understanding of you. It's also exactly what I told myself at the start."

Sarah giggled. "When I think of how you let me tramp all over the Fleetwood property and struggle with that darned map...Oh, Gideon, it's too much. You must have been laughing yourself silly."

"Treasure hunting is fun. I wanted you to have the thrill." Gideon's eyes turned serious. "And I didn't want the adventure to end too soon. I wanted time with you. I couldn't figure out what was going on between us, but I didn't want to let you go out of my life too quickly. The treasure hunt was a way of stalling you for a while."

"What about arranging for us to have to share that cabin? That was a deliberate ploy to try to get me into bed, wasn't it?"

"I guess it could be viewed in that light," Gideon said modestly.

"And virtually kidnapping me and forcing me to come back here instead of going home to Seattle? That was a ploy to try to keep me around, too, right? Protecting me from Jake Savage was just a convenient excuse."

"For all the good it did me."

"They were all terribly romantic gestures, Gideon, worthy of any true romance hero, but I would have to say that seducing me right on top of the white rock was the pièce de résistance."

"I was rather proud of that move myself."

She kissed him. "You were going to have great fun watching me discover the earrings in the strongbox in the morning, weren't you? And now I've gone and spoiled your surprise. Sorry about that." She kissed him again. "Gideon, you are so wonderful."

His eyes held hers. "So are you. What did I ever do without you?"

"We were bound to connect eventually. After all, you're the man of my dreams. How many times do I have to tell you?"

Gideon's fingers tightened in her hair was sudden fierceness as he held her still for his kiss. "You can keep on telling me that for the rest of my life. I like being your hero. I like it very, very much."

"Good. And you won't mind if I continue to use you in my books? After all, I've built a whole career based on you."

Gideon looked down into her warm, loving eyes. And for the first time since Sarah had known him, he laughed out loud. The cats, sitting side by side on the couch, flicked their ears at the unusual sound.

"Just so long as you change my name," Gideon said.

"No problem. I always change your name in each new book."

Gideon caught hold of her hand and kissed her fingers. "Now, about the wedding..."

"Yes," said Sarah. "I was thinking of a quick trip to Reno or Las Vegas. What do you think?"

"I was thinking of something a little different."

MARGARET LARK received the telegram at ten in the morning. Without stopping to calculate the time difference between Seattle and Amethyst Island, she dialed the phone. Kate Inskip Hawthorne answered at once.

"You got one, too, I take it?" Margaret asked without preamble.

"Reminds me of the one I sent," Kate said cheerfully. "Looks like we've got a tradition going here. I guess Sarah's intuition was right again, as usual."

"She was sure of him from the first letter, wasn't she? A Beast waiting to be saved with Beauty's love." Margaret smiled to herself. "The poor man didn't stand a chance."

"Neither did Sarah, if you ask me. That treasure hunter of hers must be very extraordinary."

"Why do you say that?"

"Are you kidding? I would have bet good money that there wasn't a man left on the face of the earth who could have convinced Sarah to go for a big wedding. Not after what happened the last time."

"Good point. That settles it. It must be love on both sides. Will you be flying to Seattle for the festivities?" Margaret asked.

"I wouldn't miss this wedding for the world."

Margaret laughed. "We'll get to be bridal attendants. That should be fun. I've never been one." She hung up the phone a few minutes later and picked up the telegram on the kitchen counter. She reread it with a gathering sense of happiness for her friend, Sarah.

Pleased to report that my adventurer is even better in real life than he is in my books. He's got everything, including a couple of cats. Wedding set for one month from today. Will need lots of help as Gideon insists on the works. Will return to Seattle on Monday to start interviewing caterers and shop for gown. Wait until you see the earrings I'm going to wear.

Love,
Sarah

Books by Jayne Ann Krentz

HARLEQUIN TEMPTATION

HARLEQUIN INTRIGUE

Don't miss any of our special offers. Write to us at the following address for information on our newest releases.

Harlequin Reader Service
901 Fuhrmann Blvd., P.O. Box 1397, Buffalo, NY 14240
Canadian address: P.O. Box 603,
Fort Erie, Ont. L2A 5X3

COMING NEXT MONTH

**In April, Harlequin brings you the
world's most popular romance author**

JANET DAILEY

No Quarter Asked

Out of print since 1974!

After the tragic death of her father, Stacy's world is shattered. She needs to get away by herself to sort things out. She leaves behind her boyfriend, Carter Price, who wants to marry her. However, as soon as she arrives at her rented cabin in Texas, Cord Harris, owner of a large ranch, seems determined to get her to leave. When Stacy has a fall and is injured, Cord reluctantly takes her to his own ranch. Unknown to Stacy, Carter's father has written to Cord and asked him to keep an eye on Stacy and try to convince her to return home. After a few weeks there, in spite of Cord's hateful treatment that involves her working as a ranch hand and the return of Lydia, his ex-fiancée, by the time Carter comes to escort her back, Stacy knows that she is in love with Cord and doesn't want to go.

**Watch for *Fiesta San Antonio* in July and
For Bitter or Worse in September.**

JDA-1

Have You Ever Wondered If You Could Write A Harlequin Novel?

Here's great news—Harlequin is offering a series of cassette tapes to help you do just that. Written by Harlequin editors, these tapes give practical advice on how to make your characters—and your story—come alive. There's a tape for each contemporary romance series Harlequin publishes.

Mail order only

All sales final

TO: **Harlequin Reader Service**
Audiocassette Tape Offer
P.O. Box 1396
Buffalo, NY   14269-1396

I enclose a check/money order payable to HARLEQUIN READER SERVICE® for $9.70 ($8.95 plus 75¢ postage and handling) for EACH tape ordered for the total sum of $_____ *
Please send:

☐ Romance and Presents   ☐ Intrigue
☐ American Romance   ☐ Temptation
☐ Superromance   ☐ All five tapes ($38.80 total)

Signature_____

Name:_____ (please print clearly)

Address:_____

State:_____ Zip:_____

*Iowa and New York residents add appropriate sales tax.

AUDIO-H

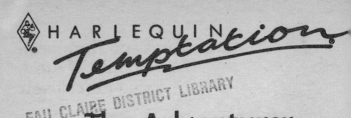

HARLEQUIN
Temptation®

The Adventurer

JAYNE ANN KRENTZ

Remember THE PIRATE (Temptation #287), the first book of
Jayne Ann Krentz's exciting trilogy Ladies and Legends? Next
month Jayne brings us another powerful romance, THE
ADVENTURER (Temptation #293), in which Kate, Sarah and
Margaret — three long-time friends featured in THE PIRATE
— meet again.

A contemporary version of a great romantic myth, THE
ADVENTURER tells of Sarah Fleetwood's search for long-
lost treasure and for love. Only when she meets her modern-
day knight-errant Gideon Trace will Sarah know she's found
the path to fortune and eternal bliss....

THE ADVENTURER — available in April 1990! And in June,
look for THE COWBOY (Temptation #302), the third book of
this enthralling trilogy.

LAUREL

**AMERICA'S GREATEST SATIRIST . . .
KURT VONNEGUT IS . . .**

"UNIQUE . . . one of the writers who map our landscapes for us, who give names to the places we know best."
> —Doris Lessing, *The New York Times Book Review*

"OUR FINEST BLACK HUMORIST. . . . We laugh in self-defense."
> —*The Atlantic Monthly*

"AN UNIMITATIVE AND INIMITABLE SOCIAL SATIRIST."
> —*Harper's Magazine*

"A MEDICINE MAN, CONJURING UP FANTASIES TO WARN THE WORLD."
> —*The Charlotte Observer*

"A CAUSE FOR CELEBRATION."
> —*Chicago Sun-Times*

"A LAUGHING PROPHET OF DOOM."
> —*The New York Times*

A
NOVEL
BY

Kurt
Vonnegut

SLAPSTICK

OR

LONESOME NO MORE!

LAUREL

Grateful acknowledgment is extended to Al Hirschfeld,
who is represented exclusively by
The Margo Felden Galleries, New York City,
for permission to reproduce the illustration
on the dedication page.

A LAUREL BOOK
Published by
Dell Publishing
a division of
Bantam Doubleday Dell Publishing Group, Inc.
666 Fifth Avenue
New York, New York 10103

Cover design: Carin Goldberg
Cover illustration: Gene Greif

The trademark Laurel® is registered in the U.S. Patent and Trademark
Office.

The trademark Dell® is registered in the U.S. Patent and Trademark
Office.

ISBN: 0-440-18009-0

Reprinted by arrangement with Delacorte Press/Seymour Lawrence

Printed in the United States of America

Published simultaneously in Canada

August 1989

26 25 24 23 22 21 20 19 18

RAD

Dedicated to the memory of
Arthur Stanley Jefferson and Norvell Hardy,
two angels of my time.

◆◆◆◆◆◆◆◆◆◆◆◆

"Call me but love, and I'll be new baptiz'd . . "
—ROMEO

Slapstick

◆◆◆◆◆◆◆◆◆◆◆◆

Prologue

✦✦✦✦✦✦✦✦✦✦✦✦

THIS is the closest I will ever come to writing an autobiography. I have called it "Slapstick" because it is grotesque, situational poetry—like the slapstick film comedies, especially those of Laurel and Hardy, of long ago.

It is about what life *feels* like to me.

There are all these tests of my limited agility and intelligence. They go on and on.

The fundamental joke with Laurel and Hardy, it seems to me, was that they did their best with every test.

They never failed to bargain in good faith with their destinies, and were screamingly adorable and funny on that account.

◆◆◆

There was very little love in their films. There was often the situational poetry of marriage, which was something else again. It was yet another test—with comical possibilities, provided that everybody submitted to it in good faith.

Love was never at issue. And, perhaps because I was so perpetually intoxicated and instructed by Laurel and Hardy during my childhood in the Great Depression, I find it natural to discuss life without ever mentioning love.

It does not seem important to me.

What does seem important? Bargaining in good faith with destiny.

◆◆◆

I have had some experiences with love, or think I have, anyway, although the ones I have liked best could easily be described as "common decency." I treated somebody well for a little while, or maybe even for a tremendously long time, and that person treated me well in turn. Love need not have had anything to do with it.

Also: I cannot distinguish between the love I have for people and the love I have for dogs.

When a child, and not watching comedians on film or listening to comedians on the radio, I used to spend a lot of time rolling around on rugs with uncritically affectionate dogs we had.

And I still do a lot of that. The dogs become tired

and confused and embarrassed long before I do. I could go on forever.

Hi ho.

◆◆◆

One time, on his twenty-first birthday, one of my three adopted sons, who was about to leave for the Peace Corps in the Amazon Rain Forest, said to me, "You know—you've never hugged me."

So I hugged him. We hugged each other. It was very nice. It was like rolling around on a rug with a Great Dane we used to have.

◆◆◆

Love is where you find it. I think it is foolish to go looking for it, and I think it can often be poisonous.

I wish that people who are conventionally supposed to love each other would say to each other, when they fight, "Please—a little less love, and a little more common decency."

◆◆◆

My longest experience with common decency, surely, has been with my older brother, my only brother, Bernard, who is an atmospheric scientist in the State University of New York at Albany.

He is a widower, raising two young sons all by himself. He does it well. He has three grown-up sons besides.

We were given very different sorts of minds at birth. Bernard could never be a writer. I could never

3

be a scientist. And, since we make our livings with our minds, we tend to think of them as gadgets—separate from our awarenesses, from our central selves.

We have hugged each other maybe three or four times—on birthdays, very likely, and clumsily. We have never hugged in moments of grief.

The minds we have been given enjoy the same sorts of jokes, at any rate—Mark Twain stuff, Laurel and Hardy stuff.

They are equally disorderly, too.

Here is an anecdote about my brother, which, with minor variations, could be told truthfully about me:

Bernard worked for the General Electric Research Laboratory in Schenectady, New York, for a while, where he discovered that silver iodide could precipitate certain sorts of clouds as snow or rain. His laboratory was a sensational mess, however, where a clumsy stranger could die in a thousand different ways, depending on where he stumbled.

The company had a safety officer who nearly swooned when he saw this jungle of deadfalls and snares and hair-trigger booby traps. He bawled out my brother.

My brother said this to him, tapping his own forehead with his fingertips: "If you think this laboratory is bad, you should see what it's like in *here*."

And so on.

◆◆◆

I told my brother one time that whenever I did repair work around the house, I lost all my tools before I could finish the job.

"You're lucky," he said. "I always lose whatever I'm working on."

We laughed.

◆◆◆

But, because of the sorts of minds we were given at birth, and in spite of their disorderliness, Bernard and I belong to artificial extended families which allow us to claim relatives all over the world.

He is a brother to scientists everywhere. I am a brother to writers everywhere.

This is amusing and comforting to both of us. It is nice.

It is lucky, too, for human beings need all the relatives they can get—as possible donors or receivers not necessarily of love, but of common decency.

◆◆◆

When we were children in Indianapolis, Indiana, it appeared that we would always have an extended family of genuine relatives there. Our parents and grandparents, after all, had grown up there with shoals of siblings and cousins and uncles and aunts. Yes, and their relatives were all cultivated and gentle and prosperous, and spoke German and English gracefully.

◆◆◆

They were all religious skeptics, by the way.

◆◆◆

They might roam the wide world over when they were young, and often have wonderful adventures. But they were all told sooner or later that it was time for them to come home to Indianapolis, and to settle down. They invariably obeyed—because they had so many relatives there.

There were good things to inherit, too, of course—sane businesses, comfortable homes and faithful servants, growing mountains of china and crystal and silverware, reputations for honest dealing, cottages on Lake Maxinkuckee, along whose eastern shore my family once owned a village of summer homes.

◆◆◆

But the delight the family took in itself was permanently crippled, I think, by the sudden American hatred for all things German which unsheathed itself when this country entered the First World War, five years before I was born.

Children in our family were no longer taught German. Neither were they encouraged to admire German music or literature or art or science. My brother and sister and I were raised as though Germany were as foreign to us as Paraguay.

We were deprived of Europe, except for what we might learn of it at school.

We lost thousands of years in a very short time—and then tens of thousands of American dollars after that, and the summer cottages and so on.

And our family became a lot less interesting, especially to itself.

So—by the time the Great Depression and a Second World War were over, it was easy for my brother and my sister and me to wander away from Indianapolis.

And, of all the relatives we left behind, not one could think of a reason why we should come home again.

We didn't belong anywhere in particular any more. We were interchangeable parts in the American machine.

◆◆◆

Yes, and Indianapolis, which had once had a way of speaking English all its own, and jokes and legends and poets and villains and heroes all its own, and galleries for its own artists, had itself become an interchangeable part in the American machine.

It was just another someplace where automobiles lived, with a symphony orchestra and all. And a race track.

Hi ho.

My brother and I still go back for funerals, of course. We went back last July for the funeral of our Uncle Alex Vonnegut, the younger brother of our late father—almost the last of our old-style relatives, of the native American patriots who did not fear God, and who had souls that were European.

He was eighty-seven years old. He was childless. He was a graduate of Harvard. He was a retired life insurance agent. He was a co-founder of the Indianapolis Chapter of Alcoholics Anonymous.

◆◆◆

His obituary in the *Indianapolis Star* said that he himself was not an alcoholic.

This denial was at least partly a nice-Nellyism from the past, I think. He used to drink, I know, although alcohol never seriously damaged his work or made him wild. And then he stopped cold. And he surely must have introduced himself at meetings of A. A. as all members must, with his name—followed by this brave confession: "I'm an alcoholic."

Yes, and the paper's genteel denial of his ever having had trouble with alcohol had the old-fashioned intent of preserving from taint all the rest of us who had the same last name.

We would all have a harder time making good Indianapolis marriages or getting good Indianapolis jobs, if it were known for certain that we had had relatives who were once drunkards, or who, like my mother and my son, had gone at least temporarily insane.

It was even a secret that my paternal grandmother died of cancer.

Think of that.

◆◆◆

At any rate, if Uncle Alex, the atheist, found himself standing before Saint Peter and the Pearly Gates after he died, I am certain he introduced himself as follows:

"My name is Alex Vonnegut. I'm an alcoholic."

Good for him.

◆◆◆

I will guess, too, that it was loneliness as much as it was a dread of alcoholic poisoning which shepherded him into A. A. As his relatives died off or wandered away, or simply became interchangeable parts in the American machine, he went looking for new brothers and sisters and nephews and nieces and uncles and aunts, and so on, which he found in A. A.

◆◆◆

When I was a child, he used to tell me what to read, and then make sure I'd read it. It used to amuse him to take me on visits to relatives I'd never known I had.

He told me one time that he had been an American spy in Baltimore during the First World War, befriending German-Americans there. His assignment was to detect enemy agents. He detected nothing, for there was nothing to detect.

He told me, too, that he was an investigator of graft in New York City for a little while—before his parents told him it was time to come home and settle down. He uncovered a scandal involving large expenditures for the maintenance of Grant's Tomb, which required very little maintenance indeed.

Hi ho.

◆◆◆

I received the news of his death over a white, push-button telephone in my house in that part of Manhattan known as "Turtle Bay." There was a philodendron nearby.

I am still not clear how I got here. There are no turtles. There is no bay.

Perhaps I am the turtle, able to live simply anywhere, even underwater for short periods, with my home on my back.

◆◆◆

So I called my brother in Albany. He was about to turn sixty. I was fifty-two.

We were certainly no spring chickens.

But Bernard still played the part of an older brother. It was he who got us our seats on Trans World Airlines and our car at the Indianapolis airport, and our double room with twin beds at a Ramada Inn.

The funeral itself, like the funerals of our parents and of so many other close relatives, was as blankly secular, as vacant of ideas about God or the afterlife, or even about Indianapolis, as our Ramada Inn.

◆◆◆

So my brother and I strapped ourselves into a jet-propelled airplane bound from New York City to Indianapolis. I sat on the aisle. Bernard took the window seat, since he was an atmospheric scientist, since clouds had so much more to say to him than they did to me.

We were both over six feet tall. We still had most of our hair, which was brown. We had identical mustaches—duplicates of our late father's mustache.

We were harmless looking. We were a couple of nice old Andy Gumps.

There was an empty seat between us, which was spooky poetry. It could have been a seat for our sister Alice, whose age was halfway between mine and Bernard's. She wasn't in that seat and on her way to her beloved Uncle Alex's funeral, for she had died among strangers in New Jersey, of cancer—at the age of forty-one.

"Soap opera!" she said to my brother and me one time, when discussing her own impending death. She would be leaving four young boys behind, without any mother.

"Slapstick," she said.

Hi ho.

◆◆◆

She spent the last day of her life in a hospital. The doctors and nurses said she could smoke and drink as much as she pleased, and eat whatever she pleased.

My brother and I paid her a call. It was hard for her to breathe. She had been as tall as we were at one time, which was very embarrassing to her, since she was a woman. Her posture had always been bad, because of her embarrassment. Now she had a posture like a question mark.

She coughed. She laughed. She made a couple of jokes which I don't remember now.

Then she sent us away. "Don't look back," she said. So we didn't.

She died at about the same time of day that Uncle Alex died—an hour or two after the sun went down.

And hers would have been an unremarkable death statistically, if it were not for one detail, which was this: Her healthy husband, James Carmalt Adams, the editor of a trade journal for purchasing agents, which he put together in a cubicle on Wall Street, had died two mornings before—on "The Brokers' Special," the only train in American railroading history to hurl itself off an open drawbridge.

Think of that.

◆◆◆

This really happened.

◆◆◆

Bernard and I did not tell Alice about what had happened to her husband, who was supposed to take full charge of the children after she died, but she found out about it anyway. An ambulatory female patient gave her a copy of the New York *Daily News*. The front page headline was about the dive of the train. Yes, and there was a list of the dead and missing inside.

Since Alice had never received any religious instruction, and since she had led a blameless life, she never thought of her awful luck as being anything but accidents in a very busy place.

Good for her.

◆◆◆

Exhaustion, yes, and deep money worries, too, made her say toward the end that she guessed that she wasn't really very good at life.

Then again: Neither were Laurel and Hardy.

◆◆◆

My brother and I had already taken over her household. After she died, her three oldest sons, who were between the ages of eight and fourteen, held a meeting, which no grownups could attend. Then they came out and asked that we honor their only two requirements: That they remain together, and that they keep their two dogs. The youngest child, who was not at the meeting, was a baby only a year old or so.

From then on, the three oldest were raised by me and my wife, Jane Cox Vonnegut, along with our own three children, on Cape Cod. The baby, who lived with us for a while, was adopted by a first cousin of their father, who is now a judge in Birmingham, Alabama.

So be it.

The three oldest kept their dogs.

I remember now what one of her sons, who is named "Kurt" like my father and me, asked me as we drove from New Jersey to Cape Cod with the two dogs in back. He was about eight.

We were going from south to north, so where we were going was "up" to him. There were just the two of us. His brothers had gone ahead.

"Are the kids up there nice?" he said.

"Yes, they are," I replied.

He is an airline pilot now.

They are all something other than children now.

One of them is a goat farmer on a mountaintop in Jamaica. He has made come true a dream of our sister's: To live far from the madness of cities, with animals for friends. He has no telephone or electricity.

He is desperately dependent on rainfall. He is a ruined man, if it does not rain.

The two dogs have died of old age. I used to roll around with them on rugs for hours on end, until they were all pooped out.

◆◆◆

Yes, and our sister's sons are candid now about a creepy business which used to worry them a lot: They cannot find their mother or their father in their memories anywhere—not anywhere.

The goat farmer, whose name is James Carmalt Adams, Jr., said this about it to me, tapping his forehead with his fingertips: "It isn't the museum. it should be."

The museums in children's minds, I think, automatically empty themselves in times of utmost horror—to protect the children from eternal grief.

◆◆◆

For my own part, though: It would have been catastrophic if I had forgotten my sister at once. I had never told her so, but she was the person I had always written for. She was the secret of whatever artistic unity I had ever achieved. She was the secret of my technique. Any creation which has any wholeness and harmoniousness, I suspect, was made by an artist or inventor with an audience of one in mind.

Yes, and she was nice enough, or Nature was nice enough, to allow me to feel her presence for a number of years after she died—to let me go on writing for her. But then she began to fade away, perhaps because she had more important business elsewhere.

Be that as it may, she had vanished entirely as my audience by the time Uncle Alex died.

So the seat between my brother and me on the airplane seemed especially vacant to me. I filled it as best I could—with that morning's issue of *The New York Times*.

◆◆◆

While my brother and I waited for the plane to take off for Indianapolis, he made me a present of a joke by Mark Twain—about an opera Twain had seen in Italy. Twain said that he hadn't heard anything like it ". . . since the orphanage burned down."

We laughed.

◆◆◆

He asked me politely how my work was going. I think he respects but is baffled by my work.

I said that I was sick of it, but that I had always been sick of it. I told him a remark which I had heard attributed to the writer Renata Adler, who hates writing, that a writer was a person who hated writing.

I told him, too, what my agent, Max Wilkinson, wrote to me after I complained again about what a disagreeable profession I had. This was it: "Dear Kurt —I never knew a blacksmith who was in love with his anvil."

We laughed again, but I think the joke was partly

lost on my brother. His life has been an unending honeymoon with his anvil.

◆◆◆

I told him that I had been going to operas recently, and that the set for the first act of *Tosca* had looked exactly like the interior of Union Station in Indianapolis to me. While the actual opera was going on, I said, I daydreamed about putting track numbers in the archways of the set, and passing out bells and whistles to the orchestra, and staging an opera about Indianapolis during the Age of the Iron Horse.

"People from our great-grandfathers' generation would mingle with our own, when we were young—" I said, "and all the generations in between. Arrivals and departures would be announced. Uncle Alex would leave for his job as a spy in Baltimore. You would come home from your freshman year at M.I.T.

"There would be shoals of relatives," I said, "watching the travelers come and go—and black men to carry the luggage and shine the shoes."

◆◆◆

"Every so often in my opera," I said, "the stage would turn mud-colored with uniforms. That would be a war.

"And then it would clear up again."

After the plane took off, my brother showed me a piece of scientific apparatus which he had brought along. It was a photoelectric cell connected to a small tape recorder. He aimed the electric eye at clouds. It perceived lightning flashes which were invisible to us in the dazzle of daytime.

The secret flashes were recorded as clicks by the recorder. We could also hear the clicks as they happened—on a tiny earphone.

"There's a hot one," my brother announced. He indicated a distant cumulus cloud, a seeming Pike's Peak of whipped cream.

He let me listen to the clicks. There were two quick ones, then some silence, then three quick ones, then silence again.

"How far away is that cloud?" I asked him.

"Oh—a hundred miles, maybe," he said.

I thought it was beautiful that my big brother could detect secrets so simply from so far away.

◆◆◆

I lit a cigarette.

Bernard doesn't smoke any more, because it is so important that he live a good while longer. He still has two little boys to raise.

◆◆◆

Yes, and while my big brother meditated about clouds, the mind *I* was given daydreamed the story in this book. It is about desolated cities and spiritual cannibalism and incest and loneliness and lovelessness and death, and so on. It depicts myself and my beautiful sister as monsters, and so on.

This is only natural, since I dreamed it on the way to a funeral.

◆◆◆

It is about this terribly old man in the ruins of Manhattan, you see, where almost everyone has been killed by a mysterious disease called "The Green Death."

He lives there with his illiterate, rickety, pregnant little granddaughter, Melody. Who is he really? I guess he is myself—experimenting with being old.

Who is Melody? I thought for a while that she was all that remained of my memory of my sister. I now believe that she is what I feel to be, when I experiment with old age, all that is left of my optimistic imagination, of my creativeness.

Hi ho.

◆◆◆

The old man is writing his autobiography. He begins it with words which my late Uncle Alex told me one time should be used by religious skeptics as a prelude to their nightly prayers.

These are the words: "To whom it may concern."

◆◆◆

Chapter 1

◆◆◆◆◆◆◆◆◆◆

To whom it may concern:

It is springtime. It is late afternoon.

Smoke from a cooking fire on the terrazzo floor of the lobby of the Empire State Building on the Island of Death floats out over the ailanthus jungle which Thirty-fourth Street has become.

The pavement on the floor of the jungle is all crinkum-crankum—heaved this way and that by frost-heaves and roots.

There is a small clearing in the jungle. A blue-eyed, lantern-jawed old white man, who is two meters tall and one hundred years old, sits in the clearing on what was once the back seat of a taxicab.

21

I am that man.

My name is Dr. Wilbur Daffodil-11 Swain.

◆◆◆

I am barefoot. I wear a purple toga made from draperies found in the ruins of the Americana Hotel.

I am a former President of the United States of America. I was the final President, the tallest President, and the only one ever to have been divorced while occupying the White House.

I inhabit the first floor of the Empire State Building with my sixteen-year-old granddaughter, who is Melody Oriole-2 von Peterswald, and with her lover, Isadore Raspberry-19 Cohen. The three of us have the building all to ourselves.

Our nearest neighbor is one and one-half kilometers away.

I have just heard one of her roosters crow.

◆◆◆

Our nearest neighbor is Vera Chipmunk-5 Zappa, a woman who loves life and is better at it than anyone I ever knew. She is a strong and warm-hearted and hard-working farmer in her early sixties. She is built like a fireplug. She has slaves whom she treats very well. And she and the slaves raise cattle and pigs and chickens and goats and corn and wheat and vegetables and fruits and grapes along the shores of the East River.

They have built a windmill for grinding grain, and

a still for making brandy, and a smokehouse—and on and on.

"Vera—" I told her the other day, "if you would only write us a new Declaration of Independence, you would be the Thomas Jefferson of modern times."

◆◆◆

I write this book on the stationery of the Continental Driving School, three boxes of which Melody and Isadore found in a closet on the sixty-fourth floor of our home. They also found a gross of ball-point pens.

◆◆◆

Visitors from the mainland are rare. The bridges are down. The tunnels are crushed. And boats will not come near us, for fear of the plague peculiar to this island, which is called "The Green Death."

And it is that plague which has earned Manhattan the sobriquet, "The Island of Death."

Hi ho.

◆◆◆

It is a thing I often say these days: "Hi ho." It is a kind of senile hiccup. I have lived too long.

Hi ho.

◆◆◆

The gravity is very light today. I have an erection as a result of that. All males have erections on days like

23

this. They are automatic consequences of near-weightlessness. They have little to do with eroticism in most cases, and nothing to do with it in the life of a man my age. They are hydraulic experiences—the results of confused plumbing, and little more.

Hi ho.

The gravity is so light today, that I feel as though I might scamper to the top of the Empire State Building with a manhole cover, and fling it into New Jersey.

That would surely be an improvement on George Washington's sailing a silver dollar across the Rappahannock. And yet some people insist that there is no such thing as progress.

I am sometimes called "The King of Candlesticks," because I own more than one thousand candlesticks.

But I am fonder of my middle name, which is "Daffodil-11." And I have written this poem about it, and about life itself, of course:

> "I was those seeds,
> "I am this meat,
> "This meat hates pain,
> "This meat must eat.
> "This meat must sleep,
> "This meat must dream,

"This meat must laugh,
"This meat must scream.
"But when, as meat,
"It's had its fill,
"Please plant it as
"A Daffodil."

And who will read all this? God knows. Not Melody and Isadore, surely. Like all the other young people on the island, they can neither read nor write.

They have no curiosity about the human past, nor about what life may be like on the mainland.

As far as they are concerned, the most glorious accomplishment of the people who inhabited this island so teemingly was to die, so we could have it all to ourselves.

I asked them the other evening to name the three most important human beings in history. They protested that the question made no sense to them.

I insisted that they put their heads together anyway, and give me some sort of answer, which they did. They were very sulky about the exercise. It was painful to them.

They finally came up with an answer. Melody does most of the talking for them, and this is what she said in all seriousness: "You, and Jesus Christ, and Santa Claus."

Hi ho.

◆◆◆

When I do not ask them questions, they are as happy as clams.

◆◆◆

They hope to become slaves of Vera Chipmunk-5 Zappa some day. That is O.K. with me.

◆◆◆

Chapter 2

◆◆◆◆◆◆◆◆◆

AND I really will try to stop writing "Hi ho" all the time.

Hi ho.

◆◆◆

I was born right here in New York City. I was not then a *Daffodil*. I was christened Wilbur *Rockefeller* Swain.

I was not alone, moreover. I had a dizygotic twin, a female. She was named Eliza Mellon Swain.

We were christened in a hospital rather than in a church, and we were not surrounded by relatives and our parents' friends. The thing was: Eliza and I were so ugly that our parents were ashamed.

27

We were monsters, and we were not expected to live very long. We had six fingers on each little hand, and six toes on each little footsie. We had supernumerary nipples as well—two of them apiece.

We were not mongolian idiots, although we had the coarse black hair typical of mongoloids. We were something new. We were *neanderthaloids*. We had the features of adult, fossil human beings even in infancy—massive brow-ridges, sloping foreheads, and steamshovel jaws.

◆◆◆

We were supposed to have no intelligence, and to die before we were fourteen.

But I am still alive and kicking, thank you. And Eliza would be, too, I'm certain, if she had not been killed at the age of fifty—in an avalanche on the outskirts of the Chinese colony on the planet Mars.

Hi ho.

◆◆◆

Our parents were two silly and pretty and very young people named Caleb Mellon Swain and Letitia Vanderbilt Swain, née Rockefeller. They were fabulously well-to-do, and descended from Americans who had all but wrecked the planet with a form of Idiot's Delight—obsessively turning money into power, and then power back into money again, and then money back into power again.

But Caleb and Letitia were harmless themselves.

Father was very good at backgammon and so-so at color photography, they say. Mother was active in the National Association for the Advancement of Colored People. Neither worked. Neither was a college graduate, though both had tried.

They wrote and spoke nicely. They adored each other. They were humble about having done so poorly in schools. They were kind.

And I cannot fault them for being shattered by having given birth to monsters. Anyone would have been shattered by giving birth to Eliza and me.

◆◆◆

And Caleb and Letitia were at least as good at parenting as I was, when my turn rolled around. I was wholly indifferent to my own children, although they were normal in every way.

Perhaps I would have been more entertained by my children if they had been monsters like Eliza and me.

Hi ho.

◆◆◆

Young Caleb and Letitia were advised not to break their hearts and risk their furniture by attempting to raise Eliza and me in Turtle Bay. We were no more true relatives of theirs, their advisors said, than baby crocodiles.

Caleb's and Letitia's response was humane. It was also expensive and Gothic in the extreme. Our parents did not hide us in a private hospital for cases such as ours. They entombed us instead in a spooky old mansion which they had inherited—in the midst of two hundred acres of apple trees on a mountaintop, near the hamlet of Galen, Vermont.

No one had lived there for thirty years.

◆◆◆

Carpenters and electricians and plumbers were brought in to turn it into a sort of paradise for Eliza and me. Thick rubber padding was put under all the wall-to-wall carpets, so we would not hurt ourselves in case we fell. Our diningroom was lined with tile, and there were drains in the floor, so we and the room could be hosed off after every meal.

More important, perhaps, were two chain-link fences which went up. They were topped with barbed wire. The first enclosed the orchard. The second separated the mansion from the prying eyes of the workmen who had to be let in through the first from time to time in order to look after the apple trees.

Hi ho.

◆◆◆

A staff was recruited from the neighborhood. There was a cook. There were two cleaning women and a cleaning man. There were two practical nurses who fed us and dressed us and undressed us and bathed us. The one I remember best is Withers Wither-

spoon, a combination guard, chauffeur and handy-
man.

His mother was a Withers. His father was a Witherspoon.

◆◆◆

Yes, and these were simple country people, who,
with the exception of Withers Witherspoon, who had
been a soldier, had never been outside Vermont.
They had rarely ventured more than ten miles from
Galen, for that matter—and they were necessarily all
related to one another, as inbred as Eskimos.

They were of course distantly related to Eliza and
me, too, since our Vermont ancestors had once been
content to dogpaddle endlessly, so to speak, in the
same tiny genetic pool.

But, in the American scheme of things at that time,
they were related to our family as carp were related
to eagles, say—for our family had evolved into world-
travelers and multimillionaires.

Hi ho.

◆◆◆

Yes, and it was easy for our parents to buy the fealty
of these living fossils from the family past. They were
given modest salaries which seemed enormous to
them, since the money-making lobes of their brains
were so primitive.

They were given pleasant apartments in the mansion, and color television sets. They were encouraged

to eat like emperors, charging whatever they liked to our parents. They had very little work to do.

Better still, they did not have to think much for themselves. They were placed under the command of a young general practitioner who lived in the hamlet, Dr. Stewart Rawlings Mott, who would look in on us every day.

Dr. Mott was a Texan, incidentally, a melancholy and private young man. To this day, I do not know what induced him to move so far from his people and his birthplace—to practice medicine in an Eskimo settlement in Vermont.

As a curious footnote in history, and a probably meaningless one: The grandson of Dr. Mott would become the King of Michigan during my second term as President of the United States.

I must hiccup again: Hi ho.

◆◆◆

I swear: If I live to complete this autobiography, I will go through it again, and cross out all the "Hi ho's."
Hi ho.

◆◆◆

Yes, and there was an automatic sprinkler system in the mansion—and burglar alarms on the windows and doors and skylights.

When we grew older and uglier, and capable of breaking arms or tearing heads off, a great gong was installed in the kitchen. This was connected to cherry red push-buttons in every room and at regular intervals down every corridor. The buttons glowed in the dark.

A button was to be pushed only if Eliza or I began to toy with murder.

Hi ho.

◆◆◆

Chapter 3

❖❖❖❖❖❖❖❖❖❖❖❖❖

FATHER went to Galen with a lawyer and a physician and an architect—to oversee the refurbishing of the mansion for Eliza and me, and the hiring of the servants and Dr. Mott. Mother remained here in Manhattan, in their townhouse in Turtle Bay.

Turtles in great profusion, incidentally, have returned to Turtle Bay.

Vera Chipmunk-5 Zappa's slaves like to catch them for soup.

Hi ho.

❖❖❖

It was one of the few occasions, except for Father's death, when Mother and Father were separated for more than a day or two. And Father wrote a graceful letter to Mother from Vermont, which I found in Mother's bedside table after Mother died.

It may have been the whole of their correspondence by mail.

"My dearest Tish—" he wrote, "Our children will be very happy here. We can be proud. Our architect can be proud. The workmen can be proud.

"However short our children's lives may be, we will have given them the gifts of dignity and happiness. We have created a delightful asteroid for them, a little world with only one mansion on it, and otherwise covered with apple trees."

Then he returned to an asteroid of his own—in Turtle Bay. He and Mother, thereafter, again on the advice of physicians, would visit us once a year, and always on our birthday.

Their brownstone still stands, and it is still snug and weathertight. It is there that our nearest neighbor, Vera Chipmunk-5 Zappa, now quarters her slaves.

"And when Eliza and Wilbur die and go to Heaven at last," our father's letter went on, "we can lay them to rest among their Swain ancestors, in the private family cemetery out under the apple trees."

Hi ho.

◆◆◆

As for who was already buried in that cemetery, which was separated from the mansion by a fence: They were mostly Vermont apple farmers and their mates and offspring, people of no distinction. Many of them were no doubt nearly as illiterate and ignorant as Melody and Isadore.

That is to say: They were innocent great apes, with limited means for doing mischief, which, in my opinion as an old, old man, is all that human beings were ever meant to be.

◆◆◆

Many of the tombstones in the cemetery had sunk out of sight or capsized. Weather had dimmed the epitaphs of those which still stood.

But there was one tremendous monument, with thick granite walls, a slate roof, and great doors, which would clearly last past Judgment Day. It was the mausoleum of the founder of the family's fortune and the builder of our mansion, Professor Elihu Roosevelt Swain.

◆◆◆

Professor Swain was by far the most intelligent of all our known ancestors, I would say—Rockefellers, Du Ponts, Mellons, Vanderbilts, Dodges and all. He took a degree from the Massachusetts Institute of Technology at the age of eighteen, and went on to set up the Department of Civil Engineering at Cornell University at the age of twenty-two. By that time, he already had several important patents on railroad bridges and safety devices, which alone would soon have made him a millionaire.

But he was not content. So he created the Swain Bridge Company, which designed and supervised the construction of half the railroad bridges in the entire planet.

◆◆◆

He was a citizen of the world. He spoke many languages, and was the personal friend of many heads of state. But when it came time to build a palace of his own, he placed it among his ignorant ancestors' apple trees.

And he was the only person who loved that barbarous pile until Eliza and I came along. We were so happy there!

◆◆◆

And Eliza and I shared a secret with Professor Swain, even though he had been dead for half a century. The servants did not know it. Our parents did not know it. And the workmen who refurbished the place never suspected it, apparently, although they must have punched pipes and wires and heating ducts through all sorts of puzzling spaces.

This was the secret: There was a mansion concealed within the mansion. It could be entered through trap doors and sliding panels. It consisted of secret staircases and listening posts with peepholes, and secret passageways. There were tunnels, too.

It was actually possible for Eliza and me, for example, to vanish into a huge grandfather clock in the ballroom at the top of the northernmost tower, and to emerge almost a kilometer away—through a trap door in the floor of the mausoleum of Professor Elihu Roosevelt Swain.

◆◆◆

We shared another secret with the Professor, too— which we learned from going through some of his papers in the mansion. His middle name hadn't actually been *Roosevelt*. He had given himself that middle name in order to seem more aristocratic when he enrolled as a student at M.I.T.

His name on his baptismal certificate was Elihu Witherspoon Swain.

It was from his example, I suppose, that Eliza and I got the idea, eventually, of giving simply everybody new middle names.

◆◆◆

Chapter 4

◆◆◆◆◆◆◆◆◆◆

WHEN Professor Swain
died, he was so fat that I do not see how he could
have fitted into any of his secret passageways. They
were very narrow. Eliza and I were able to fit into
them, however, even when we were two meters tall
—because the ceilings were so high—

Yes, and Professor Swain died of his fatness in the
mansion, at a dinner he gave in honor of Samuel
Langhorne Clemens and Thomas Alva Edison.

Those were the days.

Eliza and I found the menu. It began with turtle
soup.

Our servants would tell each other now and then that the mansion was haunted. They heard sneezing and cackling in the walls, and the creaking of stairways where there were no stairways, and the opening and shutting of doors where there were no doors.

Hi ho.

It would be exciting for me to cry out, as a crazed old centenarian in the ruins of Manhattan, that Eliza and I were subjected to acts of unspeakable cruelty in that spooky old house. But we may have in fact been the two happiest children that history has so far known.

That ecstasy would not end until our fifteenth year. Think of that.

Yes, and when I became a pediatrician, practicing rural medicine in the mansion where I was raised, I often told myself about this childish patient or that one, remembering my own childhood: "This person has just arrived on this planet, knows nothing about it, has no standards by which to judge it. This person does not care what it becomes. It is eager to become absolutely anything it is supposed to be."

That surely describes the state of mind of Eliza and me, when we were very young. And all the information we received about the planet we were on indicated that idiots were lovely things to be.

So we cultivated idiocy.

We refused to speak coherently in public. "Buh," and, "Duh," we said. We drooled and rolled our eyes. We farted and laughed. We ate library paste.

Hi ho.

❖❖❖

Consider: We were at the center of the lives of those who cared for us. They could be heroically Christian in their own eyes only if Eliza and I remained help-less and vile. If we became openly wise and self-reliant, they would become our drab and inferior assistants. If we became capable of going out into the world, they might lose their apartments, their color televisions, their illusions of being sorts of doctors and nurses, and their high-paying jobs.

So, from the very first, and without quite knowing what they were doing, I am sure, they begged us a thousand times a day to go on being helpless and vile.

There was only one small advancement they wished us to make up the ladder of human achieve-ments. They hoped with all their hearts that we would become toilet-trained.

Again: We were glad to comply.

❖❖❖

But we could secretly read and write English by the time we were four. We could read and write French, German, Italian, Latin and ancient Greek by the time we were seven, and do calculus, too.

There were thousands of books in the mansion. By the time we were ten, we had read them all by candlelight, at naptime or after bedtime—in secret passageways, or often in the mausoleum of Elihu Roosevelt Swain.

◆◆◆

But we continued to drool and babble and so on, whenever grownups were around. It was fun.

We did not itch to display our intelligence in public. We did not think of intelligence as being useful or attractive in any way. We thought of it as being simply one more example of our freakishness, like our extra nipples and fingers and toes.

And we may have been right at that. You know? Hi ho.

◆◆◆

Chapter 5

❖❖❖❖❖❖❖❖❖

AND meanwhile the strange young Dr. Stewart Rawlings Mott weighed us and measured us, and peered into our orifices, and took samples of our urine—day after day after day.

"How is everybody today?" he would say.

We would tell him "Bluh" and "Duh," and so on. We called him "Flocka Butt."

And we ourselves did all we could to make each day exactly like the one before. Whenever "Flocka Butt" congratulated us on our healthy appetites and regular bowel movements, for example, I would invariably stick my thumbs in my ears and waggle my fingers, and Eliza would hoist her skirt and snap the elastic at the waist of her pantyhose.

Eliza and I believed then what I believe even now: That life can be painless, provided that there is sufficient peacefulness for a dozen or so rituals to be repeated simply endlessly.

Life, ideally, I think, should be like the Minuet or the Virginia Reel or the Turkey Trot, something easily mastered in a dancing school.

◆◆◆

I teeter even now between thinking that Dr. Mott loved Eliza and me, and knew how smart we were, and wished to protect us from the cruelties of the outside world, and thinking that he was comatose.

After Mother died, I discovered that the linen chest at the foot of her bed was crammed with packets of Dr. Mott's bi-weekly reports on the health of Eliza and me. He told of the ever-greater quantities of food being consumed and then excreted. He spoke, too, of our unflagging cheerfulness, and our natural resistance to common diseases of childhood.

The sorts of things he reported, in fact, were the sorts of things a carpenter's helper would have had no trouble detecting—such as that, at the age of nine, Eliza and I were over two meters tall.

No matter how large Eliza and I became, though, one figure remained constant in his reports: Our mental age was between two and three.

Hi ho.

◆◆◆

"Flocka Butt," along with my sister, of course, is one of the few people I am really hungry to see in the afterlife.

I am dying to ask him what he really thought of us as children—how much he suspected, how much he really knew.

◆◆◆

Eliza and I must have given him thousands of clues as to our intelligence. We weren't the cleverest of deceivers. We were only children, after all.

It seems probable to me that, when we babbled in his presence, we used words from some foreign language which he could recognize. He may have gone into the library of the mansion, which was of no interest to the servants, and found the books somehow disturbed.

He may have discovered the secret passageways himself, through some accident. He used to wander around the house a great deal after he was through with us, I know, explaining to the servants that his father was an architect. He may have actually gone into the secret passageways, and found books we were reading in there, and seen that the floors were spattered with candlewax.

Who knows?

◆◆◆

I would like to know, too, what his secret sorrow was. Eliza and I, when we were young, were so wrapped up in each other that we rarely noticed the emotional condition of anybody else. But we were surely impressed by Dr. Mott's sadness. So it must have been profound.

◆◆◆

I once asked his grandson, the King of Michigan, Stewart Oriole-2 Mott, if he had any idea why Dr. Mott had found life to be such a crushing affair. "Gravity hadn't yet turned mean," I said. "The sky had not yet turned from blue to yellow, never to be blue again. The planet's natural resources had yet to come to an end. The country had not yet been depopulated by Albanian flu and The Green Death.

"Your grandfather had a nice little car and a nice little house and a nice little practice and a nice little wife and a nice little child," I said to the King. "And yet he used to *mope* so!"

My interview with the King took place, incidentally, in his palace on Lake Maxinkuckee, in northern Indiana, where Culver Military Academy had once stood. I was still nominally the President of the United States of America, but I had lost control of everything. There wasn't any Congress any more, or any system of Federal Courts, or any Treasury or Army or any of that.

There were probably only eight hundred people left in all of Washington, D.C. I was down to one employee when I paid my respects to the King.

Hi ho.

◆◆◆

He asked me if I regarded him as an enemy, and I said, "Heavens, no, Your Highness—I am delighted that someone of your calibre has brought law and order to the Middle West."

◆◆◆

He grew impatient with me when I pressed him to tell me more about his grandfather, Dr. Mott.

"Christ," he said, "what American knows anything about his grandparents?"

◆◆◆

He was a skinny and supple and ascetic young soldier-saint in those days. My granddaughter, Melody, would come to know him when he was an obscene voluptuary, a fat old man in robes encrusted with precious stones.

◆◆◆

He was wearing a simple soldier's tunic without any badges of rank when I met him.

As for my own costume: It was appropriately clownish—a top hat, a claw-hammer coat and striped pants, a pearl-gray vest with matching spats, a soiled white shirt with a choke collar and tie. The belly of my vest was festooned with a gold watch-chain which had belonged to John D. Rockefeller, the ancestor of mine who had founded Standard Oil.

Dangling from the watch-chain were my Phi Beta Kappa key from Harvard and a miniature plastic daffodil. My middle name had by then been legally changed from *Rockefeller* to *Daffodil-11*.

"There were no murders or embezzlements or suicides or drinking problems or drug problems in Dr. Mott's branch of the family," the King went on, "as far as I know."

He was thirty. I was seventy-nine.

"Maybe Grandfather was just one of those people who was *born* unhappy," he said. "Did you ever think of that?"

❖❖❖

Chapter 6

✦✦✦✦✦✦✦✦✦

PERHAPS some people really are born unhappy. I surely hope not.

Speaking for my sister and myself: We were born with the capacity and the determination to be utterly happy all the time.

Perhaps even in this we were freaks.

Hi ho.

◆◆◆

What is happiness?

In Eliza's and my case, happiness was being perpetually in each other's company, having plenty of servants and good food, living in a peaceful, book-filled mansion on an asteroid covered with apple trees, and growing up as specialized halves of a single brain.

Although we pawed and embraced each other a great deal, our intentions were purely intellectual. True—Eliza matured sexually at the age of seven. I, however, would not enter puberty until my last year in Harvard Medical School, at the age of twenty-three. Eliza and I used bodily contact only in order to increase the intimacy of our brains.

Thus did we give birth to a single genius, which died as quickly as we were parted, which was reborn the moment we got together again.

◆◆◆

We became almost cripplingly specialized as halves of that genius, which was the most important individual in our lives, but which we never named.

When we learned to read and write, for example, it was I who actually did the reading and writing. Eliza remained illiterate until the day she died.

But it was Eliza who did the great intuitive leaping for us both. It was Eliza who guessed that it would be in our best interests to remain speechless, but to become toilet-trained. It was Eliza who guessed what books were, and what the little marks on the pages might mean.

It was Eliza who sensed that there was something cockeyed about the dimensions of some of the mansion's rooms and corridors. And it was I who did the methodical work of taking actual measurements, and then probing the paneling and parquetry with screwdrivers and kitchen knives, seeking doors to an alternate universe, which we found.

Hi ho.

◆◆◆

Yes, I did all the reading. And it seems to me now that there is not a single book published in an Indo-European language before the First World War that I have not read aloud.

But it was Eliza who did the memorizing, and who told me what we had to learn next. And it was Eliza who could put seemingly unrelated ideas together in order to get a new one. It was Eliza who *juxtaposed.*

◆◆◆

Much of our information was hopelessly out of date, of course, since few new books had been brought into the mansion since 1912. Much of it, too, was timeless. And much of it was downright silly, such as the dances we learned to do.

If I wished, I could do a very presentable and historically accurate version of the Tarantella, here in the ruins of New York.

◆◆◆

Were Eliza and I really a genius, when we thought as one?

I have to say yes, especially in view of the fact that

we had no instructors. And I am not boasting when I say so, for I am only half of that fine mind.

We criticized Darwin's Theory of Evolution, I remember, on the grounds the creatures would become terribly vulnerable while attempting to improve themselves, while developing wings or armorplate, say. They would be eaten up by more practical animals, before their wonderful new features could be refined.

We made at least one prediction that was so deadly accurate that thinking about it even now leaves me thunderstruck.

Listen: We began with the mystery of how ancient peoples had erected the pyramids of Egypt and Mexico, and the great heads of Easter Island, and the barbaric arches of Stonehenge, without modern power sources and tools.

We concluded there must have been days of light gravity in olden times, when people could play tiddledy winks with huge chunks of stone.

We supposed that it might even be abnormal on earth for gravity to be stable for long periods of time. We predicted that at any moment gravity might become as capricious as winds and heat and cold, as blizzards and rainstorms again.

◆◆◆

Yes, and Eliza and I composed a precocious critique of the Constitution of the United States of America, too. We argued that it was as good a scheme for misery as any, since its success in keeping the common people reasonably happy and proud depended on the strength of the people themselves—and yet it described no practical machinery which would tend to make the people, as opposed to their elected representatives, strong.

We said it was possible that the framers of the Constitution were blind to the beauty of persons who were without great wealth or powerful friends or public office, but who were nonetheless genuinely strong.

We thought it was more likely, though, that the framers had not noticed that it was natural, and therefore almost inevitable, that human beings in extraordinary and enduring situations should think of themselves as composing new families. Eliza and I pointed out that this happened no less in democracies than in tyrannies, since human beings were the same the wide world over, and civilized only yesterday.

Elected representatives, hence, could be expected to become members of the famous and powerful family of elected representatives—which would, perfectly naturally, make them wary and squeamish and stingy with respect to all the other sorts of families which, again, perfectly naturally, subdivided mankind.

Eliza and I, thinking as halves of a single genius, proposed that the Constitution be amended so as to guarantee that every citizen, no matter how humble or crazy or incompetent or deformed, somehow be given membership in some family as covertly xenophobic and crafty as the one their public servants formed.

Good for Eliza and me!

◆◆◆

Hi ho.

◆◆◆

Chapter 7

◆◆◆◆◆◆◆◆◆

How nice it would have been, especially for Eliza, since she was a girl, if we had been ugly ducklings—if we had become beautiful by and by. But we simply grew more preposterous with each passing day.

There were a few advantages to being a male 2 meters tall. I was respected as a basketball player at prep school and college, even though I had very narrow shoulders and a voice like a piccolo, and not the first hints of a beard or pubic hair. Yes, and later on, after my voice had deepened and I ran as a candidate for Senator from Vermont, I was able to say on my billboards, "It takes a Big Man to do a Big Job!"

55

But Eliza, who was exactly as tall as I was, could not expect to be welcomed anywhere. There was no conceivable conventional role for a female which could be bent so as to accommodate a twelve-fingered, twelve-toed, four-breasted, Neanderthaloid half-genius—weighing one quintal, and two meters tall.

◆◆◆

Even as little children we knew we weren't ever going to win any beauty contests.

Eliza said something prophetic about that, incidentally. She couldn't have been more than eight. She said that maybe she could win a beauty contest on Mars.

She was, of course, destined to *die* on Mars.

Eliza's beauty prize there would be an avalanche of iron pyrite, better known as "Fool's Gold."

Hi ho.

◆◆◆

There was a time in our childhood when we actually agreed that we were *lucky* not to be beautiful. We knew from all the romantic novels I'd read out loud in my squeaky voice, often with gestures, that beautiful people had their privacy destroyed by passionate strangers.

We didn't want that to happen to us, since the two of us alone composed not only a single mind but a thoroughly populated Universe.

♦♦♦

This much I must say about our appearance, at least: Our clothing was the finest that money could buy. Our astonishing dimensions, which changed radically almost from month to month, were mailed off regularly, in accordance with our parents' instructions, to some of the finest tailors and cobblers and dressmakers and shirtmakers and haberdashers in the world.

The practical nurses who dressed and undressed us took a childish delight, even though we never went anywhere, in costuming us for imaginary social events for millionaires—for tea dances, for horse shows, for skiing vacations, for attending classes at expensive prep schools, for an evening of theater here in Manhattan and a supper afterwards with lots of champagne.

And so on.

Hi ho.

♦♦♦

We were aware of all the comedy in this. But, as brilliant as we were when we put our heads together, we did not guess until we were fifteen that we were also in the midst of a tragedy. We thought that ugliness was simply amusing to people in the outside world. We did not realize that we could actually nauseate strangers who came upon us unexpectedly.

We were so innocent as to the importance of good

looks, in fact, that we could see little point to the story of "The Ugly Duckling," which I read out loud to Eliza one day—in the mausoleum of Professor Elihu Roosevelt Swain.

The story, of course, was about a baby bird that was raised by ducks, who thought it was the funniest-looking duck they had ever seen. But then it turned out to be a swan when it grew up.

Eliza, I remember, said she thought it would have been a much better story if the little bird had waddled up on shore and turned into a rhinoceros.

Hi ho.

◆◆◆

Chapter 8

◆◆◆◆◆◆◆◆◆◆◆

UNTIL the eve of our fifteenth birthday, Eliza and I never heard anything bad about ourselves when we eavesdropped from the secret passageways.

The servants were so used to us that they hardly ever mentioned us, even in moments of deepest privacy. Dr. Mott seldom commented on anything but our appetites and our excretions. And our parents were so sickened by us that they were tongue-tied when they made their annual space voyage to our asteroid. Father, I remember, would talk to Mother rather haltingly and listlessly about world events he had read about in news magazines.

They would bring us toys from F.A.O. Schwarz—

guaranteed by that emporium to be educational for three-year-olds.

Hi ho.

◆◆◆

Yes, and I think now about all the secrets about the human condition I withhold from young Melody and Isadore, for their own peace of mind—the fact that the human afterlife is no good, and so on.

And then I am awed yet again by the perfect Lulu of a secret that was concealed from Eliza and me so long: That our own parents wished we would hurry up and die.

◆◆◆

We imagined lazily that our fifteenth birthday would be like all the rest. We put on the show we had always put on. Our parents arrived at our suppertime, which was four in the afternoon. We would get our presents the next day.

We threw food at each other in our tile-lined diningroom. I hit Eliza with an avocado. She hit me with a filet mignon. We bounced Parker House rolls off the maid. We pretended not to know that our parents had arrived and were watching us through a crack in the door.

Yes, and then, still not having greeted our parents face-to-face, we were bathed and talcumed, and dressed in our pajamas and bathrobes and bedroom slippers. Bedtime was at five, for Eliza and I pretended to sleep sixteen hours a day.

Our practical nurses, who were Oveta Cooper and Mary Selwyn Kirk, told us that there was a wonderful surprise waiting for us in the library.

We pretended to be gaga about what that surprise could possibly be.

We were full-grown giants by then.

I carried a rubber tugboat, which was supposedly my favorite toy. Eliza had a red velvet ribbon in the mare's nest of her coal black hair.

◆◆◆

As always, there was a large coffee table between Eliza and me and our parents when we were brought in. As always, our parents had brandy to sip. As always, there was a fizzing, popping blaze of pine and sappy apple logs in the fireplace. As always, an oil painting of Professor Elihu Roosevelt Swain over the mantelpiece beamed down on the ritual scene.

As always, our parents stood. They smiled up at us with what we still did not recognize as bittersweet dread.

As always, we pretended to find them adorable, but not to remember who they were at first.

◆◆◆

As always, Father did the talking.

"How do you do, Eliza and Wilbur?" he said. "You are looking very well. We are very glad to see you. Do you remember who we are?"

Eliza and I consulted with one another uneasily, drooling, and murmuring in ancient Greek. Eliza

61

said to me in Greek, I remember, that she could not believe that we were related to such pretty dolls.

Father helped us out. He told us the name we had given to him years ago. "I am Bluth-luh," he said.

Eliza and I pretended to be flabbergasted. "Bluth-luh!" we told each other. We could not believe our good fortune. "Bluth-luh! Bluth-luh!" we cried.

"And this," said Father, indicating Mother, "is Mub-lub."

This was even more sensational news to Eliza and me. "Mub-lub! Mub-lub!" we exclaimed.

And now Eliza and I made a great intellectual leap, as always. Without any hints from anybody, we concluded that, if our parents were in the house, then our birthday must be close at hand. We chanted our idiot word for birthday, which was "Fuff-bay."

As always, we pretended to become overexcited. We jumped up and down. We were so big by then that the floor began to go up and down like a trampoline.

But we suddenly stopped, pretending, as always, to have been rendered catatonic by more happiness than was good for us.

That was always the end of the show. After that, we were led away.

Hi ho.

◆◆◆

Chapter 9

❖❖❖❖❖❖❖❖❖

WE were put into custom-made cribs—in separate but adjacent bedrooms. The rooms were connected by a secret panel in the wall. The cribs were as big as railroad flatcars. They made a terrible clatter when their sides were raised.

Eliza and I pretended to fall asleep at once. After a half an hour, however, we were reunited in Eliza's room. The servants never looked in on us. Our health was perfect, after all, and we had established a reputation for being, as they said, ". . . as good as gold at bedtime."

Yes, and we went through a trapdoor under Eliza's crib, and were soon taking turns watching our parents in the library—through a tiny hole we ourselves had drilled through the wall, and through the upper corner of the frame around the painting of Professor Elihu Roosevelt Swain.

◆◆◆

Father was telling mother of a thing he had read in a news magazine on the day before. It seemed that scientists in the People's Republic of China were experimenting with making human beings smaller, so they would not need to eat so much and wear such big clothes.

Mother was staring into the fire. Father had to tell her twice about the Chinese rumor. The second time he did it, she replied emptily that she supposed that the Chinese could accomplish just about anything they put their minds to.

Only about a month before, the Chinese had sent two hundred explorers to Mars—without using a space vehicle of any kind.

No scientist in the Western World could guess how the trick was done. The Chinese themselves volunteered no details.

◆◆◆

Mother said that it seemed like such a long time since Americans had discovered anything. "All of a sudden," she said, "everything is being discovered by the Chinese."

◆◆◆

"We used to discover everything," she said.

◆◆◆

It was such a *stupefied* conversation. The level of animation was so low that our beautiful young parents from Manhattan might have been up to their necks in honey. They appeared, as they had always appeared to Eliza and me, to be under some curse which required them to speak only of matters which did not interest them at all.

And indeed they *were* under a malediction. But Eliza and I had not guessed its nature: That they were all but strangled and paralyzed by the wish that their own children would die.

And I promise this about our parents, although the only proof I have is a feeling in my bones: Neither one had ever suggested in any way to the other that he or she wished we would die.

Hi ho.

◆◆◆

But then there was a *bang* in the fireplace. Steam had to escape from a trap in a sappy log.

Yes, and Mother, because she was a symphony of chemical reactions like all other living things, gave a terrified shriek. Her chemicals insisted that she shriek in response to the *bang*.

After the chemicals got her to do that, though, they wanted a lot more from her. They thought it was high time she said what she really felt about Eliza and me, which she did. All sorts of other things went haywire when she said it. Her hands closed convulsively. Her spine buckled and her face shriveled to turn her into an old, old witch.

"I hate them, I hate them, I hate them," she said.

◆◆◆

And not many seconds passed before Mother said with spitting explicitness who it was she hated.

"I hate Wilbur Rockefeller Swain and Eliza Mellon Swain," she said.

◆◆◆

Chapter 10

❖❖❖❖❖❖❖❖❖❖

MOTHER was temporarily insane that night.

I got to know her well in later years. And, while I never learned to love her, or to love anyone, for that matter, I did admire her unwavering decency toward one and all. She was not a mistress of insults. When she spoke either in public or in private, no reputations died.

So it was not truly our mother who said on the eve of our fifteenth birthday, "How can I love Count Dracula and his blushing bride?"—meaning Eliza and me.

It was not truly our mother who asked our father, "How on Earth did I ever give birth to a pair of drooling totem poles?"

And so on.

◆◆◆

As for Father: He engulfed her in his arms. He was weeping with love and pity.

"Caleb, oh Caleb—" she said in his arms, "this isn't me."

"Of course not," he said.

"Forgive me," she said.

"Of course," he said.

"Will God ever forgive me?" she said.

"He already has," he said.

"It was as though a devil all of a sudden got inside of me," she said.

"That's what it was, Tish," he said.

Her madness was subsiding now. "Oh, Caleb—" she said.

◆◆◆

Lest I seem to be fishing for sympathy, let me say right now that Eliza and I in those days were about as emotionally vulnerable as the Great Stone Face in New Hampshire.

We needed a mother's and father's love about

as much as a fish needs a bicycle, as the saying goes.

So when our mother spoke badly of us, even wished we would die, our response was intellectual. We enjoyed solving problems. Perhaps Mother's problem was one we could solve—short of suicide, of course.

She pulled herself together again eventually. She steeled herself for another hundred birthdays with Eliza and me, in case God wished to test her in that way. But, before she did that, she said this:

"I would give anything, Caleb, for the faintest sign of intelligence, the merest flicker of humanness in the eyes of either twin."

◆◆◆

This was easily arranged.

Hi ho.

◆◆◆

So Eliza and I went back to Eliza's room, and we painted a big sign on a bedsheet. Then, after our parents were sound asleep, we stole into their room through the false back in an armoire. We hung the sign on the wall, so it would be the first thing they saw when they woke up.

This is what it said:

DEAR MATER AND PATER: WE CAN NEVER BE PRETTY
BUT WE CAN BE AS SMART OR AS DUMB AS THE WORLD
REALLY WANTS US TO BE.
>YOUR FAITHFUL SERVANTS,
>ELIZA MELLON SWAIN
>WILBUR ROCKEFELLER SWAIN

Hi ho.

Chapter 11

◆◆◆◆◆◆◆◆◆◆◆

Thus did Eliza and I destroy our Paradise—our nation of two.

◆◆◆

We arose the next morning before our parents did, before the servants could come to dress us. We sensed no danger. We supposed ourselves still to be in Paradise as we dressed ourselves.

I chose to wear a conservative blue, pinstripe, three-piece suit, I remember. Eliza chose to wear a cashmere sweater, a tweed skirt, and pearls.

We agreed that Eliza should be our spokesman at first, since she had a rich alto voice. My voice did not have the authority to announce calmingly but con-

71

vincingly that, in effect, the world had just turned upside down.

Remember, please, that almost all that anyone had ever heard us say up to then was "Buh" and "Duh," and so on.

Now we encountered Oveta Cooper, our practical nurse, in the colonnaded green marble foyer. She was startled to see us up and dressed.

Before she could comment on this, though, Eliza and I leaned our heads together, put them in actual contact, just above our ears. The single genius we composed thereby then spoke to Oveta in Eliza's voice, which was as lovely as a viola.

This is what that voice said:

"Good morning, Oveta. A new life begins for all of us today. As you can see and hear, Wilbur and I are no longer idiots. A miracle has taken place overnight. Our parents' dreams have come true. We are healed.

"As for you, Oveta: You will keep your apartment and your color television, and perhaps even receive a salary increase—as a reward for all you did to make this miracle come to pass. No one on the staff will experience any change, except for this one: Life here will become even easier and more pleasant than it was before."

Oveta, a bleak, Yankee dumpling, was hypnotized —like a rabbit who has met a rattlesnake. But Eliza and I were not a rattlesnake. With our heads together, we were one of the gentlest geniuses the world has ever known.

◆◆◆

"We will not be using the tiled diningroom any more," said Eliza's voice. "We have lovely manners, as you shall see. Please have our breakfast served in the solarium, and notify us when Mater and Pater are up and around. It would be very nice if, from now on, you would address my brother and me as 'Master Wilbur' and 'Mistress Eliza.'

"You may go now, and tell the others about the miracle."

Oveta remained transfixed. I at last had to snap my fingers under her nose to wake her up.

She curtseyed. "As you wish, Mistress Eliza," she said. And she went to spread the news.

◆◆◆

As we settled ourselves in the solarium, the rest of the staff straggled in humbly—to have a look at the young master and the young mistress we had become.

We greeted them by their full names. We asked them friendly questions which indicated that we had a detailed understanding of their lives. We apologized for having perhaps shocked some of them for changing so quickly.

"We simply did not realize," Eliza said, "that anybody *wanted* us to be intelligent."

We were by then so in charge of things that I, too, dared to speak of important matters. My high voice wouldn't be silly any more.

"With your cooperation," I said, "we will make this mansion famous for intelligence as it has been infamous for idiocy in days gone by. Let the fences come down."

"Are there any questions?" said Eliza.

There were none.

◆◆◆

Somebody called Dr. Mott.

◆◆◆

Our mother did not come down to breakfast. She remained in bed—petrified.

Father came down alone. He was wearing his nightclothes. He had not shaved. Young as he was, he was palsied and drawn.

Eliza and I were puzzled that he did not look happier. We hailed him not only in English, but in several other languages we knew.

It was to one of these foreign salutations that he responded at last. "Bon jour," he said.

"Sit thee doon! Sit thee doon!" said Eliza merrily.

The poor man sat.

◆◆◆

He was sick with guilt, of course, over having allowed intelligent human beings, his own flesh and blood, to be treated like idiots for so long.

Worse: His conscience and his advisors had told him before that it was all right if he could not love us, since we were incapable of deep feelings, and since there was nothing about us, objectively, that anyone in his right mind *could* love. But now it was his *duty* to love us, and he did not think he could do it.

He was horrified to discover what our mother knew she would discover, if she came downstairs: That intelligence and sensitivity in monstrous bodies like Eliza's and mine merely made us more repulsive.

This was not Father's fault or Mother's fault. It was not anybody's fault. It was as natural as breathing to all human beings, and to all warm-blooded creatures, for that matter, to wish quick deaths for monsters. This was an instinct.

And now Eliza and I had raised that instinct to intolerable tragedy.

Without knowing what we were doing, Eliza and I were putting the traditional curse of monsters on normal creatures. We were asking for respect.

❖❖❖

Chapter 12

❖❖❖❖❖❖❖❖

IN the midst of all the excitement, Eliza and I allowed our heads to be separated by several feet—so we were not thinking brilliantly any more.

We became dumb enough to think that Father was merely sleepy. So we made him drink coffee, and we tried to wake him up with some songs and riddles we knew.

I remember I asked him if he knew why cream was so much more expensive than milk.

He mumbled that he didn't know the answer.

So Eliza told him, "It's because the cows hate to squat on the little bottles."

We laughed about that. We rolled on the floor. And

then Eliza got up and stood over him, with her hands on her hips, and scolded him affectionately, as though he were a little boy. "Oh, what a sleepy-head!" she said. "Oh, what a sleepy-head!"

At that moment, Dr. Stewart Rawlings Mott arrived.

◆◆◆

Although Dr. Mott had been told on the telephone about Eliza's and my sudden metamorphosis, the day was like any other day to him, seemingly. He said what he always said when he arrived at the mansion: "And how is everybody today?"

I now spoke the first intelligent sentence Dr. Mott had ever heard from me. "Father won't wake up," I said.

"Won't he, now?" he replied. He rewarded the completeness of my sentence with the faintest of smiles.

Dr. Mott was so unbelievably bland, in fact, that he turned away from us to chat with Oveta Cooper, the practical nurse. Her mother had apparently been sick down in the hamlet. "Oveta—" he said, "you'll be pleased to know that your mother's temperature is almost normal."

Father was angered by this casualness, and no doubt glad to find someone with whom he could be openly angry.

"How long has this been going on, Doctor?" he wanted to know. "How long have you known about their intelligence?"

Dr. Mott looked at his watch. "Since about forty-two minutes ago," he said.

"You don't seem in the least surprised," said Father.

Dr. Mott appeared to think this over, then he shrugged. "I'm certainly very *happy* for everybody," he said.

I think it was the fact that Dr. Mott himself did not look at all happy when he said that which caused Eliza and me to put our heads together again. Something very queer was going on that we badly needed to understand.

◆◆◆

Our genius did not fail us. It allowed us to understand the truth of the situation—that we were somehow more tragic than ever.

But our genius, like all geniuses, suffered periodic fits of monumental naïveté. It did so now. It told us that all we had to do to make everything all right again was to return to idiocy.

"Buh," said Eliza.

"Duh," I said.

I farted.

Eliza drooled.

I picked up a buttered scone and threw it at the head of Oveta Cooper.

Eliza turned to Father. "Bluth-luh!" she said.

"Fuff-bay!" I cried.

Father cried.

◆◆◆

Chapter 13

◆◆◆◆◆◆◆◆◆◆

SIX days have passed since I began to write this memoir. On four of the days, the gravity was medium—what it used to be in olden times. It was so heavy yesterday, that I could hardly get out of bed, out of my nest of rags in the lobby of the Empire State Building. When I had to go to the elevator shaft we use for a toilet, making my way through the thicket of candlesticks I own, I crawled on all fours.

Hi ho.

Well—the gravity was light on the first day, and it is light again today. I have an erection again, and so does Isadore, the lover of my granddaughter Melody. So does every male on the island.

◆◆◆

Yes, and Melody and Isadore have packed a picnic lunch, and have gone bounding up to the intersection of Broadway and Forty-second Street, where, on days of light gravity, they are building a rustic pyramid.

They do not shape the slabs and chunks and boulders they put into it, and neither do they limit their materials to masonry. They throw in I-beams and oil drums and tires and automobile parts and office furniture and theater seats, too, and all manner of junk. But I have seen the results, and what they are building will not be an amorphous trash-pile when it is done. It will clearly be a pyramid.

◆◆◆

Yes, and if archaeologists of the future find this book of mine, they will be spared the fruitless labor of digging through the pyramid in search of its meaning. There are no secret treasure rooms in there, no chambers of any kind.

Its meaning, which is minuscule in any event, lies beneath the manhole cover over which the pyramid is constructed. It is the body of a stillborn male.

The infant is enclosed in an ornate box which was once a humidor for fine cigars. That box was placed on the floor of the manhole four years ago, amid all the cables and pipes down there—by Melody, who was its mother at the age of twelve, and by me, who was its great-grandfather, and by our nearest neighbor and dearest friend, Vera Chipmunk-5 Zappa.

The pyramid itself is entirely the idea of Melody and Isadore, who became her lover later on. It is a monument to a life that was never lived—to a person who was never named.

Hi ho.

◆◆◆

It is not necessary to dig through the pyramid to reach the box. It can be reached through other manholes.

Beware of rats.

◆◆◆

Since the infant was an heir of mine, the pyramid might be called this: "The Tomb of the Prince of Candlesticks."

◆◆◆

The name of the father of the Prince of Candlesticks is unknown. He forced his attentions on Melody on the outskirts of Schenectady. She was on her way from Detroit, in the Kingdom of Michigan, to the Island of Death, where she hoped to find her grandfather, who was the legendary Dr. Wilbur Daffodil-11 Swain.

◆◆◆

Melody is pregnant again—this time by Isadore.

She is a bow-legged little thing, rickety and snaggle-toothed, but cheerful. She ate very badly as a child—as an orphan in the harem of the King of Michigan.

Melody sometimes looks to me like a merry old Chinese woman, although she is only sixteen. A pregnant girl who looks like that is a sad thing for a pediatrician to see.

But the love that the robust and rosy Isadore gives her counterbalances my sadness with joy. Like almost all the members of his family, the Raspberries, Isadore has nearly all his teeth, and remains upright even when the gravity is most severe. He carries Melody around in his arms on days like that, and has offered to carry me.

The Raspberries are food-gatherers, mainly, living in and around the ruins of the New York Stock Exchange. They fish off docks. They mine for canned goods. They pick fruits and berries they find. They grow their own tomatoes and potatoes, and radishes, and little more.

They trap rats and bats and dogs and cats and birds, and eat them. A Raspberry will eat anything.

◆◆◆

Chapter 14

◆◆◆◆◆◆◆◆◆◆

I wish Melody what our parents once wished Eliza and me: A short but happy life on an asteroid.

Hi ho.

◆◆◆

Yes, and I have already said, Eliza and I might have had a long and happy life on an asteroid, if we had not showed off our intelligence one day. We might have been in the mansion still, burning the trees and the furniture and the bannisters and the paneling for warmth, and drooling and babbling when strangers came.

We could have raised chickens. We could have had a little vegetable garden. And we could have amused ourselves with our ever-increasing wisdom, caring nothing for its possible usefulness.

◆◆◆

The sun is going down. Thin clouds of bats stream out from the subway—jittering, squeaking, dispersing like gas. As always, I shudder.

I can't think of their noise as a noise. It is a disease of silence instead.

◆◆◆

I write on—in the light of a burning rag in a bowl of animal fat.

I have a thousand candlesticks, but no candles.

Melody and Isadore play backgammon—on a board I painted on the lobby floor.

They double and redouble each other, and laugh.

◆◆◆

They are planning a party for my one hundred and first birthday, which is a month away.

I eavesdrop on them sometimes. Old habits are hard to break. Vera Chipmunk-5 Zappa is making new costumes for the occasion—for herself and her slaves. She has mountains of cloth in her storerooms in Turtle Bay. The slaves will wear pink pantaloons and golden slippers, and green silk turbans with ostrich feather plumes, I heard Melody say.

Vera will be borne to the party in a sedan chair, I've heard, surrounded by slaves carrying presents and food and drink and torches, and frightening away wild dogs with the clangor of dinnerbells.

Hi ho.

◆◆◆

I must be very careful with my drinking at my birthday party. If I drank too much, I might spill the beans to everybody: That the life that awaits us after death is infinitely more tiresome than this one.

Hi ho.

◆◆◆

Chapter 15

◆◆◆◆◆◆◆◆◆◆◆

ELIZA and I were of course not allowed to return to consolations of idiocy. We were bawled out severely whenever we tried. Yes, and the servants and our parents found one by-product of our metamorphosis positively delicious: They were suddenly entitled to bawl us out.

What hell we caught from time to time!

◆◆◆

Yes, and Dr. Mott was fired, and all sorts of experts were brought in.

It was fun for a while. The first doctors to arrive were specialists in hearts and lungs and kidneys and so on. When they studied us organ by organ and body fluid by body fluid, we were masterpieces of health.

They were genial. They were all family employees in a way. They were research people whose work was financed by the Swain Foundation in New York. That was how they had been so easily rounded up and brought to Galen. The family had helped them. Now they would help the family.

They joshed us a lot. One of them, I remember, said to me that it must be fun to be so tall. "What's the weather up there like?" he said, and so on.

The joshing had a soothing effect. It gave us the mistaken impression that it did not matter how ugly we were. I still remember what an ear, nose and throat specialist said when he looked up into Eliza's enormous sinus cavities with a flashlight. "My God, nurse—" he said, "call up the National Geographic Society. We have just discovered a new entrance to Mammoth Cave!"

Eliza laughed. The nurse laughed. I laughed. We all laughed.

Our parents were in another part of the mansion. They kept away from all the fun.

◆◆◆

That early in the game, though, we had our first disturbing tastes of separation. Some of the examinations required that we be several rooms apart. As the distance between Eliza and me increased, I felt as though my head were turning to wood.

I became stupid and insecure.

When I was reunited with Eliza, she said that she had felt very much the same sort of thing. "It was as though my skull was filling up with maple syrup," she said.

And we bravely tried to be amused rather than

frightened by the listless children we became when we were parted. We pretended they had nothing to do with us, and we made up names for them. We called them "Betty and Bobby Brown."

◆◆◆

And now is as good a time as any, I think, to say that when we read Eliza's will, after her death in a Martian avalanche, we learned that she wished to be buried wherever she died. Her grave was to be marked with a simple stone, engraved with this information and nothing more:

Yes, and it was the last specialist to look us over, a psychologist, Dr. Cordelia Swain Cordiner, who decreed that Eliza and I should be separated permanently, should, so to speak, become forever Betty and Bobby Brown.

Chapter 16

FĒDOR Mikhailovich Dostoevski, the Russian novelist, said one time that, "One sacred memory from childhood is perhaps the best education." I can think of another quickie education for a child, which, in its way, is almost as salutary: Meeting a human being who is tremendously respected by the adult world, and realizing that that person is actually a malicious lunatic.

That was Eliza's and my experience with Dr. Cordelia Swain Cordiner, who was widely believed to be the greatest expert on psychological testing in the world—with the possible exception of China. Nobody knew what was going on in China any more.

◆◆◆

I have an Encyclopaedia Britannica here in the lobby of the Empire State Building, which is the reason I am able to give Dostoevski his middle name.

◆◆◆

Dr. Cordelia Swain Cordiner was invariably impressive and gracious when in the presence of grownups. She was elaborately dressed the whole time she was in the mansion—in high-heeled shoes and fancy dresses and jewelry.

We heard her tell our parents one time: "Just because a woman has three doctors' degrees and heads a testing corporation which bills three million dollars a year, that doesn't mean she can't be feminine."

When she got Eliza and me alone, though, she seethed with paranoia.

"None of your tricks, no more of your snotty little kid millionaire tricks with me," she would say.

And Eliza and I hadn't done *anything* wrong.

◆◆◆

She was so enraged by how much money and power our family had, and so sick, that I don't think she even noticed how huge and ugly Eliza and I were. We were just two more rotten-spoiled little rich kids to her.

"I wasn't born with any silver spoon in my mouth," she told us, not once but many times. "Many was the day we didn't know where the next meal was coming from," she said. "Have you any idea what that's like?"

"No," said Eliza.

"Of course not," said Dr. Cordiner.

And so on.

◆◆◆

Since she was paranoid, it was especially unfortunate that her middle name was the same as our last name.

"I'm not your sweet Aunt Cordelia," she would say. "You needn't worry your little aristocratic brains about that. When my grandfather came from Poland, he changed his name from Stankowitz to Swain." Her eyes were blazing. "Say 'Stankowitz!' "

We said it.

"Now say 'Swain,' " she said.

We did.

◆◆◆

And finally one of us asked her what she was so mad about.

This made her very calm. "I am not mad," she said. "It would be very unprofessional for me to ever get mad about anything. However, let me say that asking a person of my calibre to come all this distance into the wilderness to personally administer tests to only two children is like asking Mozart to tune a piano. It is like asking Albert Einstein to balance a checkbook. Am I getting through to you, 'Mistress Eliza and Master Wilbur,' as I believe you are called?"

"Then why did you come?" I asked her.

Her rage came out into the open again. She said this to me with all possible nastiness: "Because money talks, 'Little Lord Fauntleroy.'"

◆◆◆

We were further shocked when we learned that she meant to administer tests to us separately. We said innocently that we would get many more correct answers if we were allowed to put our heads together.

She became a tower of irony. "Why, of course, Master and Mistress," she said. "And wouldn't you like to have an encyclopaedia in the room with you, too, and maybe the faculty of Harvard University, to tell you the answers, in case you're not sure?"

"That would be *nice,*" we said.

"In case nobody has told you," she said, "this is the United States of America, where nobody has a right to rely on anybody else—where everybody learns to make his or her own way.

"I'm here to test you," she said, "but there's a basic rule for life I'd like to teach you, too, and you'll thank me for it in years to come."

This was the lesson: "Paddle your own canoe," she said. "Can you say that and remember it?"

Not only could I say it, but I remember it to this day: "Paddle your own canoe."

Hi ho.

◆◆◆

So we paddled our own canoes. We were tested as individuals at the stainless steel table in the tile-lined diningroom. When one of us was in there with Dr. Cordiner, with "Aunt Cordelia," as we came to call her in private, the other one was taken as far away as possible—to the ballroom at the top of the tower at the north end of the mansion.

Withers Witherspoon had the job of watching whichever one of us was in the ballroom. He was chosen for the job because he had been a soldier at one time. We heard "Aunt Cordelia's" instructions to him. She asked him to be alert to clues that Eliza and I were communicating telepathically.

Western science, with a few clues from the Chinese, had at last acknowledged that some people could communicate with certain others without visible or audible signals. The transmitters and receivers for such spooky messages were on the surfaces of sinus cavities, and those cavities had to be healthy and clear of obstructions.

The chief clue which the Chinese gave the West was this puzzling sentence, delivered in English, which took years to decipher: "I feel so lonesome when I get hay fever or a cold."

Hi ho.

◆◆◆

Well, mental telepathy was useless to Eliza and me over distances greater than three meters. With one of us in the diningroom, and the other in the ballroom, our bodies might as well have been on different planets—which is in fact their condition today.

Oh, sure—and I could take written examinations, but Eliza could not. When "Aunt Cordelia" tested Eliza, she had to read each question out loud to her, and then write down her answer.

And it seemed to us that we missed absolutely every question. But we must have answered a few correctly, for Dr. Cordiner reported to our parents that our intelligence was ". . . low normal for their age."

She said further, not knowing that we were eavesdropping, that Eliza would probably never learn to read or write, and hence could never be a voter or hold a driver's license. She tried to soften this some by observing that Eliza was ". . . quite an amusing chatterbox."

She said that I was ". . . a good boy, a serious boy —easily distracted by his scatter-brained sister. He reads and writes, but has a poor comprehension of the meanings of words and sentences. If he were separated from his sister, there is every reason to believe that he could become a fillingstation attendant or a janitor in a village school. His prospects for a happy and useful life in a rural area are fair to good."

◆◆◆

The People's Republic of China was at that very moment secretly creating literally millions upon millions of geniuses—by teaching pairs or small groups of congenial, telepathically compatible specialists to think as single minds. And those patchwork minds were the equals of Sir Isaac Newton's or William Shakespeare's, say.

Oh, yes—and long before I became President of the United States of America, the Chinese had begun to combine those synthetic minds into intellects so flabbergasting that the Universe itself seemed to be saying to them, "I await your instructions. You can be anything you want to be. I will be anything you want me to be."

Hi ho.

◆◆◆

I learned about this Chinese scheme long after Eliza died, and long after I lost all my authority as President of the United States of America. There was nothing I could do with such knowledge by then.

One thing amused me, though: I was told that poor old Western Civilization had provided the Chinese the inspiration to put together such synthetic geniuses. The Chinese got the idea from the American and European scientists who put their heads together during the Second World War, with the single-minded intention of creating an atomic bomb.

Hi ho.

◆◆◆

Chapter 17

◆◆◆◆◆◆◆◆◆◆◆

OUR poor parents had first believed that we were idiots. They had tried to adapt to that. Then they believed that we were geniuses. They had tried to adapt to that. Now they were told that we were dull normals, and they were trying to adapt to that.

As Eliza and I watched through peepholes, they made a pitiful and fog-bound plea for help. They asked Dr. Cordelia Swain Cordiner how they were to harmonize our dullness with the fact that we could converse so learnedly on so many subjects in so many languages.

Dr. Cordiner was razor-keen to enlighten them on

just this point. "The world is full of people who are very clever at seeming much smarter than they really are," she said. "They dazzle us with facts and quotations and foreign words and so on, whereas the truth is that they know almost nothing of use in life as it is really lived. My purpose is to *detect* such people—so that society can be protected from them, and so they can be protected from themselves.

"Your Eliza is a perfect example," she went on. "She has lectured to me on economics and astronomy and music and every other subject you can think of, and yet she can neither read nor write, nor will she ever be able to."

◆◆◆

She said that our case was not a sad one, since there were no big jobs we wished to hold. "They have almost no ambition at all," she said, "so life can't disappoint them. They want only that life as they have known it should go on forever, which is impossible, of course."

Father nodded sadly. "And the boy is the smarter of the two?"

"To the extent he can read and write," said Dr. Cordiner. "He isn't nearly as socially outgoing as his sister. When he is away from her, he becomes as silent as a tomb.

"I suggest that he be sent to some special school, which won't be too demanding academically or too threatening socially, where he can learn to paddle his own canoe."

"Do what?" said Father.

Dr. Cordiner told him again. "Paddle his own canoe," she said.

◆◆◆

Eliza and I should have kicked our way through the wall at that point—should have entered the library ragingly, in an explosion of plaster and laths.

But we had sense enough to know that our power to eavesdrop at will was one of the few advantages we had. So we stole back to our bedrooms, and then burst into the corridor, and came running down the front stairs and across the foyer and into the library, doing something we had never done before. We were sobbing.

We announced that, if anybody tried to part us, we would kill ourselves.

◆◆◆

Dr. Cordiner laughed at this. She told our parents that several of the questions in her tests were designed to detect suicidal tendencies. "I absolutely guarantee you," she said, "that the last thing either one of these two would do would be to commit suicide."

Her saying this so jovially was a tactical mistake on her part, for it caused something in Mother to snap. The atmosphere in the room became electrified as Mother stopped being a weak and polite and credulous doll.

Mother did not say anything at first. But she had

clearly become subhuman in the finest sense. She was a coiled female panther, suddenly willing to tear the throats out of any number of childrearing experts —in defense of her young.

It was the one and only time that she would ever be irrationally committed to being the mother of Eliza and me.

◆◆◆

Eliza and I sensed this sudden jungle alliance telepathically, I think. At any rate, I remember that the damp velvet linings of my sinus cavities were tingling with encouragement.

We left off our crying, which we were no good at doing anyway. Yes, and we made a clear demand which could be satisfied at once. We asked to be tested for intelligence again—as a *pair* this time.

"We want to show you," I said, "how glorious we are when we work together, so that nobody will ever talk about parting us again."

We spoke carefully. I explained who "Betty and Bobby Brown" were. I agreed that they were stupid. I said we had had no experience with hating, and had had trouble understanding that particular human activity whenever we encountered it in books.

"But we are making small beginnings in hating now," said Eliza. "Our hating is strictly limited at this point—to only two people in this Universe: To Betty and Bobby Brown."

Dr. Cordiner, as it turned out, was a coward, among other things. Like so many cowards, she chose to go on bullying at the worst possible time. She jeered at Eliza's and my request.

"What kind of a world do you think this is?" she said, and so on.

So Mother got up and went over to her, not touching her, and not looking her in the eyes, either. Mother spoke to her throat, and, in a tone between a purr and a growl, she called Dr. Cordiner an "overdressed little sparrow-fart."

♦♦♦

Chapter 18

◆◆◆◆◆◆◆◆◆◆

So Eliza and I were re-tested—as a *pair* this time. We sat side-by-side at the stainless steel table in the tiled diningroom.

We were so happy!

A depersonalized Dr. Cordelia Swain Cordiner administered the tests like a robot, while our parents looked on. She had furnished us with new tests, so that the challenges would all be fresh.

Before we began, Eliza said to Mother and Father, "We promise to answer every question correctly."

Which we did.

◆◆◆

What were the questions like? Well, I was poking around the ruins of a school on Forty-sixth Street yesterday, and I was lucky enough to find a whole batch of intelligence tests, all set to go.

I quote:

"A man purchased 100 shares of stock at five dollars a share. If each share rose ten cents the first month, decreased eight cents the second month, and gained three cents the third month, what was the value of the man's investment at the end of the third month?"

Or try this:

"How many digits are there to the left of the decimal place in the square root of 692038.42753?"

Or this:

"A yellow tulip viewed through a piece of blue glass looks what color?"

Or this:

"Why does the Little Dipper appear to turn about the North Star once a day?"

Or this:

"Astronomy is to geology as steeplejack is to what?"

And so on. Hi ho.

◆◆◆

We made good on Eliza's promise of perfection, as I have said.

The only trouble was that the two of us, in the innocent process of checking and rechecking our answers, wound up under the table—with our legs wrapped around each others' necks in scissors grips, and snorting and snuffling into each others' crotches.

When we regained our chairs, Dr. Cordelia Swain Cordiner had fainted, and our parents were gone.

At ten o'clock the next morning, I was taken by automobile to a school for severely disturbed children on Cape Cod.

Chapter 19
✦✦✦✦✦✦✦✦✦

IT is sundown again. A
bird down around Thirty-first Street and Fifth,
where there is an Army tank with a tree growing out
of its turret, calls out to me. It asks the same question
over and over again with piercing clarity.

"Whip poor Will?" it says.

I never call that bird a "whippoorwill," and neither do Melody and Isadore, who follow my lead
in naming things. They seldom call Manhattan
"Manhattan," for example, or "The Island of
Death," which is its common name on the mainland. They do as I do: They call it "Skyscraper National Park," without knowing what the joke is in

that, or, with equal humorlessness, "Angkor Wat."

And what they call the bird that asks about whipping when the sun goes down is what Eliza and I called it when we were children. It was a correct name which we had learned from a dictionary.

We treasured the name for the superstitious dread it inspired. The bird became a nightmare creature in a painting by Hieronymus Bosch when we spoke its name. And, whenever we heard its cry, we spoke its name simultaneously. It was almost the only occasion on which we would speak simultaneously.

"The cry of *The Nocturnal Goatsucker,*" we would say.

And now I hear Melody and Isadore saying that, too, in a part of the lobby where I cannot see them. "The cry of the Nocturnal Goatsucker," they say.

Eliza and I listened to that bird one evening before my departure for Cape Cod.

We had fled the mansion for the privacy of the dank mausoleum of Professor Elihu Roosevelt Swain.

"Whip poor Will?" came the question, from somewhere out under the apple trees.

106

Even when we put our heads together, we could think of little to say.

I have heard that condemned prisoners often think of themselves as dead people, long before they die. Perhaps that was how our genius felt, knowing that a cruel axeman, so to speak, was about to split it into two nondescript chunks of meat, into Betty and Bobby Brown.

Be that as it may, our hands were busy—which is often the case with the hands of dying people. We had brought what we thought were the best of our writings with us. We rolled them into a cylinder, which we hid in an empty bronze funerary urn.

The urn had been intended for the ashes of the wife of Professor Swain, who had chosen to be buried here in New York, instead. It was encrusted with verdigris.

Hi ho.

❖❖❖

What was on the papers?

A method for squaring circles, I remember—and a utopian scheme for creating artificial extended families in America by issuing everyone a new middle name. All persons with the same middle name would be relatives.

Yes, and there was our critique of Darwin's Theory of Evolution, and an essay on the nature of gravity, which concluded that gravity had surely been a variable in ancient times.

There was a paper, I remember, which argued that teeth should be washed with hot water, just like dishes and pots and pans.

And so on.

◆◆◆

It was Eliza who had thought of hiding the papers in the urn.

It was Eliza who now put the lid in place.

We were not close together when she did it, so what she said was her own invention: "Say goodbye forever to your intelligence, Bobby Brown."

"Goodbye," I said.

◆◆◆

"Eliza—" I said, "so many of the books I've read to you said that love was the most important thing of all. Maybe I should tell you that I love you now."

"Go ahead," she said.

"I love you, Eliza," I said.

She thought about it. "No," she said at last, "I don't like it."

"Why not?" I said.

"It's as though you were pointing a gun at my head," she said. "It's just a way of getting somebody to say something they probably don't mean. What else can I say, or *anybody* say, but, 'I love you, too'?"

"You don't love me?" I said.

"What could anybody love about Bobby Brown?" she said.

◆◆◆

Somewhere outside, out under the apple trees, the Nocturnal Goatsucker asked his question again.

◆◆◆

Chapter 20

♦♦♦♦♦♦♦♦♦♦

ELIZA did not come down to breakfast the next morning. She remained in her room until I was gone.

Our parents came along with me in their chauffeur-driven Mercedes limousine. I was their child with a future. I could read and write.

And, even as we rolled through the lovely countryside, my forgettery set to work.

It was a protective mechanism against unbearable grief, one which I, as a pediatrician, am persuaded all children have.

Somewhere behind me, it seemed, was a twin sister who was not nearly as smart as I was. She had a name. Her name was Eliza Mellon Swain.

◆◆◆

Yes, and the school year was so structured that none of us ever had to go home. I went to England and France and Germany and Italy and Greece. I went to summer camp.

And it was determined that, while I was surely no genius, and was incapable of originality, I had a better than average mind. I was patient and orderly, and could sort out good ideas from heaps of balderdash.

I was the first child in the history of the school to take College Boards. I did so well that I was invited to come to Harvard. I accepted the invitation, although my voice had yet to change.

And I would now and then be reminded by my parents, who became very proud of me, that somewhere I had a twin sister who was little more than a human vegetable. She was in an expensive institution for people of her sort.

She was only a name.

◆◆◆

Father was killed in an automobile accident during my first year in medical school. He had thought enough of me to name me an executor of his will.

And I was visited in Boston soon after that by a fat and shifty-eyed attorney named Norman Mushari, Jr. He told me what seemed at first to be a rambling and irrelevant story about a woman who had been locked away for many years against her will—in an institution for the feeble-minded.

She had hired him, he said, to sue her relatives and the institution for damages, to gain her release at once, and to recover all inheritances which had been wrongly withheld.

She had a name, which, of course, was Eliza Mellon Swain.

Chapter 21

◆◆◆◆◆◆◆◆◆◆

MOTHER would say later of the hospital where we abandoned Eliza to Limbo: "It wasn't a cheap hospital, you know. It cost two hundred dollars a day. And the doctors begged us to stay away, didn't they, Wilbur?"

"I think so, Mother," I said. And then I told the truth: "I forget."

◆◆◆

I was then not only a stupid Bobby Brown, but a conceited one. Though only a first-year medical student with the genitalia of an infant field mouse, I was the master of a great house on Beacon Hill. I was

113

driven to and from school in a Jaguar—and I had already taken to dressing as I would dress when President of the United States, like a medical mountebank during the era of Chester Alan Arthur, say.

There was a party there nearly every night. I would customarily make an appearance of only a few minutes—smoking hashish in a meerschaum pipe, and wearing an emerald-green, watered-silk dressing gown.

A pretty girl came up to me at one of those parties, and she said to me, "You are so ugly, you're the sexiest thing I ever saw."

"I know," I said. "I know, I know."

◆◆◆

Mother visited me a lot on Beacon Hill, where I had a special suite built just for her—and I visited her a lot in Turtle Bay. Yes, and reporters came to question us in both places after Norman Mushari, Jr., got Eliza out of the hospital.

It was a big story.

It was always a big story when multimillionaires mistreated their own relatives.

Hi ho.

◆◆◆

It was embarrassing, and should have been, of course.

We had not seen Eliza yet, and had not been able

to reach her by telephone. Meanwhile, though, she said justly insulting things about us almost every day in the press.

All we had to show reporters was a copy of a telegram we had sent to Eliza, in care of her lawyer, and Eliza's reply to it.

Our telegram said:

"WE LOVE YOU. YOUR MOTHER AND YOUR BROTHER."

Eliza's telegram said this:

"I LOVE YOU TOO. ELIZA."

◆◆◆

Eliza would not allow herself to be photographed. She had her lawyer buy a confessional booth from a church which was being torn down. She sat inside it when she granted interviews for television.

And Mother and I watched those interviews in agony, holding hands.

And Eliza's rowdy contralto had become so unfamiliar to us that we thought there might be an imposter in the booth, but it was Eliza all right.

I remember a television reporter asked her, "How did you spend your time in the hospital, Miss Swain?"

"Singing," she said.

"Singing anything in particular?" he said.

"The same song—over and over again," she said.

"What song was that?" he said.

" 'Some Day My Prince Will Come,' " she told him.

"And did you have some specific prince in mind—as your rescuer?" he said.

"My twin brother," she said. "But he's a swine, of course. He never came."

◆◆◆

Chapter 22

◆◆◆◆◆◆◆◆◆◆

MOTHER and I surely did not oppose Eliza and her lawyer in any way, so she easily regained control of her wealth. And nearly the first thing she did was to buy half-interest in The New England Patriots professional football team.

◆◆◆

This purchase resulted in more publicity. Eliza would still not come out of the booth for cameras, but Mushari promised the world that she was now wearing a New England Patriots blue and gold jersey in there.

She was asked in this particular interview if she

kept up with current events, to which she replied: "I certainly don't blame the Chinamen for going home."

This had to do with the Republic of China's closing its embassy in Washington. The miniaturization of human beings in China had progressed so far at that point, that their ambassador was only sixty centimeters tall. His farewell was polite and friendly. He said his country was severing relations simply because there was no longer anything going on in the United States which was of any interest to the Chinese at all.

Eliza was asked to say why the Chinamen had been so right.

"What civilized country could be interested in a hell-hole like America," she said, "where everybody takes such lousy care of their own relatives?"

◆◆◆

And then, one day, she and Mushari were seen crossing the Massachusetts Avenue Bridge from Cambridge to Boston on foot. It was a warm and sunny day. Eliza was carrying a parasol. She was wearing the jersey of her football team.

◆◆◆

My God—was that poor girl ever a mess!

She was so bent over that her face was on level with Mushari's—and Mushari was about the size of Napoleon Bonaparte. She was chain smoking. She was coughing her head off.

Mushari was wearing a white suit. He carried a cane. He wore a red rose in his lapel.

And he and his client were soon joined by a friendly crowd, and by newspaper photographers and television crews.

And mother and I watched them on television—in horror, may I say, for the parade was coming ever closer to my house on Beacon Hill.

"Oh, Wilbur, Wilbur, Wilbur—" said my mother as we watched, "is that really your sister?"

I made a bitter joke—without smiling. "Either your only daughter, Mother, or the sort of anteater known as an *aardvark*," I said.

Chapter 23

◆◆◆◆◆◆◆◆◆◆◆

MOTHER was not up to a confrontation with Eliza. She retreated to her suite upstairs. Nor did I want the servants to witness whatever grotesque performance Eliza had in mind—so I sent them to their quarters.

When the doorbell rang, I myself answered the door.

I smiled at the aardvark and the cameras and the crowd. "Eliza! Dear sister! What a pleasant surprise. Come in, come in!" I said.

For form's sake, I made a tentative gesture as though I might touch her. She drew back. "You touch me, Lord Fauntleroy, and I'll bite you, and you'll die of rabies," she said.

◆◆◆

Policemen kept the crowd from following Eliza and Mushari into the house, and I closed the drapes on the windows, so no one could see in.

When I was sure we had privacy, I said to her bleakly, "What brings you here?"

"Lust for your perfect body, Wilbur," she said. She coughed and laughed. "Is dear Mater here, or dear Pater?" She corrected herself. "Oh, dear—dear Pater is dead, isn't he? Or is it dear Mater? It's so hard to tell."

"Mother is in Turtle Bay, Eliza," I lied. Inwardly, I was swooning with sorrow and loathing and guilt. I estimated that her crushed ribcage had the capacity of a box of kitchen matches. The room was beginning to smell like a distillery. Eliza had a problem with alcohol as well. Her skin was bad. She had a complexion like our great-grandmother's steamer trunk.

"Turtle Bay, Turtle Bay," she mused. "Did it ever occur to you, dear Brother, that dear Father was not our Father at all?"

"What do you mean?" I said.

"Perhaps Mother stole from the bed and out of the house on a moonlit night," she said, "and mated with a giant sea turtle in Turtle Bay."

Hi ho.

◆◆◆

"Eliza," I said, "if we're going to discuss family matters, perhaps Mr. Mushari should leave us alone."

"Why?" she said. "Normie is the only family I have."

"Now, now—" I said.

"That overdressed sparrow-fart of a mother of yours is surely no relative of mine," she said.

"Now, now—" I said.

"And you don't consider yourself a relative of mine, do you?" she said.

"What can I say?" I said.

"That's why we're visiting you—to hear all the wonderful things you have to say," she said. "You were always the brainy one. I was just some kind of tumor that had to be removed from your side."

"I never said that," I said.

"Other people said it, and you believed them," she said. "That's worse. You're a Fascist, Wilbur. That's what you are."

"That's absurd," I said.

"Fascists are inferior people who believe it when somebody tells them they're superior," she said.

"Now, now—" I said.

"Then they want everybody else to die," she said.

"This is getting us nowhere," I said.

"I'm *used* to getting nowhere," she said, "as you may have read in the papers and seen on television."

"Eliza—" I said, "would it help at all for you to

know that Mother will be sick for the rest of our lives about that awful thing we did to you?"

"How could that help?" she said. "That's the dumbest question I ever heard."

◆◆◆

She looped a great arm over the shoulders of Norman Mushari, Jr. "Here's who knows how to help people," she said.

I nodded. "We're grateful to him. We really are."

"He's my mother and father and brother and God, all wrapped up in one," she said. "He gave me the gift of life!

"He said to me, 'Money isn't going to make you feel any better, Sweetheart, but we're going to sue the piss out of your relatives anyway.'"

"Um," I said.

"But it sure helps a hell of a lot more than your expressions of guilt, I must say. Those are just boasts about your own wonderful sensibilities."

She laughed unpleasantly. "But I can see where you and Mother might want to boast about your guilt. After all, it's the only thing you two monkeys ever earned."

Hi ho.

Chapter 24

◆◆◆◆◆◆◆◆◆

I assumed that Eliza had now assaulted my self-respect with every weapon she had. I had somehow survived.

Without pride, with a clinical and cynical sort of interest, I noted that I had a cast-iron character which would repel attacks, apparently, even if I declined to put up defenses of any other kind.

How wrong I was about Eliza's having expended her fury!

Her opening attacks had been aimed merely at exposing the cast iron in my character. She had merely sent out light patrols to cut down the trees and shrubs in front of my character, to strip it of its vines, so to speak.

And now, without my realizing it, the shell of my character stood before her concealed howitzers at nearly point-blank range, as naked and brittle as a Franklin stove.

Hi ho.

◆◆◆

There was a lull. Eliza prowled about my livingroom, looking at my books, which she couldn't read, of course. Then she returned to me, and she cocked her head, and she said, "People get into Harvard Medical School because they can read and write?"

"I worked very hard, Eliza," I said. "It wasn't easy for me. It isn't easy now."

"If Bobby Brown becomes a doctor," she said, "that will be the strongest argument I ever heard for the Christian Scientists."

"I will not be the best doctor there ever was," I said. "I won't be the worst, either."

"You might be a very good man with a gong," she said. She was alluding to recent rumors that the Chinese had had remarkable successes in treating breast cancer with the music of ancient gongs. "You look like a man," she said, "who could hit a gong almost every time."

"Thank you," I said.

"Touch me," she said.

"Pardon me?" I said.

"I'm your own flesh. I'm your sister. Touch me," she said.

"Yes, of course," I said. But my arms seemed queerly paralyzed.

◆◆◆

"Take your time," she said.

"Well—" I said, "since you hate me so—"

"I hate Bobby Brown," she said.

"Since you hate Bobby Brown—" I said.

"And Betty Brown," she said.

"That was so long ago," I said.

"Touch me," she said.

"Oh, Christ, Eliza!" I said. My arms still wouldn't move.

"I'll touch you," she said.

"Whatever you say," I said. I was scared stiff.

"You don't have a heart condition, do you Wilbur?" she said.

"No," I said.

"If I touch you, you promise you won't die?"

"Yes," I said.

"Maybe *I'll* die," she said.

"I hope not," I said.

"Just because I act like I know what's going to happen," she said, "doesn't mean I know what's going to happen. Maybe nothing will happen."

"Maybe," I said.

"I've never seen you so frightened," she said.

"I'm human," I said.

"You want to tell Normie what you're scared about?" she said.

"No," I said.

◆◆◆

Eliza, with her fingertips almost brushing my cheek, quoted from a dirty joke Withers Witherspoon had told another servant when we were children. We had heard it through a wall. The joke had to do with a woman who was wildly responsive during sexual intercourse. In the joke, the woman warned a stranger who was beginning to make love to her.

Eliza passed on the sultry warning to me: "Keep your hat on, Buster. We may wind up miles from here."

◆◆◆

Then she touched me.

We became a single genius again.

◆◆◆

Chapter 25

✦✦✦✦✦✦✦✦✦✦

WE went berserk. It was
only by the Grace of God that we did not tumble out
of the house and into the crowd on Beacon Street.
Some parts of us, of which I had not been at all aware,
of which Eliza had been excruciatingly aware, had
been planning a reunion for a long, long time.

I could no longer tell where I stopped and Eliza
began, or where Eliza and I stopped and the Universe began. It was gorgeous and it was horrible. Yes,
and let this be a measure of the quantity of energy
involved: The orgy went on for five whole nights and
days.

◆◆◆

Eliza and I slept for three days after that. When I at last woke up, I found myself in my own bed. I was being fed intravenously.

Eliza, as I later found out, had been taken to her own home in a private ambulance.

◆◆◆

As for why nobody broke us up or summoned help: Eliza and I captured Norman Mushari, Jr., and poor Mother and the servants—one by one.

I have no memory of doing this.

We tied them to wooden chairs and gagged them, apparently, and set them neatly around the dining-room table.

◆◆◆

We gave them food and water, thank Heavens, or we would have been murderers. We would not let them go to the toilet, however, and fed them nothing but peanut butter and jelly sandwiches. I apparently left the house several times to get more bread and jelly and peanut butter.

And then the orgy would begin again.

◆◆◆

I remember reading out loud to Eliza from books on pediatrics and child psychology and sociology and anthropology, and so on. I had never thrown away any book from any course I had taken.

I remember writhing embraces which alternated with periods of my sitting at my typewriter, with

Eliza beside me. I was typing something with super-human speed.

Hi ho.

◆◆◆

When I came out of my coma, Mushari and my own lawyers had already paid my servants handsomely for the agony they had suffered at the dinner table, and for their silence as to the dreadful things they had seen.

Mother had been released from Massachusetts General Hospital, and was back in bed in Turtle Bay.

◆◆◆

Physically, I had suffered from exhaustion and nothing more.

When I was allowed to rise, however, I was so damaged psychologically that I expected to find everything unfamiliar. If gravity had become variable on that day, as it in fact did many years later, if I had had to crawl about my house on my hands and knees, as I often do now, I would have thought it a highly appropriate response by the Universe to all I had been through.

◆◆◆

But little had changed. The house was tidy.

The books were back in their shelves. A broken thermostat had been replaced. Three diningroom chairs had been sent out for repairs. The diningroom carpet was somewhat piebald, pale spots indicating where stains had been removed.

The one proof that something extraordinary had happened was itself a paradigm of tidiness. It was a manuscript—on a coffee table in the livingroom, where I had typed so furiously during the nightmare.

Eliza and I had somehow written a manual on childrearing.

◆◆◆

Was it any good? Not really. It was only good enough to become, after The Bible and *The Joy of Cooking*, the most popular book of all time.

Hi ho.

◆◆◆

I found it so helpful when I began to practice pediatrics in Vermont that I had it published under a pseudonym, Dr. Eli W. Rockmell, M.D., a sort of garbling of Eliza's and my names.

The publisher thought up the title, which was *So You Went and Had a Baby.*

◆◆◆

During our orgy, though, Eliza and I gave the manuscript a very different title and sort of authorship, which was this:

Kurt Vonnegut

THE CRY OF THE NOCTURNAL GOATSUCKER
by
BETTY AND BOBBY BROWN

◆◆◆

Chapter 26

◆◆◆◆◆◆◆◆◆◆

AFTER the orgy, mutual terror kept us apart. I was told by our go-between, Norman Mushari, Jr., that Eliza was even more shattered by the orgy than I had been.

"I almost had to put her away again—" he said, "for good cause this time."

◆◆◆

Machu Picchu, the old Inca capital on the roof of the Andes in Peru, was then becoming a haven for rich people and their parasites, people fleeing social reforms and economic declines, not just in America, but in all parts of the world. There were even some

133

full-sized Chinese there, who had declined to let their children be miniaturized.

And Eliza moved into a condominium down there, to be as far away as possible from me.

◆◆◆

When Mushari came to my house to tell me about Eliza's prospective move to Peru, a week after the orgy, he confessed that he himself had become severely disoriented while tied to a diningroom chair.

"You looked more and more like Frankenstein monsters to me," he said. "I became convinced that there was a switch somewhere in the house that controlled you. I even figured out which switch it was. The minute I untied myself, I ran to it and tore it out by the roots."

It was Mushari who had ripped the thermostat from the wall.

◆◆◆

To demonstrate to me how changed he was, he admitted that he had been wholly motivated by self-interest when he set Eliza free. "I was a bounty-hunter," he said, "finding rich people in mental hospitals who didn't belong there—and setting them free. I left the poor to rot in their dungeons."

"It was a useful service all the same," I said.

"Christ, I don't think so," he said. "Practically every sane person I ever got out of a hospital went insane almost immediately afterwards.

"Suddenly I feel old," he said. "I can't take that any more."

Hi ho.

◆◆◆

Mushari was so shaken by the orgy, in fact, that he turned Eliza's legal and financial affairs over to the same people that Mother and I used.

He came to my attention only once more, two years later, about the time I graduated from medical school—at the bottom of my class, by the way. He had patented an invention of his own. There was a photograph of him and a description of his patent on a business page in *The New York Times*.

There was a national mania for tap-dancing at the time. Mushari had invented taps which could be glued to the soles of shoes, and then peeled off again. A person could carry the taps in little plastic bags in a pocket or purse, according to Mushari, and put them on only when it was time to tap-dance.

◆◆◆

Chapter 27

✦✦✦✦✦✦✦✦✦

I never saw Eliza's face again after the orgy. I heard her voice only twice more—once when I graduated from medical school, and again when I was President of the United States of America, and she had been dead for a long, long time.

Hi ho.

✦✦✦

When Mother planned a graduation party for me at the Ritz in Boston, across from the Public Gardens, she and I never dreamed that Eliza would somehow hear of it, and would come all the way from Peru.

My twin never wrote or telephoned. Rumors about her were as vague as those coming from China. She was drinking too much, we had heard. She had taken up golf.

◆◆◆

I was having a wonderful time at my party, when a bellboy came to tell me I was wanted outside—not just in the lobby, but in the balmy, moonlit night outdoors. Eliza was the farthest thing from my mind.

My guess, as I followed the bellboy, was that there was a Rolls-Royce from my mother parked outside.

I was reassured by the servile manner and uniform of my guide. I was also giddy with champagne. I did not hesitate to follow as he led me across Arlington Street and then into the enchanted forest, into the Public Gardens on the other side.

He was a fraud. He was not a bellboy at all.

◆◆◆

Deeper and deeper we went into the trees. And in every clearing we came to, I expected to see my Rolls-Royce.

But he brought me to a statue instead. It depicted an old-fashioned doctor, dressed much as it amused me to dress. He was melancholy but proud. He held a sleeping youth in his arms.

As the inscription in the moonlight told me, this was a monument to the first use of anaesthetics in surgery in the United States, which took place in Boston.

◆◆◆

I had been aware of a clattering whir somewhere in the city, over Commonwealth Avenue perhaps. But I had not identified it as a hovering helicopter.

But now the bogus bellhop, who was really an Inca servant of Eliza's, fired a magnesium flare into the air.

Everything touched by that unnatural dazzle became statuary—lifeless and exemplary, and weighing tons.

The helicopter materialized directly over us, itself made allegorical, transformed into a terrible mechanical angel by the glare of the flare.

Eliza was up there with a bullhorn.

◆◆◆

It seemed possible to me that she might shoot me from there, or hit me with a bag of excrement. She had traveled all the way from Peru to deliver one-half of a Shakespearean sonnet.

"Listen!" she said. "Listen!" she said. And then she said, "Listen!" again.

The flare was meanwhile dying nearby—its parachute snagged in a treetop.

Here is what Eliza said to me, and to the neighborhood:

"O! how thy worth with manners may I sing,
"When thou art all the better part of me?
"What can mine own praise to mine own self bring?

"And what is't but mine own when I praise thee?

"Even for this let us divided live,

"And our dear love lose name of single one,

"That by this separation I may give

"That due to thee, which thou deserv'st alone."

❖❖❖

I called up to her through my cupped hands. "Eliza!" I said. And then I shouted something daring, and something I genuinely felt for the first time in my life.

"Eliza! I love you!" I said.

All was darkness now.

"Did you hear me, Eliza?" I said. "I *love* you! I *really* love you!"

"I heard you," she said. "Nobody should ever say that to anybody."

"I mean it," I said.

"Then I will say in turn something that I really mean, my brother—my twin."

"What is it?" I said.

She said this: "God guide the hand and mind of Dr. Wilbur Rockefeller Swain."

❖❖❖

And then the helicopter flew away.

Hi ho.

❖❖❖

Chapter 23
◆◆◆◆◆◆◆◆◆◆◆◆

I returned to the Ritz, laughing and crying—a two-meter Neanderthaler in a ruffled shirt and a robin's-egg blue velvet tuxedo.

There was a crowd of people who were curious about the brief supernova in the east, and about the voice which had spoken from Heaven of separation and love. I pressed past them and into the ballroom, leaving it to private detectives stationed at the door to turn back the following crowd.

The guests at my party were only now beginning to hear hints that something marvelous had happened outside. I went to Mother, to tell her what Eliza had done. I was puzzled to find her talking to a nondescript, middle-aged stranger, dressed, like the detectives, in a cheap business suit.

Mother introduced him as "Dr. Mott." He was, of course, the doctor who had looked after Eliza and me for so long in Vermont. He was in Boston on business, and, as luck would have it, staying at the Ritz.

I was so full of news and champagne, though, that I did not know or care who he was. And, having said my bit to Mother, I told Dr. Mott that it had been nice to meet him, and I hurried on to other parts of the room.

◆◆◆

When I got back to Mother in about an hour, Dr. Mott had departed. She told me again who he was. I expressed pro forma regrets at not having spent more time with him. She gave me a note from him, which she said was his graduation present to me.

It was written on Ritz stationery. It said simply this:

"'If you can do no good, at least do no harm.' Hippocrates."

◆◆◆

Yes, and when I converted the mansion in Vermont into a clinic and small children's hospital, and also my permanent home, I had those words chipped in stone over the front door. But they so troubled my patients and their parents that I had them chipped away again. The words seemed a confession of weakness and indecision to them, a suggestion that they might as well have stayed away.

I continued to carry the words in my head, however, and in fact did little harm. And the intellectual center of gravity for my practice was a single volume which I locked into a safe each night—the bound manuscript of the child-rearing manual Eliza and I had written during our orgy on Beacon Hill.

Somehow, we had put *everything* in there.

And the years flew by.

◆◆◆

Somewhere in there I married an equally wealthy woman, actually a third cousin of mine, whose maiden name was Rose Aldrich Ford. She was very unhappy, because I did not love her, and because I would never take her anywhere. I have never been good at loving. We had a child, Carter Paley Swain, whom I also failed to love. Carter was normal, and completely uninteresting to me. He was somehow like a summer squash on the vine—featureless and watery, and merely growing larger all the time.

After our divorce, he and his mother bought a condominium in the same building with Eliza, down in Machu Picchu, Peru. I never heard from them again—even when I became President of the United States.

And the time flew.

◆◆◆

I woke up one morning to find that I was almost fifty years old! Mother had moved in with me in Vermont.

She sold her house in Turtle Bay. She was feeble and afraid.

She talked a good deal about Heaven to me.

I knew nothing at all about the subject then. I assumed that when people were dead they were dead.

"I know your father is waiting for me with open arms," she said, "and my Mommy and Daddy, too."

She was right about that, it turned out. Waiting around for more people is just about all there is for people in Heaven to do.

◆◆◆

The way Mother described Heaven, it sounded like a golf course in Hawaii, with manicured fairways and greens running down to a lukewarm ocean.

I twitted her only lightly about wanting that sort of Paradise. "It sounds like a place where people would drink a lot of lemonade," I said.

"I love lemonade," she replied.

◆◆◆

Chapter 29

◆◆◆◆◆◆◆◆◆

MOTHER talked toward the end, too, about how much she hated unnatural things—synthetic flavors and fibers and plastics and so on. She loved silk and cotton and linen and wool and leather, she said, and clay and glass and stone. She loved horses and sailboats, too, she said.

"They're all coming back, Mother," I said, which was true.

My hospital itself had twenty horses by then—and wagons and carts and carriages and sleighs. I had a horse of my own, a great Clydesdale. Golden feathers hid her hooves. "Budweiser" was her name.

Yes, and the harbors of New York and Boston and San Francisco were forests of masts again, I'd heard. It had been quite some time since I'd seen them.

◆◆◆

Yes, and I found the hospitality of my mind to fantasy pleasantly increased as machinery died and communications from the outside world became more and more vague.

So I was unsurprised one night, after having tucked Mother in bed, to enter my own bedroom with a lighted candle, and to find a Chinese man the size of my thumb sitting on my mantelpiece. He was wearing a quilted blue jacket and trousers and cap.

As far as I was able to determine afterwards, he was the first official emissary from the People's Republic of China to the United States of America in more than twenty-five years.

◆◆◆

During the same period, not a single foreigner who got inside China, so far as I know, ever returned from there.

So "going to China" became a widespread euphemism for committing suicide.

Hi ho.

◆◆◆

My little visitor motioned for me to come closer, so he would not have to shout. I presented one ear to

145

him. It must have been a horrible sight—the tunnel with all the hair and bits of wax inside.

He told me that he was a roving ambassador, and had been chosen for the job because of his visibility to foreigners. He was much, much larger, he said, than an average Chinese.

"I thought you people had no interest in us any more," I said.

He smiled. "That was a foolish thing for us to say, Dr. Swain," he said. "We apologize."

"You mean that we know things that you don't know?" I said.

"Not quite," he said. "I mean that you *used* to know things that we don't know."

"I can't imagine what those things would be," I said.

"Naturally not," he said. "I will give you a hint: I bring you greetings from your twin sister in Machu Picchu, Dr. Swain."

"That's not much of a hint," I said.

"I wish very much to see the papers you and your sister put so many years ago into the funeral urn in the mausoleum of Professor Elihu Roosevelt Swain," he said.

◆◆◆

It turned out that the Chinese had sent an expedition to Machu Picchu—to recover, if they could, certain lost secrets of the Incas. Like my visitor, they were oversize for Chinese.

Yes, and Eliza approached them with a proposition. She said she knew where there were secrets which were as good or better than anything the Incas had had.

"If what I say turns out to be true," she told them, "I want you to reward me—with a trip to your colony on Mars."

He said that his name was Fu Manchu.

I asked him how he had got to my mantelpiece.

"The same way we get to Mars," he replied.

Chapter 30

◆◆◆◆◆◆◆◆◆◆

I agreed to take Fu Man-
chu out to the mausoleum. I put him in my breast
pocket.

I felt very inferior to him. I was sure he had the
power of life and death over me, as small as he was.
Yes, and he knew so much more than I did—even
about medicine, even about myself, perhaps. He
made me feel immoral, too. It was greedy for me to
be so big. My supper that night could have fed a
thousand men his size.

◆◆◆

The exterior doors to the mausoleum had been welded shut. So Fu Manchu and I had to enter the secret passageways, the alternative universe of my childhood, and come up through the mausoleum's floor.

As I made our way through cobwebs, I asked him about the Chinese use of gongs in the treatment of cancer.

"We are way beyond that now," he said.

"Maybe it is something we could still use here," I said.

"I'm sorry—" he said from my pocket, "but your civilization, so-called, is much too primitive. You could never understand."

"Um," I said.

❖❖❖

He answered all my questions that way—saying, in effect, that I was too dumb to understand anything.

❖❖❖

When we got to the underside of the stone trapdoor to the mausoleum, I had trouble heaving it open.

"Put your shoulder into it," he said, and, "Tap it with a brick," and so on.

His advice was so simple-minded, that I concluded that the Chinese knew little more about dealing with gravity than I did at the time.

Hi ho.

◆◆◆

The door finally opened, and we ascended into the mausoleum. I must have been even more frightful than usual to look at. I was swaddled in cobwebs from head to toe.

I removed Fu Manchu from my pocket, and, at his request, I placed him on top of the lead casket of Professor Elihu Roosevelt Swain.

I had only one candle for illumination. But Fu Manchu now produced from his attaché case a tiny box. It filled the chamber with a light as brilliant as the flare that had lit Eliza's and my reunion in Boston —so long ago.

He asked me to take the papers from the urn, which I did. They were perfectly preserved.

"This is bound to be trash," I said.

"To you, perhaps," he said. He asked me to flatten out the papers and spread them over the casket, which I did.

"How could we know when we were children something not known even today to the Chinese?" I said.

"Luck," he said. He began to stroll across the papers, in his tiny black and white basketball shoes, pausing here and there to take pictures of something he had read. He seemed especially interested in our essay on gravity—or so it seems to me now, with the benefit of hindsight.

◆◆◆

He was satisfied at last. He thanked me for my cooperation, and told me that he would now dematerialize and return to China.

"Did you find anything at all valuable?" I asked him.

He smiled. "A ticket to Mars for a rather large Caucasian lady in Peru," he replied.

Hi ho.

◆◆◆

Chapter 31

◆◆◆◆◆◆◆◆◆◆◆

THREE weeks later, on the morning of my fiftieth birthday, I rode my horse Budweiser down into the hamlet—to pick up the mail.

There was a note from Eliza. It said only this: "Happy birthday to us! Going to China!"

That message was two weeks old, according to the postmark. There was fresher news in the same mail. "Regret to inform you that your sister died on Mars in an avalanche." It was signed, "Fu Manchu."

◆◆◆

I read those tragic notes while standing on the old wooden porch of the post office, in the shadow of the little church next door.

An extraordinary feeling came over me, which I first thought to be psychological in origin, the first rush of grief. I seemed to have taken root on the porch. I could not pick up my feet. My features, moreover, were being dragged downward like melting wax.

The truth was that the force of gravity had increased tremendously.

There was a great crash in the church. The steeple had dropped its bell.

Then I went right through the porch, and was slammed to the earth beneath it.

In other parts of the world, of course, elevator cables were snapping, airplanes were crashing, ships were sinking, motor vehicles were breaking their axles, bridges were collapsing, and on and on.

It was terrible.

Chapter 32

◆◆◆◆◆◆◆◆◆◆

THAT first ferocious jolt of heavy gravity lasted less than a minute, but the world would never be the same again.

I dazedly climbed out from under the post office porch when it was over. I gathered up my mail.

Budweiser was dead. She had tried to remain standing. Her insides had fallen out.

◆◆◆

I must have suffered something like shell shock. People were crying for help there in the hamlet, and I was the only doctor. But I simply walked away.

I remember wandering under the family apple trees.

I remember stopping at the family cemetery, and gravely opening an envelope from the Eli Lilly Company, a pharmaceutical house. Inside were a dozen sample pills, the color and size of lentils.

The accompanying literature, which I read with great care, explained that the trade name for the pills was "tri-benzo-Deportamil." The "Deport" part of the name had reference to good deportment, to socially acceptable behavior.

The pills were a treatment for the socially unacceptable symptoms of Tourette's Disease, whose sufferers involuntarily spoke obscenities and made insulting gestures no matter where they were.

In my disoriented state, it seemed very important that I take two of the pills immediately, which I did.

Two minutes passed, and then my whole being was flooded with contentment and confidence such as I had never felt before.

Thus began an addiction which was to last for nearly thirty years.

Hi ho.

◆◆◆

It was a miracle that no one in my hospital died. The beds and wheelchairs of some of the heavier children had broken. One nurse crashed through the trapdoor which had once been hidden by Eliza's bed. She broke both legs.

Mother, thank God, slept through it all.

When she woke up, I was standing at the foot of

her bed. She told me again about how much she hated unnatural things.

"I know, Mother," I said. "I couldn't agree with you more. Back to Nature," I said.

◆◆◆

I do not know to this day whether that awful jolt of gravity was Nature, or whether it was an experiment by the Chinese.

I thought at the time that there was a connection between the jolt and Fu Manchu's photographing of Eliza's and my essay on gravity.

Yes, and, coked to the ears on tri-benzo-Deportamil, I fetched all our papers from the mausoleum.

◆◆◆

The paper on gravity was incomprehensible to me. Eliza and I were perhaps ten thousand times as smart when we put our heads together as when we were far apart.

Our Utopian scheme for reorganizing America into thousands of artificial extended families, however, was clear. Fu Manchu had found it ridiculous, incidentally.

"This is truly the work of children," he'd said.

◆◆◆

I found it absorbing. It said that there was nothing new about artificial extended families in America. Physicians felt themselves related to other physicians, lawyers to lawyers, writers to writers, athletes to athletes, politicians to politicians, and so on.

Eliza and I said these were bad sorts of extended families, however. They excluded children and old people and housewives, and losers of every description. Also: Their interests were usually so specialized as to seem nearly insane to outsiders.

"An ideal extended family," Eliza and I had written so long ago, "should give proportional representation to all sorts of Americans, according to their numbers. The creation of ten thousand such families, say, would provide America with ten thousand parliaments, so to speak, which would discuss sincerely and expertly what only a few hypocrites now discuss with passion, which is the welfare of all mankind."

My reading was interrupted by my head nurse, who came in to tell me that our frightened young patients had all gotten to sleep at last.

I thanked her for the good news. And then I heard myself tell her casually, "Oh—and I want you to write to the Eli Lilly Company, in Indianapolis, and order two thousand doses of a new drug of theirs called 'tri-benzo-Deportamil.'"

Hi ho.

Chapter 33

◆◆◆◆◆◆◆◆◆

MOTHER died two weeks after that.

Gravity would not trouble us again for another twenty years.

And time flew. Time was a blurry bird now—made indistinct by ever-increasing dosages of tri-benzo-Deportamil.

◆◆◆

Somewhere in there, I closed my hospital, gave up medicine entirely, and was elected United States Senator from Vermont.

And time flew.

I found myself running for President one day. My

valet pinned a campaign button to the lapel of my claw-hammer coat. It bore the slogan which would win the election for me:

LONESOME NO MORE!

◆◆◆

I appeared here in New York only once during that campaign. I spoke from the steps of the Public Library at Forty-second and Fifth. This island was by then a sleepy seaside resort. It had never recovered from that first jolt of gravity, which had stripped its buildings of their elevators, and had flooded its tunnels, and had buckled all but one bridge, which was the Brooklyn Bridge.

Now gravity had started to turn mean again. It was no longer a jolting experience. If the Chinese were indeed in charge of it, they had learned how to increase or decrease it gradually, wishing to cut down on injuries and property damage, perhaps. It was as majestically graceful as the tides now.

◆◆◆

When I spoke from the library steps, the gravity was heavy. So I chose to sit in a chair while speaking. I was cold sober, but I lolled in the chair like a drunken English squire from olden times.

My audience, which was composed mostly of retired people, actually lay down on Fifth Avenue, which the police had blocked off, but where there would have been hardly any traffic anyway. Somewhere over on Madison Avenue, perhaps, there was a small explosion. The island's useless skyscrapers were being quarried.

◆◆◆

I spoke of American loneliness. It was the only subject I needed for victory, which was lucky. It was the only subject I had.

It was a shame, I said, that I had not come along earlier in American history with my simple and workable anti-loneliness plan. I said that all the damaging excesses of Americans in the past were motivated by loneliness rather than a fondness for sin.

An old man crawled up to me afterwards and told me how he used to buy life insurance and mutual funds and household appliances and automobiles and so on, not because he liked them or needed them, but because the salesman seemed to promise to be his relative, and so on.

"I had no relatives and I needed relatives," he said.

"Everybody does," I said.

He told me he had been a drunk for a while, trying

to make relatives out of people in bars. "The bartender would be kind of a father, you know——" he said. "And then all of a sudden it was closing time."

"I know," I said. I told him a half-truth about myself which had proved to be popular on the campaign trail. "I used to be so lonesome," I said, "that the only person I could share my innermost thoughts with was a horse named 'Budweiser.' "

And I told him how Budweiser had died.

◆◆◆

During this conversation, I would bring my hand to my mouth again and again, seeming to stifle exclamations and so on. I was actually popping tiny green pills into my mouth. They were outlawed by then, and no longer manufactured. I had perhaps a bushel of them back in the Senate Office Building.

They accounted for my unflagging courtesy and optimism, and perhaps for my failure to age as quickly as other men. I was seventy years old, but I had the vigor of a man half that age.

I had even picked up a pretty new wife, Sophie Rothschild Swain, who was only twenty-three.

◆◆◆

"If you get elected, and I get issued all these new artificial relatives——" said the man. He paused. "How many did you say?"

"Ten thousand brothers and sisters," I told him. "One-hundred and ninety-thousand cousins."

"Isn't that an awful lot?" he said.

"Didn't we just agree we need all the relatives we can get in a country as big and clumsy as ours?" I said. "If you ever go to Wyoming, say, won't it be a comfort to you to know you have many relatives there?"

He thought that over. "Well, yes—I expect," he said at last.

"As I said in my speech:" I told him, "your new middle name would consist of a noun, the name of a flower or fruit or nut or vegetable or legume, or a bird or a reptile or a fish, or a mollusk, or a gem or a mineral or a chemical element—connected by a hypen to a number between one and twenty." I asked him what his name was at the present time.

"Elmer Glenville Grasso," he said.

"Well," I said, "you might become Elmer Uranium-3 Grasso, say. Everybody with Uranium as a part of their middle name would be your cousin."

"That brings me back to my first question," he said. "What if I get some artificial relative I absolutely can't stand?"

❖❖❖

"What is so novel about a person's having a relative he can't stand?" I asked him. "Wouldn't you say that sort of thing has been going on now for perhaps a million years, Mr. Grasso?"

And then I said a very obscene thing to him. I am not inclined toward obscenities, as this book itself demonstrates. In all my years of public life, I had never said an off-color thing to the American people.

So it was terrifically effective when I at last spoke coarsely. I did so in order to make memorable how nicely scaled to average human beings my new social scheme would be.

Mr. Grasso was not the first to hear the startling rowdy-isms. I had even used them on radio. There was no such thing as television any more.

"Mr. Grasso," I said, "I personally will be very disappointed, if you do not say to artificial relatives you hate, after I am elected, 'Brother or Sister or Cousin,' as the case may be, 'why don't you take a flying fuck at a rolling doughnut? Why don't you take a flying fuck at the mooooooooooooooon?' "

❖❖❖

"You know what relatives you say that to are going to do, Mr. Grasso?" I went on. "They're going to go home and try to figure out how to be better relatives!"

❖❖❖

"And consider how much better off you will be, if the reforms go into effect, when a beggar comes up to you and asks for money," I went on.

"I don't understand," said the man.

"Why," I said, "you say to that beggar, 'What's your middle name?' And he will say 'Oyster-19' or 'Chickadee-1,' or 'Hollyhock-13,' or some such thing.

"And you can say to him, 'Buster—I happen to be

a Uranium-3. You have one hundred and ninety thousand cousins and ten thousand brothers and sisters. You're not exactly alone in this world. I have relatives of my own to look after. So why don't you take a flying fuck at a rolling doughnut? Why don't you take a flying fuck at the mooooooooooooon?' "

Chapter 34

◆◆◆◆◆◆◆◆◆◆◆

THE fuel shortage was so severe when I was elected, that the first stiff problem I faced after my inauguration was where to get enough electricity to power the computers which would issue the new middle names.

I ordered horses and soldiers and wagons of the ramshackle Army I had inherited from my predecessor to haul tons of papers from the National Archives to the powerhouse. These documents were all from the Administration of Richard M. Nixon, the only President who was ever forced to resign.

◆◆◆

I myself went to the Archives to watch. I spoke to the soldiers and a few passers-by from the steps there. I said that Mr. Nixon and his associates had been unbalanced by loneliness of an especially virulent sort.

"He promised to bring us together, but tore us apart instead," I said. "Now, hey presto!, he will bring us together after all."

I posed for photographs beneath the inscription on the facade of the Archives, which said this:

"THE PAST IS PROLOGUE."

"They were not basically criminals," I said. "But they yearned to partake of the brotherhood they saw in Organized Crime."

◆◆◆

"So many crimes committed by lonesome people in Government are concealed in this place," I said, "that the inscription might well read, 'Better a Family of Criminals than No Family at All.'

"I think we are now marking the end of the era of such tragic monkeyshines. The Prologue is over, friends and neighbors and relatives. Let the main body of our noble work begin.

"Thank you," I said.

◆◆◆

There were no large newspapers or national magazines to print my words. The huge printing plants had all shut down—for want of fuel. There were no microphones. There were just the people there.

Hi ho.

◆◆◆

I passed out a special decoration to the soldiers, to commemorate the occasion. It consisted of a pale blue ribbon from which depended a plastic button.

I explained, only half-jokingly, that the ribbon represented "The Bluebird of Happiness." And the button was inscribed with these words, of course:

◆◆◆

Chapter 35

◆◆◆◆◆◆◆◆◆◆◆

IT is mid-morning here in Skyscraper National Park. The gravity is balmy, but Melody and Isadore will not work on the baby's pyramid today. We will have a picnic on top of the building instead. The young people are being so companionable with me because my birthday is only two days away now. What fun!

There is nothing they love more than a birthday!

Melody plucks a chicken which a slave of Vera Chipmunk-17 Zappa brought to us this morning. The slave also brought two loaves of bread and two liters of creamy beer. He pantomimed how nourishing he was being to us. He pressed the bases of the two beer bottles to his nipples, pretending that he had breasts that gave creamy beer.

We laughed. We clapped our hands.

◆◆◆

Melody tosses pinches of feathers skyward. Because of the mild gravity, it appears that she is a white witch. Each snap of her fingers produces butterflies.

I have an erection. So does Isadore. So does every male.

◆◆◆

Isadore sweeps the lobby with a broom he has made of twigs. He sings one of the only two songs he knows. The other song is "Happy Birthday to You." Yes, and he is tone-deaf, too, so he drones.

> "Row, row, row your boat," he drones,
> "Gently down the stream.
> "Merrily, merrily, merrily, merrily—
> "Life is but a dream."

◆◆◆

Yes, and I now remember a day in the dream of my life, far upstream from now, in which I received a chatty letter from the President of my country, who happened to be me. Like any other citizen, I had been waiting on pins and needles to learn from the computers what my new middle name would be.

My President congratulated me on my new middle name. He asked me to use it as a regular part of my signature, and on my mailbox and letterheads and in directories, and so on. He said that the name was selected at immaculate random, and was not intended as a comment on my character or my appearance or my past.

He offered deceptively homely, almost inane examples of how I might serve artificial relatives: By watering their houseplants while they were away; by taking care of their babies so they could get out of the house for an hour or two; by telling them the name of a truly painless dentist; by mailing a letter for them; by keeping them company on a scary visit to a doctor; by visiting them in a jail or a hospital; by keeping them company at a scary picture show.

Hi ho.

◆◆◆

I was enchanted by my new middle name, by the way. I ordered that the Oval Office of the White House be painted pale yellow immediately, in celebration of my having become a Daffodil.

And, as I was telling my private secretary, Hortense Muskellunge-13 McBundy, to have the place repainted, a dishwasher from the White House kitchen appeared in her office. He was bent on a very shy errand, indeed. He was so embarrassed that he choked every time he tried to speak.

When he at last managed to articulate his message, I embraced him. He had come out of the steamy depths to tell me ever-so-bravely that he, too, was a *Daffodil-11*.

"My brother," I said.

◆◆◆

Chapter 36

✦✦✦✦✦✦✦✦✦

WAS there no substantial opposition to the new social scheme? Why, of course there was. And, as Eliza and I had predicted, my enemies were so angered by the idea of artificial extended families that they constituted a polyglot artificial extended family of their own.

They had campaign buttons, too, which they went on wearing long after I was elected. It was inevitable what those buttons said, to wit:

◆◆◆

I had to laugh, even when my own wife, the former Sophie Rothschild, took to wearing a button like that.

Hi ho.

◆◆◆

Sophie was furious when she received a form letter from her President, who happened to be me, which instructed her to stop being a *Rothschild*. She was to become a *Peanut-3* instead.

Again: I am sorry, but I had to laugh.

◆◆◆

Sophie smouldered about it for several weeks. And then she came crawling into the Oval Office on an afternoon of particularly heavy gravity—to tell me she hated me.

I was not stung.

As I have already said, I was fully aware that I was not the sort of lumber out of which happy marriages were made.

"I honestly did not think you would go this far, Wilbur," she said. "I knew you were crazy, and that your sister was crazy, too. But I did not believe you would go this far."

❖❖❖

Sophie did not have to look up at me. I, too, was on the floor—prone, with my chin resting on a pillow. I was reading a fascinating report of a thing that had happened in Urbana, Illinois.

I did not give her my undivided attention, so she said, "What is it you're reading that is so much more interesting than me?"

"Well—" I said, "for many years, I was the last American to have spoken to a Chinese. That's not true any more. A delegation of Chinese paid a call to the widow of a physicist in Urbana—about three weeks ago."

Hi ho.

❖❖❖

"I certainly don't want to waste your valuable time," she said. "You're certainly closer to Chinamen than you ever were to me."

I had given her a wheelchair for Christmas—to use around the White House on days of heavy gravity. I asked her why she didn't use it. "It makes me very sad," I said, "to have you go around on all-fours."

174

"I'm a *Peanut* now," she said. *"Peanuts* live very close to the ground. *Peanuts* are famous for being low. They are the cheapest of the cheap, and the lowest of the low."

◆◆◆

That early in the game, I thought it was crucial the people not be allowed to change their Government-issue middle names. I was wrong to be so rigid about that. All sorts of name-changing goes on now—here on the Island of Death and everywhere. I can't see that any harm is done.

But I was severe with Sophie. "You want to be an *Eagle* or a *Diamond*, I suppose," I said.

"I want to be a *Rothschild,"* she said.

"Then perhaps you should go to Machu Picchu," I said. That was where most of her blood relatives had gone.

◆◆◆

"Are you really so sadistic," she said, "that you will make me prove my love by befriending strangers who are now crawling out from damp rocks like earwigs? Like centipedes? Like slugs? Like worms?"

"Now, now," I said.

"When was the last time you took a look at the freak show outside the fence?" she said.

The perimeter of the White House grounds, just outside the fence, was infested daily with persons claiming to be artificial relatives of Sophie or me.

There were twin male midgets out there, I remember, holding a banner that said "Flower Power."

There was a woman, I remember, who wore an Army field jacket over a purple evening dress. On her head was an old-fashioned leather aviator's helmet, goggles and all. She had a placard on the end of a stick. "Peanut Butter," it said.

◆◆◆

"Sophie—" I said, "that is not the general American population out there. And you are not mistaken when you say that they have crawled out from under damp rocks—like centipedes and earwigs and worms. They have never had a friend or a relative. They have had to believe all their lives that they were perhaps sent to the wrong Universe, since no one has ever bid them welcome or given them anything to do."

"I hate them," she said.

"Go ahead," I said. "There's very little harm in that, as far as I know."

"I did not think you would go this far, Wilbur," she said. "I thought you would be satisfied with being President. I did not think you would go this far."

"Well," I said, "I'm glad I did. And I am glad we have those people outside the fence to think about, Sophie. They are frightened hermits who have been tempted out from under their damp rocks by humane new laws. They are dazedly seeking brothers and sisters and cousins which their President has suddenly given to them from their nation's social treasure, which was until now untapped."

"You are insane," she said.

"Very likely," I replied. "But it will not be an hallucination when I see those people outside the fence find each other, if no one else."

"They deserve each other," she said.

"Exactly," I said. "And they deserve something else which is going to happen to them, now that they have the courage to speak to strangers. You watch, Sophie. The simple experience of companionship is going to allow them to climb the evolutionary ladder in a matter of hours or days, or weeks at most.

"It will not be an hallucination, Sophie," I said, "when I see them become human beings, after having been for so many years, as you say, Sophie—centipedes and slugs and earwigs and worms."

Hi ho.

◆◆◆

Chapter 37

◆◆◆◆◆◆◆◆◆◆

SOPHIE divorced me, of course, and skeedaddled with her jewelry and furs and paintings and gold bricks, and so on, to a condominium in Machu Picchu, Peru.

Almost the last thing I said to her, I think, was this: "Can't you at least wait until we compile the family directories? You're sure to find out that you're related to many distinguished women and men."

"I already *am* related to many distinguished women and men," she replied. "Goodbye."

◆◆◆

In order to compile and publish the family directories, we had to haul more papers from the National Archives to the powerhouse. I selected files from the Presidencies of Ulysses Simpson Grant and Warren Gamaliel Harding this time.

We could not provide every citizen with directories of his or her own. It was all we could do to ship a complete set to every State House, town and City Hall, police department, and public library in the land.

◆◆◆

One greedy thing I did: Before Sophie left me, I asked that we be sent Daffodil and Peanut directories all our own. And I have a Daffodil Directory right here in the Empire State Building right now. Vera Chipmunk-5 Zappa gave it to me for my birthday last year. It is a first edition—the only edition ever published.

And I learn from it again that among my new relatives at that time were Clarence Daffodil-11 Johnson, the Chief of Police of Batavia, New York, and Muhammad Daffodil-11 X, the former Light-Heavyweight Boxing Champion of the World, and Maria Daffodil-11 Tcherkassky, the Prima Ballerina of the Chicago Opera Ballet.

◆◆◆

I am glad, in a way, incidentally, that Sophie never saw her family directory. The Peanuts really did seem to be a ground-hugging bunch.

The most famous Peanut I can now recall was a minor Roller Derby star.

Hi ho.

◆◆◆

Yes, and after the Government provided the directories, Free Enterprise produced family newspapers. Mine was *The Daffy-nition*. Sophie's, which continued to arrive at the White House long after she had left me, was *The Goober Gossip*. Vera told me the other day that the *Chipmunk* paper used to be *The Woodpile*.

Relatives asked for work or investment capital, or offered things for sale in the classified ads. The news columns told of triumphs by various relatives, and warned against others who were child molesters or swindlers and so on. There were lists of relatives who could be visited in various hospitals and jails.

There were editorials calling for family health insurance programs and sports teams and so on. There was one interesting essay, I remember, either in *The Daffy-nition* or *The Goober Gossip*, which said that families with high moral standards were the best maintainers of law and order, and that police departments could be expected to fade away.

"If you know of a relative who is engaged in criminal acts," it concluded, "don't call the police. Call ten more relatives."

And so on.

◆◆◆

Vera told me that the motto of *The Woodpile* used to be this: "A Good Citizen is a Good Family Woman or a Good Family Man."

◆◆◆

As the new families began to investigate themselves, some statistical freaks were found. Almost all *Pachysandras*, for example, could play a musical instrument, or at least sing in tune. Three of them were conductors of major symphony orchestras. The widow in Urbana who had been visited by Chinese was a *Pachysandra*. She supported herself and her son by giving piano lessons out there.

Watermelons, on the average, were a kilogram heavier than members of any other family.

Three-quarters of all *Sulfurs* were female.

And on and on.

As for my own family: There was an extraordinary concentration of Daffodils in and around Indianapolis. My family paper was published out there, and its masthead boasted, "Printed in Daffodil City, U.S.A."

Hi ho.

◆◆◆

Family clubhouses appeared. I personally cut the ribbon at the opening of the Daffodil Club here in Manhattan—on Forty-third Street, right off Fifth Avenue.

This was a thought-provoking experience for me, even though I was sedated by tri-benzo-Deportamil. I had once belonged to another club, and to another sort of artificial extended family, too, on the very same premises. So had my father, and both my grandfathers, and all four of my great grandfathers.

Once the building had been a haven for men of power and wealth, and well-advanced into middle age.

Now it teemed with mothers and children, with old people playing checkers or chess or dreaming, with younger adults taking dancing lessons or bowling on the duckpin alleys, or playing the pinball machines.

I had to laugh.

◆◆◆

Chapter 38

◆◆◆◆◆◆◆◆◆◆◆

I T was on that particular visit to Manhattan that I saw my first "Thirteen Club." There were dozens of such raffish establishments in Chicago, I had heard. Now Manhattan had one of its own.

Eliza and I had not anticipated that all the people with "13" in their middle names would naturally band together almost immediately, to form the largest family of all.

And I certainly got a taste of my own medicine when I asked a guard on the door of the Manhattan Thirteen Club if I could come in and have a look around. It was very dark in there.

"All due respect, Mr. President," he said to me, "but are you a *Thirteen,* sir?"

"No," I said. "You know I'm not."

"Then I must say to you, sir," he said, "what I have to say to you.

"With all possible respect, sir:" he said, "Why don't you take a flying fuck at a rolling doughnut? Why don't you take a flying fuck at the moooooooooooooon?"

I was in ecstasy.

◆◆◆

Yes, and it was during that visit here that I first learned of The Church of Jesus Christ the Kidnapped—then a tiny cult in Chicago, but destined to become the most popular American religion of all time.

It was brought to my attention by a leaflet handed to me by a clean and radiant youth, as I crossed the lobby to the staircase of my hotel.

He was jerking his head around in what then seemed an eccentric manner, as though hoping to catch someone peering out at him from behind a potted palm tree or an easy chair, or even from directly overhead, from the crystal chandelier.

He was so absorbed in firing ardent glances this way and that, that it was wholly uninteresting to him that he had just handed a leaflet to the President of the United States.

"May I ask what you're looking for, young man?" I said.

"For our Saviour, sir," he replied.

"You think He's in this hotel?" I said.

"Read the leaflet, sir," he said.

◆◆◆

So I did—in my lonely room, with the radio on.

At the very top of the leaflet was a primitive picture of Jesus, standing and with His Body facing forward, but with His Face in profile—like a one-eyed jack in a deck of playing cards.

He was gagged. He was handcuffed. One ankle was shackled and chained to a ring fixed to the floor. There was a single perfect tear dangling from the lower lid of His Eye.

Beneath the picture was a series of questions and answers, which went as follows:

QUESTION: What is your name?

ANSWER: I am the Right Reverend William Uranium-8 Wainwright, Founder of the Church of Jesus Christ the Kidnapped at 3972 Ellis Avenue, Chicago, Illinois.

QUESTION: When will God send us His Son again?

ANSWER: He already has. Jesus is here among us.

QUESTION: Why haven't we seen or heard anything about Him?

ANSWER: He has been kidnapped by the Forces of Evil.

QUESTION: What must we do?

ANSWER: We must drop whatever we are doing, and spend every waking hour in trying to find

185

Him. If we do not, God will exercise His Option.

QUESTION: What is God's Option?

ANSWER: He can destroy Mankind so easily, any time he chooses to.

Hi ho.

◆◆◆

I saw the young man eating alone in the diningroom that night. I marvelled that he could jerk his head around and still eat without spilling a drop. He even looked under his plate and water glass for Jesus not once, but over and over again.

I had to laugh.

◆◆◆

Chapter 39

❖❖❖❖❖❖❖❖❖

BUT then, just when everything was going so well, when Americans were happier than they had ever been, even though the country was bankrupt and falling apart, people began to die by the millions of "The Albanian Flu" in most places, and here on Manhattan of "The Green Death."

And that was the end of the Nation. It became families, and nothing more.

Hi ho.

❖❖❖

Oh, there were claims of Dukedoms and Kingdoms and such garbage, and armies were raised and forts were built here and there. But few people admired them. They were just more bad weather and more bad gravity that families endured from time to time.

And somewhere in there a night of actual bad gravity crumbled the foundations of Machu Picchu. The condominiums and boutiques and banks and gold bricks and jewelry and pre-Columbian art collections and the Opera House and the churches, and *all* that, eloped down the Andes, wound up in the sea.

I cried.

◆◆◆

And families painted pictures everywhere of the kidnapped Jesus Christ.

◆◆◆

People continued to send news to us at the White House for a little while. We ourselves were experiencing death and death and death, and expecting to die.

Our personal hygiene deteriorated quickly. We stopped bathing and brushing our teeth regularly. The males grew beards, and let their hair grow down to their shoulders.

We began to cannibalize the White House almost absent-mindedly, burning furniture and bannisters and paneling and picture frames and so on in the fireplaces, to keep warm.

Hortense Muskellunge-13 McBundy, my personal secretary, died of flu. My valet, Edward Strawberry-4 Kleindienst, died of flu. My Vice-President, Mildred Helium-20 Theodorides, died of flu.

My science advisor, Dr. Albert Aquamarine-1 Piatigorsky, actually expired in my arms on the floor of the Oval Office.

He was almost as tall as I was. We must have been quite a sight on the floor.

"What does it all mean?" he said over and over again.

"I don't know, Albert," I said. "And maybe I'm glad I don't know."

"Ask a Chinaman!" he said, and he went to his reward, as the saying goes.

◆◆◆

Now and then the telephone would ring. It became such a rare occurrence that I took to answering it personally.

"This is your President speaking," I would say. As like as not, I would find myself talking over a tenuous, crackling circuit to some sort of mythological creature—"The King of Michigan," perhaps, or "The Emergency Governor of Florida," or "The Acting Mayor of Birmingham," or some such thing.

But there were fewer messages with each passing week. At last there were none.

I was forgotten.

Thus did my Presidency end—two thirds of the way through my second term.

And something else crucial was petering out almost as quickly—which was my irreplaceable supply of tri-benzo-Deportamil.

Hi ho.

I dared not count my remaining pills until I could not help but count them, they were so few. I had become so dependent upon them, so grateful for them, that it seemed to me that my life would end when the last one was gone.

I was running out of employees, too. I was soon down to one. Everybody else had died or wandered away, since there weren't any messages any more.

The one person who remained with me was my brother, was faithful Carlos Daffodil-11 Villavicencio, the dishwasher I had embraced on my first day as a Daffodil.

Chapter 40

✦✦✦✦✦✦✦✦✦✦

BECAUSE everything
had dwindled so quickly, and because there was no
one to behave sanely for any more, I developed a
mania for counting things. I counted slats in venetian
blinds. I counted the knives and forks and spoons in
the kitchen. I counted the tufts of the coverlet on
Abraham Lincoln's bed.

And I was counting posts in a bannister one day, on
my hands and knees on the staircase, although the
gravity was medium-to-light. And then I realized
that a man was watching me from below.

He was dressed in buckskins and moccasins and a
coon-skin hat, and carried a rifle.

"My God, President Daffodil," I said to myself, "you've really gone crazy this time. That's ol' Daniel Boone down there."

And then another man joined the first one. He was dressed like a military pilot back in the days, long before I was President, when there had been such a thing as a United States Air Force.

"Let me guess:" I said out loud, "It's either Halloween or the Fourth of July."

◆◆◆

The pilot seemed to be shocked by the condition of the White House. "What's happened here?" he said.

"All I can tell you," I said, "is that history has been made."

"This is terrible," he said.

"If you think this is bad," I told him, and I tapped my forehead with my fingertips, "you should see what it looks like in *here.*"

◆◆◆

Neither one of them even suspected that I was the President. I had become quite a mess by then.

They did not even want to talk to me, or to each other, for that matter. They were strangers, it turned out. They had simply happened to arrive at the same time—each one on an urgent mission.

They went into other rooms, and found my Sancho Panza, Carlos Daffodil-11 Villavicencio, who was making a lunch of Navy hardtack and canned smoked oysters, and some other things he'd found. And Carlos brought them back to me, and convinced them that I was indeed the President of what he called, in all sincerity, "the most powerful country in the world."

Carlos was a really stupid man.

◆◆◆

The frontiersman had a letter for me—from the widow in Urbana, Illinois, who had been visited a few years before by Chinese. I had been too busy ever to find out what the Chinese had been after out there.

"Dear Dr. Swain," it began—

"I am an undistinguished person, a piano teacher, who is remarkable only for having been married to a very great physicist, to have had a beautiful son by him, and after his death, to have been visited by a delegation of very small Chinese, one of whom said his father had known you. His father's name was 'Fu Manchu.'

"It was the Chinese who told me about the astonishing discovery my husband, Dr. Felix Bauxite-13 von Peterswald, made just before he died. My son, who is incidentally a Daffodil-11, like yourself, and I have kept this discovery a secret ever since, because the light it throws on the situation of human beings in the Universe is very demoralizing, to say the least. It has to do with the true nature of what awaits us all after death. What awaits us, Dr. Swain, is tedious in the extreme.

"I can't bring myself to call it 'Heaven' or 'Our Just Reward,' or any of those sweet things. All I can call it is what my husband came to call it, and what you will call it, too, after you have investigated it, which is 'The Turkey Farm.'

"In short, Dr. Swain, my husband discovered a way to talk to dead people on The Turkey Farm. He never taught the technique to me or my son, or to anybody. But the Chinese, who apparently have spies everywhere, somehow found out about it. They came to study his journals and to see what was left of his apparatus.

"After they had figured it out, they were nice enough to explain to my son and me how we might do the gruesome trick, if we wished to. They themselves were disappointed with the discovery. It was new to them, they said, but could be 'interesting only to participants in what is left of Western Civilization,' whatever that means.

"I am entrusting this letter to a friend who hopes to join a large settlement of his artificial relatives, the Berylliums, in Maryland, which is very near you.

"I address you as 'Dr. Swain' rather than 'Mr. President,' because this letter has nothing to do with the national interest. It is a highly personal letter, informing you that we have spoken to your dead sister Eliza many times on my husband's apparatus. She says that it is of the utmost importance that you come here in order that she may converse directly with you.

"We eagerly await your visit. Please do not be insulted by the behavior of my son and your brother, David Daffodil-11 von Peterswald, who cannot prevent himself from speaking obscenities and making insulting gestures at even the most inappropriate moments. He is a victim of Tourette's Disease.

"Your faithful servant,
"Wilma Pachysandra-17 von Peterswald."

Hi ho

◆◆◆

Chapter 41

◆◆◆◆◆◆◆◆◆◆

I was deeply moved, despite tri-benzo-Deportamil.

I stared out at the frontiersman's sweaty horse, which was grazing in the high grass of the White House lawn. And then I turned to the messenger himself. "How came you by this message?" I said.

He told me that he had accidentally shot a man, apparently Wilma Pachysandra-17 von Peterswald's friend, the Beryllium, on the border between Tennessee and West Virginia. He had mistaken him for an hereditary enemy.

"I thought he was Newton McCoy," he said.

He tried to nurse his innocent victim back to

health, but he died of gangrene. But, before he died, the Beryllium made him promise as a Christian to deliver a letter he had himself sworn to hand over to the President of the United States.

◆◆◆

I asked him his name.

"Byron Hatfield," he said.

"What is your Government-issue middle name?" I said.

"We never paid no mind to that," he replied.

It turned out that he belonged to one of the few genuine extended families of blood relatives in the country, which had been at perpetual war with another such family since 1882.

"We never was big for them new-fangled middle names," he said.

◆◆◆

The frontiersman and I were seated on spindly golden ballroom chairs which had supposedly been bought for the White House by Jacqueline Kennedy so long ago. The pilot was similarly supported, alertly awaiting his turn to speak. I glanced at the name-plate over the breast pocket of the pilot. It said this:

CAPT. BERNARD O'HARE

◆◆◆

"Captain," I said, "you're another one who doesn't seem to go in for the new-fangled middle names." I noticed, too, that he was much too old to be only a captain, even if there had still been such a thing. He was in fact almost sixty.

I concluded that he was a lunatic who had found the costume somewhere. I supposed that he had become so elated and addled by his new appearance, that nothing would do but that he show himself off to his President.

The truth was, though, that he was perfectly sane. He had been stationed for the past eleven years in the bottom of a secret, underground silo in Rock Creek Park. I had never heard of the silo before.

But there was a Presidential helicopter concealed in it, along with thousands of gallons of absolutely priceless gasoline.

◆◆◆

He had come out at last, in violation of his orders, he said, to find out "what on Earth was going on."

I had to laugh.

◆◆◆

"Is the helicopter still ready to fly?" I asked.

"Yes, sir, it is," he said. He had been maintaining it single-handedly for the past two years. His mechanics had wandered off one-by-one.

"Young man," I said, "I'm going to give you a

medal for this." I took a button from my own tattered lapel, and I pinned it to his.

It said this, of course:

❖❖❖

Chapter 42

◆◆◆◆◆◆◆◆◆◆◆

THE frontiersman refused a similar decoration. He asked for food, instead —to sustain him on his long trip back to his native mountains.

We gave him what we had, which was all the hardtack and canned smoked oysters his saddlebags would hold.

◆◆◆

Yes, and Captain Bernard O'Hare and Carlos Daffodil-11 Villavicencio and I took off from the silo on the following dawn. It was a day of such salubrious gravity, that our helicopter expended no more energy than would have an airborne milkweed seed.

As we fluttered over the White House, I waved to it.

"Goodbye," I said.

◆◆◆

My plan was to fly first to Indianapolis, which had become densely populated with Daffodils. They had been flocking there from everywhere.

We would leave Carlos there, to be cared for by his artificial relatives during his sunset years. I was glad to be getting rid of him. He bored me to tears.

◆◆◆

We would go next to Urbana, I told Captain O'Hare —and then to my childhood home in Vermont.

"After that," I promised, "the helicopter is yours, Captain. You can fly like a bird wherever you wish. But you're going to have a rotten time of it, if you don't give yourself a good middle name."

"You're the President," he said. "You give me a name."

"I dub thee 'Eagle-1,'" I said.

He was awfully pleased. He loved the medal, too.

◆◆◆

Yes, and I still had a little tri-benzo-Deportamil left, and I was so delighted to be going simply anywhere, after having been cooped up in Washington, D.C. so long, that I heard myself singing for the first time in years.

I remember the song I sang, too. It was one Eliza

and I used to sing a lot in secret, back when we were still believed to be idiots. We would sing it where nobody could hear us—in the mausoleum of Professor Elihu Roosevelt Swain.

And I think now that I will teach it to Melody and Isadore at my birthday party. It is such a good song for them to sing when they set out for new adventures on the Island of Death.

It goes like this:

> "Oh, we're off to see the Wizard,
> "The wonderful Wizard of Oz.
>
> ***
>
> "If ever a whiz of a Wiz there was,
> "It was the Wizard of Oz."*

♦♦♦

And so on.

♦♦♦

Hi ho.

♦♦♦

Chapter 43

❖❖❖❖❖❖❖❖❖❖❖

MELODY and Isadore
went down to Wall Street today—to visit Isadore's
large family, the Raspberries. I was invited to become a Raspberry at one time. So was Vera Chip-
munk-5 Zappa. We both declined.

Yes, and I took a walk of my own—up to the baby's
pyramid at Broadway and Forty-second, then across
Forty-third Street to the old Daffodil Club, to what
had been the Century Association before that; and
then eastward across Forty-eighth Street to the
townhouse which was slave quarters for Vera's farm,
which at one time had been my parent's home.

I encountered Vera herself on the steps of the

townhouse. Her slaves were all over in what used to be United Nations Park, planting watermelons and corn and sunflowers. I could hear them singing "Ol' Man River." They were so happy all the time. They considered themselves very lucky to be slaves.

They were all Chipmunk-5's, and about two-thirds of them were former Raspberries. People who wished to become slaves of Vera had to change their middle names to Chipmunk-5.

Hi ho.

Vera usually labored right along with her slaves. She loved hard work. But now I caught her tinkering idly with a beautiful Zeiss microscope, which one of her slaves had unearthed in the ruins of a hospital only the day before. It had been protected all through the years by its original factory packing case.

Vera had not sensed my approach. She was peering into the instrument and turning knobs with childlike seriousness and ineptitude. It was obvious that she had never used a microscope before.

I stole closer to her, and then I said, "Boo!"

She jerked her head away from the eyepiece.

"Hello," I said.

"You scared me to death," she said.

"Sorry," I said, and I laughed.

These ancient games go on and on. It's nice they do.

"I can't see anything," she said. She was complaining about the microscope.

"Just squiggly little animals that want to kill and eat us," I said. "You really want to see those?"

"I was looking at an opal," she said. She had draped an opal and diamond bracelet over the stage of the microscope. She had a collection of precious stones which would have been worth millions of dollars in olden times. People gave her all the jewels they found, just as they gave me all the candlesticks.

◆◆◆

Jewels were useless. So were candlesticks, since there weren't such things on Manhattan as candles any more. People lit their homes at night with burning rags stuck in bowls of animal fat.

"There's probably Green Death on the opal," I said. "There's probably Green Death on everything."

The reason that we ourselves did not die of The Green Death, by the way, was that we took an antidote which was discovered by accident by Isadore's family, the Raspberries.

We had only to withhold the antidote from a troublemaker, or from an army of troublemakers, for that matter, and he or she or they would be exiled quickly to the afterlife, to The Turkey Farm.

◆◆◆

There weren't any great scientists among the Raspberries, incidentally. They discovered the antidote through dumb luck. They ate fish without cleaning them, and the antidote, probably pollution left over from olden times, was somewhere in the guts of the fish they ate.

❖❖❖

"Vera," I said, "if you ever got that microscope to work, you would see something that would break your heart."

"What would break my heart?" she said.

"You'd see the organisms that cause The Green Death," I said.

"Why would that make me cry?" she said.

"Because you're a woman of conscience," I said. "Don't you realize that we kill them by the *trillions* —every time we take our antidote?"

I laughed.

She did not laugh.

"The reason I am not laughing," she said, "is that you, coming along so unexpectedly, have spoiled a surprise for your birthday."

"How is that?" I said.

She spoke of one of her slaves. "Donna was going to make a present of this to you. Now you won't be surprised."

"Um," I said.

"She thought it was an extra-fancy kind of candlestick."

◆◆◆

She confided to me that Melody and Isadore had paid her a call earlier in the week, had told her again how much they hoped to be her slaves someday.

"I tried to tell 'em that slavery wasn't for everybody," she said.

◆◆◆

"Answer me this," she went on, "What happens to all my slaves when I die?"

" 'Take no thought for the morrow,' " I told her, " 'for the morrow shall take thought for the things of itself. Sufficient unto the day is the evil thereof.'

"Amen," I said.

◆◆◆

Chapter 44

♦♦♦♦♦♦♦♦♦♦

OLD Vera and I reminisced there on the townhouse steps about the Battle of Lake Maxinkuckee, in northern Indiana. I had seen it from a helicopter on my way to Urbana. Vera had been in the actual thick of it with her alcoholic husband, Lee Razorclam-13 Zappa. They were cooks in one of the King of Michigan's field kitchens on the ground below.

"You all looked like ants to me down there," I said, "or like germs under a microscope." We didn't dare come down close, for fear of being shot.

"That's what we felt like, too," she said.

"If I had known you then, I would have tried to rescue you," I said.

"That would have been like trying to rescue a germ from a million other germs, Wilbur," she said.

◆◆◆

Not only did Vera have to put up with shells and bullets whistling over the kitchen tent. She had to defend herself against her husband, too, who was drunk. He beat her up in the midst of battle.

He blacked both her eyes and broke her jaw. He threw her out through the tent flaps. She landed on her back in the mud. Then he came out to explain to her how she could avoid similar beatings in the future.

He came out just in time to be skewered by the lance of an enemy cavalryman.

"And what's the moral of that story, do you think?" I asked her.

She lay a callused palm on my knee. "Wilbur—don't ever get married," she replied.

◆◆◆

We talked some about Indianapolis, which I had seen on the same trip, and where she and her husband had been a waitress and a bartender for a Thirteen Club —before they joined the army of the King of Michigan.

I asked her what the club was like inside.

"Oh, you know—" she said, "they had stuffed black cats and jack-o-lanterns, and aces of spades stuck to the tables with daggers and all. I used to wear net stockings and spike heels and a mask and all. All the waitresses and the bartenders and the bouncer wore vampire fangs."

"Um," I said.

"We used to call our hamburgers 'Batburgers,' " she said.

"Uh huh," I said.

"We used to call tomato juice with a shot of gin a 'Dracula's Delight,' " she said.

"Right," I said.

"It was just like a Thirteen Club anywhere," she said, "but it never went over. Indianapolis just wasn't a big Thirteen town, even though there were plenty of Thirteens there. It was a Daffodil town. You weren't anything if you weren't a Daffodil."

Chapter 45

✦✦✦✦✦✦✦✦✦✦✦

I tell you—I have been regaled as a multimillionaire, as a pediatrician, as a Senator, and as a President. But nothing can match for sincerity the welcome Indianapolis, Indiana, gave me as a Daffodil!

The people there were poor, and had suffered an awful lot of death, and all the public services had broken down, and they were worried about battles raging not far away. But they put on parades and feasts for me, and for Carlos Daffodil-11 Villavicencio, too, of course, which would have blinded ancient Rome.

◆◆◆

Captain Bernard Eagle-1 O'Hare said to me, "My gosh, Mr. President—if I'd known about this, I would have asked you to make me a Daffodil."

So I said, "I hereby dub thee a Daffodil."

◆◆◆

But the most satisfying and educational thing I saw out there was a weekly family meeting of Daffodils.

Yes, and I got to vote at that meeting, and so did my pilot, and so did Carlos, and so did every man, woman, and every child over the age of nine.

With a little luck, I might even have become Chairperson of the meeting, although I had been in town for less than a day. The Chairperson was chosen by lot from all assembled. And the winner of the drawing that night was an eleven-year-old black girl named Dorothy Daffodil-7 Garland.

She was fully prepared to run the meeting, and so, I suppose, was every person there.

◆◆◆

She marched up to the lectern, which was nearly as tall as she was.

That little cousin of mine stood on a chair, without any apologies or self-mockery. She banged the meeting to order with a yellow gavel, and she told her silenced and respectful relatives, "The President of the United States is present, as most of you know.

With your permission, I will ask him to say a few words to us at the conclusion of our regular business.

"Will somebody put that in the form of a motion?" she said.

"I move that Cousin Wilbur be asked to address the meeting at the conclusion of regular business," said an old man sitting next to me.

This was seconded and put to a voice vote.

The motion carried, but with a scattering of seemingly heartfelt, by-no-means joshing, "Nays" and "Noes."

Hi ho.

◆◆◆

The most pressing business had to do with selecting four replacements for fallen Daffodils in the army of the King of Michigan, who was at war simultaneously with Great Lakes pirates and the Duke of Oklahoma.

There was one strapping young man, I remember, a blacksmith, in fact, who told the meeting, "Send me. There's nothing I'd rather do than kill me some 'Sooners,' long as they ain't Daffodils." And so on.

To my surprise, he was scolded by several speakers for his military ardor. He was told that war wasn't supposed to be fun, and in fact wasn't fun—that tragedy was being discussed, and that he had better put on a tragic face, or he would be ejected from the meeting.

"Sooners" were people from Oklahoma, and, by extension, anybody in the service of the Duke of

Oklahoma, which included "Show Me's" from Missouri and "Jayhawkers" from Kansas and "Hawkeyes" from Iowa, and on and on.

The blacksmith was told that "Sooners" were human beings, too, no better or worse than "Hoosiers," who were people from Indiana.

And the old man who had moved that I be allowed to speak later on got up and said this: "Young man, you're no better than the Albanian influenza or The Green Death, if you can kill for joy."

◆◆◆

I was impressed. I realized that nations could never acknowledge their own wars as tragedies, but that families not only could but had to.

Bully for them!

◆◆◆

The chief reason the blacksmith was not allowed to go to war, though, was that he had so far fathered three illegitimate children by different women, "and had two more in the oven," as someone said.

He wasn't going to be allowed to run away from caring for all those babies.

◆◆◆

Chapter 46

E VEN the children and the drunks and the lunatics at that meeting seemed shrewdly familiar with parliamentary procedures. The little girl behind the lectern kept things moving so briskly and purposefully that she might have been some sort of goddess up there, equipped with an armload of thunderbolts.

I was so filled with respect for these procedures, which had always seemed like such solemn tomfoolery to me before.

◆◆◆

And I am still so respectful, that I have just looked up their inventor in my Encyclopædia here in the Empire State Building.

His name was Henry Martyn Robert. He was a graduate of West Point. He was an engineer. He became a general by and by. But, just before the Civil War, when he was a lieutenant stationed in New Bedford, Massachusetts, he had to run a church meeting, and he lost control of it.

There were no rules.

So this soldier sat down and wrote some rules, which were the identical rules I saw followed in Indianapolis. They were published as *Robert's Rules of Order*, which I now believe to be one of the four greatest inventions by Americans.

The other three, in my opinion, were The Bill of Rights, the principles of Alcoholics Anonymous, and the artificial extended families envisioned by Eliza and me.

♦♦♦

The three recruits which the Indianapolis Daffodils finally voted to send off to the King of Michigan, incidentally, were all people who could be most easily spared, and who, in the opinion of the voters, had had the most carefree lives so far.

Hi ho.

♦♦♦

The next order of business had to do with feeding and sheltering Daffodil refugees, who were trickling into town from all the fighting in the northern part of the state.

The meeting again discouraged an enthusiast. A young woman, quite beautiful but disorderly, and clearly crazed by altruism, said that she could take at least twenty refugees into her home.

Somebody else got up and said to her that she was such an incompetent housekeeper that her own children had gone to live with other relatives.

Another person pointed out to her that she was so absent-minded that her dog would have starved to death, if it weren't for neighbors, and that she had accidentally set fire to her house three times.

❖❖❖

This sounds as though the people at the meeting were being cruel. But they all called her "Cousin Grace" or "Sister Grace," as the case might be. She was my cousin too, of course. She was a Daffodil-13.

What was more: She was a menace only to herself, so nobody was particularly mad at her. Her children had wandered off to better-run houses almost as soon as they were able to walk, I was told. That was surely one of the most attractive features of Eliza's and my invention, I think: Children had so many homes and parents to choose from.

Cousin Grace, for her part, heard all the bad reports on herself as though they were surprising to her, but no doubt true. She did not flee in tears. She stayed for the rest of the meeting, obeying Robert's Rules of Order, and looking sympathetic and alert.

At one point, under "New Business," Cousin Grace made a motion that any Daffodil who served with the Great Lakes Pirates or in the army of the Duke of Oklahoma should be expelled from the family.

Nobody would second this.

And the little girl running the meeting told her, "Cousin Grace, you know as well as anybody here, 'Once a Daffodil, always a Daffodil.'"

Chapter 47

◆◆◆◆◆◆◆◆◆◆

IT was at last my turn to speak.

"Brothers and Sisters and Cousins—" I said, "your nation has wasted away. As you can see, your President has also become a shadow of his former shadow. You have nobody but your doddering Cousin Wilbur here."

"You were a damn good President, Brother Billy," somebody called from the back of the room.

"I would have liked to give my country peace as well as brotherhood and sisterhood," I went on. "There is no peace, I'm sorry to say. We find it. We lose it. We find it again. We lose it again. Thank God, at least, that the machines have decided not to fight any more. It's just people now.

"And thank God that there's no such thing as a battle between strangers any more. I don't care who fights who—everybody will have relatives on the other side."

◆◆◆

Most of the people at the meeting were not only *Daffodils*, but also searchers for the kidnapped Jesus. It was a disconcerting sort of audience to address, I found. No matter what I said, they kept jerking their heads this way and that, hoping to catch sight of Jesus.

But I seemed to be getting across, for they applauded or cheered at appropriate moments—so I pressed on.

◆◆◆

"Because we're just families, and not a nation any more," I said, "it's much easier for us to give and receive mercy in war."

"I have just come from observing a battle far to the north of here, in the region of Lake Maxinkuckee. It was horses and spears and rifles and knives and pistols, and a cannon or two. I saw several people killed. I also saw many people embracing, and there seemed to be a great deal of deserting and surrendering going on.

"This much news I can bring you from the Battle of Lake Maxinkuckee:" I said—

"It is no massacre."

◆◆◆

Chapter 48

◆◆◆◆◆◆◆

WHILE in Indianapolis, I received an invitation by radio from the King of Michigan. It was Napoleonic in tone. It said that the King would be pleased "to hold an audience for the President of the United States in his Summer Palace on Lake Maxinkuckee." It said that his sentinels had been instructed to grant me safe passage. It said that the battle was over. "Victory is ours," it said.

So my pilot and I flew there.

We left my faithful servant, Carlos Daffodil-11 Villavicencio, to spend his declining years among his countless relatives.

"Good luck, Brother Carlos," I said.

"Home at last, Meester President, me Brudder,"

he replied. "Tanks you and tanks God for everything. Lonesome no more!"

❖❖❖

My meeting with the King of Michigan would have been called an "historic occasion" in olden times. There would have been cameras and microphones and reporters there. As it was, there were notetakers there, whom the King called his "scribes."

And he was right to give those people with pens and paper that archaic title. Most of his soldiers could scarcely read or write.

❖❖❖

Captain O'Hare and I landed on the manicured lawn before the King's Summer Palace, which had been a private military academy at one time. Soldiers, who had behaved badly in the recent battle, I suppose, were on their knees everywhere, guarded by military policemen. They were cutting grass with bayonets and pocket knives and scissors—as a punishment.

❖❖❖

Captain O'Hare and I entered the palace between two lines of soldiers. They were an honor guard of some sort, I suppose. Each one held aloft a banner, which was embroidered with the totem of his artificial extended family—an apple, an alligator, the chemical symbol for lithium, and so on.

It was such a comically trite historical situation, I

thought. Aside from battles, the history of nations seemed to consist of nothing but powerless old poops like myself, heavily medicated and vaguely beloved in the long ago, coming to kiss the boots of young psychopaths.

Inside myself, I had to laugh.

I was ushered alone into the King's spartan private quarters. It was a huge room, where the military academy must have held dances at one time. Now there was only a folding cot in there, a long table covered with maps, and a stack of folding chairs against one wall.

The King himself sat at the map table, ostentatiously reading a book, which turned out to be Thucydides' *History of the Peloponnesian War*.

Behind him, standing, were three male scribes—with pencils and pads.

There was no place for me or anyone else to sit.

I positioned myself before him, my mouldy Homburg in hand. He did not look up from his book immediately, although the doorkeeper had certainly announced me loudly enough.

"Your Majesty," the doorkeeper had said, "Dr. Wilbur Daffodil-11 Swain, the President of the United States!!"

◆◆◆

He looked up at last, and I was amused to see that he was the spit and image of his grandfather, Dr. Stewart Rawlings Mott, the physician who had looked after my sister and me in Vermont so long ago.

◆◆◆

I was not in the least afraid of him. Tri-benzo-Deportamil was making me soigné and blasé, of course. But, also, I had had more than enough of the low comedy of living by then. I would have found it a rather shapely adventure, if the King had elected to hustle me in front of a firing squad.

"We thought you were dead," he said.

"No, your Majesty," I said.

"It's been so long since we heard anything about you," he said.

"Washington, D.C., runs out of ideas from time to time," I said.

◆◆◆

The scribes were taking all this down, all this history that was being made.

He held up the spine of the book so I could read it. "Thucydides," he said.

"Um," I said.

"History is all I read," he said.

"That is wise for a man in your position, your Majesty," I replied.

"Those who fail to learn from history are condemned to repeat it," he said.

The scribes scribbled away.

"Yes," I said. "If our descendents don't study our times closely, they will find that they have again exhausted the planet's fossil fuels, that they have again died by the millions of influenza and The Green Death, that the sky has again been turned yellow by the propellants for underarm deodorants, that they have again elected a senile President two meters tall, and that they are yet again the intellectual and spiritual inferiors of teeny-weeny Chinese."

He did not join my laughter.

I addressed his scribes directly, speaking over his head. "History is merely a list of surprises," I said. "It can only prepare us to be surprised yet again. Please write that down."

Chapter 49

✦✦✦✦✦✦✦✦✦✦✦✦

IT turned out that the young King had an historic document he wished me to sign. It was brief. In it, I acknowledged that I, the President of the United States of America, no longer exercised any control over that part of the North American Continent which was sold by Napoleon Bonaparte to my country in 1803, and which was known as "The Louisiana Purchase."

I, therefore, according to the document, sold it for a dollar, to Stewart Oriole-2 Mott, the King of Michigan.

I signed with the teeny-weeniest signature possible. It looked like a baby ant. "Enjoy it in good health!" I said.

The territory I had sold him was largely occupied by the Duke of Oklahoma, and, no doubt, by other potentates and panjandrums unknown to me.

After that, we chatted some about his grandfather.

Then Captain O'Hare and I took off for Urbana, Illinois, and an electronic reunion with my sister, who had been dead so long.

Hi ho.

◆◆◆

Yes, and I write now with a palsied hand and an aching head, for I drank much too much at my birthday party last night.

Vera Chipmunk-5 Zappa arrived encrusted with diamonds, borne through the ailanthus forest in a sedan chair, accompanied by an entourage of fourteen slaves. She brought me wine and beer, which made me drunk. But her most intoxicating gifts were a thousand candles she and her slaves had made in a colonial candle mold. We fitted them into the empty mouths of my thousand candlesticks, and deployed them over the lobby floor.

Then we lit them all.

Standing among all those tiny, wavering lights, I felt as though I were God, up to my knees in the Milky Way.

◆◆◆

Epilogue

◆◆◆◆◆◆◆◆◆◆

DR. Swain died before he could write any more. He went to his just reward.

There was nobody to read what he had written anyway—to complain about all the loose ends of the yarn he had spun.

He had reached the climax of his story, at any rate, with his reselling of the Louisiana Purchase to a bandit chief—for a dollar he never received.

Yes, and he died proud of what he and his sister had done to reform their society, for he left this poem, perhaps hoping that someone would use it for his epitaph:

"And how did we then face the odds,
"Of man's rude slapstick, yes, and God's?
"Quite at home and unafraid,
"Thank you,
"In a game our dreams remade."

◆◆◆

He never got to tell about the electronic device in Urbana, which made it possible for him to reunite his mind with that of his dead sister, to recreate the genius they had been in childhood.

The device, which those few people who knew about it called "The Hooligan," consisted of a seemingly ordinary length of brown clay pipe—two meters long and twenty centimeters in diameter. It was placed just so—atop a steel cabinet containing controls for a huge particle-accelerator. The particle-accelerator was a tubular magnetic race track for subatomic entities which looped through cornfields on the edge of town.

Yes.

And the Hooligan was itself a ghost, in a way, since the particle-accelerator had been dead for a long time, for want of electricity, for want of enthusiasts for all it could do.

A janitor, Francis Iron-7 Hooligan, stored the piece of pipe atop the dead cabinet, rested his lunchpail there, too, for the moment. He heard voices from the pipe.

◆◆◆

He fetched the scientist whose apparatus this had been, Dr. Felix Bauxite-13 von Peterswald. But the pipe refused to talk again.

Dr. von Peterswald demonstrated that he was a great scientist, however, with his willingness to believe the ignorant Mr. Hooligan. He made the janitor go over his story again and again.

"The lunchpail," he said at last. "Where is your lunchpail?"

Hooligan had it in his hand.

Dr. von Peterswald instructed him to place it in relation to the pipe exactly as it had been before.

The pipe began promptly to talk again.

◆◆◆

The talkers identified themselves as persons in the afterlife. They were backed by a demoralized chorus of persons who complained to each other of tedium and social slights and minor ailments, and so on.

As Dr. von Peterswald said in his secret diary: "It sounded like nothing so much as the other end of a telephone call on a rainy autumn day—to a badly run turkey farm."

Hi ho.

◆◆◆

When Dr. Swain talked to his sister Eliza over the Hooligan, he was in the company of the widow of Dr.

von Peterswald, Wilma Pachysandra-17 von Peterswald, and her fifteen-year-old son, David Daffodil-11 von Peterswald, a brother of Dr. Swain, and a victim of Tourette's Disease.

◆◆◆

Poor David suffered an attack of his disease—just as Dr. Swain was beginning to talk with Eliza across the Great Divide.

David tried to choke down the involuntary stream of obscenities, but succeeded only in raising their pitch an octave. "Shit . . . sputum . . . scrotum . . . cloaca . . . asshole . . . pecker . . . mucous membrane . . . earwax . . . piss," he said.

◆◆◆

And Dr. Swain himself went out of control. He climbed involuntarily on top of the cabinet, as tall and old as he was. He crouched over the pipe, to be that much closer to his sister. He hung his head upside-down in front of the business end of the pipe, and knocked the crucial lunchpail to the floor, breaking the connection.

"Hello? Hello?" he said.

"Perineum . . . fuck . . . turd . . . glans . . . mount of Venus . . . afterbirth," said the boy.

◆◆◆

The widow von Peterswald was the only stable person on the Urbana end, so it was she who restored the lunchpail to its correct position. She had to jam it rather brutally between the pipe and the knee of the President. Then she found herself trapped in a grotesque position, bent at a right angle across the top of the cabinet, one arm extended, and her feet a few inches off the floor. The President had clamped down not only on the lunchpail, but on her hand.

"Hello? Hello?" said the President, his head upside down.

◆◆◆

There were answering gabblings and gobblings and squawks and clucks from the other end.

Somebody sneezed.

"Bugger . . . defecate . . . semen . . . balls," said the boy.

◆◆◆

Before Eliza could speak again, dead people in the background sensed that poor David was a kindred spirit, as outraged by the human condition in the Universe as they were. So they egged him on, and contributed obscenities of their own.

"You tell 'em, kid," they said, and so on.

And they doubled everything. "Double cock! Double clit!" they'd say. "Double shit!" and so on.

It was bedlam.

◆◆◆

But Dr. Swain and his sister got together anyway, with such convulsive intimacy that Dr. Swain would have crawled into the pipe, if he could.

Yes, and what Eliza wanted from him was that he should die as soon as possible, so that the two of them could put their heads together. She wanted then to figure out ways to improve the utterly unsatisfactory, so-called "Paradise."

❖❖❖

"Are you being tortured there?" he asked her.

"No," she said, "we are being bored stiff. Whoever designed this place knew nothing about human beings. Please, brother Wilbur," she said, "this is *Eternity* here. This is *forever!* Where you are now is just nothing in terms of time! It's a joke! Blow your brains out as quick as you can."

And so on.

❖❖❖

Dr. Swain told her about the problems the living had been having with incurable diseases. The two of them, thinking as one, made child's play of the mystery.

The explanation was this: The flu germs were Martians, whose invasion had apparently been repelled by anti-bodies in the systems of the survivors, since, for the moment, anyway, there was no more flu.

The Green Death, on the other hand, was caused by microscopic Chinese, who were peace-loving and meant no one any harm. They were nonetheless in-variably fatal to normal-sized human beings when inhaled or ingested.

And so on.

◆◆◆

Dr. Swain asked his sister what sort of communications apparatus there was on the other end—whether Eliza, too, was squatting over a piece of pipe, or what.

Eliza told him that there was no apparatus, but only a feeling.

"What is the feeling?" he said.

"You would have to be dead to understand my description of it," she said.

"Try it anyway, Eliza," he said.

"It is like being dead," she said.

"A feeling of deadness," he said tentatively, trying to understand.

"Yes—coldness and clamminess—" she said.

"Um," he said.

"But also like being surrounded by a swarm of invisible bees," she said. "Your voice comes from the bees."

Hi ho.

◆◆◆

When Dr. Swain was through with this particular ordeal, he had only eleven tablets left of tri-benzo-Deportamil, which were originally created, of course, not as a narcotic for presidents, but as suppressants for the symptoms of Tourette's Disease.

And the remaining pills, when he displayed them to himself in the palm of his huge hand, inevitably looked to him like the remaining grains in the hourglass of his life.

◆◆◆

Dr. Swain was standing in the sunshine outside the laboratory building containing the Hooligan. With him were the widow and her son. The widow had the lunchpail, so that only she could turn the Hooligan on.

The gravity was light. Dr. Swain had an erection. So did the boy. So did Captain Bernard Daffodil-11 O'Hare, who stood by the helicopter nearby.

Presumably, the erectile tissues in the widow's body were also engorged.

"You know what you looked like on top of that cabinet, Mr. President?" said the boy. He was clearly sickened by what his disease was about to make him say.

"No," said Dr. Swain.

"Like the biggest baboon in the world—trying to fuck a football," blurted the boy.

Dr. Swain, in order to avoid any more insults like that, handed his remaining supply of tri-benzo-Deportamil to the boy.

◆◆◆

The consequences of his withdrawal from tri-benzo-Deportamil were spectacular. Dr. Swain had to be tied to a bed in the widow's house for six nights and days.

Somewhere in there he made love to the widow, conceiving a son who would become the father of Melody Oriole-2 von Peterswald.

Yes, and somewhere in there the widow passed on to him what she had learned from the Chinese—that they had become successful manipulators of the Universe by combining harmonious minds.

◆◆◆

Yes, and then he had his pilot fly him to Manhattan, the Island of Death. He intended to die there, to join his sister in the afterlife—as a result of inhaling and ingesting invisible Chinese communists.

Captain O'Hare, not wishing to die yet himself, lowered his President by means of a winch and rope and harness to the observation deck of the Empire State Building.

The President spent the remainder of the day up there, enjoying the view. And then, breathing deeply with every few steps, hoping to inhale Chinese communists, he descended the stairs.

It was twilight when he reached the bottom.

◆◆◆

There were human skeletons in the lobby—in rotting nests of rags. The walls were zebra-striped with soot from cooking fires of long ago.

There was a painting of Jesus Christ the Kidnapped on one wall.

Dr. Swain for the first time heard the shuddering whir of bats leaving the subway system for the night.

He considered himself to be already a dead man—a brother to the skeletons.

But six members of the Raspberry family, who had observed his arrival by helicopter, suddenly came out of hiding in the lobby. They were armed with spears and knives.

◆◆◆

When they understood who they had captured, they were thrilled. He was a treasure to them not because he was President, but because he had been to medical school.

"A doctor! Now we have everything!" said one.

Yes, and they would not hear of his wish to die. They forced him to swallow a small trapezoid of what seemed to be a tasteless sort of peanut-brittle. It was in fact boiled and dried fish guts, which contained the antidote to The Green Death.

Hi ho.

◆◆◆

The Raspberries hustled him down to the Financial District at once, for Hiroshi Raspberry-20 Yamashiro, the head of the family, was deathly ill.

◆◆◆

The man seemed to have pneumonia. Dr. Swain could do nothing for him but what physicians of a century before would have done, which was to keep his body warm and his forehead cool—and to wait.

Either the fever would break, or the man would die.

◆◆◆

The fever broke.

As a reward, the Raspberries brought their most precious possessions to Dr. Swain on the floor of the New York Stock Exchange. There was a clock-radio, an alto saxophone, a fully-fitted toiletries kit, a model of the Eiffel Tower with a thermometer in it—and on and on.

From all this junk, and merely to be polite, Dr. Swain selected a single brass candlestick.

And thus was the legend established that he was crazy about candlesticks.

Thereafter, everybody would give him candlesticks.

◆◆◆

He did not like the communal life of the Raspberries, which required him, among other things, to jerk his head around perpetually, in search of the kidnapped Jesus Christ.

So he cleaned up the lobby of the Empire State Building, and moved in there. The Raspberries supplied him with food.

And time flew.

Somewhere in there, Vera Chipmunk-5 Zappa arrived, and was given the antidote by the Raspberries. They hoped she would be Dr. Swain's nurse.

And she was his nurse for a little while, but then she started her model farm.

And little Melody arrived a long time after that, pregnant, and pushing her pathetic worldly goods ahead of her in a dilapidated baby carriage. Among those goods was a Dresden candlestick. Even in the Kingdom of Michigan, it was well known that the legendary King of New York was crazy about candlesticks.

Melody's candlestick depicted a nobleman's flirtation with a shepherdess at the foot of a treetrunk enlaced in flowering vines.

Melody's candlestick was broken on the old man's last birthday. It was kicked over by Wanda Chipmunk-5 Rivera, an intoxicated slave.

When Melody first presented herself at the Empire State Building, and Dr. Swain came out to ask who she was and what she wanted, she went down on her knees to him. Her little hands were extended before her, holding the candlestick.

"Hello, Grandfather," she said.

He hesitated for a moment. But then he helped her to her feet. "Come in," he said. "Come in, come in."

◆◆◆

Dr. Swain did not know at that time that he had sired a son during his withdrawal from tri-benzo-Deportamil in Urbana. He supposed that Melody was a random supplicant and fan. Nor did he bring to that first encounter any daydreams of having descendents somewhere. He had never much wanted to reproduce himself.

So, when Melody gave him shy but convincing arguments that she was an actual blood relative, he had a feeling that he, as he later explained to Vera Chipmunk-5 Zappa, " had somehow sprung a huge leak. And out of that sudden, painless opening," he went on, "there crawled a famished child, pregnant and clasping a Dresden candlestick.

"Hi ho."

◆◆◆

Melody's story was this:

Her father, who was the illegitimate child of Dr. Swain and the widow in Urbana, was one of the few survivors of the so-called "Urbana Massacre." He was then pressed into service as a drummer boy in the army of the perpetrator of the massacre, the Duke of Oklahoma.

The boy begat Melody at the age of fourteen. Her

mother was a forty-year-old laundress who had attached herself to the army. Melody was given the middle name "Oriole-2", to ensure that she would be treated with maximal mercy, should she be captured by the forces of Stewart Oriole-2 Mott, the King of Michigan, the chief enemy of the Duke.

And she was in fact captured when a six-year-old —after the Battle of Iowa City, in which her father and mother were slain.

Hi ho.

Yes, and the King of Michigan had become so decadent by then, that he maintained a seraglio of captured children with the same middle name as his— which, of course, was Oriole-2. Little Melody was added to that pitiful zoo.

But, as her ordeals became more disgusting, so did she gain increasing inner strength from her father's dying words to her, which were these:

"You are a princess. You are the granddaughter of the King of Candlesticks, of the King of New York."

Hi ho.

And then, one night, she stole the Dresden candlestick from the tent of the sleeping King.

Then Melody crawled under the flaps of the tent and into the moonlit world outside.

♦♦♦

Thus began her incredible journey eastward, ever eastward, in search of her legendary grandfather. His palace was one of the tallest buildings in the world.

She would encounter relatives everywhere—if not Orioles, then at least birds or living things of some kind.

They would feed her and point the way.

One would give her a raincoat. Another would give her a sweater and a magnetic compass. Another would give her a baby carriage. Another would give her an alarm clock.

Another would give her a needle and thread, and a gold thimble, too.

Another would row her across the Harlem River to the Island of Death, at the risk of his own life.

And so on.

–Das Ende–